YOU CAN'T GO HOME AGAIN

Jeff didn't feel much like eating after everything that had happened, but he poured a small amount of cold cereal into a bowl and sprinkled on some sugar and added milk. He found a spoon and sat down to eat. When he pulled a napkin from the dispenser on the table, a piece of folded paper came out with it and landed on the table in front of him.

He could see that something was written on the inside in ink. Large, block letters had been gone over so many times they almost tore through the paper in several places.

Jeff's hand was trembling as he picked up the paper and unfolded it. He scanned the jagged, childish scrawl, unable to believe what he was seeing.

LEAVE THIS HOUSE RIGHT NOW!
BEFORE WHAT HAPPENED TO JUDY
— HAPPENS TO YOU!!!

HAUTALA'S HORROR AND SUPERNATURAL SUSPENSE

GHOST LIGHT (4320, $4.99)
Alex Harris is searching for his kidnapped children, but only the ghost of their dead mother can save them from his murderous rage.

DARK SILENCE (3923, $5.99)
Dianne Fraser is trying desperately to keep her family—and her own sanity—from being pulled apart by the malevolent forces that haunt the abandoned mill on their property.

COLD WHISPER (3464, $5.95)
Tully can make Sarah's every wish come true, but Sarah lives in teror because Tully doesn't understand that some wishes aren't meant to come true.

LITTLE BROTHERS (4020, $4.50)
The "little brothers" have returned, and this time there will be no escape for the boy who saw them kill his mother.

NIGHT STONE (3681, $4.99)
Their new house was a place of darkness, shadows, long-buried secrets, and a force of unspeakable evil.

MOONBOG (3356, $4.95)
Someone—or something—is killing the children in the little town of Holland, Maine.

MOONDEATH (1844, $3.95)
When the full moon rises in Cooper Falls, a beast driven by bloodlust and savage evil stalks the night.

Available wherever paperbacks are sold, or order direct from the Publisher. Send cover price plus 50¢ per copy for mailing and handling to Penguin USA, P.O. Box 999, c/o Dept. 17109, Bergenfield, NJ 07621. Residents of New York and Tennessee must include sales tax. DO NOT SEND CASH.

RICK HAUTALA

TWILIGHT TIME

ZEBRA BOOKS
KENSINGTON PUBLISHING CORP.

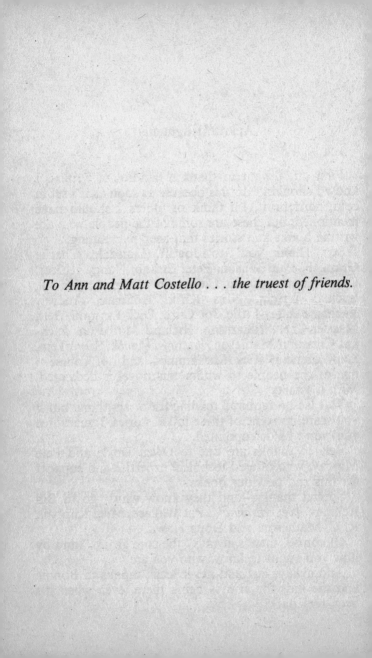

To Ann and Matt Costello . . . the truest of friends.

Acknowledgments

First off, I want to thank a handful of writers. I know I shouldn't do this because as soon as it's set in cold, hard print, I'll think of others I should have mentioned, but these are some of the people who are writing books and stories that keep *me* reading.

So "Thank you" to: Joe R. Lansdale, Charlie Grant, F. Paul Wilson, Peter Straub, Nancy Holder, Dean Koontz, Doug Clegg, Ed Gorman, Tim (T. Lucien) Wright, Nina Kiriki Hoffman, Andrew Vachss, Bentley Little, Joe Citro, Dick Laymon, Beth Massie, Chet Williamson, Richard Matheson, Richard Christian Matheson, Kathryn Ptacek, Steve Tem, Scott Ciencin, Rick McCammon and—of course— one of the people to whom this novel is dedicated, Matt Costello.

This isn't a required reading list or anything, but if you scare up some of these folks' stories, I guarantee you won't be disappointed.

Belated thanks are due to Owen Doyle and Pete Murray, who offered technical expertise and support for this and previous books.

Special thanks—and they know why!—go to Bill Relling *(Aye, carumba!)*, Pat Wallace, Mike Kimball, R. C. Matheson, and Doug Hawk.

Of course, there's always "the core group," and by now you ought to know who you are.

And always last and never least, thanks to Bonnie and the kids for always being there, even when it's been *very* dark!

Dum spiro, spero

Prologue: In the Dark

The darkness in the room seemed to flicker with a raw energy of its own, an energy that was stronger than any light that could have penetrated it.

The boy sobbed as he huddled in the darkness, his legs drawn up against his chest. He threaded his fingers together and squeezed them so tightly they began to tingle. Leaning against the cold wall, he stared into the darkness. It was so deep, he could no longer distinguish if it was inside him or outside him.

Perhaps it was both, he thought.

Perhaps he *was* the darkness.

It didn't really matter.

He knew that he was still alive only because he could feel the clammy slick of tears that streaked his face. Every breath he took burned like there was a hot spark lodged in his throat.

Time meant nothing to him here.

He could have been sitting in this room for an hour or a day or a week.

It didn't matter.

He was alone.

He knew that much.

All alone!

He tried hard not to imagine that he had shriveled until he was nothing more than a speck of dust, floating in a vast, eternal black void, a void without meaning or form. He wanted to believe that he was still a little boy, that hot blood and vibrant energy still flowed inside his body. He clung desperately to the hope that one day he would once again run through the woods and play baseball on Saturday mornings with his friends, that he would someday climb trees again, and go swimming at the beach. He knew he had once been alive, had tasted the cold, smooth taste of ice cream and smelled the fresh breeze following a rainstorm, but those memories were now so distant they felt as though they belonged to someone else.

Yes, someone else.

For now, all he knew was that he was surrounded by a darkness that squeezed in on him from all sides, filling him with a stabbing sense of loneliness. He wanted to cry out, to release his feelings, but he couldn't.

No, he was all cried out.

Sometime . . . maybe soon—it didn't matter when time had no meaning—they would come for him; but he honestly couldn't decide which was worse—sitting here all alone in darkness, or being out in the open air where *they* could get him.

Here, though, he was terrified. There was no one to touch him . . . no one to hold him . . . no one to hear him cry out or to wipe the tears from his eyes and tell him everything would be all right.

Here, he was alone.

All alone . . .

Until some timeless moment later, he heard . . . something.

In the darkness, a sound fluttered against his ears like the powdery touch of unseen moth wings.

He stiffened, feeling his folded hands squeeze together even tighter. Blood thundered in his ears with a hot, rapid pulse.

Were they coming for him now?

Were they going to take him out into the blinding brightness again and do more of those horrible things to him?

He shrank back, begging the darkness to carry him away, to take him down . . . all the way down into death, if need be, if that's what was necessary to get away from . . .

Them!

As hard as he tried to convince himself that he had made the sound or imagined it, his body was knotted with tension as he stiffened and waited to hear the sound repeated. It had almost sounded like someone . . .

Sighing.

The heavy hammering of his pulse filled his ears like thunder. He could feel hot pressure building up in his neck, a pressure that made his head feel like it was about to explode . . . a pressure that almost strangled him as he craned his head forward, trying to hear better.

But his pulse seemed to block out all other sounds.

Then, after the span of several heartbeats, from out of the darkness, there came a soft brushing sound that reminded him of rotting cloth, tearing. Choking tension took hold of his throat and wouldn't let go as he sat back against the cold wall, cringing and waiting.

The sound grew louder, hissing like the harsh grinding of sand underfoot, and then he *felt* it—a warm presence bearing down on him from out of the darkness.

He almost cried out . . . he wanted to cry out, but his throat was sealed off. He couldn't take even the tiniest of breaths as he waited to feel the cold touch of this unseen presence. White spots of light shot across his vision like exploding comets. His throat made a loud clicking sound when he tried to swallow a gulp of air to quench the fire in his chest. He could feel the darkness pressing in against him, squeezing him until he felt as though he were encased in cement.

And then a voice, whispering and raw, filled the darkness.

" . . . are you here? . . ."

He couldn't speak, but he was amazed that—somehow—he found the strength and courage to reach one hand out blindly into the darkness. He felt around on the cold floor until he came in contact with something. Panic seized him when he felt a hand clasp around his wrist and start to squeeze tightly.

" . . . don't worry . . . ," said the voice.

It was as fragile as thin glass, but it pierced the darkness and made him feel a subtle current of warmth as the hand fumbled down, and fingers entwined his own. Then the hand started to pull him forward.

"Don't worry, Jeff," the voice rasped, broken from crying. "Don't worry . . . I'm here . . . I still love you."

Part One

Many are the forms of what is unknown.
　　　　　　　　　　—Euripides

That they could treat me so!
I, the mind of the past, to be driven under the ground
outcast, like dirt!
　　　　　　　　　　　—Aeschylus

Chapter One
Old Pain

"So, you think you might have overreacted to all of this, then, is that it?"

Pressing his clenched fist hard against his mouth, Jeff Wagner nodded as he sawed his teeth back and forth over his lower lip. For the last several minutes—*Goddamn, but it felt like hours!*—he had been pacing back and forth across the office floor, his shoes whispering on the thick pile carpet; but now he stopped short and turned to look at Walter Ingalls, his therapist.

"Yeah," Jeff said, painfully aware of how fragile his voice sounded. "Yeah . . . definitely . . . I think I overreacted."

"And do you have any idea why?" Walter asked.

Walter was slouching back in his cushioned chair, his head tilted forward as he stared at Jeff over the top edge of his bifocals. His folded hands were placed comfortably across the rounded expanse of his stomach. As always, Walter was wearing a faded tweed sport coat, beige Dockers, a wrinkled blue Oxford cloth dress shirt, and his trademark blue-and-purple diamond-design necktie. What little hair he had left, thin blond wisps that lifted with the slightest passing breeze, was swept straight back, making his forehead look exceptionally white and wide. Jeff's first impression upon meeting him eight years ago, when he had first started therapy, was that Walter looked like an alien, a Martian, perhaps, with an overdeveloped cranium to contain his enlarged brain.

"I mean, of course," Walter added, "other than your obvious concern for your sister's health."

"Yeah," Jeff said softly.

He realized he'd been holding his breath, so he let it out in a long, whistling hiss.

"Umm . . . my sister."

He shook his head and squinted his eyes in an attempt to keep them from tearing up, but his vision started to blur. Turning away from Walter, he wiped away the tears with the heel of his hand as he looked out the window, past the busy streets and rows of buildings to the purple shaded wrinkles of the distant Rocky Mountains. Fast-moving fair-weather clouds dotted the wide arc of blue sky like puffs of cotton. Their shadows shifted rapidly across the distant foothills, making the ground look like it was dark, churning water instead of the solid ground Jeff knew it was. In the distance, the line of mountains stood out in sharp relief against the sky. Mount Evans seemed so close he thought he could almost reach out and touch it as it floated mirage-like on the horizon, looking like a razor's edge slicing across the sky. It was another beautiful autumn afternoon in Denver, but Jeff could find absolutely no pleasure in it.

"Well," Walter said after clearing his throat, "it's entirely understandable that you're upset about what happened to Judy."

Jeff snapped his head up and glared at Walter. "It didn't *happen* to her! *She* did it! *She's* the one who tried to kill herself!"

"So, do you want to talk about it? Care to tell me what happened?"

"That's why I called and asked if you could fit me in today," Jeff snapped. Sighing, he closed his eyes and started to massage his neck as he rotated his head back and forth. It didn't come close to relieving the iron rod of tension that was jamming up inside his spine. He could feel his shoulder muscles contracting, and already there was a cold, hard pulsing behind his eyes. He knew he was going to have one *bitch* of a headache, if not right now, then very soon.

"I was in class . . . teaching my—ahh, my freshman course in Ancient History when Gladys Tyler, the office secretary, came to the door." He sniffed with tight laughter and shook his head. "It's funny, but as soon as I saw her face—goddamn! I *knew* something was wrong."

"Did she look worried or concerned in any way?" Walter offered.

Jeff shook his head tightly. "No, not really. I just knew that something had happened. You know, I feel as though sometimes I can . . . I can *sense* when something bad's going to happen."

"You don't think that this *feeling* you had was because you were expecting something bad to happen, do you?" Walter said, sounding more declarative than inquisitive.

Jeff snorted another short burst of laughter that almost sent snot flying from his nose. A heavy pulse throbbed behind his eyes.

"Come on, Walter!" he said, trying to keep from shouting. "After eight years, you ought to know me well enough to know that I'm *always* expecting something bad to happen. Always!"

Walter raised his eyebrows, but he wasn't going to rise to the bait.

"So," he said calmly, his eyes looking almost lazy, "what did she say?"

Jeff narrowed his eyes as he continued to rub his forehead, wishing to Heaven that the steadily increasing *thump-thump* of pain would subside. "She just knocked on the door. Then she leaned her head into the room and told me that my wife was on the phone in the department office. As soon as she said that, I *knew* something bad had happened."

"But you didn't know what . . . or to whom."

Jeff shook his head.

"No, but of course my first thought was that something had happened to Robin—"

In the center of his head, the pain was growing steadily stronger, throbbing like a pulsating light that grew brighter with each flash. A thick, sour taste filled the back of Jeff's throat.

"And why do you think you immediately thought it had anything to do with Robin?"

Jeff covered his mouth with one hand and shook his head. The motion made a flash of light streak across his vision.

"I have no idea," he said, hearing the raw rasp of his voice. "I mean I . . . once you have kids, it's only natural that you worry about them all the time, isn't it?" He waved his hands in front of his face for emphasis.

"Well, I don't think it's healthy to worry *all* the time," Walter said without a trace of condescension in his voice.

"Yeah, but—you know, we just moved into the house on Downing Street last spring. It's a nice place, beautiful house overlooking Washington Park and all, but the traffic out there is horrible, so—yeah, on a nice day like this, my first thought was that she was on her bike or something, and she just went shooting out into the road, or maybe she got hit by a car or something while crossing the street to go play in the park."

"But wouldn't she have left for school by eight o'clock?"

Jeff nodded. "Sure she would, but I didn't think of that—not at first, anyway. I excused myself from the class, telling the students they could leave if I wasn't back within fifteen minutes, and went down to the office."

Walter nodded and, lowering his voice, said, "And that's when you found out about your sister."

Again, Jeff's eyes started to sting, but he blinked them furiously, trying to keep the tears at bay. He couldn't say anything, so he just stood there in front of the opened window, nodding his head up and down. The pain behind his eyes was almost intolerable.

"We don't have to talk about this if you don't want to, you know," Walter said, using his mellow, let's-go-with-the-flow voice.

"No, I *want* to talk about it," Jeff said, perhaps a tad too forcefully. He turned and started pacing back and forth in front of the window. "I *have* to talk about it. It's been . . . how long? Almost six months, now, since I stopped coming to you. I . . . I thought I was cured, you know?"

"Well, you certainly have made a great deal of progress since we started working together," Walter said.

"Yeah, but—I mean, if I've made such great progress, why does something like this upset me so much?"

He could hear the twisted pain in his own voice as he looked over at Walter and wished, although he knew better, that his therapist could just snap his fingers and everything would be all right. Jeff knew therapy didn't work like that, but from time to time, it didn't stop him from wishing that it did—especially in situations like this, when he was feeling so vulnerable.

But *why,* he wondered, why the hell was he feeling so much pressure?

Sure, he was concerned about what had happened to his sister. Who wouldn't be? But what bothered him almost as much was that, as soon as he got the message that his wife had called, he had been so convinced, so positive that something bad had happened to Robin. After eight years of therapy, he would have thought he could cut right to the heart of the matter and see what was *really* bothering him, but—apparently—he wasn't quite "cured" enough.

"You mean you're upset about your sister?"

"No!" Jeff shouted.

He punched his clenched fist into his open palm, making a wet smacking sound. Cold tension filled his stomach. He could feel his testicles shrivel and suck up into his body cavity as he continued to pace back and forth. The air in Walter's office seemed entirely too thin to breathe, and from somewhere a cold draft of air made him shiver in spite of the sweat that had broken out on his brow. He suddenly stopped pacing and sat down heavily in the plush chair beside Walter's desk. Groaning softly, he started rubbing his brow again.

"Would you like a drink of water? An aspirin, maybe?" Walter asked.

Jeff nodded and held out his hand as Walter opened a bottle of Excedrin and shook two pills into his hand. He went over to the watercooler and washed the pills down with several gulps of almost numbingly cold water.

"You'll feel better in a minute or two," Walter said.

"Yeah," Jeff replied, his voice hushed.

After a moment of silence, Walter cleared his throat and said, "You were saying? . . ."

"Umm—yeah," he said, slumping back in the seat and letting it surround him. "I mean—sure I'm wor-

ried about my sister. Of *course* I am! But what bugs me
almost as much is, why the hell, as soon as I think
anything's wrong, do I immediately think something's
happened to *Robin?*"

Walter shrugged, making the padded shoulders of
his jacket wrinkle up and almost touch his ears.

"I would think you would have a better handle on
that than I would," he said mildly. "How old is
Robin? Is she six now?"

"Yeah, she just turned six last July," Jeff said, letting his shoulders drop. His whole body sagged as
though he was utterly defeated, but still the pain
throbbed behind his eyes. For a few seconds, he closed
his eyes and sighed, letting his mind fill with an image
of his daughter—her long, dark hair framing her thin
face; her wide, almond-shaped eyes, so much like her
mother's; and her smile, so wide and genuine. God,
she was a beautiful child, and he felt no guilt admitting
to himself that she was the center of his life.

"You have kids of your own, right?" Jeff asked in a
trembling voice.

Walter nodded. "Yup. A boy and a girl. They're
both off to college now. Alice is a junior, majoring in
economics at Tulane, and Tod's a freshman at D.U."

"So you must know what it's like, when you feel as
though your children mean everything, I mean absolutely *everything* to you, right?"

"Sure I do," Walter said simply.

"Especially when they're little, right?" Jeff said.
"When they're so . . . so defenseless against the world.
You feel as though you'd do anything . . . I mean
anything to protect them, and that you . . . you'd
probably lose your mind or something if anything ever
happened to them, right?"

Walter nodded. "Absolutely, but I think there's a
fine line between being protective and being *over*protective."

"Fuck, don't I ever *know* that!"

Again in frustration, Jeff smacked the flat of his palm with his fist. He winced as another jolt of pain rocketed through his head.

"So," Walter went on, "I'd suggest what you need to think about is, why? Why would you feel so instantly concerned, to the point where—well, you said so yourself—even after you found out that it wasn't Robin, but your sister, Judy, you weren't able to go back and continue your class?"

Jeff felt a sudden jolt of anger directed at Walter. He tried not to say anything, but he couldn't stop himself from leaning forward and shouting, "Well for Christ's sake, who the fuck wouldn't be upset? I just found out my sister tried to . . . to *kill* herself? How the fuck am I supposed to feel?"

Completely unfazed by the outburst, Walter sat back and simply nodded.

"I never said that I blame you for anything you might think or feel," he said calmly, "but you still haven't gotten to the core of the problem here about your reaction . . . your *over*reaction. Why do you think this upset you so?"

Covering his face with both hands, Jeff took a deep breath and let it out slowly. The air rushing between his fingers sounded like Darth Vader, breathing.

"We've done a lot of work over the years, Jeff," Walter went on, "but you have to keep in mind that it's still all process, not product. All of it! There's no single point at which I'm going to stamp you with a rubber stamp that says totally cured. The fact that you felt that you needed to come in and see me again is encouraging. You've demonstrated that you know you have to work through these things as they arise, as life throws them at you. Sometimes they're hard to take. *Damned* hard. I understand completely how you must feel about what happened to your sister."

"What *she* did to *herself,*" Jeff said hollowly.

"Yes, what she did! You've told me a lot about her over the years, and I completely sympathize with how you must be feeling."

Jeff looked at him but said nothing.

"As regards your overreaction about your daughter—well, I'd say there must still be some issues that you have to bring out into the open. This kind of reaction could have a basis in something that happened to you, back when you were about the same age as she is now. It could be connected with something that's been buried in your memory. From what you've told me about your parents—"

"Yeah," Jeff said, interrupting him with a snort of repressed laughter. "My goddamned parents!"

"Well, from what you've told me about them, how you always felt they were never around for you while you were growing up, I'm not at all surprised that you might err on the other side of caution and be perhaps—and I emphasize the word *perhaps*—a little bit *too* overprotective."

"But in a world like ours, how much is *too* overprotective? Can you tell me that?"

Walter shrugged. "Well, I'd guess it's safe to say it's too much when every time something goes wrong, you think it's happened to your child."

"Umm . . . yeah," Jeff said, nodding listlessly. By now, he'd almost grown accustomed to the pulsating pain in his head. "I mean—I can see that." He took a shuddering breath and held it for a moment.

"And Robin is *how* old again?"

"She's six," Jeff replied, his voice now sounding pale and dispirited.

"Six years old," Walter echoed, his voice resonating deeply. "Does that particular age ring any bells for you?"

For several seconds, Jeff remained silent, just sitting

there, rubbing his forehead, and listening to the soft whisper of his pulse in his ears. He wished desperately that the sound would blot out of his mind the memories that were stirring within him. An icy chill gripped him and made him shiver. He barely recognized his own voice when he whispered, "Yeah . . . it rings a bell for me, all right."

"Oh, really?" Walter leaned forward, his eyebrows raised. "So tell me about it."

Jeff looked at Walter, suddenly angry at the way the man seemed always just to sit there as though he were in judgment of his psyche.

"Yeah," Jeff said, feeling a sudden white flash of fear. "That's how old Jeremy . . . my little brother was . . . when he . . . when he—"

His throat caught, and his voice cut off sharply. He felt the hot track of a tear run down his cheek.

"—when he *what?*" Walter said, prodding him once the silence had gone on a bit too long.

Jeff's eyes were brimming with tears as he stared at his therapist. His throat was constricted, and although his lips moved, no sound would come out. The cold, tingling tightness was squeezing in on him, and he felt as though his head was going to explode. Finally, in a voice that was little more than a gasp, he managed to say, "When he . . . when Jeremy . . . died."

Jeff let out a shuddering gasp and slumped back in the chair feeling totally exhausted.

"My brother Jeremy was . . . six years old when he . . . when he drowned in the river . . ."

"You've mentioned that to me before," Walter said, narrowing his eyes and nodding sympathetically. "Is there anything else you want to add?"

"I was—I was supposed to be—to be watching him," Jeff said, his voice breaking on just about every word. He squeezed his eyes shut, no longer concerned about the tears that were flowing from his eyes. The pain in his head receded, but only because there was the sharper pain of this memory.

"We were—playing—down by the river, and I was just—I just left him there—it was only for a few minutes while I went off to—to do something by myself. I don't even remember what it was, but when I . . . when he . . . when I came back, he was . . . he was gone, and we—we never saw him again."

"You've told me all of that before," Walter said. He took a tissue from the dispenser on his desk and handed it to Jeff, who started blotting the tears from his eyes. "I just wanted you to make the connection for yourself."

Jeff stiffened and looked at him. "So what you're suggesting is, I'm overreacting about all of this just because Robin's now the same age Jeremy was when he died, that I think it was somehow *my* fault, *my* responsibility, is that it?"

"No," Walter said quietly. "I'm not suggesting that. *You* are."

Jeff closed his eyes and sobbed silently for several seconds, but at last he straightened up, blew his nose into the tissue, and looked squarely at Walter.

"Okay," he said. His voice still sounded raw and unnaturally high, but it was a shade stronger. "So I've made the connection. *Now* what?"

Walter shrugged and shook his head. "I'd say that's entirely up to you, don't you think?"

"Well . . . yeah, I suppose so, but . . ."

"So, what are you going to do?"

Jeff cleared his throat, and after a moment he said, "Well, shit, I'm going to have to go back home . . . to Maine, to help my sister. I know *that* much."

"I see."

"I mean, there's no way around it, is there?" His voice sounded forceful, as though even now he was trying hard to convince himself. "I *have* to go back home and . . . and deal with all of this."

"And you don't like that," Walter offered. "You feel very uncomfortable about it?"

In a flash, Jeff felt his anger rise at Walter again. Sometimes he didn't like it at all the way he just sat there, pompously illuminating the obvious.

"Of *course* I don't like it!" he shouted, squeezing his fist tightly. Pain jolted inside his head, almost making him cry out. "I haven't been back home since—well, since my folks died in 1978. I had to go back for their funeral, but that was more than fifteen years ago."

"And you haven't seen your sister since then?"

Jeff shook his head. "No, she's come out here a few times and visited us. Once ever year or two. It's a lot easier—and cheaper—for her to fly out here than it is for all of us to fly back East."

"I see," Walter said, nodding. He stroked his chin thoughtfully and for a moment stared past Jeff at the view outside his office window. "So tell me, Jeff, in one word—the first thing that pops into your head, how do you feel about going back to Maine?"

"Scared."

The word was out of his mouth before he could stop it. Grunting with surprise, he covered his mouth with his hand as though he could somehow take the word back.

"Scared," Walter repeated softly.

His voice had a calming lilt to it, but the word sent a wash of chills through Jeff.

"Fuckin'-A, I'm scared," Jeff said, having to fight back the freezing surge of nervousness that was steadily tightening around him.

"And can you tell me what—exactly—you are afraid of?"

Jeff narrowed his eyes and looked at Walter. He could feel his insides trembling. He wasn't even sure if he'd be able to speak, but he finally cleared his throat and said, "You know damned right well what I'm most afraid of." His voice was little more than a twisted hiss.

Walter nodded again but said nothing. For several seconds—seconds that seemed like hours to Jeff—the office was silent except for the crackling sound made by the radiator and the faint hiss of traffic passing by outside.

"So what am I going to do about it?" he finally said, his voice rising to a plaintive whine. "What the hell am I going to do if . . . if *they* come back?"

Walter smiled reassuringly, but Jeff thought his smile looked more like a grimace, the frozen rictus he imagined would be plastered across a dead person's face.

"You're telling me you're afraid that your alter personalities might begin to reassert themselves again, is that it?"

Every muscle in Jeff's body contracted.

"You're damned right I am," he said.

"Even though we've been through eight years of therapy and have gone through the entire integration process."

Again, what Walter said sounded more like a statement than a question.

Jeff bit his lower lip and nodded.

"But you *do* realize that you still can go into the safe room, don't you?"

Biting down harder onto his lower lip, Jeff nodded again. The motion sent a sharp spike of pain through his head.

"And you know that you can go there, in your mind, any time you want and talk to any of those other personalities, right?"

Jeff didn't answer. He just sat there, staring blankly ahead. His head suddenly felt extraordinarily heavy, as though his neck could no longer support it. The room seemed to be closing in on him from all sides, and at the edges of his vision, he saw dark, shifting curtains drifting inward.

"You realize by now that none of your multiple personalities were ever real, I hope. You're convinced of that, aren't you? That they're really just fragmented aspects of your own personality that *seemed* to be distinct? You realize that, don't you?"

Jeff wanted to reply, but his mouth felt like it was filled with cotton, and he couldn't begin to form any words out of the chaos that was raging inside his mind.

Walter leaned forward and placed both hands on the top of his desk, looking for a moment as though he was preparing to vault over it.

"Don't forget that, Jeff," he said in a deep, earnest voice. "You still have that *safe* room. You *always* have it, and you can go there whenever you want to or need to and talk to any of them."

Blinking his eyes rapidly, Jeff looked at him, and saw the genuine concern and caring intensity in Walter's eyes. It helped pull him back . . . a little. He stopped nodding his head and, after licking his lips, he said in a croaking voice, "Yeah . . . I know that."

Walter pointed his index finger at him and shook it. "Well, don't you forget it!" he said, his voice low and commanding. "You hear me? Any time you think you need to, you just go there and talk to them. See what they have to say."

Jeff's head was still hammering as he rose to his feet, preparing to go. He looked at Walter and nodded as he held his hand out for him to shake.

"Don't worry," he said. His head hurt so bad he could hardly concentrate on what he was saying. "I won't forget."

*   *   *

As he drove along Pena Boulevard, heading toward Denver International Airport, a hard, cold lump of apprehension formed in Jeff's stomach. He wished now that he had let Sally do the driving. He was wound up enough as it was about flying and going back to Maine; he sure as hell didn't need the added hassle of dealing with all this traffic.

"What the devil is this, anyway?" he asked through gritted teeth. "Is *everyone* flying out of Denver today?"

A woman driving a small red Honda sped past him on the left and then darted in front of him with little room to spare. Jeff tapped the brake pedal with his foot and at the same time punched the horn once, hard.

"Christ, another coat of paint, and that asshole would've hit us!"

"You shouldn't swear, Daddy," Robin piped from the backseat.

"Yeah, you can take it easy, you know. You've still got plenty of time before your flight," Sally said. She smiled reassuringly as she patted his arm, but her touch made him flinch.

"Yeah, except I don't have any idea how to find my way around out here," Jeff said.

"The airport's still too new," Sally said mildly. "No one knows their way around yet."

"Yeah, especially people like that fu—, like that idiot who just cut me off," Jeff said, glaring ahead at the small red car. It was several cars ahead of him, still weaving in and out of traffic. "With my luck, I'll probably be sitting next to that asshole on the plane."

"Come *on,* Daddy! Watch your language!" Robin squealed from behind him.

"Okay, sorry . . . sorry. I-I'm just feeling a little bit tense," he said, and concluded with a tight laugh.

They drove in silence for a while until Robin leaned

over the front seat, pointed at the distant roof line of the terminal, and said, "You know, I *still* think they look like a whole bunch of Indian teepees."

Jeff glanced at her over his shoulder and smiled, but the knot in his stomach didn't go away; it got even harder when he recalled how terrified he had been— *God, had it been just yesterday?*—that something had happened to her. His eyes stung as the thought came to him—again—of how he thought he would absolutely lose his mind if anything ever happened to his little girl.

"Yeah, they sure do," he said, his voice trembling as he flicked his gaze back and forth between his daughter and the road ahead. Thankfully, the red Honda was out of sight.

"I don't think it looks as bad as everybody says," Sally offered. She was obviously picking up on his nervousness, so she gave his arm a firm squeeze just above the elbow. This time Jeff didn't pull away from her.

"You know, we could still plan to fly out in a day or two and join you," Sally said. "Doctor Schober told me I could have as much time off as I wanted, no problem."

Jeff shook his head as he glanced at her. The slanting early morning sunlight illuminated his wife's face, making her pale blue eyes sparkle like wet marbles. Every highlight in her dark hair seemed alive with cold fire, and her skin looked as smooth and pale as polished marble.

God, she's beautiful! Jeff thought, and the knot in his stomach tightened even more. *What the hell is someone as gorgeous as her doing with a schmuck like me?*

He shifted uncomfortably in the car seat, painfully aware of the tight grip he had on the steering wheel. His knuckles were nearly bone-white in the morning sun.

The hands of a dead man, he thought, and couldn't repress the shudder that reached up his back.

Again he glanced at Robin in the backseat and was amazed at how much she looked like a miniature version of her mother. Jeff had always had to look hard to see any of his own family resemblances in his daughter's face, and that was just fine with him. He hoped to Heaven that his daughter—and any other children he and Sally might eventually have, and Lord knows they had been trying!—would *never* take after his side of the family!

"Well?" Sally said, when Jeff didn't respond. She applied a bit more pressure to the grip she had on his arm. "Are you *sure* you don't want us to come?"

"Huh?" Jeff said, shaking his head as though dazed. "Oh, yeah. I'm sure I don't need you there."

"Well *thanks* a *lot!*" Sally said. She pulled away from him and, leaning against her door, stared straight ahead out the front window.

"Oh, come on, Sally. It's not like that," Jeff said, but Sally continued to stare straight ahead. They were all silent for a while until Jeff snapped on his turn signal and pulled into the right lane for short-term parking. Robin let out a low gasp as she stared up at a plane that was just taking off with an earsplitting roar and blast of blue exhaust. Her face was pressed flat against the glass, smearing the window.

As they were approaching the parking lot, Jeff sighed and, reaching out, took Sally firmly by the hand.

"It's not like that, and you know it," he said softly, hoping that Robin was so involved with watching the planes taking off that she wasn't picking up on any of the tension between them. "Not at all. I just—"

He squeezed her hand and almost choked on the wave of tension that tightened his throat.

"I won't be there all that long, and I think it's

. . . it's—" He nodded his head toward Robin in the backseat. "We couldn't get someone to cover Robin for the time, and I don't want to . . . you know, I don't think she needs to be exposed to—you know, to what's been going on."

"I know. I understand," Sally said, nodding as she placed her other hand on top of his. Jeff was painfully aware of how warm and full of strength her grip was while his own hand felt as stiff and cold as a dead man's. The stinging in his eyes got steadily worse, but he blinked away the tears as he pulled to a stop in front of the curb at a taxi stand in front of the terminal building. His hand was shaking as he shifted the car into park.

"Hey, aren't you going to park in the lot?" Sally asked, giving him another hard look.

Biting his lower lip, Jeff shook his head. "I don't think so. Hey, why pay a dollar or two just to park for a half hour or so. We can say goodbye here, and—"

"But I wanted a ride on the people mover. You promised!" Robin shouted as she leaned over the front seat, her hands clenched into fists.

Jeff gritted his teeth and shook his head firmly. "Some other time, sweetheart. I just want to get going for today."

"But you *promised!*"

"I know I did, but not today, all right?" Jeff said. He cast a meaningful glance at Sally.

"Your father's right, dear," Sally said. "Besides, you've already missed your school bus. I don't want you missing very much of school today."

"But Daddy, you *promised!*"

"Another time, sweetheart," Jeff said, twisting around and reaching over the seat to cup her face with one hand. "I don't even know my way around in here, and I-I just want to find the right gate and get on the plane so I can get to Maine and help Aunt Judy. You understand, don't you?"

"Yeah, but you promised," Robin repeated. There was now a note of grudging acceptance in her voice.

"Hey, when I get back, I promise we'll do something fun, okay? And don't worry, I'll call you every day. Maybe I'll even bring you back a real live Maine lobster or something."

"Lobster . . . *yuck!*" Robin said, wrinkling her nose.

"Well, then, I'll think of something," Jeff said as he mussed her hair. "Come on, give daddy a kiss goodbye."

Robin practically dived into the front seat as she wrapped her arms around her father's neck and pulled his face against hers to plant a big, wet kiss on his cheek. Jeff almost started crying again as he realized that he wouldn't be seeing his little girl for a few days, possibly as much as a week. Closing his eyes and inhaling deeply the scent of her hair, he clung to his daughter almost desperately. After a moment, he opened his eyes and looked at his wife over Robin's shoulder. Sighing heavily, he broke the embrace.

"Come on . . . you, too," he said as he held his arms out to Sally. She leaned forward and gave him a tight squeeze, and then pulled back a bit to kiss him firmly on the lips. Their kiss lengthened until the sound of a beeping car's horn drew their attention. Jeff glanced out the back of the car and saw the airport security van that had pulled up behind them. The officer in the car, an elderly man with thick, white hair, was smiling, but he pointed up at the TAXI STAND—NO PARKING ZONE sign and waved at them to move along.

Jeff reached into the backseat for his suitcase, snapped open the driver's door, and stepped out onto the road. A cold breeze tugged at his coat collar, and he shivered again, feeling a wave of loneliness, of desertion. Sally slid over behind the steering wheel while

Robin scrambled into the passenger's seat. Sally rolled down the window, and Jeff leaned down close to her.

"Don't worry," he said after kissing her again, this time on the cheek. "I'll call you just as soon as I get there. And you—" He pointed at Robin. "Buckle that seat belt!"

"Okay."

Again, the security cop tooted his horn, and Jeff stepped away from the car as Sally shifted into drive. They waved to each other, and Robin leaned forward and blew him a kiss with a wide sweep of both arms. Jeff gave her a big smile, but it didn't match at all what he was feeling inside as he watched the car slowly pull away from the curb. The cold, lonely ache in his stomach was even worse as he stepped up onto the sidewalk and watched the car disappear around the wide curving road. The security car eased past him, and the policeman inside smiled and gave him a friendly wave. Jeff nodded, but for several seconds he just stood there on the sidewalk, staring blankly at where he had last seen the family car.

The only thought in his mind was, *God, I don't know what I would do if something happened to either one of them while I was gone.*

After a long search for the United Airlines desk and the correct gate, and an even longer wait before boarding, Jeff was finally seated in the plane a little after nine o'clock. He had bought a newspaper and a copy of *Newsweek* for the flight at the news kiosk, but so far hadn't been able to concentrate on either of them. He'd been assigned a window seat but was hoping to change it if the plane wasn't filled. For the last fifteen minutes or so, while the ground crew refueled and went through the preflight check, he just sat there staring out past the wing at the long stretch of runway.

Beyond the runway was the flat, brown expanse of the prairie. In spite of the October morning chill, the air was shimmering with the heat of the sun rebounding from the asphalt.

Had it really been sixteen years since he had been back to Maine?

The last time he'd gone home had been in 1978, the year after he had graduated from UCLA, for his parents' funeral. His parents, John and Margaret, had died together in a boating accident while vacationing in Florida. Jeff had always thought their deaths seemed somehow appropriate, considering how often they had left him and his sister behind and gone off on their vacations. All the while Jeff and Judy were growing up, their parents often acted as if they didn't even have children. In many ways, Jeff viewed his parents as children who had never fully taken on the responsibilities of adulthood and parenthood.

And both of their children—he and Judy—had suffered because of it.

After eight years of therapy, Jeff realized that the way he had been raised was one of the major reasons why he worked so hard at maintaining a family life for Sally, Robin, and himself. Because as a child he and his sister were always being pawned off, usually staying out at the farm with Uncle Kirby and Aunt Mildred for weeks at a time, they had never felt the real security of a loving family. Now that Jeff had a wife and child of his own, he wanted to make damned sure he gave them something he'd never had . . . something it had taken him damned near eight years of therapy even to begin to get a handle on.

But sixteen years!

God, how could it have been *that* long?

His childhood in Maine now seemed like a dream, a distant memory that belonged to someone else, not to him, or else a psychic trace left over from a previous

lifetime. Ever since his marriage to Sally right after
college, through all the years they had both worked at
low-paying "shit" jobs so he could finish graduate
school and get his doctorate, and especially since he
had taken the job as a history professor at D.U., all he
had known—all he *wanted* to know—was his life in
Colorado.

To *hell* with Maine!

Having their first child, Robin, had merely added to
all of the things that distanced him from Cape Higgins, the town where he had grown up, and the child
he had once been. Time and time again as a therapeutic exercise, he had mentally written the words *Cape
Higgins, Maine* onto an imaginary piece of paper and
shredded it so he wouldn't have to think about it ever
again. And if his sister hadn't stayed there, living in the
old family homestead, he never would have thought
about it again.

But now—against his will—he had to go back.

Judy needed help.

He could feel the internal tension, the pressure of
who he *had* been as opposed to who he was *now,*
building up steadily inside him. He didn't consider
himself a particularly religious person, but he now
found himself praying to Heaven that he would be
able to handle this visit . . . and he hoped to hell that
he wouldn't have any type of relapse that would bring
back any of his old problems . . . problems like all
those different voices he used to hear, whispering inside his head . . . and the feelings he would get from
time to time that he wasn't always who he thought he
was, that he was someone else . . . and the fear he had
that he did things—or things happened—that he had
no awareness of until later, when one of his internal
voices would tell him about it. As he stared out at the
stretch of prairie, thoughts like this filled his mind with
a dull, gnawing terror.

"Hey, nice day to fly, don't 'cha think?"

The loud, boisterous voice, speaking so suddenly and so close to him, made Jeff turn around with a start.

"Sorry, I didn't mean to startle you," said the overweight, balding man as he dropped into the seat beside Jeff. The man grunted as he leaned forward and stuffed a battered briefcase underneath the seat in front of him. Then he reached up and turned on both overhead fans, and directed them toward his sweating face. He took a handkerchief from his jacket pocket and wiped his forehead a few times.

"M'name's Will . . . Will Bartlett. What's yours?"

Jeff was a bit taken aback by the plump warmth of the man's sweaty grip. As soon as they broke contact, he leaned forward and surreptitiously wiped his hand on his pant leg.

"Uhh—Jeff . . . I'm Jeff Wagner."

"Well, pleased to meet 'cha, Jeff. So, where you heading this fine day?"

Still feeling a bit distracted, Jeff glanced around the cabin as though looking for a stewardess who would acknowledge that a mistake had been made, that this man was not supposed to be sitting next to him; but all of the stewardesses seemed occupied with getting ready for takeoff.

"I have uh . . . an hour stopover in Chicago," Jeff said. "I'm on my way to Portland, Maine."

"Maine, huh? Lobster-land—the pine-tree state," Will said, his fleshy face breaking into a wide smile. "Nice place. Beautiful. I've been there three or four times, mostly for business. You going there for a little vacation, are ya?"

"Actually, no," Jeff said, shifting in his seat and trying to put another inch or two of distance between him and Will. "My . . . uh, there's been a family emergency that I have to attend to."

"Oh, so sorry to hear that," Will said, clucking his tongue as he shook his head. Already, his brow was bathed with sweat again, and his face had a disconcerting red flush.

"Me," Will went on, "I'm on my way to a convention in Detroit. I sell life insurance."

"That's nice," Jeff said.

Without anything more to say, he turned to look out the window again, staring past his own ghostlike reflection in the glass to the prairie beyond. He was painfully aware of Will's motions as he shifted his bulk from side to side, settling into his seat. The heavy scent of the man's antiperspirant almost choked him, but he was grateful the man didn't need a shower. That would have made the flight to Chicago unbearable. After a while—once Will apparently had caught the hint that Jeff wasn't in a talkative mood—he was left to his own thoughts again. The flight attendants ran through the safety regulations and emergency procedures—as if any of their suggestions were going to help if the plane dropped forty thousand feet!—and then the jets began to roar as the airplane taxied for takeoff.

The force of the takeoff pressed Jeff back against his seat. He opened his mouth and wiggled his jaw back and forth, hoping to relieve the pressure that was building up in his ears. Leaning close to the window and looking down at the rapidly receding prairie, he watched the reflection of his face skimming like a thin mirage across the dun-colored earth and then the sky. Cold tension filled him, and he tried desperately to push aside the impression he had that his face was nothing but a mask—unblinking and lifeless.

He licked his lips and swallowed with difficulty, already missing his family. He wondered if Sally and Robin were still down there, parked somewhere on the side of the road and watching for his plane to take off, or if they had already left to get Robin to school on time. As the horizon stretched out and bowed down, and the sunlight shifted slowly across his face, the plane banked to the east and then leveled off.

The cold knot in Jeff's stomach tightened even more. He couldn't tear his gaze away from his reflection in the window, and he couldn't stop wondering—as he had so much over the last ten years—if he really *knew* that person he was looking at.

And beneath that thought was another, deeper worry.

He couldn't help but wonder if he would ever see his wife and child again.

Chapter Two

Conversation in a Dark Room: #1

"Hey, come on! I know there's someone in here. I can hear you breathing."

I take a deep breath and hold it, listening as I lean my head back against the wall. I am vaguely surprised that the wall feels so soft. Even the floor of the room is spongy and warm, like a foam cushion that's been left out in the sun. I don't remember the room ever being like this before, but then again, it's been a long time since I've been in here. I place my fingers on the floor beside me and push, trying to determine what I'm sitting on.

The room is lost in total darkness, but I know this is the same room. I'm not exactly sure how I know this, but I'm positive it's the same only . . . different. There's a subtle smell in the air that's vaguely familiar, a certain *feeling* to the darkness that identifies the room for me like a long-lost friend . . . or maybe it's the deep, barely audible noise humming so low it rattles my teeth.

Whatever it is, I know perfectly well *where* I am; and just as surely, I know that I'm not alone.

"Come on, you can talk to me. Tell me who you are. I know you're in here."

"So take a guess."

Every muscle in my body tenses the instant I hear the voice, sounding so close to me. It hits my ears like a sudden hammer blow from out of the darkness, but four words quickly spoken aren't enough for me to identify it. I need more. At least now I know I'm not alone.

"Come on, then. You don't have to be afraid. You can talk to me, you know."

"I know that," says the voice, again with a close suddenness that catches me off guard. Pins and needles sweep like a dash of cold water up my arms. There still haven't been quite enough words for me to identify the speaker, but I know I recognize the voice. It's been a long time since I've been here.

"Look, I have the door locked, so nobody else can get in here, if that's what you're afraid of."

The dark room trembles with expectant silence as I wait for a reply.

"Come on. Say something. Why the hell are you playing this game with me? Is it Sammy?"

"Guess again," says the voice with just a trace of mocking humor.

I can feel my anger rising. Beads of sweat break out on my brow. I wipe them away with my forearm. My armpits feel cold and clammy.

"Come on, you can talk to me," I say, making an effort to keep my voice steady and low. I don't want any trace of my rising anxiety to show.

"It's been a while, hasn't it?" I continue. "We must have a lot to talk about."

After a long pause, the voice says, "Yeah, I guess we do."

"Alexander!" I practically shout as I lean forward, trying to pierce the darkness. "It's you, isn't it?"

"Very good, Jeff. I'm impressed."

"So . . . Alexander . . . How the hell have you been?"

"You should know," replies Alexander in a voice as smooth as oil.

"Yeah, I guess I should," I say, sniffing with laughter. "But you tell me."

I shift my position and, on impulse, reach out into the darkness in an attempt to touch Alexander. I want at least to shake hands with him, but he draws back, knowing that I can't touch him. I've never been able to touch any of the people I talk to in this room. It's one of the unwritten rules. Usually I accept that, but right now, I'm feeling so lost, so vulnerable that I feel almost compelled to try. I *need* some human contact.

"So," I say after a moment, my voice tightening with tension, "I guess you must know all about what's happened . . . with Judy, I mean."

I stare into the darkness which is so intense it begins to flicker with shifting curtains of dark energy. I feel as though I'm suspended in a dark, dimensionless void. For all I know, I could be falling . . . spinning head over heels into the darkness. Washes of pinprickling heat alternating with bone-deep cold sweep up my back and over my neck. Faintly, I can hear a low, steady roar that reminds me of . . . something.

Damn!

I can't quite place it.

"Of *course* I know what happened to Judy," Alexander says. The way his voice lifts up at the end signals that he isn't quite through speaking. I wait, and after a long pause, Alexander adds, "Wait a second, are you talking about what happened recently? Or do you mean what happened . . . well, you know . . . back . . . before?"

"No, I-I mean what just happened," I say. The tension nearly strangles me.

"Yeah," says Alexander. "It's too bad, really, isn't it? I mean, your poor sister . . . she's just never been happy, has she?"

My lips feel hot and chapped, as though I'm leaning too close to an unseen fire. I lick them furiously before speaking again.

"No," I say, my voice not much more than a croak. "I-I don't think you could say she's ever been . . . happy. I mean *really* happy."

"Or very lucky," Alexander says. "I mean, after two failed marriages, a miscarriage the one and only time she ever really wanted to get pregnant, and a job in an insurance company she's had since high school, working for a boss she absolutely loathes. No, I'd have to say it's a rather sad situation, really." Again that long, expectant pause as I wait for him to finish his thoughts. "It's no wonder she tried to kill herself."

"Who . . . well, I mean, who can say why," I offer.

Alexander lowers his voice to a rumbling, accusatory tone. "I would think, Jeff, that *you* would know more than anyone else."

A sticky, sour taste floods the back of my throat, the taste I always get whenever I'm going to throw up.

"Wh-why would you say something like that?" I ask, no longer able to control the shaking in my voice; but even before the words are out of my mouth, my face flushes as I anticipate Alexander's response.

"Oh, come on, now, Jeff!" Alexander says, sounding almost as though he's spitting. "Do you mean to tell me that we have to go through all of that all over again?" He lets out an exasperated sigh that sounds like a leaky radiator. "Sheesh!"

The darkness of the room seems to deepen. I try to take a deep breath, but the air feels thick in my throat and lungs, like warm honey, smothering, impossible to breathe.

"Do I *really* need to remind you about what you and she *did* together?" Alexander says.

I shake my head slowly from side to side, feeling it press back hard against the cushiony wall. Funny, I think, but I always remembered the walls as being hard, like stone. And the room is usually a lot cooler than this. Sweat is streaming down my sides, tickling my ribs.

"I thought we'd been through all of that . . . well, at least enough times so you'd finally accept it and forget about it," Alexander says. "I mean, after all, you *were* only children at the time, right?"

"Yeah, I know, but—"

"But *what?*"

"But that doesn't necessarily excuse it, you know?"

"No, I don't suppose it does," Alexander says, followed by a heavy breath. "But still, I wonder . . ."

There is a long pause. As I wait for Alexander to continue, the roaring sound rises louder all around me. I feel myself sway sickeningly to one side. Vertigo grips me, and I moan out loud, shifting my weight in an attempt to compensate.

"What?" I shout, feeling suddenly angry. "You wonder what? Tell me, you son of a bitch! What do you wonder?"

"Well . . ." Alexander says, letting his voice drag teasingly. "I just wonder . . . I mean, I wasn't there at the time, you know, but I've always been curious if you and she . . . you know, if you and your sister ever really went all the way, if you know what I mean."

I choke on my anger and am unable to say anything.

"I mean, like you always told me, you were—what? Ten years old at the time, weren't you? And she was twelve? I just don't see how you could have—you

know, could have gotten it up, as they say, and really
done it."

"I-I don't want to go over all of this again," I say.
The sour taste flooding my mouth makes me suddenly
panicky that I am going to throw up. I don't want to
do that here in the dark room.

"Hey, I didn't bring it up," Alexander says, his
voice sounding smooth and all innocence now.

"Oh yes you did," I say, almost snarling. "I know
I sure as hell didn't want to talk about it."

"Oh, but maybe you *did*," Alexander offers.
"Maybe that's what's been bugging you all along, ever
since you heard that Judy tried to kill herself. Maybe
that's why you came here in the first place, to talk this
over with me . . . Again! You must remember how, all
these years, I've been telling you just to forget about it
and get on with your life. I have, haven't I?"

"Yeah, but I . . . I can't."

"And why is that?"

My throat makes a loud sound when I swallow, but
words fail me.

"Maybe you should, you know?" Alexander goes
on. "Just forget about it. Look at what it's doing to
you. This one little thing from back when you were a
kid is making you a goddamned nervous wreck."

"Well, look at what it did to *Judy,* for Christ's
sake!" I suddenly shout.

"Maybe . . . and maybe not," Alexander replies
coolly. "Did you ever stop to think that what she
did—what she *tried* to do—might have absolutely
nothing to do with what you and she did back then?
Did you ever even *consider* that?"

I shrug, even though I know the motion is wasted in
the total darkness of the room.

"Well, think about it for a minute, Jeff. Why do you
think anything that has to do with Judy, with *her* life
and *her* decisions and some of the shit that's happened

to her has to revolve around you? Do you *really* think
you're all *that* goddamned important?"

"No, I-I'm not saying that . . . not at all," I reply.
Again, my face feels flushed. "I just know how much
it's bothered me ever since it happened, and I would
think that it—that it would—"

"That it would *what?*" Alexander says. He doesn't
shout at all, but his voice has the power of command.

"I . . . I don't know," I say, my voice barely a
whisper.

"Maybe—and I'm not calling you a liar or anything, you understand, but just *maybe* you never even
really *did* it with her, you know? Have you ever
thought about that?"

"Jesus Christ! Why do you have to keep saying *did*
it?" I shout as my anger stiffens my resolve. "Can't
you come right out and say it? Come to think of it, I
don't think you ever have. Maybe *you're* the one who
can't accept what happened. Maybe *you're* the one
who can't let it go."

"Okay, then," Alexander says. He clears his throat,
and I hear him inhale sharply through his nose. "I'll
say it if it will make you happy. Maybe you never did
fuck your sister. Is that what you want to hear? Or
even if you did *fuck* her—even if you took that little
ten-year-old prick of yours and stuck it up into her
cunt, maybe it doesn't even count. You keep telling me
you were just kids at the time. So maybe it doesn't
even *count* as real *fucking,* huh? You've certainly
fucked since then. Did it feel like the same thing?"

"Shut up," I scream. "Just shut the fuck up! Go
away! I didn't even want to talk to you in the first
place."

"Oh, you didn't, huh?"

"No, I . . . I . . ." My voice trails away. I cover my
face with both hands and start to sob. The cold ache
of loneliness fills me, and I know—even with Alexan-

der's voice all around me here in the dark room—that
I am alone . . .

Alone!

"It's just that sometimes . . . you know, sometimes
we were . . . we were scared and . . . and we were
all we had for . . . for comfort and . . . and for . . .
for . . ."

"Say it!" Alexander commands.

I take a deep breath and hold it until my lungs began
to hurt.

"Go on! . . . Say it!"

"For . . . *love,*" I say at last. The last word sounds
like a fading, dying gasp.

I sit stiffly, waiting for a reply, but Alexander says
nothing. I shiver, suddenly convinced that I am alone
in the dark room. As I reach out blindly into the
darkness, my fingers come to rest on something small
. . . it feels like cardboard . . . a folded book of matches.

I know on some deep level that there isn't really a
book of matches in my hand, that I have created it just
as I have created the dark room in my mind; but the
cold, dry lump in my throat gets even colder and drier
as I flip open the matchbook and run my fingers across
the tops of the matches. My hands are trembling as I
tear off a match. By feel, I find the scratch board on
the back of the packet. Holding my breath, I position
the match and then drag it slowly across the scratch
board. There is a loud sandpaper scratch, and then a
roaring sputter as a small flame erupts in the darkness.
It curls like a wicked orange flower with flame-tinged
petals.

My mind is a chaos of thoughts as I stare at the
flame and then raise the burning match up to my face.
The motion reminds me of lighting a cigarette, back
when I used to smoke. Jagged purple afterimages flash
across my vision like holes in the darkness. The brightness of the flame, as small as it is, makes my eyes sting.

For what seems like several seconds, my heart stops beating. My skin goes suddenly cold when I look up and see a face materialize slowly out of the darkness in front of me. The features seem to resolve out of the pitch-black as if the darkness itself is taking on form and substance.

I want to cry out as the face, ghoulishly underlit by the match, resolves and leans closer to me with a wide, leering smile. The eyes catch the firelight, but they seem to absorb it rather than reflect it back.

The eyes of a dead man!

The thought hits me with a soul-deep shiver, but there is no way I can say those words out loud as I stare in mute horror at my own face.

Every muscle in my body contracts violently. I suddenly lurch forward and let out a loud, gargling scream just as my eyes snap open . . .

Jeff found himself leaning awkwardly to one side, his head pressed against the cold glass of the airplane's rounded, rectangular window. He was staring at the double reflection of his own fear-widened eyes.

"Whoa!" said a booming voice so close behind him it made him jump. "Hey, Jeff, you all right there?"

The only thought that cut through Jeff's blinding panic was—*Thank God! At least that's not Alexander's voice!*

Turning his head around slowly, his neck aching, Jeff looked over at the frowning, florid face of Will Bartlett. Will's brow was wrinkled with concern, and all Jeff could think was how relieved Will must be that he didn't die on him, right here in his seat.

"Boy, you must've been having one *hell* of a dream there, buddy," Will said, laughing nervously. "I know it's kinda early in the day, but whadda ya say you lemme buy you a drink, huh?"

Chapter Three
Dark Landing

Because of a delay in Chicago, Jeff's plane was approaching Portland, Maine, quite a bit behind schedule. It was almost five-thirty in the evening when the NO SMOKING and FASTEN SEAT BELTS signs lit up. Somewhere over Vermont or New Hampshire, Jeff had watched the sun set, glowing with a harsh orange light that had rimmed the western horizon like a blazing brushfire.

As the landing gear *thunked* into place and the jet engines whined loudly, shaking the plane with sudden deceleration, Jeff checked his watch and realized that it was only three-thirty back home in Colorado.

Still daylight.

Robin would have gotten home from school only about an hour or so ago. He sighed, thinking how his life back home already seemed so remote, like it was more than two time zones away—like it was a lifetime or two away. He couldn't stop wondering what Sally and Robin might be doing at this exact moment. They could be making plans to go out for supper, maybe to Beau Jo's, Robin's favorite pizza place. Or maybe they were together in the kitchen, preparing an early supper and talking about where Daddy might be right now and how much they missed him.

He sure as hell knew he missed both of them!

Jeff felt relieved, knowing that Maine was already cloaked in darkness by the time the plane began its descent. Lights of houses and cars on the roads flickered in the dark, looking like an expansive miniature village. He was happy to be spared having to see much of the landscape, but no matter how much he tried not to, he couldn't help but try to identify certain landmarks. With all the lights, the city looked a lot more spread out than he remembered, although it was still nowhere near as big as Denver.

As the jet swung heavily around, he caught a glimpse of the half-moon that was riding high above a cloudbank to the east. Pale, silvery light was cast over the dark expanse of ocean, making it look like beaten pewter. Somewhere off to his right, directly due south of Portland and Cape Elizabeth, was Cape Higgins. He couldn't see it, but he could imagine what it must look like—a dark curlicue of land that stuck out into the ocean like a flattened fishhook.

"Son of a bitch," he whispered, his face so close to the window his breath fogged the glass. "Son of a goddamned fucking bitch!" His voice hitched in his throat, and he had to take a sudden, shuddering breath to keep from crying.

He stared at his distorted reflection in the window and watched as his jaw muscles clenched and unclenched, grinding his teeth back and forth. His eyes seemed to glimmer with a dull, unnatural light, and when he tried to analyze the expression on his face objectively, he thought he looked like someone who was close to the breaking point. Thankfully, Will Bartlett had said goodbye in Chicago, and for the second leg of his trip, Jeff had sat alone, so there was no one to hear him sigh or try to pry out of him what might be bothering him.

And—*shit!*—he had *plenty* on his mind!

He'd been unable to concentrate on reading the *Denver Post* or *Newsweek* throughout the flight, and so had slept fitfully, his mind filling with bizarre, unnerving dreams. Once he was awake and tried to capture the images, however, they dissolved away like cotton candy left out in the rain. He was certain of one thing—that he hadn't gone back into the dark room to talk to anyone else. He felt good about that. After months of feeling like he didn't want to do that anymore, he was starting to wonder whether or not he really needed to.

Maybe it would be better, he thought, if he just dealt with this whole situation with Judy on his own, handling things as things came up.

Maybe he was finally beyond needing any kind of psychological crutch.

Maybe . . .

Jeff caught glimpses of the landing lights, strobing blue-and-white beacons in the darkness that guided the plane in for a landing. The plane jolted when it touched down, and the wheels squealed on the asphalt as the roaring backwash of the engines blocked out every other sound, making everything vibrate. Jeff watched the landing field lights streak past as the jet slowed down and then taxied up to the accordion gate.

Even before the seat belt lights went off, passengers started crowding into the narrow aisle as they wrestled down their carry-on luggage from the overhead compartments. Feeling drawn and a bit spacey, Jeff was swept along with the crowd down the gangway to the waiting room. Friends and relatives, some of them looking quite worried because of the delay, noisily greeted arriving passengers, but Jeff felt a cold pang in

his chest, knowing that the only person who might
have come to greet him was in the hospital.

Everyone made their way down the escalator to the
luggage carousels on the first level. Feeling in no particular hurry, Jeff followed along behind the push of
the crowd. After he picked up his baggage, two over-
stuffed canvas flight bags, he walked over to the Hertz
desk and rented a car. Figuring that it didn't make
much sense to spend any more money than he had
to for transportation, he chose an economy car. His
return-flight ticket was for Saturday. He planned to be
in town only for a few days unless something else
happened.

He tried not to think about things like that.

Just be cool, be practical, he kept reminding himself.
*Remember what Alexander said: you're here to help
Judy, and that's all. Stop worrying so damned much
about yourself!*

The automatic doors separated, and he stepped out
into the cool night air. Sighing again, he dropped his
baggage on the sidewalk and rotated his head, hoping
to relieve the crick in his neck. He scanned the road,
looking for the man who was supposed to bring his car
around, and took a deep breath. A shiver went
through him. The fresh smell of the night air was tangy
with a briny smell.

The ocean wasn't very far away.

Just knowing that sent another chill racing through
him. No matter *how* long he had lived in Colorado, he
recognized the smell of the ocean and knew that it was
something he would never be able to forget.

After waiting a few minutes, he saw a red Honda
Civic dart around the corner and pull to an abrupt
stop at the curb. Leaving the engine running, the
driver hopped out of the car and took the rental papers from Jeff.

Jeff's stomach was rumbling with hunger as he

opened the car door, threw his luggage onto the back-seat, and slid in behind the steering wheel. His first thought was to get something to eat before he found a motel for the night, so he followed the thin stream of traffic out of the airport, then took a left turn onto Western Avenue and headed out toward the Maine Mall.

He could see that things around Portland had changed dramatically in the last sixteen years, at least out here by the mall. The mall had been here a long time, going on thirty years, but back when Jeff lived in Maine, there had been no more than a few other businesses nearby. Now there was a long stretch of outdoor shopping areas on both sides of the road—restaurants, clothing stores, book and record stores, department stores, and several hotels, including the round towers of the Sheraton. As he approached the stoplight at one intersection, Jeff caught sight of a Deering Ice Cream shop on the left. Without using his turn signal, he cut across the street and pulled into the parking lot. A loud, trailing horn blast behind him let him know just how much he had pissed off someone.

After he was seated in a booth and had ordered a cheeseburger, French fries, coleslaw, and coffee, Jeff went to the pay phone he had seen by the cashier's station and looked up the number for Maine Medical Center. He dialed the number for the front desk and asked to speak with someone who could tell him where his sister was. He identified himself and then gave the woman on the phone Judy's name. He listened to the rapid *click-click* as she typed something into a computer. After a few seconds, she informed him that Judy Lennox had been admitted on Sunday night and was now in room 613. When he asked if there was anyone who could tell him how his sister was doing, the receptionist told him that the computer only indicated her room number and that she had been admitted by Doctor Delano. Jeff asked if he could speak with Doctor Delano and was put on hold as he was transferred several times between various departments.

All this time, Jeff kept glancing over at his table to see if his supper had arrived, but—at least tonight—the service was a bit slow. For once, he was happy about that. Eventually he got connected with a woman who said her name was Nurse Farley, and that she was the duty nurse in charge of admissions in the emergency room.

"As far as I know, your sister's doing just fine now," Mrs. Farley said. "She was admitted and taken up to P-6 shortly after she was treated in the E.R. If you want to know any more than that, you might want to check with her family doctor. He's listed here as Doctor Jefferson."

"Yes, I know who he is," Jeff replied, a bit snappily. "I—that is, my wife has already spoken to him." He had no idea what P-6 was, and he didn't ask.

"Well, Doctor Delano treated her when she first arrived on Sunday night. He isn't here right now, but we do expect him first thing in the morning. Or should I switch you over to someone in P-6."

"No, but . . . uh, well, should I make an appointment to see Doctor Delano or something?"

"That's entirely up to you." Nurse Farley sounded completely disinterested in helping him beyond the bare essentials. "I could leave him a message that you called, if you'd like."

"Yes, I'd appreciate that. By the way, what time are visiting hours at the hospital?" Jeff asked.

He glanced over at his table and saw that the waitress was walking toward his seat with a cheeseburger plate and coffee urn. She placed both items carefully onto the table. Looking a bit confused for a moment, she glanced around the restaurant until she saw Jeff at the pay phone. He signaled to her with a quick nod of the head that he would be right over.

"If you are immediate family, you can—"

"I already told you," Jeff said, wishing that he didn't sound quite so angry. It must be the flight—and the circumstances—that were making him feel so edgy and hostile. "We're talking about my *sister* here! I just want to get some idea how she's doing."

"Well, I can't tell you that. All I know is she's been admitted and is on P-6."

"When can I see her, then?"

"Well, regular visiting hours are nine to eleven in the morning and one to four in the afternoon, but there are restricted vising hours for P-6. You can come up any time after nine o'clock tomorrow morning, but you'll have to check in at the front desk first. I'm sure you'll be allowed to see her."

"Thank you," Jeff said, pondering her use of the word *allowed.* "I-I'm sorry if I sounded a bit cranky. You see, I, uh, just got in from Colorado, and I'm still a bit fried from the flight. Should I—well, I'm not exactly sure where I'll be staying tonight, but should I call back and leave you a telephone number where you or Doctor Delano can reach me?"

"I don't think that will be necessary as long as her family doctor knows how to reach you. You should give Doctor Jefferson a call."

"I will," Jeff said. "He has my telephone number at home, in Colorado. I, umm, I'll probably be staying at a motel while I'm in town."

As soon as Jeff had realized and accepted the fact that he would have to come back to Maine, he had told Sally that he would probably be staying at Judy's house in order to save money, but actually he had no intention of staying there. In fact, the thought of driving out to Cape Higgins was the furthest thing from his mind. There was no way in hell he wanted to see his

hometown or the old homestead again, much less stay
there a few nights. Judy had been living at home with
her parents following her first divorce, and after their
parents had died, she had bought out Jeff's half of the
property. That had suited Jeff just fine because the
mere thought of seeing his boyhood home left him
feeling cold and shaky.

No, contrary to what he had *suggested* to Sally—
and he had never *promised* her otherwise—he was
planning on staying in a motel the whole time he was
here in Maine. He figured he'd call Sally once he found
a place and tell her he'd decided to do this so he would
be closer to the hospital, even though he knew that was
a lie. Christ, he didn't even plan to drive out to Cape
Higgins out of curiosity. For all he cared, the whole
fucking town could break off from the mainland and
sink into the goddamned ocean!

"I'll come by first thing tomorrow morning, then,"
Jeff said. "And thanks again for all your help."

"You're welcome," Nurse Farley said, still sounding as though she could care less.

Jeff hung up the phone, but he suddenly felt too
weak in the knees to walk back over to the booth. He
leaned forward and, resting his head on the telephone,
took a deep, trembling breath. Just talking to someone
about his sister had made him feel completely drained
of strength. He wondered how he was going to be able
to handle actually seeing her. He wiped the back of his
neck with the flat of his hand, not at all surprised at
how slick with sweat it was.

When he realized someone was standing behind
him, waiting to use the telephone, he turned and
walked slowly back to where his meal was waiting. By
the time he was seated and took a bite of his cheeseburger, it was already lukewarm. He considered sending it back and asking the chef to reheat it, but he
decided that it wasn't worth the hassle. Sighing heavily

and slouching back in the padded seat, he ate the rest of his meal slowly and in silence. He tried to fill his mind with thoughts about Sally and Robin, and how happy he would be to get back home with them, but other thoughts kept intruding. He couldn't stop wondering how in the name of Christ he was going to find the strength to face his sister in the morning.

God All-fucking-mighty! She really did it! She really tried to kill herself!

All through the meal, a tiny voice that didn't sound anything like the usual voice of his thoughts was whispering in the back of his mind—*Yeah, she fucking tried to kill herself, all right, and it was all because of you, Jeff! It was all your fault, you lousy son of a bitch!*

"Do you miss me?"

"You know I do, Daddy. When are you coming home?"

"In a few days, honey pie. Are you being a good girl for your mother?"

"Of course I am."

"What did you do for supper tonight? No, wait. Let me guess. I'll bet you went out for pizza at Beau Jo's. Am I right?"

"How'd you know?"

"Ohh, daddies have a special way of knowing. Say, honeypie, is Mommy right there? I'd like to talk with her for a minute."

"No, she's in the shower right now. You want me to go get her?"

"No, this is a collect call, so I don't want to run up the bill. Have you got a pencil and paper handy?"

"Just a sec. Let me look. . . . Okay, I'm ready."

"Tell her that I'm at the Days Inn in South Portland. Room 37. Here, let me give you the number."

While he was talking, Jeff had been doodling on the

memo pad beside the phone. He read off the number
at the top of the page as he drew messy spirals around
it.

"You got that, Robin? Remember, now, that's
room 37. Make sure you tell Mommy, okay?"

"I will. I wrote it down."

"Good girl. Hey, you don't happen to know if
Mommy's heard anything more from the doctor about
Aunt Judy, do you?"

"We were out for quite a while, but there weren't
any messages when we came home. I checked, 'cause
I've been expecting a call from Trisha."

"Well, then, you just tell Mommy that my plane
landed safely. I'm really tired, so I'm gonna go to bed
soon."

"It's not even seven o'clock yet."

"Well, it's almost nine o'clock out here. Make sure
you tell Mommy I'll give her a call tomorrow night,
after I see Aunt Judy, okay? Can you remember that?"

"Of course I can. I hope you come home soon,
Daddy. I really miss you."

"I miss you, too, honey pie. Be a good girl, okay?"

"I sure will."

"That's my girl. Bye, love. And give Mommy a great
big kiss for me, okay?"

"I will. Bye-bye, Daddy."

"Bye, honey pie."

The next morning, Jeff was feeling incredibly uncomfortable as he sat in the small, padded chair that
was wedged between two paper- and book-littered
desks in what passed for an office in the hospital's
emergency room.

After his phone conversation with Robin, his sleep
had been fitful and plagued by disturbing dreams
which he couldn't remember once he woke up. Long

before dawn, he had gotten out of bed, gone into the bathroom, shaved and taken a long hot shower, then dressed and gone out for breakfast at the nearby Deering Ice Cream shop. In the hotel lobby, he had picked up a copy of the *Portland Press Herald,* but he was too distracted to do much more than scan the headlines. The day was mild for so late in October. Even out by the mall, with Interstate 95 so close, there was a fresh, bracing smell in the air that had almost raised Jeff's spirits.

. . . almost.

Using the phone at the front of the restaurant again, he had called Maine Medical Center to make sure Doctor Delano would be there when he arrived. Other than Judy's regular doctor, whom he had called but had gotten only an answering service, Delano was the only name Jeff had. Nurse Farley certainly hadn't been very helpful. Jeff wanted desperately to speak with someone, whoever was in charge before he went to visit his sister in case he needed to be prepared for something. He'd had more than enough coffee at breakfast, and now, after waiting in the office for nearly half an hour, his bladder felt like it was about to burst. He wondered if he had time to try to find a rest room. Worse yet, he felt so wound up he was trembling all over. His hands were cold and slick with sweat, and the pressure building up inside his head made it feel like it was about to explode. Now and again he closed his eyes and stared into the internal darkness, mentally asking if there was anyone there he could talk to.

He got no reply.

No, it looked like he was on his own with this one.

After he had been waiting more than half an hour, a thin, dark-haired young man wearing a loose-fitting green O.R. shirt and pants breezed into the room and swung the door shut behind him. The pocket protector in his shirt pocket was lined with an array of colored pens. A stethoscope dangled around his neck, the sounding diaphragm tucked into his shirt pocket. He was wearing new, white sneakers that squeaked on the floor with every step he took. In his left hand, he held a clipboard, which he stared at while drumming it with the fingertips of his right hand. His face was so pale he looked as though he hadn't been to the beach once last summer. If this was Doctor Delano, Jeff thought he didn't look old enough to be out of college, much less a doctor.

Whistling between his teeth and frowning, the man shook his head before looking up at Jeff. "Boy, it's been one helluva morning already, and there isn't even a full moon." He looked at Jeff as if noticing him for the first time and said, "Hi, I'm Doctor Delano. Sorry to keep you waiting."

He held his hand out for Jeff to shake. Jeff was self-conscious about how clammy his own hand must feel.

"What can I do for you?" Delano said. "I had a message here that you wanted to see me."

"Yes, it's—uh, I'm Jeff Wagner. Judy Lennox's brother," Jeff said. "I called last night."

"Right," Delano said, still sounding a bit distracted as he tapped his fingers against the clipboard. "She was admitted on—umm, it was Sunday evening, as I recall."

The doctor hiked one leg up onto one of the desks and leaned forward, looking intently for a moment at the clipboard he was holding. He nodded and grunted softly to himself as he scanned the top page. When he didn't seem to be forthcoming with anything else, Jeff cleared his throat and said, "So, what can you tell me about her situation? I mean, without betraying any patient confidentiality or anything, can you tell me exactly what happened to my sister? How's she doing?"

It took Jeff a great deal of effort to keep his voice from breaking.

"Well, Mr. . . . uh, Mr. Wagner, was it?"

"Call me Jeff."

"Right—Jeff. Well, your sister tried to kill herself with an overdose of sleeping pills. As far as I know, she's doing fine now, but to be perfectly candid with you, I'd have to say that I think she's a very disturbed woman. Hey, I'm just an emergency room physician here, not a psychologist, but it was pretty obvious to me that she has some quite serious psychological problems. Especially after what she tried to do. I took care of her immediate medical situation, but her family doctor. . . . Who's her regular doctor again?"

"It's Doctor Jefferson."

"Right, Marty Jefferson. Good man. Of course, he could fill you in a lot better than I can, I'm sure. He should be checking in on her regularly, too."

"I called him last night and again this morning, but I haven't gotten to speak with him yet," Jeff said.

Delano nodded. "You might want to check with his office and see if he'll be in today. I'm sure you realize, though, that her case also has to be evaluated by the psych unit. Doctor Jennifer Grant is head of that department."

"Wait a second, my sister's in the *psych* ward?"

"That's where we send people who try to kill themselves. P-6. It's up on the sixth floor."

"I see," Jeff said as a cold rush moved up his spine. He was unable to speak further, so he simply nodded and stared at his hands, which were folded in his lap. He was squeezing them so tightly his fingers were staring to tingle.

When Doctor Delano spoke again, his voice thundered in Jeff's ears.

"I have no idea if she's mentioned this to anyone at the hospital or to her regular doctor, but do you know, has she been seeing a therapist on a regular basis?"

Jeff shrugged. "I—I'm really not sure," he said, surprised that his voice sounded as normal as it did. "I mean—you know, it's not exactly something a lot of people want to talk about." He ended with a nervous chuckle which he was positive communicated to the doctor that *he* had been seeing a shrink.

After a short silence, Delano cleared his throat and said, "Well . . . as to the particulars, a—ummm." He squinted as he focused on the top sheet on his clipboard again. "Ms. Vera Becker got a call from your sister on Sunday evening, at approximately six P.M. She reported that your sister said she had called to tell her that she wouldn't be in to work in the morning. Apparently they work together and share rides to work."

"Right," Jeff said shakily. "She works at UNUM—Union Mutual—in South Portland."

Doctor Delano glanced at him, and the inquisitive expression on his face made Jeff squirm a bit in the chair. He couldn't stop feeling like *he* was the one being assessed here, but he told himself to stop thinking so damned much about himself and show more concern for Judy.

"Anyway, Ms. Becker reported that when she asked your sister why she wouldn't be at work in the morning, your sister replied, quite calmly, so I understand, that she would no doubt be dead by then. She then went on to tell Ms. Becker that she had just taken an overdose of sleeping pills, which her family doctor had prescribed for her, and was just waiting to drift off. Do you know if your sister had a sleeping disorder?"

"No, I mean . . . I have no idea," Jeff said, narrowing his eyes and thoughtfully shaking his head. "I mean, she's my sister, but we didn't do a very good job of keeping in touch, you know. I've been living in Denver for the last ten years. Just flew in last night, in fact."

"I see," Doctor Delano said, nodding as he glanced again at the paperwork in front of him. "Well, before she went over to your sister's house, Ms. Becker had the presence of mind to call the town rescue unit and give them your sister's address. If she hadn't, your sister might in fact be dead right now, and you'd be talking to a funeral director instead of me. She's lucky to be alive."

"I realize that," Jeff said. "Exactly how serious do you think this . . . attempt was?" Jeff shivered at the thought and was unable to say the word *suicide*.

Doctor Delano shrugged. "Again, I'd have to say that's something you'll have to discuss either with her regular doctor or with Doctor Grant, but my initial impression was that your sister is a very high-strung individual." He shrugged and slapped his clipboard against his thigh. "Who can say how serious it was? Is this the first time she's ever done anything like this?"

Jeff nodded and said, "Uh-huh. As far as I know."

A sharper jolt of guilt lanced through him, and he couldn't help but think that he knew *exactly* the reason why after all these years his sister would try something like that. Her life had been a mess . . . had been, ever since that first time they had . . . fooled around with each other. After two lousy marriages and living alone, working a job she hated but felt trapped in, no wonder.

Jeff closed his eyes for a moment and thought he heard another voice, whispering softly to him, but when he opened his eyes and looked around, he guessed it was just someone passing by outside in the hall.

"Well, then," Doctor Delano said, "in an instance like this, I would speculate that, because she called her

friend and told her exactly what she had done, this was
more of a cry for help rather than a genuine, serious
attempt to kill herself. As it was, they got her to the
hospital just in time so we could get her stomach
pumped out and stabilize her vitals. I can't mince
words with you. It was damned close."

Jeff looked up at the doctor, wanting desperately to
say something, but he couldn't quite put the chaos of
his thoughts into words. As if he were reading Jeff's
mind, Doctor Delano went on, "As for any long term
physical effects—no, I don't think you'll have to
worry. I'm sure they're keeping a very close watch on
her, and I'm positive she'll be fine in a few days. However, as to the *psychological* aspects . . . well, as I said,
I'm not a psychologist, I'm just a doctor, but if your
sister *isn't* under therapeutic care, she certainly *should*
be. Of course, the staff here at the hospital will fully
evaluate her before she's allowed to go back home."

"Of course," Jeff echoed softly. "That certainly
makes sense."

Even as he was speaking, he heard the same faint
voice whisper again, and this time he could tell that it
wasn't out in the hallway; it was inside his mind.

*Well, now, that makes two for two, doesn't it, Jeffy-
boy? Both you and your sister seeing a shrink. Christ on
a cross! What the hell did your parents do to you to drive
both of you fucking nuts?*

Jeff's throat made a loud *click* sound, and his body
went suddenly rigid.

No way! he thought as a wave of frantic panic
washed through him. *There's no fucking way I'm nuts!*

He clenched his hands into tight fists and punched
his thighs once, hard. Then, feeling embarrassed, he
looked up at Doctor Delano and smiled sheepishly.

"I'm not the one to talk to, really," Doctor Delano
said. "You'll have to speak with Doctor Grant if you

want more information. Hey, what can I say? All I did
was save her life."

Jeff leaned back in the chair and inhaled deeply as
he shook his head. "You said she's on the sixth floor,
right?" He released the tension in his fists and forced
a thin smile as he stood up.

"You can check at the front desk for the room
number or go straight on up," Delano said.

Jeff extended his hand to Delano. "I want to thank
you for taking the time to talk to me." They shook
hands, then he turned toward the door.

As Jeff was leaving, Delano leaned forward and
indicated a right-hand turn with a sweep of his clipboard. "There's a bank of elevators just around the
next corner and down quite a ways on your left. I'm
sure you'll have to check in at the desk on P-6 before
they'll let you see her."

Jeff nodded. "Thanks for your time," he said, but
when he glanced back at Delano, he was already
hunched over his clipboard, flipping through the pages
and muttering to himself. Jeff left the office, shutting
the door quietly behind him, and started down the
corridor toward the elevators.

Jesus Christ, she looks like she's already dead!

After checking with the nurse at the front desk, Jeff
was standing outside his sister's room—number 613—
and looking in at her. Behind his back, he clutched the
small stuffed black bear he had bought for her in the
gift shop downstairs.

The closed blinds sliced the dull yellow glow of
morning sunlight into narrow strips that rippled like a
tiger's stripes across the floor and bed. Judy was lying
on her back with her hands folded across her chest.
Her eyes were closed as though she was sleeping, but
there was a tension in her body, a stiffness that indi-

cated she might be wide-awake and just faking sleep.

She looks like a corpse, laid out in a funeral home. He recalled what Doctor Delano had said, about how lucky she was that they got to her in time, otherwise he would be talking to a funeral director.

Jeff took one step into the doorway and stopped. Cupping his hand over his mouth, he cleared his throat.

Instantly, Judy's eyes snapped opened. Her gaze went unfocused for a few seconds as she looked around, blinking her eyes; then she saw him there in the doorway. For just a moment, her face lit up with an expression of genuine surprise and pleasure, but her smile quickly melted, and she shifted her gaze away from him. Jeff thought he saw her shoulders hitch once with a repressed sob.

"Hey," he said, taking a few more tentative steps into the room. The sterile, antiseptic hospital smell stung his nose and made his stomach lurch.

"Hey yourself," Judy said in a low, thick whisper.

She sounded as though she hadn't been talking much lately; either that, or else she was medicated. She blinked her eyes again a few times, then slid her glance in his direction, looking steadily at him. Her eyes were glassy, and they glowed with an odd lambent light.

"So, when'd you get here?" she asked.

"Flew in last night," Jeff said.

"What day is it, anyway?"

"It's—uh, it's Wednesday."

"Jesus, *Wednesday* already?" Judy said, disbelief coloring her voice. She shook her head lazily. "It feels like . . . like I dunno. Like I've been here only a couple of hours or . . . forever."

Jeff shrugged and gave her a twisted smile, trying his damnedest to appear completely casual, but the most pressing thing on his mind was to ask her why—why in the *hell* had she done something as stupid as try to commit suicide. But he knew that wasn't the best way to start, so instead he brought the stuffed animal out from behind his back and presented it to her.

"Here ya go," he said, laughing tightly. "I thought you might like a little company. They don't let you bring flowers up here, you know, because of allergies or whatever."

"Yeah . . . whatever," Judy said listlessly.

"If you feel up to reading or anything, I can go back down and buy you a book or a handful of magazines."

Judy shrugged. The motion made the bedsheets and plastic mattress cover crinkle. She still regarded him with a glazed, distant expression that convinced him, now, that she was indeed heavily medicated. Pilled to the gills. She seemed to be having a hell of a time, focusing her eyes. When she didn't reach out for the toy right away, which Jeff now thought had been a foolish thing to buy, he propped it up at the foot of her bed and said, "There. He can keep an eye on you from down here."

After a moment of silence, Jeff stepped forward, leaned down, and gave her a gentle hug and a kiss on the cheek. He was surprised by how warm and soft her cheek felt, but he tried not to think about it.

"They treating you okay here, are they?"

Judy looked at him again, then smiled weakly. "The food's shit," she said, her voice still sounding like sandpaper, "and I could sure use a glass of wine 'bout now."

"Yeah, I'll bet," Jeff said.

He picked up the plastic cup filled with ice water that was on her bed stand. Holding the straw in place, he brought it up to her mouth so she could sip it without lifting her head. "How about some Sebago Light instead?"

"Come on, Jeff!" Judy said. She winced with the effort as she suddenly shifted up onto her elbows and snatched the cup away from him. "I'm not a fucking invalid, you know."

Avoiding the straw, she raised the cup to her mouth and took several gulps, then licked her lips. The glazed look never left her eyes.

"I didn't think you were," Jeff said, a bit defensively. "I just thought you might want to rest a bit."

"Yeah, sure" Judy said, a slight sneer curling her upper lip. "I want to rest, all right, but they wake you up every other goddamned hour around here, it seems, just to ask how you're sleeping." She took another sip of water, then replaced the plastic cup on the bed stand. "So, did Sally and Robin come out with you?"

Jeff shook his head. "Naw . . . Sally couldn't get the time off from work." The back of his neck flushed at the lie, but he ignored it as he took Judy's hand and gave it a gentle squeeze.

"How are they both?"

"Oh, they're doing great. Robin's growing up so fast. She's in first grade already and loving it. Sally's still working at the doctor's office, but she enjoys her work, and it helps round out the budget, you know."

"Umm." Judy nodded, and again—for just an instant—her eyes went unfocused. "And how about you, little brother?"

Jeff shrugged. "I'm hanging in there."

Judy didn't press him for details, so for the next several seconds, the room filled with silence. Finally, when he was just starting to get uncomfortable, Jeff cleared his throat and said, "So tell me, Jude. Truthfully. How are you feeling?"

For the span of several heartbeats, Judy regarded him with a cold, steady stare. Her lips looked pale and drawn as she bit down on them. When she took a deep breath, the air whistled in her nose like a heating teakettle. Jeff still held onto her hand, glad that she made no attempt to pull away or shake off his grip.

"I've been better, Jeffy," she said and let out a loud gasp. "I've been a whole *hell* of a lot better."

Jeff nodded but said nothing. His eyes were stinging fiercely, and he had to resist the strong impulse to throw himself at her and give her the biggest hug he could manage. Feeling drained, both emotionally and physically, he only had the strength to hold onto her hand and smile at her.

He was burning to ask her straight out why she had tried to kill herself, but besides thinking that it might not be therapeutically good for her to deal with the issue head-on—especially with him—he was too scared to bring it up because of the deep core of burning guilt he felt. He couldn't stop thinking that he knew damned well what was at the heart of his sister's problems.

Jesus! Just forget about it, will you? a faint but demanding voice whispered in his mind. *Stop thinking about yourself all the time! Did you ever stop to consider that what she tried to do might have absolutely nothing to do with what you and she did back when you were kids?*

Jeff was suddenly very aware of how uncomfortably hot the hospital room was. He shifted from one foot to the other and took a deep breath, but the walls seemed to close in on him a bit.

"Do you want me to open the curtains?" he asked. "Get some fresh air in here?"

He let go of her hand and started toward the windows, but then stopped when Judy rolled her head back and forth on the pillow.

"No," she said weakly. "I like it like this . . . nice and dark."

"Oh, sure . . . fine," Jeff said.

He came back to her bedside and looked down at her. Before he could think of anything else to say, she started talking. Her voice was still low and raw, but her words sent a razor-edged chill up his back.

"You know," she said, "I always kind of hoped that it would be like this . . . death, I mean . . . I thought that if I took enough pills, I would just . . . sort of . . . drift off, softly . . . quietly."

"Come on, Jude. Don't talk like that," Jeff said.

Tension was making his body wire-tight, and the burning in his eyes was getting worse, but he wouldn't let himself cry. He couldn't! Not in front of his sister.

"Seriously," Judy said. "I want to . . . I *have* to talk about it. My shrink told me that it's good for me to talk about it. I wanted to understand it, you see? Death. I always pictured it as being sort of like—well, like you just walk into a dark, silent room . . . maybe a room like this. Soft and warm and quiet."

She looked at Jeff as though expecting him to say something, but he couldn't speak.

"After I'd taken those sleeping pills, I started to drift off, but I didn't . . . I couldn't go all the way with it. Maybe I was scared to let go all the way, or maybe I had a premonition or something and knew that I wasn't going to die, that it wasn't my time yet. I don't know. Maybe I didn't *really* want to die, and all along knew that I'd end up in the hospital instead, but— Jesus, Jeff!" Her voice broke, and a pained expression fixed her face in a grimace. "I kept *trying* to give up control, to just . . . let go, you know? . . . To just fade away."

When she looked up at him again, Jeff was surprised to see that her eyes weren't tearing up. Her face seemed slack, perfectly relaxed, as though there was absolutely no connection between what she was saying and how she really felt about it.

"That's what I've always pictured death to be like— just this big, soft, dark cushion, and I was just gonna fall over backwards, rolling and tumbling until I finally landed on it and was swallowed up by it."

Jeff closed his eyes a moment, imagining the tingling fright and the funny feeling he got in his stomach whenever he was flying and the plane was descending to land.

Judy rolled her eyes and sighed deeply, sounding like an old person who was feeling nostalgic, recalling her lost childhood.

"Yeah . . . ," she said. Her voice faded to a raspy murmur. "Just a big . . . soft . . . dark fall into . . . absolutely nothing."

Choking on his emotion, Jeff gripped his sister's hand with both of his and squeezed it as tightly as he could.

"Well *I'm* glad you didn't make it," he said, his voice breaking on nearly every word. "Because you *can't* do it! I won't *let* you do this to me or . . . or to yourself."

Judy looked up at him with such complete emotional detachment that he wondered—he hoped to hell that it was her medication that was doing this to her, but he thought he saw a used-up lifelessness deep inside his sister's eyes. He shuddered, thinking she looked like someone who had simply given up completely. After a few seconds of silence, Judy's eyes fluttered and then slowly closed. Her body settled, and her breathing became deep and regular. The hard line of her mouth relaxed only a little bit. Her lips still looked thin and bloodless.

"I *mean* it, Jude," Jeff said, no longer caring that tears were streaming down his face. His shoulders shook with his sobs. "Honest to Christ, I do! You *have* to hang in there . . . if for nothing else, then at *least* for *me!*"

He interlocked his fingers with hers and squeezed

tightly. When he spoke again, something dark stirred deep inside his mind, and he had the unnerving feeling that someone else, not he, was saying these words.

"Don't worry, Jude . . . I'm here . . . I still love you."

Chapter Four
Recovering

Jeff couldn't believe what a relief it was to get back outside.

It was a little bit past eleven o'clock when the electronic double doors whooshed shut behind him and he started down the sidewalk toward the street. His legs felt all rubbery, almost unable to support him as he walked slowly past the people who were entering and leaving the hospital. He had parked his rental car on one of the side streets, about half a mile away from the hospital. He couldn't recall the street name, but right now, the only thing on his mind was getting back to the motel so he could take a long, hot shower, get something to eat, and then—maybe—take a nap.

If he could sleep, that is.

As he waited on the curb to cross the street, a wild shiver raced through him. He tried to convince himself that it was from the chill in the air and had nothing to do with Judy's situation or anything she had said to him, but he couldn't get out of his mind the mental image of his sister, lying there in the hospital bed.

Christ, she had looked so out of it, like she was already half-dead!

Again there was a stinging in his eyes and a cold twist of guilt deep in his gut.

Because of the steady flow of traffic, he couldn't cross right away, so rather than wait, he started walking up the hill, away from the hospital. He was so preoccupied, trying to think of something he could do to help his sister, that he wasn't paying much attention to where he was going.

But he knew there wasn't much, if anything, he could do.

Right now, the hospital—*P-6 . . . the "psycho" ward*—was the best place for Judy. She was under the constant care of mental health professionals, and there wasn't anything he could do, other than show up for the next few days to check on how she was doing. He had an appointment to see Doctor Grant later that afternoon, but he was convinced, now, that it wasn't going to do much good.

No, he knew it was going to take Judy a long time to make a complete comeback—if she *ever* did. His return-flight ticket was for Saturday—and that was the end of it. He sniffed with cynical laughter as he continued up the street, away from the hospital.

He felt guilty that he hadn't planned to spend more time with Judy, making sure she got her wheels back on the road, but—shit, he had his own family and job, a life of his own back in Colorado. Financially and time-wise, he couldn't very well afford to hang around Portland for several more days, maybe even weeks, hoping to find some little thing he could do to help her out. All he could do, he told himself, was make sure she had all the support and services she would need to pull herself through.

He remembered, now, seeing two or three get well cards on Judy's windowsill. She had never left her hometown since high school, so she had her own friends who would watch out for her. Doctor Delano had mentioned the one who had called the rescue unit.

What was her name?

Vera Becker, wasn't it?

Yeah, maybe he should look her up in the phone book, give her a call, and make sure he could count on her to be there for Judy once she got out of the hospital. He told himself that maybe during semester break in December, he and the whole family might come out to Maine and spend some time with Judy, even if it meant having to go out to the house in Cape Higgins.

Before he realized it, Jeff had passed the street where his car was parked, and he found himself up on the Western Promenade, looking out over the salt flats toward South Portland. The maple trees were mostly stripped bare by now. Their thick, dark branches looked like skeletal hands against the pale sky. In the distance, Jeff could see Portland Jetport and a long, curving stretch of Interstate 295 that crossed the Fore River. Sunlight sparkled like a shower of silver coins on the water. In the distance, a jet arrowed up into the sky from the airport, leaving behind a thick stream of gray exhaust to mark its passage. The air was so cold and clear, he could see all the way to the mountains in New Hampshire.

Jeff realized that his car was parked down the hill, but rather than turn back now, he kept walking until he came to a small park area that overlooked the river. There were three chipped and fading green park benches in a semicircle, aimed out at the view. On one of them sat a couple of old men, bundled up in heavy woolen coats. They both had their arms folded across their chests and were leaning back as they stared out at the scenery. Their eyes followed the flow of traffic as if they wished they could be going someplace. Neither one of them was talking, but they seemed happy enough just to be alive, watching the world go by.

Jeff wondered if they were patients from the hospi-

tal, out for a stroll, or else a couple of homeless men.
He considered sitting down on one of the other
benches, but he felt suddenly self-conscious, as if his
worry and guilt showed on his face like a tattoo. Instead, he kept walking, picking up his pace until he
was practically running, his arms pumping like pistons
at his sides. At this high point of land, the wind blowing in off the ocean was brisk and cold, but Jeff narrowed his eyes and took a deep breath, letting it burn
in his lungs.

Yeah, he thought, picking up his pace even more,
this is what I need . . . just burn it up!

Once he crested the hill and had a good view out
across the bay to the oil tanks in South Portland, he
clenched his fists tightly and pushed himself to run
faster. Wind whistled in his ears like the steady hiss of
escaping steam. He concentrated on the sound of his
own breathing and the steady *slap-slap* of his sneakers
on the asphalt. The sounds were almost hypnotic, and
with every step, his worries and concerns seemed to
melt away.

Oh, they were still there, all right; but their nagging
tug seemed to lessen as he indulged himself in the
release of pure, physical activity. Back home in Denver, he exercised semi-regularly at best. Over the past
few years, he had noticed, along with his thinning hair,
a thickening of his waist and a shortness of breath, but
he had never been one for jogging, opting instead for
racquetball and tennis. He was mildly amused that he
would start running now.

*Probably out of desperation. What the hell are you
running away from, anyway?*

The thought whispered in his mind, barley audible
above the rushing sound of the wind in his ears.

Nothing! Nothing at all! he replied to his own
thought, but very faintly, he thought he heard the
sound of laughter.

I just need time to think, that's all . . . time to let all of this sink in, he thought, but—once again—he thought he heard the faint chuffing sound of laughter. It could have been an echo of the sound of his sneakers, scuffing on the sidewalk, but he didn't think so.

He rounded the corner and passed a fenced-in school yard, then started down the hill. The street was slightly familiar from back when he used to live in Maine, but it seemed almost like it was someone else's memory.

He had no idea where or how far he planned to run. He simply gritted his teeth, clenched his fists, and kept running. His feet plowed through windblown piles of dead leaves that had gathered like snowdrifts on the sidewalk.

Hell, he might run all the way over to the Eastern Prom and back, if he thought that would even relieve, much less eliminate the pressure of his own thoughts.

A cold, bracing sweat broke out on his brow, and he felt a deep, internal burn in his leg and shoulder muscles.

It felt good.

For the first time in his life, Jeff thought he could understand why some people actually enjoyed running. His experience had always been that there's a threshold of pain which he could never quite push himself past, but this time—somehow—he seemed to have skipped that, or at least not noticed it. He was pumping his arms, his whole body moving like a smooth-running, well-oiled machine. He sucked in every breath through his nose deep into his lungs, then puffed it out his mouth. Cold drops of sweat skittered like tiny fingers down the back of his neck.

Goddamn! I feel alive! he thought, but then there came a twinge of guilt when another voice whispered that he probably hadn't felt *this* alive in years . . . if ever!

His feet pounded the pavement as he turned left,
rounding the corner, and started up a slight grade that
brought him past an old graveyard. The black
wrought-iron fence looked like it badly needed a new
coat of paint. Many of the gravestones were tumbled
over. Some of them had spray-painted graffiti on
them—symbols and initials that Jeff didn't recognize.

He slowed his pace once he reached the top of the
hill, then started down. He took another left turn onto
a side street that was lined with three- and four-story
apartment buildings and private homes. He was hoping he was lucky enough to have picked the street he
had parked on, but no such luck. He found himself
back at the Western Prom.

He didn't slow his pace as he started down the road
until he came to the right-hand turn. Pine Street. That
was it, and up ahead, he saw the red Honda. Uttering
a low grunt, he broke into a full-tilt dash. The wind
screamed in his ears, and his breath roared like a bellows. He ran for all he was worth until he came up to
the car and collapsed across it, leaning his head onto
his folded arms on the top of the car.

The air stung his lungs, and his legs felt like rubber,
but he still felt more invigorated than tired as he
straightened up and stretched, then dug the car keys
out of his pocket. He was still panting hard as he drove
away. Just before the turn that would take him down
to Congress Street, he glanced into his rearview mirror
at the receding reflection of the hospital building.

Just as he had expected, his conversation with Doctor Grant didn't tell him much than he hadn't already
figured out for himself. What it all boiled down to was,
Judy would be in the hospital for another day or two
for observation and then, as long as Doctor Grant and
her personal physician were satisfied that her condi-

tion had stabilized, and she had made an appointment to start seeing a therapist, she would be sent home. Hospital beds were at a premium these days, especially in P-6.

The news that Judy might be going home soon was news Jeff wasn't all that happy to hear, but at least it beat some of the alternatives he had imagined.

Around three o'clock in the afternoon he poked his head into Judy's room again, but she was sleeping, so he decided not to disturb her and went back to the motel. He called Judy's doctor and left his number with the secretary, so Doctor Jefferson knew how to get in touch with him. After a short nap, which was filled with disturbing dreams, he got up and, with nothing better to do, went to the Maine Mall to do a bit of shopping. He bought Robin a large, stuffed red lobster, and for Sally a very tasteful white sweatshirt with the word MAINE sewn in bold, plaid letters.

After a quick stop at the Waldenbooks to pick up a few magazines and the new John Grisham novel, he headed back to the motel to wait until it was suppertime. There were no messages waiting for him, from either Jefferson or his wife.

And exactly what problems do you expect? asked a voice in his mind. *Are you afraid something's happened to Robin or Sally while you're gone? Or do you think Judy might try to kill herself again . . . try and succeed this time?*

Jeff tried not to think along those lines.

He left the motel and drove around town until he found a Chinese restaurant called Panda Garden, where he ate a marvelous supper. After that, he considered taking in a movie at the Maine Mall theater across the street from his motel but decided against it. Back in the motel room, he tried to interest himself in reading but couldn't concentrate, so he watched about half of a movie on Pay Per View, made a quick phone call home to fill Sally in on Judy's progress, and then went to bed.

As usual, he didn't sleep very well. This was getting to be a bad habit, he thought. Most of the night, he tossed and turned and ended up staring at either the ceiling or the flashing red digits of the alarm clock. His mind was filled with dark worries and concerns about his sister, his family, and himself. When he finally drifted off to sleep, his dreams were filled with haunting, terrifying images. Several times he awoke with a start, thinking someone had spoken to him in the darkness. He would look frantically around the room but, of course, there was no one there. In the morning, he remembered none of the details of his dreams, just the disoriented, depressed feeling they left him with.

He was out of bed long before the alarm went off.

"Well Jesus Christ, *there* you are," Judy shouted as soon as Jeff appeared in the doorway.

Caught a bit off guard by her greeting, Jeff walked into the room with a twisted, almost guilty grin on his face. The blinds were open, and a pale wash of sunlight lit up the hospital room with an almost cheery glow. Although the angle was different, outside the window he could see pretty much the same view of the Fore River and I-295 he had seen yesterday from the Western Promenade. He noticed that the stuffed bear he had given her yesterday was perched on the windowsill, lined up alongside eight get well cards.

"So how come you're so damned late today?" Judy asked. She was sitting up in bed and, although her hair was disheveled from sleep, her face looked bright and alert.

"Late . . . ?"

"Well, yeah . . . you're later than you were yesterday. I've been sitting here for the past hour or more, just waiting for you to show up."

"Is that so?"

He looked at his sister, surprised to see her looking so alive, so fully animated. There was actually a bloom of color in her cheeks that didn't look like makeup, and her eyes had a natural, alert sparkle. Her excited smile seemed to be completely genuine.

"Well, aren't we the bright and chipper one this morning," Jeff said as he walked over to the bed and gave her a hug and a light kiss on the cheek. He couldn't help but think that either the medication she was taking was finally working, or else the doctor had changed it to something else.

Or maybe—just maybe—she was back to being herself again.

Naw! said a low, almost snarling voice in the back of his mind. *She was NEVER all THAT cheery!*

"I'm feeling a *lot* better today," Judy said with a high lilt to her voice. "I slept like a baby last night, and today—God! I feel like I could whip the whole world!"

"Hey, that's great," Jeff said. He had to force himself to sound cheery because he couldn't remove the dark suspicion that this was all a facade. How could she go from being so doped up, practically a vegetable yesterday to this in a mere twenty-four hours? It didn't seem possible. No matter what was causing it, Jeff knew, after eight years of being in therapy himself, that it had to be temporary. The one thing any permanent changes took was time . . . lots of time and hard, inner work.

"The doctor said I'll probably be able to go home tomorrow," Judy said. Her voice sounded so bubbly, it was almost obnoxious. "I could have checked in to JBI for a while, but I don't think I need to."

"JBI?"

"Jackson Brook Institute," Judy said with a slight

shrug. "The psych hospital in South Portland over by the mall."

"Oh," Jeff said.

He just stood there, looking at her as though he expected, any second now, to see a crack in the mask, but her smile and enthusiasm seemed completely genuine.

"So, you—ah, you're really feeling *that* much better, huh?" he asked.

His stomach dropped when, for just an instant, he saw the trace of a dark cloud pass across Judy's face. She cocked her mouth to one side as though gnawing on the inside of her cheek, and squinted at him. A pleading, almost frantic look crept into her eyes, but it quickly passed.

"God, I can't *wait* to get out of here," she said in a low, almost conspiratorial voice. She pursed her lips and shook her head tightly. "I mean, I don't want to be in here—I don't *have* to be here. This place is really scary!"

Swallowing hard, Jeff took a breath and said, "Well, what you did was pretty scary, too, you know." It was a tough thing to say, but he knew he *had* to say it.

Judy's gaze hardened as she looked up at him. He could see how weak, how vulnerable she was beneath it all. He didn't want to say or do anything that might throw her back into her downward spiral; but then again, he sure as hell didn't want her to be released if she was still going to be a danger to herself, either. He wondered how he could *ever* trust her not to try to kill herself again. What would it take for her to earn back that kind of trust?

You CAN'T trust her, ever again! said a dry, rattling voice in his mind. *And you already know damned right well why she tried to do it in the first place! That hasn't changed. None of it's changed, and you can bet your ass she'll try it again!*

Jeff stiffened, feeling the blood drain from his face. He hoped to hell his thoughts didn't show in his expression.

"Are you sure you're . . . you know, that you're really okay now? The doctor really told you that you could go home tomorrow?"

Nodding eagerly, Judy reached out and grabbed his hand. She laced her fingers through his and started to squeeze. There was something frighteningly familiar about the grip she had on his hand—something more than just how he remembered holding hers yesterday. A cold, tingling tension filled his stomach.

"I mean it, Jude," he said in a trembling voice.

Against his will, tears began to fill his eyes.

"You had me scared . . . I mean, *really* scared!"

"I-I know that," Judy said haltingly with downcast eyes. "I . . . I don't know why I did what I did, but I'm sorry." She looked at him, pleading in her eyes as she sucked in a breath. "Come on, Jeff. You have to believe me when I say I'm sorry."

"But can you say it?"

Judy stared at him, looking confused for a moment. He saw her eyes beginning to fill with tears, too.

"Say . . . what?" she said in a shattered whisper.

"You know what."

Judy took another deep breath, almost swallowing the air. Then she looked Jeff straight in the eyes and said, "I don't know why I tried to . . . to kill myself. Is that what you want me to say?"

Jeff nodded.

A single tear spilled from his eye and carved a warm track down his cheek. Sniffing, he wiped it away with the back of his hand. He shuddered when he reached out and cupped her face with his hand. Her skin felt so warm, so alive. He couldn't imagine how it would feel stone-cold dead.

"We're all we got, you know," he said, his voice

twisting with emotion as more tears ran from his eyes.

Judy nodded. Plump tears were rolling down her face, too, falling like dime-sized raindrops onto her folded hands and sheets.

"I *mean* it!" he said, more forcefully. "You and me . . . we're all we've got!"

"I . . . I know that," Judy whispered, looking at him and smiling bravely.

Jeff's heart sank when he saw—not his sister as the forty-year-old woman she was now, but his sister when she was a little girl—a small, frightened twelve-year-old girl.

His voice almost broke when he said, "We're all we've *ever* had, you know."

"I . . . know that," Judy said.

Reaching up, she pulled him close and hugged him so tightly she almost crushed the breath out of him. They stayed like that for several seconds, both of them sobbing; then they broke off, and Jeff straightened up.

"You're sure, though?" he asked. "You're absolutely sure that you're ready . . . to go home, I mean?"

Biting her lower lip and rolling her eyes around the room, Judy nodded. "I can't *wait* to get the hell out of here! I mean—Jeez, they have *crazy* people up here!"

Jeff smiled at her attempted joke but then got serious again.

"And they have you lined up with a good therapist and all? They're supposed to—"

"Yes, yes! I'm all set, Jeff. Honest, you can stop worrying so much, okay? I have an appointment to meet with a woman therapist—what's her name? Ruth Jenkins, I think is her name. I have it written down somewhere, but I've got an appointment to meet her tomorrow afternoon. Look, I've had plenty of time to think things over the last few days, and I . . . I don't know for sure why I was so down, why I tried what I did, but I promise you I won't do it again! Do you believe me?"

Jeff nodded, but a voice in the back of his mind whispered, *Oh, yeah, like hell you do!*

"I was hoping I could ask you a favor," Judy said. "Just a little favor."

Jeff smiled at her. "Sure . . . anything," he said.

"Well, if they really are planning to let me go home tomorrow, I don't want to leave this place looking like . . . like this." She raised her hands like she'd been asked a question she couldn't possibly answer. "I was wondering if you could swing by the house and pick up a few things for me, my makeup bag and maybe some fresh clothes."

Jeff opened his mouth as if to say something, but nothing came out.

"Anything will do," Judy said. "Just grab something out of the closet and get some lipstick and face stuff from the bathroom. It's all right there on the counter, I think. I just want to look as good as I can, you know? You're not a woman, but I'm sure you understand."

Jeff was speechless for another second or two, but he finally managed to say, "At your . . . house."

He was staring at her, and he couldn't shut off the voice that was yelling inside his mind.

No! No way, buddy! Not the old house! There's no way you can go out there!

"Can you do me that one, little favor?"

Jeff couldn't believe it when he forced a smile and nodded. His voice sounded flat, like someone else's when he said, "Yeah, sure thing. First thing this afternoon, I'll drive out."

But even as he said it, he knew he was lying. There was no way he was going to go out to Judy's house on Cape Higgins.

No fucking way in hell!

Chapter Five
Back Home

On Friday morning, Jeff and Judy were driving along Route 77, heading toward Cape Higgins. Rain was blowing in off the ocean and beating so hard against the car that the windshield wipers were having a tough time keeping up with it even at high speed. Stripped of their leaves, the oaks and maples that lined the road looked black and oily against the lowering gray sky. In the long stretches of woods along either side of the road, mist clung to the ground, wafting like heavy smoke between rain-darkened pines. It didn't take long for the steady *slap-slap* of the wipers and the high, hissing sound of tires on wet pavement to get on Jeff's nerves. The radio was on WGMX, a classic rock station, but when John Denver's song "Back Home Again" came on, Jeff quickly changed the station to some classical music.

Yes-sir-ee, he thought, repressing a shudder, *isn't this just a Jim-dandy day to be driving out here for the first time in—how long? Christ, sixteen years!*

In a different mood, it might have struck him as almost funny how the approach to town hadn't changed all that much, especially considering how

much the surrounding Portland area seemed to have
expanded since he'd last been home. Sure, along the
road he saw a lot of houses and a few new businesses,
including a large Shop 'n Save that hadn't been there
when he was growing up, but there was an essential
character, a certain *feel* to the road and the approach
to town that hadn't changed one bit. He realized that
he and his reactions to his hometown were the only
things that had really changed.

"I saw that you had a lot of get well cards at the
hospital," he said, just trying to make conversation.
"Who were they from?"

Judy was silent for a moment as she chewed the
inside of her cheek. She looked like she was carefully
weighing her response.

"Mostly friends from work," she finally replied.
"Oh, and Sally and Robin sent me one. That was
really nice."

She stopped talking abruptly, and the pause was so
obvious that Jeff glanced over at her.

"Mostly? . . . ," he said.

"Well, yeah . . ."

Her eyelids fluttered as she stared straight ahead at
the road. "And . . . uh, well, I also got a card from
Aunt Mildred and Uncle Kirby, if you can believe,"
she said, her voice lowering almost to a whisper.

"No shit," Jeff said. He whistled between his teeth
and nodded. He tried to say something else, but something caught in his throat, and he swallowed hard,
trying to make it go down.

"Yeah," Judy said. "I have no idea how they knew
I was in the hospital."

"Well I sure as hell didn't tell them," Jeff said, fighting the high quaver in his voice. "How are they doing,
anyway? I never hear from them any more, not even at
Christmas. Do they still live out at the farm?"

"Of course they do," Judy said, sniffing with laughter. "I don't think they'll *ever* leave that place . . . not until they die."

Jeff couldn't help but notice the nervous edge in her voice as well. "Umm, they must be getting up there."

Judy nodded. "They're both in their sixties, but I don't see them all that much. No more than I have to, actually. I never go out to visit them. I might see them around town every now and then, but that's about it."

"And I'll bet you Kirby's still driving that same old rusty pickup truck, too."

"Not the same one," Judy said, "but he's still driving an old truck, and it still looks like it's being held together with baling wire and spit. Smokes like a bastard, too."

"What, the truck . . . or Uncle Kirby?"

"The truck, of course," Judy said sourly. "Why, don't you know? Smoking is a sin! A vice of the Devil! Do you actually think Uncle Kirby would do something as *evil* as smoke a cigarette?"

Jeff nodded, trying to keep his expression impassive, but all he could think about was how miserable he and his sister had been whenever they had to stay with their Aunt Mildred and Uncle Kirby at the farm out on Bridge Road while their mother and father were off on one of their many vacations. The property bordered the Libby River, and—at least when Jeff was growing up, it had been an active farm. No doubt, as they got older, his aunt and uncle had to cut back on the amount of farming they did, but he could picture Kirby, thin and grizzled, out there working the fields, raising vegetables to sell to the summer tourists.

"I take it Kirby's still thumping the ole Bible like he used to, then, huh?" Jeff said.

He laughed out loud, trying to make light of his comment, but he heard—and was positive Judy also heard—the dry catch in his throat.

Judy looked at him and shook her head sharply. "I

told you, Jeff. I don't see them or talk to them anymore, but—" She snorted loudly. "Yeah, I'd guess they're both still . . . still—"

Her voice faded for a moment as she stared straight ahead at the rain-slick road. It could have been just the way the dim light of the day caught her eyes, but Jeff thought he saw her eyes clouding up and filling with tears.

". . . I'm sure he's still *filled* with the *glory* of the *Lord!"*

She said this last bit with the joyous, rising lilt of a televangelist, but the sarcasm was obvious. There wasn't a trace of humor in her expression.

After an awkward pause, Jeff finally said, "Yeah, you're probably right." It was obvious Judy didn't want to talk about them, and he would just as soon end the discussion now, too. He tried to think of something else to talk about but came up dry, so they drove for a while in silence.

As they neared the center of town, passing familiar houses and roads, Jeff found himself wishing that he didn't feel so goddamned tense. He tried to convince himself that it was just because Judy had mentioned their aunt and uncle. Like her, he would just as soon never see them again, either. The few memories he had of the times he had stayed with them were absolutely terrible. Like the rest of his life—his *former* life in Cape Higgins—he just wanted to forget all about them and move on.

I'm just here to help get Judy settled, and that's all; then I'm outta here, he kept reminding himself.

Tomorrow morning, he would get back on a plane and fly back to his *real* life in Colorado. As far as he was concerned, he was going to drop Judy off at her front door, maybe he'd walk her up to the door and make sure she got inside okay, but after that, he was going to get back in the car, turn around, and head back to the motel as quickly as possible. There was no way he wanted even to consider going inside the house with her, much less spend any part of the day there once he made sure she was all set.

Besides, she had an appointment with her shrink this afternoon, and she probably wanted to get cleaned up, maybe take a nap before then.

No, from here on out, Judy was going to have to take care of herself.

There were plenty of things about the old family house and his memories of growing up there that Jeff would just as soon forget. After eight years of therapy, he knew he *had* forgotten some—maybe a *lot* of what he'd gone through. Maybe he'd done that on purpose, but therapy had dredged up many of them, and most of them were much too painful to think about for very long. And *all* of them—every single goddamned thing he could think of that had been screwing up his life— seemed to be tied to his living and growing up in that house and in this town. It amazed him sometimes that Judy still lived in Cape Higgins, that she had never moved away, that she was still living in the same damn house! How could she? After all, her memories of growing up here couldn't be that much better than his—especially, he thought guiltily, the memory of what they had done together.

Yeah, and you loved it, too, didn't you? whispered a low, grating voice in his mind. *You think about it a lot, don't you? Come on, you can admit it. You enjoyed the hell out of fucking her back then, right? So go on! Admit it—at least to yourself. Admit that you've thought about doing it with her again, too. Haven't you? I said "HAVEN'T YOU?"* Christ, yes, you have. Just look at her, Jeff! Don't you ever wonder why she's acting so nervous and wired around you? Well, maybe it's not because she's embarrassed that she tried to kill herself. Maybe it's because she wants it, too, and she knows you* *want to do it! Did you ever think about that, Jeffy-boy?*

Jeff's voice sounded different to him when, just to break his train of thought, he glanced at Judy and said, "I—ah, I hope you liked those things I picked out for you . . . I mean that makeup and stuff."

Judy looked over at him with a crooked smile on her face.

"Well, they weren't exactly my color, Jeff," she said, almost laughing out loud. "What you got me would really look better on a blonde."

Biting his lower lip, Jeff shrugged as he slowed for the blinking yellow light that marked the center of town. He had such a tight grip on the steering wheel that the palms of his hands began to tingle. In spite of himself, he glanced over to the right, fully expecting to see the Cove Variety Store, but now, instead, there was a Mobile gas station and mini-mart. He sighed and almost said something about it to Judy but let his comment die.

"I still don't see why you didn't just zip out to the house and pick up my stuff like I asked," Judy said once they were past the Mobile station and had turned left onto Long Shore Drive.

Jeff shrugged again. "It was just as easy to pick up a few things at the pharmacy out by the Mall," he said.

Judy sniffed. "Well, it would have been nice to have something to wear other than what I had on when they brought me in," she said. "Besides, it's a waste of money if the makeup's not the right color, now, isn't it?"

Jeff smiled apologetically as he glanced over at her.

"Yeah, I suppose it is," he said. "But I—you know, I forgot to get a key from you before I left the hospital yesterday, anyway."

"Oh, yeah—right. You could have come back for it. And anyway—do you mean to tell me that you wouldn't know where to look for a key?"

Again, Jeff shrugged. His ears were burning, and he wished to hell she'd just let this whole thing drop.

"Well, for your information," she went on, "I still keep a spare one on the nail under the top step of the back porch. I'll bet you a dollar just out of habit that's where you would have looked first."

Jeff shook his head in quick denial. "Isn't that funny? I honestly didn't even remember that," he said, cringing at his own lie. The truth was, he knew damned well where Judy kept her spare key—the family had *always* kept one there. But he never had any intention of coming out here yesterday to get the few things Judy had asked for, and he sure as hell wouldn't be coming out here right now if he hadn't felt an obligation to help her before he left for Denver in the morning.

His heart gave a cold, hard thump in his chest when he slowed for the right-hand turn onto Oak Street. At the beginning of the road, he could see that the moss-covered stone wall marking Old Man Murray's property was still standing. It looked much smaller than he remembered it, and one section of it had collapsed, making it look like a huge, gap-toothed smile. Sodden, brown leaves littered the road and nestled in the spaces between the fallen stones.

Jeff felt a twinge of nostalgia when he recalled all the times he had played out here on that wall with his friends, pretending it was either a fort or a castle. There had been Johnny Holder, and the twins, Jimmy and Ray Makkonen, and his best friend, Eddie Dearborn. His memories might at times feel distant to him, like they belonged to someone else, but this stone wall was a tangible reminder that he had grown up here, had lived on this street. Sure, maybe over the years he had lost touch with all of his childhood friends, but from time to time he couldn't help but wonder where they were now. The last he had heard, Johnny had married a woman doctor and was living in California. Ray had died several years ago in a hunting accident up north. He had no idea whatever became of Jimmy. He knew from what Judy had told him that Eddie Dearborn was a town cop, but they had lost touch right after high school.

Hell, Jeff thought, *they might just as well all be dead.*

For so many years, he had tried to distance himself from his family home and this town and his own memories, but now he couldn't deny that they were his. He shivered again, trying to grasp how time had slipped away, that *he* had been the little boy who, on lush, spring evenings, had played out here . . . who on buzzing summer days had ridden his bike down this road, heading downtown to buy candy and soda at Cove Variety or over to the old school yard to play baseball or to the beach; and who in winter's icy grip had waited by the wall every morning at seven o'clock, sometimes even in predawn darkness, for the school bus to arrive.

Forgetting himself for a moment, Jeff sighed heavily. Judy immediately picked up on it.

"Been a while, huh?" she said, looking over at him with a twisted smile.

Clenching his teeth together, Jeff nodded. *Jesus, this is it! I can't turn back now!*

The bare trees lining both sides of Oak Street seemed to reach toward him like grasping hands as he drove slowly down the street toward the family home. He couldn't help but peer ahead, anticipating the first instant when he would see the roofline of the house through the autumn-stripped trees. He was surprised to see a new road that angled off to the left. It wasn't marked by a town street sign yet, but at the corner was a fancy hand-carved wooden sign with gold letters on a pale blue background that said, MURRAY HILL ESTATES.

Jeff looked at his sister and raised one eyebrow. *"Estates?"* he said. "My-my, aren't we getting fancy around here."

Judy snickered. "Yeah, well, after Old Man Murray died—oh, it must have been at least five years ago—his son and daughter, you remember them. Cindy and Pete. Well, they subdivided the old property into house lots and made a killing. Pete's a contractor, you know, and he built almost all of the houses out here, too."

Jeff and Judy had, of course, known Cindy and Pete Murray back when they were kids, but the Murray kids had been several years ahead of him in school, so they had never really been friends. Pete used to pick on him now and then, but he never beat him up or anything.

"Go ahead," Judy said. "Drive on down there and take a look around. They've got some pretty fancy places, and one hell of a view of the ocean. I'll bet the taxes are a killer, though."

"Umm . . . I'll bet," Jeff said.

He slowed and almost took the turn just to avoid going to the old house, but because he wanted to get all of this over with as soon as possible, he decided not to and followed the street as it veered around to the right.

"Naw . . . I think I'll pass . . . for now," he said, biting his lower lip and shaking his head. "It's funny how, the way I remember it, it always seemed like we lived out here in the middle of nowhere, but now—" He rubbed his jawline, and his frown deepened. "I don't know . . . now everything seems so . . . so small and close. Even the road is so friggin' narrow."

"It's probably because you're used to living out West now, with lots of wide, open spaces. We own enough land so the nearest house to me is still more than half a mile away, so I still have my privacy."

"Umm, have you met any of the new neighbors?"

Judy scowled and shook her head. "No, not really, other than passing them by on the street either coming or going. Some of the kids show up for trick or treating or to sell Girl Scout cookies or whatever, but it's kind of a snooty little development, actually. Lots of yuppies."

"Hey, aren't we yuppies, too?"

Judy shook her head tightly. "Not really. My bank account seems to be going steadily downward, so I guess that makes me—what? A duppie . . . a *downwardly* mobile urban professional."

Jeff laughed at her joke but, because of his own nervousness, perhaps a bit too heartily.

"Yeah, but I'll bet you can't help but feel like you've lost some of your privacy," he said. "Don't you feel like the town's closing in on you?"

"Not really," Judy said, shrugging and shaking her head as if it didn't matter. "But one thing I know for sure, Old Man Murray never wanted to cut up his land like that. He's probably spinning in his grave, but Cindy and Pete are happy. From what I hear, they made a killing, selling those lots."

"That's progress, I guess."

Jeff was still feeling uncomfortable. It seemed as though any topic he or Judy brought up made him feel that way. He said nothing as he rounded the last curve in the road. Leaning over the steering wheel and looking ahead, he caught his first glimpse of the old homestead through the trees. His skin went ice-cold, and he held his breath until his lungs began to hurt. He felt as though someone had just punched him—hard—in the ribs.

"Jesus . . . ," he whispered, more of a gasp than a word.

The wipers were slapping back and forth, smearing his view, but as far as he could see, the house hadn't changed that much if at all. It stood out, a dark, brooding silhouette against the gray sky.

For just an instant, Jeff felt as though he had been magically transported back some thirty years, and he was an eight year old boy just coming home after being away for a while. Waves of shivers raced through him. His foot involuntarily lifted off the gas pedal, and the car slowed almost to a stop.

"What is it?" Judy said. "Is something the matter?"

Biting his lower lip, Jeff shook his head and said, "No, it's just . . . I . . ."

His voice faded away as he took the turn into the driveway and then pulled to a stop in front of the house. He stared up at it silently.

Looking at it objectively, the house seemed ordinary enough. It was a large, two-storied building of early twentieth-century style with a high, peaked roof of slate gray shingles. The windows reflected back the rain-laden sky like flat, dimensionless mirrors. A long breezeway connected the main part of the house to the dilapidated barn, which obviously served now as Judy's garage. Jeff was surprised to see that his old basketball hoop, now rusty and bent down, was still hanging from above the barn door. The house had been painted gray when Jeff was a boy, but now there were few—if any—traces of color left, having been worn away by weather and salty winds. Even the white trim around the windows was peeling and looked as faded as old bone. Thick silver threads of water dripped from the broken-down spouts. Like a relic from another age, a television antenna, bent in the middle and missing several crossbars, was strapped to the central chimney.

The bare trees that surrounded the house swayed against the sky like long, bony fingers. In the front yard, thick tussocks of yellow grass and weeds were beaten flat by the rain that swept across the yard in brisk gusts. A sheeting stream of water ran down the incline of the driveway and disappeared into a road-side ditch that was choked with thick, brown weeds.

Jeff wanted to say something, to hurry things along if nothing else, but his mind was a raging maelstrom of confused thoughts and memories. He couldn't quite grasp that this had been his home all those years ago. It all looked like something out of a terrible dream . . . a dream he might be having back home in Colo-rado.

"You might as well pull up as close to the side door as you can get," Judy said as she nudged Jeff's shoul-der.

Jeff shook his head as though momentarily dazed, then took his foot off the brake and inched the car closer to the house. Rain hissed against the car roof. Usually Jeff thought that sound was soothing, but now it set his teeth on edge.

"Let me get that stuff for you," Jeff said, reaching into the backseat and grabbing the two bags that con-tained Judy's belongings. Once he had the bags firmly in hand, he looked at his sister and said, "You ready to make a run for it? We're gonna get wet no matter how fast we move, so make sure you have your key ready."

Judy held up her key ring and jangled it.

"Are you going to come in and have a little some-thing before you take off?"

Jeff didn't reply right away, but it wasn't because he hadn't made up his mind; he simply wasn't able to speak. After clearing his throat, he shook his head and managed to say, "No, I've—ah, gotta get going."

"You sure?" Judy said, giving him an intense, ques-tioning look.

Jeff nodded, hoping to hell this wasn't a plea for him to stay with her because she still wasn't feeling quite strong enough to deal with being back home. He was feeling quite fragile himself and wasn't sure how much longer he could maintain being a support for her.

"I . . . I'm sure," he said in a tight voice.

Leaving the car running with the wipers slapping back and forth, he snapped open his door at the same time Judy opened hers. The cold blast of wind-driven rain took his breath away, but he hugged Judy's bags close to his chest and ran for the front door like a football player heading for the goal line. He heard the sloppy sounds of his own feet and Judy's on the wet pavement, and then they were both huddled underneath the shelter of the breezeway, panting heavily. When he looked at her, with her rain-plastered hair in dark squiggles on her forehead, he couldn't help but laugh.

"Jesus, you look like a drowned rat," he said, barely able to hear himself above the sound of the rain beating the roof.

"Thanks a lot," Judy replied, her teeth chattering wildly. Her hands were shaking as she tried to fit the key into the lock and kept missing. "You don't look so great yourself."

She finally got the key into the slot and turned it, but when she tried to push the door open, it stuck. Sighing with frustration, she twisted to one side and bumped it open with her hip.

"It always gets this way when it's raining," she said with an apologetic laugh. "The wood gets wet and swells up or something."

Jeff nodded, but once the door was open and Judy had stepped inside the shelter of the breezeway, he stayed where he was on the top step, looking in at her. He silently passed the two bags to her, then looked around nervously, at a complete loss for words. Even out here in the breezeway, he caught a whiff of a familiar smell and remembered *exactly* how the house used to smell inside. He shivered again, harder, and pushed back the flood of memories.

"Are you sure you don't want to come in and dry off before you leave? I can heat up some water for coffee or tea."

Jeff shook his head forcefully but found it difficult to look her straight in the eye.

"No thanks. Really. I'd just as soon get back to the motel and start packing. My flight is first thing in the morning, and I'd just as soon relax. It's been a pretty stressful couple of days."

"Tell me about it," Judy said, but Jeff thought he could tell by her expression that she knew right well that he was just making excuses.

"I—uh, I can give you a call later today, maybe tonight after you . . . uh, see that therapist," he offered. "You *do* remember that you have an appointment this afternoon, don't you?"

"Yeah, yeah. Don't worry. I won't forget about it."

"And you're sure you're feeling all right . . . about everything, I mean?"

Judy gave him a twisted half-smile and reached out to place one hand gently on his shoulder.

"Yeah," she said in a low, husky voice. "I'm fine now . . . honest."

"Well then . . . ," Jeff said, shrugging nervously and slapping his hands against his legs. "I guess I'd might as well be going then."

He took a deep breath and finally found the courage to look his sister straight in the eyes.

"You take care of yourself, now, you hear me?"

"I said *don't worry,*" Judy said. Her face was dripping wet, and it looked pale and small, framed in the doorway. She still had her hand on his shoulder, and she gave him a bracing squeeze.

"Well I *do* worry," Jeff said, finding it difficult to

control his voice. "Honest to shit, Jude, I *mean* it! You're really important to me, and I—"

"If I'm so damned important to you, then how come you live halfway across the fucking country?"

Jeff swallowed hard but couldn't reply. Judy continued to stare at him for several seconds, looking like she wanted to say something else, something really important, but she remained silent.

Last chance! a voice whispered softly in Jeff's mind. *Are you sure you don't want to admit it to her now? Go on! Tell her, for Christ's sake! Tell her how much you've been thinking about her! Tell her how much you want to DO it with her again! Jesus Christ, man! Tell her you still want to fuck her!*

"No, I . . . ," Jeff said, but that was all he could manage. He lowered his head and shook it sadly, fighting back the tears.

"Hey, thanks . . . thanks for everything you've done," Judy said in a voice that sounded thin and shaky. "I really do appreciate how you've helped me out."

Jeff shrugged. "What do you expect?" he said, trying to sound light but knowing he didn't.

Leaning forward suddenly, Judy gave him a quick kiss on the cheek. Then, clutching the two bags tightly to her chest, she walked to the side door and tried to open it. That door was stuck too, but it opened with a loud clatter when she gave it a solid kick down low.

"See ya later then," she said, almost dismissively over her shoulder as she went inside and closed the door behind her.

"Yeah," Jeff said, barely a whisper. "Later."

He felt like a fool, standing there on the top step with the wind and rain tugging at his back. Pulling his collar tightly around his neck, he ducked his head down and ran back to the waiting car. As he backed out of the driveway, before he pulled away, he looked up at the house and saw Judy, standing there in the living-room window, looking out at him. She had her arms folded across her chest, and one hand raised to cover her mouth as though she were trying to stop herself from calling out to him. Her figure looked eerily translucent through the rain-streaked glass, and as he drove away, the last impression he had was that his sister looked like a ghost, trapped in the old family house . . . a ghost who stared longingly out at a world she knew she would never be a part of again.

Chapter Six

Conversation in a Dark Room: #2

"Who's there?"

"Just me."

"Who? . . . Is that you, Karl?"

"What, you were expecting the Pope or something?"

I am sitting on the floor in the dark room, not even sure if my eyes are opened or closed. Darkness closes around me like a tight-fitting glove. I shift my position, encircling my legs with my arms, and grip my wrists tightly. I take a deep, shuddering breath, surprised at how warm the air feels . . . as if it were summertime, and the living was easy . . .

"No, but I . . . How the hell have you been, Karl?"

There is a pause that goes on almost too long. I am beginning to think Karl might have left the room, but then I hear him sigh and say, "Oh, I'm getting along all right. It's been a while since I've talked to . . . to anyone."

"Really?"

"Really."

"So you don't know anything about what's been happening, then, huh?"

I hear a soft rustling sound of cloth, as if Karl is shrugging.

"Happening with what?"

"With me and my . . . uh, sister . . ."

"You mean when you and she—"

"No, no, not that. Something else. Just a few days ago, Judy tried to . . ." The words form in my mind, but I have a tough time saying them. "She tried to kill herself."

"Well, can't say as I blame her," Karl replies. His voice is low and sounds despondent. "I mean, after what you and she have been through and all."

I am about to respond, but I hesitate, suddenly not sure what Karl is talking about. Does he mean what had just happened recently, or is he referring to something that happened back when we—or I was a kid?

"I heard Sammy saying something about how he thought you and Judy were going to do it again . . . you know, make love."

"No way," I reply in a constricted voice. "Sammy's full of shit."

"As usual," Karl says. "I told him that, too. That he's full of shit. He was going on and on about how you only married Sally because she looks so much like your sister, and how what your only *real* problem is, you won't just admit that's what you always wanted—to be married to your sister."

"I told you, he's full of shit," I say, feeling my anger rise even as a cold twisting sensation fills my gut. "Of course I . . . I *care* about her. I mean, shit—I don't want anything bad to happen to her. She tried to kill herself, you know."

"Yeah, you already told me that," Karl says. His voice has a strange reverberation in the darkness, and it seems to be coming at me from several directions at once. "But—Christ, man, she's your sister! What are you supposed to do, just let her go through with it?"

"Exactly my point. Of course not!"

"I mean—shit, yeah, she's had it tough, no doubt about it. To tell you the truth, I was really worried about her a lot right after her second marriage fell apart. She was close to the edge then, too."

"Who could blame her," I say, thinking I sound a little lame. "But do you have any idea what might have prompted it this time?"

"None whatsoever," Karl replies. "Unless it had something to do with what you guys have been through . . . especially like what good ole Bible-thumpin' Kirby and Mildred did to the both of you."

My body tenses, and I lean forward, trying to pierce the swelling darkness with my eyes. I know I won't be able to see Karl. I've never seen anyone here in the safe room. That's part of the deal. Everyone can come in here and talk freely as long as no one ever looks at anyone else.

"What do you mean?" I say, my voice edging higher. "What do you know? I mean about what Uncle Kirby and Aunt Mildred might have . . . done?"

"Jesus, Jeff, you're an adult now! Don't you think you can dispense with this *uncle* and *aunt* bullshit?"

"Yeah . . . sure, but what do you know about it? What aren't you telling me? Do you remember something that I don't?"

"That all depends, I guess," Karl says, letting his voice rise temptingly. "I mean, sure, I remember some things—"

"Like what? Jesus Christ, Karl, tell me! I've taken enough shit from Sammy and Alexander and some of the others, but I thought I could always count on you to tell me everything you know."

"Sure you can. It's just . . . well, don't you think it'd be better if you remembered it yourself?"

"Not if you were there. Tell me anything you remember about what Uncle—I mean, what Kirby and Mildred did."

"Can you tell me—honestly—that you don't remember?"

I gnaw on my lower lip and think for a moment in silence.

"I know I never liked being around them—I think mostly because they were always talking about the Bible and God's will and all that."

"Think about it, though," Karl says. "Try to remember what happened some of those times you stayed with them while your parents were away on vacation."

"My folks took off like that a lot. I think my sister and I spent at least a couple of weeks with Kirby and Mildred every summer out at the farm."

"Oh, yeah. Sometimes *more* than a couple of weeks. One summer you were there almost the whole of summer vacation."

"Really?" I say, shaking my head. "I don't remember that . . . not very clearly, anyway."

"But come on, Jeff, do you mean to tell me you don't remember anything about the Bible lessons?"

"No, I . . ."

My voice drifts off as a cold, clutching fear wraps around me and squeezes. My breath is lodged in my throat, and I feel my eyes, bugging out of my head.

"Oh, Jesus!" I whisper. My voice hisses like a snake in the darkness. "Oh, *shit!* . . . Yes, *yes* I *do* remember!"

"Go on. Tell me."

I swallow and lick my lips furiously before I can speak.

"I remember how Mildred used to . . . used to read to us from the Bible . . . right after supper."

"Yes? . . ."

"Yeah, and if we . . . if we didn't pay attention and answer her questions correctly—"

"Go on," Karl says, his voice drawling.

"Then Kirby would ask us if he had to *beat* the lessons into us. Shit, yes, I remember now. That's why we were so afraid of him—especially him, but Mildred was almost as bad. She never hit us or anything. She always left that to her husband, but she'd grind us with those Bible stories until we could recite them in our sleep."

"Yeah, and even *then,* I'll bet Kirby would give you each a beating—'a *Godly* whooping,' wasn't that what he used to call it?"

"Shit . . . yes," I say, barely above a whisper.

"But do you mean to tell me that up until right now, you never even remembered any of that?" Karl asks. He sounds completely incredulous.

A cold sweat breaks out on my forehead, and a burning dryness starts choking me so I can't answer.

"Come on, Jeff. You don't expect me to believe that you *never* remembered all the 'whoopings' you took! Get real, man! How could you forget? After so many years of therapy, how could you not remember that kind of abuse?"

"Honest," I say, my voice croaking horribly. "I . . . not until just now, I . . . I didn't remember it."

I'd been holding my breath so long it hurt my chest, so I let it out in a long sigh that sounds like a cold wind, whistling in the eaves of a house.

"Well, I find that rather difficult to believe," Karl says, his voice loaded with sarcasm. "You might not want to admit it to Alexander and the others, but you can admit it to me, you know. I'd say you probably *did* remember it, remembered it very vividly, but you just never told anyone, not even your shrink or your wife. Isn't that so?"

"No, honest," I reply, feeling totally shaken. I take

another breath, but it feels like sand entering my lungs.
"But if *you* knew so much about it, how come you
never said anything to me? We've talked lots of times
in here. I would think you would have said *something*
before now."

"Hey, I can't tell you everything! I mean—shit, it
just never came up before, I guess—and besides, don't
you think it's better if you dredge up this shit on your
own? You can't expect me to sit around here in the
dark and start listing all your deep, dark secrets, you
know. Christ, some of them you might not even *want*
to hear . . . you might not be *able* to hear."

"Oh, yeah? Try me," I say, a bit surprised by the
sudden surge of courage I feel.

"Well, for one thing, did you ever stop to think that
maybe that's why you and Judy started doing what
you did in the first place?"

"What, do you mean . . . sleeping together?"

"Of course I do," Karl snaps, sounding as though
he's just lost his last ounce of patience. "You two
started sleeping together, and then one thing led to
another. You were—what? Ten years old, and Judy
was twelve, wasn't she, when you first did it—or at
least *tried* to do it?"

"I . . . I don't remember exactly."

"There you go with this *I don't remember* bullshit!
Well, then trust me on this, okay? You were ten and
she was twelve. And you were at Kirby and Mildred's
house the first time you did it."

"How do you know that?"

"Don't ask. Believe me, I know. You were supposed
to be sleeping in separate bedrooms upstairs. Your
aunt and uncle slept downstairs—"

"That's right—in the room off the living room."

"Yeah, but late at night, once you were sure they
were asleep, Judy would tiptoe into your bedroom and

slip into bed with you. Don't you remember how you used to hug each other until you fell asleep?"

I swallow noisily, but it doesn't stop the burning in my throat.

"Sure I—uh, I remember that I was scared a lot . . . when I was trying to go to sleep. I was always afraid that Kirby would catch us and beat us even more."

"So you *do* remember it."

"It's coming back to me," I say weakly.

"Well, do you remember there was a streetlight right outside the bedroom window? Remember how you would watch the branches blowing back and forth, imagining that they were hands, clawing at the windows? Come on, you *must* remember at least *that* much!"

"Yeah, I do."

"And you must remember that that's when Judy used to come in and slip into bed with you, and how then you started fooling around, feeling each other up. Eventually, as scared as you both were, you started touching each other's private places."

"Jesus, stop it!" I shout. "Stop it right now! I don't want to talk about this!"

I suddenly lurch forward in the darkness and swing my fist out in front of myself, but I don't connect with anything.

"Why not?" Karl says in a low, calm voice that I find completely irritating. "I think what you mean is, you don't want to *hear* it, just like I said."

"Whatever!" I say, feeling every muscle in my body tense. My eyes are stinging, and I know I'm going to start crying soon. "I just don't need to have you rub my face in it, for Christ's sake! We were kids! We were scared out of our minds!"

"That's exactly what I'm talking about," Karl replies, still sounding calm and in complete control.

"Who else did you have to turn to? Either one of you? You needed to find love *somewhere,* from *someone,* right? You sure as hell weren't getting it from your parents. They farmed you out whenever they had a chance to get away. And you sure as shit never got it from Kirby and Mildred. Come on, remember how you used to think they were so angry all the time, and that they beat you because they were pissed that they never had kids of their own. That's why they took it out on you."

"Yeah . . . I remember," I whisper. "They used to say things like that all the time, how if we were their children, they'd make sure they brought us up right, in the ways of the Lord."

"My point exactly," Karl says smoothly. "Look, I want to get going now. This isn't exactly my idea of fun, so you take care of yourself, now, you hear me?"

"Yeah."

"And don't let Sammy or Alexander or anyone else grind you down about what you and Judy did, okay? You *had* to do it to survive, for Christ's sake. As far as I'm concerned, you didn't do anything that was perverted or sick. You did it because you needed love."

"Yeah," I say, my voice sounding ragged and raw. "Love."

"And you tell me, just what's so goddamned bad about needing love? Huh?"

Chapter Seven
Flight Home

Jeff had no idea what time it was when he awoke with a start to find himself slouched in a chair in the dimly lit motel room. For several heart-stopping seconds, he looked around, trying desperately to figure out where he was and what he had been doing, but he was confused by the vague images and distant memories that flooded his mind. Opening his eyes wide, he tried hard to make sense of his surroundings, and then—like an electric shock—it suddenly came back to him.

He was in Maine . . . in a motel room . . . He had just come back from Cape Higgins . . . from seeing his sister . . .

Groaning aloud, he stretched his left arm out and looked at the luminous dial of his wristwatch. The dull green numbers read 2:49.

He felt something crusty on his chin, and when he wiped it away with the back of his hand, he realized he must have been drooling in his sleep. When he licked the inside of his mouth, his teeth felt like they were coated with fur.

Shit, it's almost three in the morning, he thought

after a moment's consideration. He had gotten back from Judy's house—when? Sometime in the early afternoon. After a quick lunch, he had come back to the motel room to shower and start packing for his flight home in the morning. He hadn't had any urgent plans; his only consideration had been to get the hell away from the old family home and the memories it stirred within him.

His neck was stiff, so he sat forward and rotated it a few times, listening to the faint crackle of his spine. Tiny white lights spiraled like fireflies in his field of vision. Then, once he thought he was ready, he planted his feet firmly on the floor, stood up, and stretched his arms over his head.

"Ahh, *shit*," he groaned.

He could feel the stiff resistance of his muscles as he took a few tentative steps forward. His legs felt all rubbery and weak, as if he had been standing up or running for hours. He wondered if he was finally paying the price for that morning jog he'd taken out by the hospital a few days ago. His stomach was growling with hunger, but he figured it was much too late to call room service, and in Portland, Maine, there probably weren't that many all-night diners. Sighing heavily, he stripped down to his underwear, pulled back the bedcovers, and slid into the bed.

"Yeah . . . just fuck it," he whispered softly, wondering why, if he had been asleep in the chair for the last maybe six or eight hours, did he feel so damned exhausted?

He pulled the covers up to his chin and scrunched his eyes tightly shut, but from then until the first traces of gray morning light filtered between the curtains, sleep only teased him. He kept drifting in and out of sleep, and all the while he was plagued by disturbing dreams that mixed his sister's current problems with twisted memories of the abuse he had suffered as a

child from his aunt and uncle. It all melded to create
a vague, nameless threat that at times felt like it was
directed at him, but then it blended, as dreams will,
into something that threatened his whole family.

When he saw his watch flash 6:15, he finally gave up
trying to sleep and got out of bed.

His flight was at 9:35 that morning, and he wanted
to get to the airport at least an hour ahead of time so
he could return his rented car, check in, and get his
boarding pass. By seven o'clock, he had shaved, show-
ered, and dressed, putting on his usual Oxford cloth
shirt, sweater, jeans, and sneakers. He found a soft
rock station on the radio and sang along with a Bea-
tles' tune as he packed his bags. Once he was ready to
go, he put his luggage into the car and went out for
breakfast.

The waitress who had served him every morning so
far was there again. She greeted him cheerfully, and
he, feeling almost like a regular as he settled into his
booth, joked with her. But as far as he was concerned,
she and everyone else in Maine could be just as
friendly as they liked, there was no way he was going
to miss one goddamned thing about this state once he
got back to his "real" life in Colorado. Sure, he would
no doubt still be concerned about how Judy was
doing, but they could stay in touch by phone and mail
as they had over the years.

Nothing had changed between them . . . not really.

He got to the airport even earlier than he expected,
returned the car, and went to the United desk to check
in. After that, he saw that he still had more than an
hour to kill, so he headed over to the Jetport News to
buy a few treats for the flight. As he rounded the
corner into the small store, he bumped into and almost
knocked over a display of Stephen King books that
had been decorated with stick-on Halloween jack-o'-
lanterns and angel's hair cobwebs.

"Whoa, are you all right there?" a woman's voice called out.

For a moment, Jeff thought he was hallucinating when he looked up and saw the woman behind the counter. She was wearing a filmy black dress that hung in tatters, and a tall, pointed witch's hat. Her face was made up with thick, black wrinkle lines, and there was a round, red wart almost the size of a Ping-Pong ball on the end of her nose.

She caught his startled expression and, smiling, said, "Just trying to get into the spirit of things."

"Oh, yeah . . . that's right," Jeff said, a bit bemused.

"You're the third customer who's bumped into that coming around the corner. I guess I'd better move it."

"Good idea," Jeff said.

He frowned, thinking this sales clerk was maybe carrying things a little bit too far as he selected a pack of gum and a roll of peppermint Life Savers and placed them on the counter. On impulse, he also picked up a copy of the *Portland Press Herald.* After paying for his things, he went out into the lobby to sit and wait.

The time passed slowly.

He read as much of the newspaper as he cared to read, then sat with his arms folded across his chest, his eyes closed as he waited for the flight to be called. Once he was in his seat in the jet, he settled back again and closed his eyes.

Christ! he thought for at least the dozenth time already this morning, *for as much as I slept last night, I sure as shit am tired!*

Once again, he had a window seat, so he propped his head on one of the thin airline pillows, closed his eyes, and tried to fall asleep as the jet took off and started winging its way westward.

As he dozed fitfully, a new face invaded his dreams, mixing and blending with stark images of his wife, his daughter, and his sister. It was the crackled and wrinkled face of an old woman—a witch, who leered at him, her face frighteningly underlit as she rolled bulging, bloodshot eyes that were the color of old ivory. She cackled wildly, exposing the rotten stumps of her teeth. At times, Jeff, in his dream, would think that the witch's face looked a bit like that of his Aunt Mildred, and he startled himself awake several times when he thought that she—or Uncle Kirby, who he thought might be standing behind her, shrouded in shadow—had hold of a thick, leather strap—a belt—and was swinging it at him.

There had been another long layover in Chicago, so it was getting on toward evening by the time the landing gear locked into place, and the jet came screaming down out of the sky. Jeff heaved more than one deep sigh of relief when he saw the brown, shadowed stretch of prairie rushing closer and closer, and then felt the jet shudder as it touched down. He was still feeling more exhausted than rested as he grabbed his carry-on bags and waited to slip into the flow of disembarking passengers. By the time he was out of the landing gate, finished his wait at the luggage carousel, and headed into the lobby, he was feeling a curious mixture of relief and gathering apprehension as he scanned the waiting crowd, looking for his wife and daughter.

"Daddy!" he heard someone—a little girl—shriek, but when he turned to look, it wasn't Robin. Jeff felt a cold sinking in his heart as he wondered if Sally had forgotten what time he was arriving . . . or if she had gotten stuck in the rush-hour traffic . . . or if—

Jesus Christ! No! Don't think it!

—if something had happened to her or Robin or *both* of them while he was away.

Cold sweat broke out on his forehead, and his insides felt all bubbly as he jostled along with the crowd, desperately hoping to see Sally and Robin soon. His heart gave a solid thump, and his eyes began to sting with tears the instant he caught sight of them. They were waiting off to one side. Robin was bouncing up and down on tiptoes, her hands clenched in front of her.

"Well, well, well, and don't you look *gorgeous,*" he said, dropping his bags and scooping her up into his arms as she rushed toward him.

Robin squealed as she wiggled in his embrace, winding both arms around his neck and hugging him so hard she almost hurt his neck. She gave him a loud, smacking kiss on the cheek.

"I don't think anyone here is being met by anyone more beautiful than you," he said as he gently lowered her to the floor.

"That goes for you, too," he said, locking eyes with Sally and stepping closer so he could hug her and kiss her full on the lips. "I missed you." His voice was low and gravelly. "A *lot!*"

"I missed you, too," Sally said, but there was a flat lifelessness to her voice, as though something was bothering her. Maybe he was the only one who caught it, but it was definitely there.

"Geez, you look really beat," Sally said.

"Yeah, I am," Jeff replied. "God, no matter how hard I try, I just can't seem to sleep on a plane. Maybe it's because I'm sitting up or something."

"Umm . . . maybe."

He noticed that Sally didn't maintain eye contact when she spoke to him, so he knew that *something* was definitely wrong. He was going to ask her what, but he picked up Sally's unspoken signal that it was something she didn't want to talk about right now.

"Hey, let me carry one of those for you, Daddy," Robin said as she made a grab for the smaller of his travel bags. She gripped the leather handle and tried to pick it up but couldn't.

"God, Daddy, what have you *got* in there?" she said, frowning.

"Well, *maybe* there's a little surprise in there for you."

"I hope you didn't bring me one of those icky *lobsters* you were talking about," Robin said. She wrinkled her nose in disgust and took a cautious step away from her father, eyeing the luggage as if she was expecting it to explode.

"Oh, no . . . nothing of the sort," Jeff replied, smiling and shaking his head. "But—here. I can carry my own luggage."

He caught Sally's sidelong glance and, smiling widely, gave her a wink, but felt a chill in his gut when he saw the pinched, worried expression on her face.

Jesus Christ! he thought. *What the hell is bothering her?*

She was doing her best to keep from blurting out whatever was on her mind, but she obviously didn't want to talk about it in front of Robin. Jeff immediately started clicking through the various possibilities.

Without him around for a few days, what if she had finally worked up the courage to tell him she wasn't happy with him and wanted a divorce? Or what if she had been to the doctor's and found out that she—or maybe Robin!—had some serious, possibly terminal disease? Or had she received bad news from her job? What if she had been fired or replaced? Or maybe it was his own job! What if she had heard about some more budget cuts at the University, and he was losing his job?

Telling himself just to calm down, that things would sort themselves out in their own time, he picked up and hefted his bags, and then the three of them started the long trek toward the exit. While Robin bubbled on and on about how *great* it was to have her daddy home again, Sally and Jeff kept exchanging meaningful glances. Once or twice, when Robin had run a few paces ahead of them, jumping and skipping merrily, Jeff started to open his mouth, but each time Sally would signal for him to be quiet.

"Boy, this airport sure is *huge,* isn't it?" Jeff said, ruffling Robin's hair as she walked along beside him, her hand clutching his arm just above the elbow.

"Yeah," Robin said. "I really liked that subway."

"The people mover," Jeff said, smiling. "Yeah, that was fun, huh? And it sure beats walking."

"I just hope I can remember where the hell I parked the car," Sally said softly. Her voice had a nervous edge to it, and Jeff couldn't stop himself from thinking that it was something else that was bothering her, not where she had left the car. "Now, let me see . . . I know I wrote down the parking lot number somewhere." She started searching through her purse until she found the sheet of paper she had torn out of her pocket notebook. "Ah-hah. Here it is."

As soon as they were outside, Jeff leaned his head back, looked up at the sky, and in spite of the exhaust fumes that swirled in the air, took a long, hissing inhalation.

"Ahh," he said, smiling as he turned to face Sally. "You can't smell even a *trace* of the ocean. I like it like that."

Sally said nothing, but it looked to Jeff as though a dark bank of storm clouds had shifted across her eyes.

It took them the better part of fifteen or twenty minutes to find their car, and by the time they had, Jeff's hands were aching from carrying his luggage. Sally gave him the car keys and stood close beside him as he opened up the back of the Volvo station wagon and placed his luggage inside. He was going crazy with curiosity—and worry—to find out what was bugging

Sally, and had been hoping that this would give them a chance to talk, but Robin stood beside them as if she were overseeing the job—too close for them to talk.

"So," Robin asked, bouncing excitedly up and down on her toes once the car was loaded, "are you going to take me out for ice cream, Daddy? I've been waiting all *day* for you to get home."

"Oh, I don't know, sweetie," Jeff said tiredly. "I'm really beat after such a long flight."

"Ahh, come on," she said.

"Robin," Sally said sharply.

His daughter glanced quickly at her mother, then back to him with such a pouting, trembling lip that he knew he wouldn't be able to handle it if she started to cry. He considered for a moment and then, taking a deep breath, said, "Well . . . okay." He came around to the side of the car and unlocked the back door. "As long as you hop right in and buckle up *real* quick, I'll take you."

"Yippie!" Robin shouted as she did a spinning turn on one toe. She darted over to the car door and opened it, then threw herself onto the backseat, and slammed the door shut behind her before Jeff could say another word.

"Okay," she shouted, as she shifted back and forth, settling into the seat, and glanced over the backseat at her parents. She pulled the shoulder strap across her chest and snapped it. "I'm all buckled up, too."

Jeff couldn't help but laugh out loud. "If only you moved that fast whenever I told you it was time to get ready for bed," he said. When he turned to look at Sally again, he saw that worry was still darkening her eyes. His hand was shaking, and he desperately wanted to say something as he reached up and grabbed the trunk lid, and then slammed it shut. The sound echoed like a gunshot in the parking garage. He started to turn, out of habit heading to the driver's side, but Sally snagged his sleeve, pulling him up short.

"What is it, Sal?" he asked, his voice barely above a whisper as he looked deeply into his wife's eyes.

For several long, drawn-out seconds, Sally didn't say anything as she looked at him, her lower lip trembling with a repressed sob. A car taking a sharp turn somewhere in the garage made a loud, squealing sound that startled them both. They both looked to see if they could see it, then looked at each other again.

Jeff cast a nervous glance at Robin, who was waiting impatiently in the car. He could feel the car shaking from her bouncing in her seat.

"What *is* it? Can you talk about it now?"

Sally bit down hard on her lower lip, making it go bloodless. Her whole face seemed to pale as her eyes flickered madly, blinking back the tears that were building up.

"Jesus, Sal, come on," Jeff said, feeling suddenly fearful and desperate. "Whatever it is—"

"About an hour ago . . . just as we were leaving for the airport . . . I got a call—"

"Yes!"

"Hey! Come on! Hurry up!" Robin shouted, her voice muffled from inside the car.

"From Maine," Sally said, and with those two words, Jeff felt as if the air pressure suddenly doubled. Everything seemed to be pushing against him with unbearable pressure. His voice was a pathetic croak when he said, "My sister?"

"Yes . . . your sister," Sally said, not caring now as her tears began to fall. "They . . . found her."

"What do you mean?" Jeff grabbed her by both arms and gave her a rough shake. "What the hell are you talking about?"

"She . . . she did it."

Jeff almost asked, *Did what?* but he was stunned into

silence because he knew in an instant *exactly* what
Judy had done.

"Oh, no," he said. He sagged back against the car
and covered his face with both hands, feeling like a
balloon that had suddenly lost all of its air. "No
. . . no . . . no," he said in a broken voice. "This can't
be happening!"

"I . . . I'm sorry, honey," Sally said as she leaned
forward and hugged him tightly against herself, almost crushing the breath out of him. He felt as frail as
a baby in her embrace. "Her friend—I-I don't remember her name—but she had come over to . . . to check
on her this afternoon, to see how she was doing, and
she . . . she found her . . ."

"Jesus, no!"

Sally took a breath, a loud, ragged gasp. "She was
. . . was in the . . . the bathtub. She had—"

"No!" Jeff shouted. *"Don't tell me!"* His voice
echoed dully in the cavernous parking garage. He
clenched both fists and started punching both sides of
his head as if he could somehow beat the thought or
the reality of what had happened out of his brain.

"Jesus, no! . . . No! . . . *No!"* he wailed, rolling his
eyes and looking up at the dark ceiling of the parking
garage and imagining that it was slowly, silently cav-
ing in on him.

He started shaking his head from side to side as he
squeezed his eyes tightly shut, wishing to God he could
somehow stop the burning sensation that was tearing
through him like a house fire. Hot streams of tears
were running down his cheeks now, and a thick, salty
taste had flooded the back of his throat.

"Come on, you guys!" Robin shouted, jumping up
and down in her seat and making the car bounce.
"You two can do all the huggin' and kissin' you want
after we get home!"

Jeff was trembling all over, feeling suddenly drained

of all life and hope. He closed his eyes and wished desperately that he would drop dead himself right there on the spot.

How could she do it? he thought.

That was the only clear thought that pierced the raging maelstrom inside his mind.

How in the hell could she do this to herself . . . and to me?

Chapter Eight
Grim Preparations

"Hello, Jeff. My answering service relayed the message that you had called earlier this morning. What is it? Are you still in Maine, or are you back home now?"

Just hearing Doctor Ingalls's voice helped . . . at least a little bit. Jeff squeezed his eyes tightly shut for a moment and tried to focus his thoughts.

"Yeah, I-I'm back home," he said.

He was alone in the house. Sally had hustled Robin outside to play as soon as she realized that it was Jeff's therapist returning his call.

"I hadn't heard from you," Doctor Ingalls said, "but I've been wondering if everything went all right for you back East."

"Well—no, actually, you see . . . ah, something—something happened."

"So tell me about it," Doctor Ingalls said.

His voice sounded so calm and rational that, for just an instant, Jeff felt as though there might actually be a spark of hope left; then he remembered the reason he had called.

"It's my . . . my sister," he said, trying hard to keep his voice from breaking. "She . . . she did it."

"Did it? Did what? What do you mean?"

"She . . . she killed herself."

"Oh, God. I'm awfully sorry to hear that." There was silence on the line for a second or two; then Doctor Ingalls spoke again. "Did this happen while you were out there?"

Jeff felt a cold jab of loss and almost started crying, but he fought hard to control his emotions. "Uh, no—no, she . . . it happened the day I left, after I'd already gotten onto the plane . . . sometime in the afternoon, from what I understand."

"Oh, I'm *so* sorry to hear that," Doctor Ingalls repeated. For just a flash, Jeff found himself questioning his therapist's sincerity, but then he chalked it up to his own emotional turmoil.

"Are you? . . . Do you think we could—that I could see you sometime today?"

"Geez, I'm really sorry, Jeff, but I'm calling you from down in Cortez. We're here visiting my wife's parents. It's her father's birthday today, and we're not planning to leave until tomorrow. I won't be back at my office until sometime tomorrow afternoon."

For a moment, Jeff said nothing. What could he say? He certainly didn't want to beg. Aware of how sweaty his grip was on the phone receiver, he shifted the phone to his other hand, closed his eyes, and took a deep, calming breath.

"We can certainly talk about it now, if you'd like," Doctor Ingalls said in a mild voice.

"Yeah," Jeff replied, feeling utterly defeated, "I . . . I guess so."

Squeezing his eyes tightly shut, he thought for a moment; then, his voice catching with emotion several times, he told his therapist about his short stay in Maine, especially about his concern that his sister hadn't been ready to be released from the hospital, and about the almost overpowering fear he had experienced when he had driven her out to the old homestead.

"Well," Doctor Ingalls said once Jeff was finished, "By the sound of it, I'd say you handled things very well—certainly as well as could be expected. You did everyth—"

"But Jesus! She's dead!" Jeff shouted, suddenly squeezing the receiver so hard an icy numbness spread up his arm to his elbow. *"Jesus Christ!* If I had done *everything,* then I could have . . . I could have . . . then she wouldn't be dead now, would she?"

"Well, I—"

"Would she?" Jeff shouted even louder. "But she's dead! Do you understand? *Dead!"*

"Yes, I understand," Doctor Ingalls said. He was silent for a moment as Jeff listened to himself breathing heavily into the phone. At last, the doctor said softly, "But you know damned well, Jeff, that you can't take responsibility for anything that happened—for what *she* decided to do."

"But I—I let her down," Jeff said, his voice breaking. He could hold them back no longer, and hot tears flooded from his eyes. Sniffing loudly, he wiped his face with the back of his hand. "I-I was supposed to *be* there . . . be there *for* her, don't you see? And I . . . I let her *down!"*

"But you *were* there for her, Jeff," Doctor Ingalls replied mildly. "I don't think you're being very fair to yourself, saying something like that."

Even through his own misery and choking panic, Jeff could hear the genuine concern in his therapist's voice.

"You didn't let *anyone* down. In fact, I'd say you did everything you could have—certainly more than most brothers would have done for their brother or sister in a similar situation, let me tell you. You have absolutely nothing to blame yourself for!"

"But she's *dead* now, and I . . . I can't help stop thinking that I—I could have stopped her somehow! I could have saved her!"

"Tell me, how could you have done that?"

"I—I don't know, but I could have done *something* else to help her!"

"You don't know that for a certainty," Doctor Ingalls said.

"But if I had maybe stayed with her another day or two . . . if I had done something else . . . I—I don't know what, but *something* to help her, to give her whatever the fuck it was she needed!"

"Seriously, Jeff, how can you even pretend to know what she might have needed?"

"Jesus, she needed someone to love her," Jeff said, his voice cracking with every word. "Is that so bad, wanting someone to love?"

As soon as the words were out of his mouth, Jeff cringed, remembering that they were almost exactly the same words Karl had spoken to him in the dark room. He shivered, recalling the conversation he'd had with Karl. He couldn't stop from wondering when it had taken place. Why, he wondered, while he was sitting in that chair in the motel, had he lost . . . How many hours had it been? Six? Eight? Maybe more?

"No," Doctor Ingalls said, "there's absolutely nothing wrong with wanting love, but you can't hold yourself responsible because your sister didn't find it."

Jeff grunted, then was silent for a moment as his mind filled with a confusion of thoughts and emotions. Yesterday afternoon, he had talked to the local police and asked that they take Judy over to Marcigliano's Funeral Home, in South Portland, the same funeral home he and Judy had used when their parents had died. His whole body went numb when he tried to picture the actuality that right now, even as he was on the phone with Doctor Ingalls, his sister was in a funeral home, lying on a cold, marble slab. His breath came in shallow, burning gulps, and every muscle in his body felt like it was drawn as taut as a bowstring.

"Did you hear me?" Doctor Ingalls said, his voice taking on a commanding edge that Jeff had rarely—if ever—heard in it before. "I'm telling you that you did *everything* you could, but there's no way you can assume responsibility for anything your *sister* chose to do. You're not being fair to yourself *or* to her."

"Yeah, but . . . but what if—"

Jeff stopped himself short. He knew exactly what he had been about to say, but there was no way he could force the words out of his mouth. A dark and not-so-nameless fear was coiling like a cold, fat snake in his gut. All he could think was, there was no way in hell he could say what he was thinking, not over the phone. No, he had to *see* Doctor Ingalls and *talk* to him in person. That was the only way he might be able to express the deepest, darkest fears that were churning like poison deep inside him.

"What if *what*, Jeff?" Doctor Ingalls said, his voice still sounding gentle, but now also prodding.

"Well, you see, I—I have to fly back to Maine . . . to take care of the funeral arrangements and settle Judy's affairs, settle her will and all," Jeff said after a moment. "I'm going to ask for an extended leave of absence from the University."

"That makes sense, I suppose, but are you sure you're up to doing all of that . . . I mean, after everything you just went through?"

Jeff swallowed hard and shook his head, even though he knew the motion was wasted.

"I *have* to! Don't you see that? There's no one else who *can* do it!"

"Well, then, will your wife be going out there with you this time?"

Again, Jeff didn't answer him right away as a rush

of confused thoughts swept through him. He realized that he wouldn't be going back to Maine in the first place if he didn't feel somehow responsible or guilty—

Yes, guilty as hell!

—for not doing *something* to prevent Judy from killing herself. But as much as he would have liked to have Sally come with him for emotional support, on a deeper level he felt as though this was something he *had* to do alone. Last night, and again this morning, she had offered to come with him, but he had dissuaded her, using the dual excuse of not being able to find someone to take care of Robin, and Sally's responsibilities at her own job. When she had suggested that Robin could also come with them, he had reacted with an irrational outburst, telling her that there was no way in hell he wanted Robin to be at his sister's funeral—not at six years old! They hadn't even told Robin yet that her aunt Judy had died.

But Jeff had another, stronger reason. There was no way he wanted his daughter to see his hometown or the house in which he had grown up. Sally had made it clear that she understood there were too many tangled emotions tied up in that place for him, but even this afternoon, she had been subtly pushing him to let both of them come with him. Once—but only once—she had even suggested that she was worried about him, having to face all of this on his own.

"She—uh, no, Sally can't get away right now," Jeff said after a lengthening moment. "You know, because of her job and . . . and getting coverage for Robin." He hoped the lie wasn't *too* obvious in his voice.

"I understand," Doctor Ingalls said, and Jeff was grateful that he didn't press him any more on the issue. "And you're sure you feel up to handling this?"

"No," Jeff said, honestly. "I don't feel up to it at all, but it's something I *have* to do!"

"You're sure of that," Doctor Ingalls said, as much

statement as question. "I mean, she must have some good friends locally, or another relative living nearby who could take care of the arrangements."

"No, Judy and I talked about this years ago," Jeff said. Cold sweat ran down his sides from his armpits. "She set me up as executor of her will . . . you know, because she's been living all this time in the family house and all."

"Sure, I understand," Doctor Ingalls went on, "but having just been back to Maine, and considering everything that's happened now, I wish you could tell me that you feel strong enough. I would think—in fact, I can tell just by the tone of your voice that your trip has stirred up some things for you. Do you want to talk about any of it right now?"

"For Christ's sake! Why do you think I called?" Jeff shouted, his voice breaking as his face flushed with anger.

He suddenly jumped when he heard what sounded like someone out in the kitchen. Thinking Sally and Robin might have come back inside, he lowered his voice as he heaved himself up off the couch to go check.

"Well—yeah, while I was out there, I-I had a kind of breakthrough. I remembered something from my childhood that I had blocked out completely. Judy reminded me of it, as a matter of fact."

"Oh, really? Do you want to tell me about it?"

Jeff grunted in response and cradled the phone under his chin as he walked out into the kitchen. There was no one there. Pulling the lacy curtain aside and looking out the window, he could see Sally and Robin playing in the backyard, tossing a Frisbee back and forth. He closed his eyes for a moment and gritted his teeth, silently wishing that the scene really was as peaceful and pleasant as it looked on the surface, but he was painfully aware of the dark fears that eddied like silent, deadly tides just beneath the surface.

"I—yes, I *do* want to talk about it," Jeff said, gaining a slight measure of control over himself. "That's why I was hoping to see you before I had to fly back East tomorrow."

"When's your flight scheduled?"

"First thing in the morning, I have to go to the university to talk with my department head about getting some personal time off. Then I'm flying out at— umm, around ten o'clock."

"Whether or not you're granted the leave of absence?" Doctor Ingalls asked.

"Uh-huh. That's right."

"You won't be jeopardizing your job or anything, will you?"

Jeff snorted with laughter. "I'm sure Professor Murchison—he's the head of the history department, will give me a hard time about it, but I'm tenured, so as long as we can arrange for a replacement, he can't fire me for it."

"Well," Doctor Ingalls said, "as I already told you, I won't be back until late tomorrow afternoon, so if there's no way you could postpone your flight, I guess I won't be able to see you. But you mentioned a breakthrough of some kind."

Jeff was silent for a moment as he considered what to say. Again, a cold, clutching fear took hold of him, tightening around his chest. The most disturbing thing about it was, he *knew* exactly what was bothering him. The only thing he questioned was, would he have the courage to say it to *anyone?* At least so far, he hadn't even mentioned it to Sally, and he wondered now if he had the courage to talk to his therapist about it.

"You know," Doctor Ingalls said as the pause on the line lengthened, "if you don't want to talk about it, I'd understand completely. Talking on the telephone can feel so impersonal. Besides, you've got enough other things as it is to deal with. As much as I don't like it, though, the best I can offer you now is to say that I'll be back in Denver late tomorrow afternoon. I guess I won't be able to see you until after you get back from Maine."

"No, it . . . it's not that," Jeff said, inwardly cringing. "I mean, I don't mind talking on the phone. I just hope you won't mind if I call you from Maine . . . you know, if things get really hairy."

"Not at all. So tell me. What was this breakthrough you mentioned?"

Haltingly, his voice catching several times, Jeff started to tell Doctor Ingalls about how, in talking to Judy, he had remembered how he and his sister had both been abused by their aunt and uncle whenever they had stayed at their house, and how that had led to their first sexual encounter. He was looking for Doctor Ingalls to reassure him that he was definitely making progress if he could face up to something like this, but he could tell, just by the way his therapist was listening and saying nothing more than an occasional "Uh-huh . . . uh-huh," that he half-suspected Jeff was keeping something else from him.

And he was!

Always at the back of his mind, there was that nagging thought about the "missing time" he'd experienced that last night in Maine.

Ever since Sally had told him what had happened to Judy, he couldn't stop wondering exactly *how* long he had been sitting in that chair in his motel room, having that conversation in the "dark room" with Karl. He knew he had come back to the motel sometime in the early afternoon, and that it had been almost three o'clock in the morning when he had finally gone to bed, but other than that talk with Karl, which couldn't have taken more than fifteen minutes, half an hour at the most, he couldn't remember anything else that he had done, not even if he had called Sally to make sure she knew when to pick him up at the airport. Had he *really* been sitting there in that chair the whole time?

It didn't seem possible, and he couldn't stop wondering if, sometime during that time, he had gone and done something else . . . perhaps something like take a drive back out to the house in Cape Higgins. He was surprised, in fact, that the policeman he had spoken with hadn't mentioned it.

The internal pressure building up inside him was almost intolerable, and he wished to God he could just blurt it out to Doctor Ingalls, but he couldn't make himself say the words. The grinding worry was a cold, hard knot that tightened around his heart and spread through his body like a slow, numbing poison.

But in all that time, from early afternoon until three in the morning, what the hell happened? . . . Did I do anything else?

He couldn't stop wondering this, even as he went on talking almost automatically about how Aunt Mildred and Uncle Kirby used to punish him and his sister, sometimes beating them with a belt or piece of wood, all the while lecturing them about the *Holy Bible* and how they had to *"get right"* with God, or else rot in hell!

He knew he couldn't mention his *real* concern to Doctor Ingalls because he hardly dared to phrase it silently even to himself, but there was a question, gnawing away at the dark core of his heart.

While I was in the dark room . . . having that talk with Karl . . . did one of my other personalities, after all these years of therapy, reassert itself? . . . Did one of the people . . . who must still be—somewhere—inside my mind . . . take control of me . . . and make me . . . do something? . . . Something I don't remember?

* * *

On Monday morning, after a nearly sleepless night, Jeff was up before dawn, packing for his trip back to Maine. He sat down at the counter in the kitchen to eat breakfast with Sally, but his stomach was so knotted with tension, he ate very little. Robin didn't have to get up until seven o'clock, so they let her sleep. After breakfast and a cup of coffee that was already sitting sour in his stomach, he left for campus.

The air was crisp and clear. Miles to the west, the Rockies, lit by the first rays of the morning sun, shone bright gold against the brightening blue sky. Long, thin shadows stretched out across the campus as Jeff pulled into the faculty parking lot and parked his car. The sour tension in his stomach only got worse as he walked up the stairway to the side door of the Mary Reed Building, which housed the History Department. Few students and faculty were about at this early hour, but Jeff knew Professor Murchison usually showed up at the office before seven o'clock. He felt so nervous he was shaking as he walked into the history department office and asked Elizabeth Knowles, the office secretary, if Murchison was in.

"Oh, he should be," she said, hardly looking up from the open file drawer she was rifling through.

Jeff nodded his thanks.

"There's fresh coffee in the pot, if you'd like," she said.

"Uh, no—no thanks," Jeff replied.

He turned and walked down the short, picture-lined corridor to the department head's closed office door. Gritting his teeth and clenching his fist tightly, he rapped on the wooden door hard enough to make the frosted, wire-mesh window rattle.

"I'm in. You're out," Murchison shouted, sounding much too chipper for this time of morning.

Jeff eased the door open and entered. Murchison was leaning back in his roller chair with his feet propped up on his desk. A heavy book with yellowed pages was open and resting in his lap.

"Well, hello, Jeff. How are you? Back from Maine, I see," Murchison said, looking up at him over his reading glasses. There always seemed to be a false heartiness in Murchison's voice. It usually bothered Jeff, but today he chose to ignore it, and simply smiled grimly and nodded.

"Not for long, I'm afraid," he said in a low, controlled voice.

Murchison closed the book on his finger to mark his place, swung his feet off his desk, and leaned forward. Planting one elbow on his desktop, he took off his reading glasses and dangled them beside his ear.

"Oh?" Murchison said, one bushy eyebrow rising like a thick, black comma.

"Yeah, you see, my sister . . . passed away," Jeff said. "I have to go back home to Maine for her funeral."

Home, Jeff thought, his body quaking subtly. *Jesus, was that just a slip, or for some ungodly reason do I still think of Maine as home?*

"Oh, I'm sorry to hear that. Truly sorry," Murchison said.

For almost the first time in his life since he had known the man, Jeff thought he detected a tone of genuine sincerity in his department head's voice.

"Yeah—well, you see, she'd been sick . . . for quite some time, actually, and—and . . . well . . ." Jeff ended lamely, simply shrugging and clapping his hands together. "She just didn't pull through."

"Was it cancer?" Murchison said, his expression darkening.

"No, it was . . . something else," Jeff said. The back

of his neck was burning at the lie, but he saw no reason to tell Murchison that Judy had committed suicide.

"Well, that's too bad, Jeff. You have my sympathies."

"Thanks, but what I wanted to see you about was the possibility of arranging for some personal time off," Jeff said, not allowing a moment of silence. "I know I just took a week off, but—you see, she was . . . I'm the only family she has—that is, *had* left—"

Another lie, he thought, inwardly cringing, *because there's always Uncle Kirby and Aunt Mildred.*

"And I feel I have to do this . . . for her. I was hoping you could approve another personal leave of absence for me."

Murchison craned his neck to one side and stared up at the ceiling for a moment as he scratched the corner of his mouth with the end piece of his glasses. After a moment, he drew a deep breath and shook his head. "I'm really sorry, Jeff," he said, "but you know the policies as well as I do. You've already taken more days than I should have allowed. As much as I'd like to, I can't give you any more time off, especially not with pay."

"Oh, I understand that," Jeff said. "I don't care about the pay. I just need the time off."

"Well, how long were you thinking you'd need?"

Jeff shrugged. "I'm not sure exactly. There's the funeral arrangements, of course, and then I suppose I'll have to take care of her personal affairs—you know, close her bank account, take care of her will, go through her possessions in the house. I'll probably end up donating most of her clothes and furniture to Goodwill or whatever. And I'm going to put the house up for sale. That'll take—I don't know. Maybe a week or two, I'd guess."

"At least that, I would think," Murchison replied. "You must realize, however, that if we hire a substitute for while you're gone, you'll be responsible for covering the costs."

Jeff nodded tightly.

"I was hoping that—given the circumstance—you could waver that . . . at least some of it."

Murchison frowned and shook his head. "I'm sorry, but I can't do that, even under these circumstances. Believe me, I would if I could."

That's bullshit, and you know it, Jeff thought.

A wave of anger directed at Murchison swept through him, but he let it pass and hoped it didn't show. Glancing at his watch, he said, "Well, my flight's in a couple of hours, so I guess I don't have any other choice. Can you arrange for someone to cover my classes?"

"Oh, sure. No problem," Murchison said. "Don't worry about a thing on this end, okay? Just do what you have to do. I know a couple of graduate assistants who I'm sure won't mind filling in for you."

He lifted the heavy book from his lap and placed it on his desk. Rising to his feet, he extended his hand to Jeff and said, "I'm truly sorry to hear about your sister. I hope things go well for you out there . . . as well as they could, anyway, given the situation."

"Yeah . . . thanks," Jeff said, shaking hands with him weakly.

With that, he turned and left the office. His stomach was so full of tension, he went straight to the nearest rest room and threw up what little breakfast he had eaten.

"Last chance," Sally said.

"What?"

"This is your last chance. If you want me and Robin to come out there with you, I'm giving you one last chance to say so. We could catch a plane this afternoon or tomorrow, I'm sure."

Jeff had dropped his carry-on luggage and was standing with Sally to one side of the security gate at the airport. He stared blankly at his wife as he shook his head slowly, trying to pull his mind away from the descending spiral of thoughts he'd been caught in for the last two days. He had said his goodbyes to Robin earlier that morning. Rather than have her miss any school time, they had dropped her off early at school on their way out to the airport.

Echoing throughout Concourse B, a woman's voice was announcing over the intercom that United Airlines, Flight 303, leaving for Chicago was now boarding at Gate B-16.

"Well, I guess that's mine," Jeff said, a trace wistfully.

He took hold of Sally's arms and pulled her close to him so he could give her a kiss. All around them, people were noisily hurrying by, but when Jeff looked into his wife's dark eyes before kissing her, he felt—for just an instant—a moment of peace and serenity, and maybe even hope that things really would work out all right after all. When he saw the genuine trust and love reflected in her eyes, he felt absolutely rotten that he hadn't been completely honest with her about what he was thinking and feeling. Just before their lips met, he almost broke down and blurted out what was *really* on his mind, but his voice choked off when he tried to speak, and he tried to lose himself in the warmth of her affection.

"I'm gonna miss you," Sally said.

"Not as much as I'll miss you," Jeff replied, still holding onto her.

Sally gave him a twisted smile to acknowledge that she recognized the exchange they always had whenever one of them was going away without the other. She cleared her throat and said, "You know, I didn't really know your sister all that well, but I . . . I feel really bad about what happened, you know."

Jeff nodded. "Yeah, tell me about it."

"Especially for you." She caught a grip on both of his arms and gave him an emphatic shake. "I mean it, honey. I just don't like it that you're going out there all on your own. Are you *sure* you're gonna be all right?"

" 'Course I am," Jeff said, painfully aware of how shaky his voice must sound. "Stop worrying so damned much, will you?"

"How can I not worry?" Sally replied, frowning as she looked up at him. "But . . . well, I guess as long as this isn't just some *macho* thing you think you have to do to . . . you know, to prove yourself. It isn't, is it?"

Jeff shook his head and forced a smile. "Of course it isn't."

"What I mean is, though, if you're going to have a tough time with it and all, I want to be there to help you get through it."

Yeah, right! Like I was there for Judy when she needed me? Jeff thought but didn't say.

"I know you do, but stop worrying, okay? I'll be fine . . . honest," he said. "And I promise, I'll call you every night, okay?"

Sally nodded, and he hugged her again, squeezing her tightly, almost desperately before giving her another long, lingering kiss.

"I love you, Sal," he whispered into her ear.

"I love you, too," Sally replied, her breath hot on the back of his neck.

Jeff stepped back and looked at her. She was smiling weakly at him, but he could tell it was a great effort for her not to cry. A hot stinging sensation filled his own eyes, and his hands were trembling as he picked up his luggage and then moved slowly over toward the conveyor belt beside the metal detector. Reluctant to

leave, but knowing that he had to, he kept turning
around, glancing back at her. He couldn't get rid of
that gloomy, fatalistic feeling that had gripped him.

Is this the last time I'll ever see her? he wondered.

Sally stood there, waving to him, smiling bravely
and blowing him kisses; but the whole time, Jeff
couldn't stop himself from mentally phrasing the question that had been in his mind almost constantly since
he had first heard that Judy had killed herself. At
different times, it had sounded like different voices
speaking inside his head, but they all said the same
thing.

Did I do it? . . .

*Did I—or one of my personalities—go back to the
house in Cape Higgins . . . and kill her? . . . Kill Judy?
. . . And then arrange things to look like she had committed suicide?*

Oh, dear God, is THAT what I did?

Part Two

These are no fancies of affliction. They are clear, and real, and here . . .
—Aeschylus

Fortune is dark; she moves, but we cannot see the way,
nor can we pin her down by science and study her.
—Euripides

Chapter Nine

Long Lost

Jeff had given it a lot of thought during the flight from Denver and had decided that in order to save money, especially now that Murchison was making him pay for the substitute teacher, he had no choice but to stay at Judy's house for the time he was in Maine.

But that didn't mean he had to *like* the idea . . . not in the least.

The prospect of sleeping in the old family homestead even one night made his stomach churn with sour acid, but there was no way around it. Besides paying for two round-trip airfares within a week, he had run up quite a bill on his Visa card, staying at the motel last time. For this trip, he was going to have to cut corners, at least until he found out how much money Judy had left behind. He decided to rent a car rather than use hers only because it didn't feel right

It was almost 6:30 P.M. and already dark as he drove east on Route 77, heading out of South Portland toward Cape Higgins. The dark, curving road unspooled in front of his headlights. He couldn't believe it had been only three days ago that he had driven this same road, taking Judy home from the hospital.

God, how could it have been that short a time?

It felt like it had been at least a whole lifetime ago, if not more. He shivered and almost started to cry whenever he remembered that his sister was now dead in the cellar of Marcigliano's Funeral Home.

A mile or so from the center of town, he saw a new-looking Shop'n Save supermarket in a strip mall. He slowed the car and took the turn into the parking lot. Pulling to a stop near the front door, he let his breath out in a gasping rush as he leaned his head back and stretched out his arms, bracing the steering wheel. His eyes hurt like hell, and his body was gripped with wire-tight tension. After a moment, he opened the car window and took a few deep breaths of the damp, salty air; then he got out, locked the car, and walked into the store.

He had no doubt that it was just fatigue from the flight combined with the bright fluorescent lights inside the store that made his eyes start watering as soon as the automatic doors whooshed shut behind him. He felt momentarily confused, almost blinded by the bright riot of colorful displays surrounding him as he fumbled to grab a shopping cart and started up the produce aisle. Of course, he picked a cart with a front wheel that didn't work right.

By the time he reached the end of the first aisle, he had the beginnings of a headache. Dull pressure pulsed in his temples. He considered going straight to the first-aid aisle and grabbing a bottle of aspirin, but he gritted his teeth and made his way slowly up and down the various aisles, gathering the few things he thought he might need. Before long, his shopping cart was jam-packed with items: instant coffee, sugar, boxes of breakfast cereal, peanut butter, crackers, and canned soups. He was just rounding the corner, heading toward the beer cooler, when he saw someone—a woman—up ahead of him. The instant he saw her, he let out a soft grunt of surprise and jerked back.

"Jesus Christ! . . . No way," he whispered.

He started to turn around, but just at that instant, the woman looked up from her shopping list, saw him, and seemed to recognize him.

On reflex, he swung his cart around, but he miscalculated the arc and knocked into a display of Ritz crackers. His face flushed with embarrassment. His chest felt like it was being squeezed by a steadily tightening steel band as he fumbled to straighten out the boxes he had knocked out of place. Then he pushed his shopping cart to the head of the aisle and stopped, his back toward the woman he had seen. The hot pounding in his temples got stronger with each pulse.

No way! No way that could be her! he thought, feeling a cold rush of desperation.

But even if it is, even if she saw me, she couldn't have recognized me!

With the flat of his hand, he tried to wipe away the cold sheen of sweat that had broken out on his forehead.

His back was still to her, but he was burning to turn around and look again, to see if she had seen him. The back of his neck was prickling as if she—or *someone*—were staring intensely at his back and walking slowly toward him. He cringed, waiting for the touch of her hand on his shoulder. His shoulder muscles bunched with tension, and white spikes of light shot across his vision.

Slowly, so he wouldn't wrench his neck, he started to turn around and, holding his breath, looked. He had hoped the woman would be gone, but she was still there at the end of the aisle, and she was looking straight at him with a curious expression on her face, a mixture of shock and pleasure as if she had recognized him immediately but couldn't quite believe who she was seeing.

"Jeff? . . ."

Above the rattling hum of the overhead fluorescent lights, he could barely hear her voice, calling out his name. It was more like a whisper inside his head. The pulsing pain behind his eyes spiked higher.

"Jeff Wagner? . . . Is that really you?"

He cringed when he heard the click of her heels on the linoleum floor as she started up the aisle toward him. His first impulse was to head off into another aisle as fast as he could, pretend he hadn't heard her and hope she concluded—immediately—that she had been mistaken, but he could *feel* her presence, steadily closing the gap between them.

"Excuse me? . . . Sir?" the woman called out.

There was an excited edge in her voice that Jeff immediately recognized from years ago. He felt like a turtle, trying to retreat into his shell as he hunched his shoulders, turned around slowly, and looked at her. She was no more than ten feet away. As soon as they made eye contact, a wide smile broke out across her face, and she tossed her arms up into the air in genuine surprise and joy.

"Oh, my God! It *is* you! Jeff! What the hell are you doing back here?"

Wincing with internal pain, Jeff licked his lips and tried to say something, but his throat was sealed off. He was sure he must look like a deranged person, standing there and gaping silently at the woman.

"Come on, Jeff. Don't tell me you don't even recognize me! It's me, Katherine . . . Katherine Foster."

"Kat?" Jeff finally managed to say.

The vibration of his voice in his head made his headache explode like a firecracker inside his skull. His face felt like it was going to crack open as he forced himself to smile back at her. His grip on the shopping-cart handle tightened, whitening his knuckles. His throat went instantly dry.

"Well, I'll be a son of a bitch," Jeff said, forcing a false, hearty laugh. "Kat! How have you been? It's been a long time."

"No kidding," Katherine said.

She stopped short a few feet away from him, but he could tell by the way she was poised that she had been about to give him a big hug and kiss, and had pulled back only at the last instant. Hardly able to believe his eyes, he took her all in, and he had to admit that he liked what he saw.

Katherine Foster, his high-school sweetheart for three years, looked as though she hadn't aged much if at all since high school. She still had her slim build, and her figure had improved if anything. Her medium-length hair was still dark brown with not a trace of gray, and her face was as young-looking and wrinkle-free as ever. The light caught her blue eyes and made them glow with a pale fire. Her smile, the thing most people first seemed to notice about her, was as wide and bright as it had ever been. She looked at least ten years younger than the late thirties he knew she was.

"You're looking great, Kat," Jeff said, and he meant it.

Katherine smiled modestly, glancing at the floor for a moment. "Thanks," she said. "You're looking pretty damned good yourself."

Despite his headache, Jeff forced a smile and patted the slight bulge of his belly. "Well, I work at it some. Do a little jogging a couple of times a week."

"Yeah, but—my God! I-I can't believe it's really you?" Katherine said. "The last I heard, you were teaching in Denver. Are you still living out there?"

Jeff nodded. "Yeah, at the University of Denver. D.U."

"So what the devil are you doing back in town,

anyway? I remember how you vowed you would *never* come back to this place."

Before Jeff could answer, she caught herself and, looking embarrassed, covered her mouth with her hand and nodded.

"Oh, that's right. Your sister," she said, her voice lowering to a whisper. "I heard about that." She sucked in a breath. "I-I'm terribly sorry."

"Umm . . . yeah," Jeff said, feeling even more uncomfortable. He narrowed his eyes, wishing the pain would recede. As awkward as this was, he couldn't deny how good it was to see Kat again. "I—uh, I had to come back to take care of things . . . you know, put the house up for sale and all."

"I see," Katherine said, nodding as she stroked her chin thoughtfully.

It might have been merely the mention of Judy's death; or maybe, Jeff thought, he wasn't hiding his discomfort talking to her very well. Maybe it was just the aftershock of her initial greeting, or perhaps she was suddenly embarrassed, remembering how much they used to be in love. Whatever it was, *something* was obviously making Katherine feel suddenly uncomfortable. She shifted from one foot to the other and looked to Jeff as though she had something more to say but had no idea where or how to start. For several seconds, they both just stood there, silently staring at each other. Before either of them could say anything to break the awkward silence, a young boy, no more than ten or eleven years old, came wheeling around the corner at the far end of the aisle. Catching Katherine's attention, he waved and called out to her.

"Hey, Mom! There you are!" He started up the aisle toward them. "What the heck are you doing, anyway? I thought you were in a hurry to get home."

Jeff looked at Katherine and raised one eyebrow in spite of the jolt of pain it sent through his head.

"Mom?" he said, smiling as he watched the boy dash up the aisle and come to a screeching stop beside Katherine.

"Yup," Katherine said, hugging the boy with one arm as she ruffled his hair. "This is Danny. Danny, I'd like you to meet a—a *very* dear old friend of mine."

"Well, I'm not *that* old," Jeff said with a high laugh.

"This is Jeff Wagner," Katherine said, smiling. "He's a friend of mine from high school."

"That's Dan, not Danny," the boy said, looking sharply at Jeff and giving him a quick, appraising nod as he held out his hand for Jeff to shake. "Pleased to meet'cha."

"Me, too . . . Dan," Jeff said. He was surprised by the firmness of the boy's handshake. Dan was a good-looking kid, with his mother's wide smile but dark eyes and darker hair, no doubt inherited from his father.

Jeff couldn't deny the sudden sinking feeling he got in his stomach as he tried to absorb the fact that this was Katherine's kid. He knew the feeling was irrational. After all, he was married himself and had a child of his own; but he realized that, from the instant he had seen her, he had been secretly hoping that Katherine had never married or had any children. He realized now what it was: He had wanted to keep his memory of her as fresh and innocent as she had been when they had been boyfriend and girlfriend back in high school. Having children—especially one Danny's age—only reinforced the feeling that time was slipping away.

Yeah, just like it did for Judy! whispered a voice in the back of his mind.

"So, Kat," Jeff said after a lengthening moment. He sucked in a sharp breath, hoping to push back his headache. "I'd have to guess, since you're shopping out here, that you're still living in town, huh?"

"Oh, yeah," Katherine said, beaming her bright smile. "I have a great job in town as a secretary at a lawyer's office. I'm living on Wescott Street, you know, just past the old schoolhouse. You know, Danny's in the fourth grade now, and he even has Mrs. Pinkham for a teacher."

"You don't say," Jeff said, smirking as he eyed Danny. "And I'll bet she still pours on the old homework, doesn't she?"

"I guess so," Danny said. He shrugged, obviously uncomfortable to be the object of their attention.

"Gosh, she must be *ancient* by now," Jeff said, glancing back at Katherine.

"Yeah," Katherine said, laughing. "I don't think she'll *ever* die."

"We all do, Kat," Jeff said, suddenly serious.

By now, his headache was so bad he was afraid he was going to fall down if he didn't do something about it soon. All around him, the bright colors of product displays swirled and blended. He knew he was standing still, holding tightly to the shopping-cart handle, but the checkerboard floor pattern suddenly looked like it was rippling. Waves of subtle motion bounced Jeff up and down, almost throwing him off balance. He knew he had to get away from Katherine, if only because he didn't want her to see him so shaken.

"I—uh, you know, I have one hell of a headache . . . probably from the flight," he said, rubbing his brows vigorously with one hand. "I really should get going."

Katherine smiled and nodded.

"Yeah, come on, Mom," Danny said. "If we don't hurry, we'll be late for open house at school."

She looked longingly at Jeff, as though she wasn't quite ready to leave. Jeff couldn't deny feeling as though some kind of unspoken message had passed between them, either. It was tough, he told himself, to encounter a long-lost girlfriend after so many years and not feel *something*. Although he felt a twinge of guilt, thinking about Sally back in Denver, he had to admit that it was great to see Katherine again. He just wished it didn't stir up in him thoughts about all the "might-have-beens" in his life.

Yeah, whispered a voice in his mind, *like how Judy might have still been alive if you had done something to help her!*

"Well, it's been really great to see you," he said. "In spite of the—uh, circumstance."

His voice sounded flat and hollow in his ears as another sharp jolt of pain lanced behind his eyes.

"You, too," Katherine said.

Jeff couldn't help but notice the reluctance in her posture as she started to turn around and walk away with Danny.

"Maybe I'll have you over for dinner while you're here," Katherine said when she was a few paces away from him.

"I'd like that," Jeff replied in spite of himself. The truth was, he felt extremely uncomfortable around her. He couldn't deny that the old spark seemed to be there, fanning back to life.

"Where are you staying?"

"At the old house," Jeff said, almost choking on the words.

Katherine unleashed her beaming smile and said, "Okay, I'll call you then."

Jeff nodded and waved, then stood there watching as she walked to the end of the aisle and then rounded the corner. Once she was gone, he let his breath out in a long, trailing *whoosh,* then closed his eyes and vigorously rubbed his forehead. As he stared into the swirling, pain-laced darkness behind his eyes, he couldn't stop wondering which would be worse—for her to go ahead and call to invite him over . . . or for her to forget all about her promise.

* * *

A nearly full moon shed a cold, silvery glow over the house and front yard as Jeff got out of his rented car. A cold, knife-edge wind was blowing in off the ocean, sending fallen leaves skittering and clicking like old bones across the driveway. Bare tree branches swayed back and forth, clawing like frantic hands against the starry night sky. The streetlight out in front of the house cast long, thin shadows of branches that looked like deep, jagged fractures in the earth.

Jeff shivered and pulled his collar up tightly around his neck as he walked around to the back of the house. Through gaps in the trees, he caught glimpses of the ocean, shimmering like beaten silver in the moonlight. The view—something he had seen hundreds, probably thousands of times while growing up here—seemed equally familiar and frighteningly foreign to him. He was almost overwhelmed by the sense that—some-how—he didn't belong here . . . not anymore, anyway.

Bending over, he reached under the top step of the porch and felt around until he found the key that was hanging on the nail right where it had always been. When he took it from the nail and stood up, gripping it tightly in his hand, he noticed that he was breathing rapidly. Casting his gaze back and forth, as though expecting to see *something,* he walked back around front to the breezeway door. His teeth were chattering, and his hands were shaking as he slipped the key into the lock and gave it a quick turn. At first, the tumblers didn't fall, and Jeff was thinking that the key might be for the front door, but then, with a little more pressure, the lock clicked.

"Jesus Christ," he muttered under his breath as he twisted the doorknob and pushed the door inward. He was expecting it to still be stuck like it had been the last

time he had been here, but it opened easily, chattering
on rusted hinges as it swung wide.

Once again, just like a few days ago when he had
dropped Judy off at the house, as soon as he stepped
into the breezeway, his nostrils were assailed by a dry,
musty smell which he found instantly familiar.

It was a smell from his childhood . . . the distinctive
smell of his old home.

A dryness clutched at his throat, and he licked his
upper lip. Opening the side door, which had been left
unlocked, he reached his hand in around the doorjamb
into the house and found the light switch. Even after
all these years, out of pure habit he knew exactly where
it was. He snapped the switch, and immediately a soft,
yellow glow that seemed almost welcoming spilled out
into the breezeway, lighting up the floor and the lower
half of his legs. He realized he'd been holding his
breath and let it out in a long, whistling sigh.

Leaving both doors open, he ran back and forth
between the house and car three times before he got his
luggage and all of the groceries inside. He piled the
bags of groceries on the kitchen counter beside the
refrigerator, and put his luggage by the door leading
into the living room. Then he closed the outside doors
on the chilly night, making sure to lock both of them.
Exhausted, he pulled out a chair at the kitchen table
and sat down to catch his breath and take a moment
to try to absorb the fact that he was really here. Subtle
currents of fear ran through him like teasing jolts of
electricity.

The kitchen was pretty much as he remembered it.
Sometime in the past, Judy had bought a new stove
and refrigerator, and had a new floor put in, a tan-
and-white tile pattern. The walls were painted yellow
instead of the dingy brown they had once been, but
other than feeling perhaps a bit smaller than he re-

membered it, this was the same kitchen he remembered from growing up.

And it wouldn't take much, he thought, to imagine that he was a kid once again—that his mother was standing by the stove, cooking supper, and he was sitting here, impatiently waiting for something to eat after a hard day at play or at school. For some reason, he clearly remembered one particular night—it must have been in his junior year during the autumn, on a night much like this for it to come back so vividly. Following an argument between him and Katherine, he had sat at the kitchen table, his chair in almost this exact same spot, as he remembered, and unloaded his problems and worries to his mother, who—for about the only time in his life he could remember—had given him uncharacteristic attention and even offered a bit of advice.

"She's not the only fish in the sea," his mother had said; and, as he recalled, he had answered her: "Yeah, but I wonder if I have the right bait."

It should have been a sweet memory, but like everything else about his childhood, it was laced with the bitterness of regret about other memories and times that were now passed and gone, and a childhood that had been shadowed by hurt feelings, unmet needs, and missed opportunities.

Like Katherine . . .

Seeing her tonight had stirred up the muck of memories about the good times they'd had together, and how right up until their senior year in high school, other than an occasional misunderstanding, they had talked about getting married. All of their friends, even their parents seemed to think of them as a couple as surely as if the date had already been set.

And why hadn't they stayed together? Jeff asked himself.

You know damned well, answered a voice in his mind, so loud and clear it made Jeff jump.

But he knew the answer.

It was because he had been so goddamned anxious to get away from home, to get out of Cape Higgins and never come back. More than anything else, he had worried that, if he married a hometown girl—even someone as nice as Katherine, he might *never* get out of town. So what had been his solution? He dumped her in their senior year—rather coldheartedly, as he recalled with a twist of guilt, and then applied to all out-of-state colleges, most of them outside of New England. He had left that next September without ever really talking to her again even though many mutual friends told him how much she still loved him.

But—apparently—those wounds had healed.

But seeing how good Katherine had looked tonight, seeing that the years hadn't worn her down and turned her into the dour, bitter person he had been afraid he and everyone else he knew would become in adulthood, Jeff couldn't help but wonder what his life would have been like if he hadn't left her.

The only thing he knew for sure was, he would have turned out to be an entirely different person; it was impossible to say if he would have been better or worse off.

But Katherine had been out of his life for going on twenty years. She no doubt was happily married . . . as he was basically happily married. His mother and father had been dead for sixteen years, and now his sister was dead. In a few days, probably on Thursday morning, Judy would be buried in the cemetery plot next to their parents, and that would be the end of his last connection to this town. He kept reminding himself that he had come back here simply to handle the funeral arrangement and to sell the old family homestead. After that, he would go back to his life in Colorado.

But there's a cemetery plot right next to Judy, Mom, and Dad, reserved for me!

The thought sent a chill zipping up his back.

Just to do *something* to get his mind away from such thoughts, he took a bottle from the six-pack of Samuel Adams beer he had bought, found a bottle opener in one of the kitchen drawers, and popped the top. Leaning back against the counter, he took a long, noisy gulp.

"Ahh, that's more like it," he said.

The beer hit his stomach like a cold fist. He smacked his lips and smiled as he wiped his mouth on his sleeve. He knew what he had to do was push aside whatever unnerving thoughts he might have about being here and look at things objectively. This was a sad situation, no way around it, but like Doctor Ingalls had told him, he couldn't blame himself for any choices Judy might have made, either in her life or how she chose to end it. He had to hang in there and handle things by keeping focused on practical matters. He couldn't let nagging little things like unsettled memories of his childhood or even seeing Katherine bother him so damned much.

He glanced over at the telephone on the wall, still in the same place it had always been, and remembered that he should give Sally a call to let her know he had arrived safely. Before he did that, though, he wanted to take a quick tour through the house to acclimate himself to it, so, beer bottle in hand, he moved from the kitchen through the dining room and into the living room, turning on lights as he went. Because he didn't want to leave any part of the house in darkness, he left all the lights on behind him.

Of course, Judy had different furniture from what his parents had when he was a kid, but the space, the atmosphere, the "feeling" of each room still seemed so familiar, as if the walls had absorbed the life that had been lived within the house and now, like heated stones, was slowly radiating it back. The entire downstairs seemed to be loaded with dark, distant memories, none of which Jeff wanted to dwell upon for very long. He became almost wistful as he finished his circuit of the downstairs and walked back into the kitchen. He wasn't quite ready to go upstairs. The prospect of actually seeing his old bedroom unnerved him enough so he was actually considering sleeping downstairs on the couch just to avoid seeing it. He caught himself wondering if Judy had saved his old bed or any of his other furniture, or if she had converted his bedroom into something else—a sewing room, perhaps.

But he would check that out later . . . if at all.

Right now, his beer bottle was empty, and he was debating whether or not he should have another. He usually didn't drink very much, but finally, figuring *what the hell?* he grabbed another bottle from the refrigerator and flipped off the cap. Sitting down again, he leaned back and put both feet up on the kitchen table, something his mother would never have allowed, and sipped his beer slowly, savoring the taste. He closed his eyes and tried to let his thoughts wander and not dwell on all the bad things that had happened, especially the sadness of Judy's death. But the longer he sat there, the bleaker his thoughts became. Ten minutes later, after he had finished his second beer, he felt all tense. He was just getting up to call Sally, wanting to hear a friendly voice, when the telephone rang.

The sudden sound of it made him jump out of his chair with a shout of surprise. Thinking it must be Sally calling him, he darted over to the wall phone and snatched up the receiver before the second ring.

"Hello?" he said.

"Who—who's this?" said a woman's voice, sounding both tense and curious.

Jeff knew right away that it wasn't Sally or Katherine. He couldn't place the voice and was instantly suspicious.

"You tell me," he said sharply. "Who is *this?*"

"Is this . . . did I call Judy Lennox's house?"

"Who *is* this?" Jeff repeated. His anger rose at the woman's presumption, but he also felt a strengthening current of fear inside him. His gaze shifted nervously to the kitchen window and the black square of night outside. He told himself it was crazy to think—as he had expected—there would be a face in the window.

"Why, this is Vera Becker," the woman on the other end of the line said. "I'm a friend . . . of Judy's. Could I please ask you who you are and what you're doing in her house?"

Jeff thought he recognized the name but couldn't quite place it. Then in a flash it came to him. Vera Becker was the woman the doctor in the emergency room told him had found Judy the night she had first tried to kill herself.

"I'm Jeff . . . Jeff Wagner. I'm Judy's brother."

"Oh, Jeff," Vera said, her voice dropping as she sighed with relief. "For God's sake, why didn't you say so?"

I just did, Jeff thought, but he let it go.

"I—ah, just got in from Denver," he went on, closing his eyes a moment and feeling his exhaustion. "You *do* know that Judy . . . died, don't you?"

"Yes, yes. I know. I-I'm so sorry."

Her voice choked off with emotion. Jeff heard her sob, then take a steadying breath.

"But . . . you see, just a little while ago, I drove out past the house just to make sure everything was all right," Vera said, "and I saw lights on inside. I didn't

think a burglar would be all that blatant, but . . . well,
it's a good thing I decided to call the house before I
called the police, huh?"

"Yeah, I guess so," Jeff said tiredly. "Look, Vera,
I'm really beat from the flight and all. It's really been
a tough couple of days—"

"For me, too," Vera said.

Again, Jeff could hear the tightness in her voice.

"She's over at Marcigliano's, but I haven't even
begun to make the funeral arrangements. You don't
happen to know if Judy attended a church regularly,
do you?"

"No, I have no idea."

"Umm," Jeff grunted. "Well, I'll probably contact
whoever's the minister at the Congregational church
where we used to go as kids. Look—uh, why don't you
give me your phone number, and I'll let you know
once everything's arranged, okay?"

"Yes, I'd appreciate that, Jeff," she said.

Again her voice caught, and Jeff could tell she was
crying as she dictated her number twice to make sure
he got it.

"Judy was, she was a—a really good friend," Vera
said, nearly choking on every word. "And I . . . I'm
really gonna miss her something *terrible.*"

"Yeah, I know," Jeff said, nodding sympathetically
and feeling his own eyes begin to sting. "This has been
real tough on me, too. But I . . . before I forget, I want
to thank you for . . . for everything you did, you know,
to . . . to try to help and all."

He paused, waiting for Vera to reply, but she was
crying so hard now, she wasn't able to speak.

"I really appreciate it," he said as a single teardrop
squeezed from his eye and ran down his cheek, into the
corner of his mouth. It tasted salty. "I'll call you as
soon as I've spoken to the minister, okay? But look, I

have to call my family back home, now, so we'll . . . I'll give you a call sometime tomorrow, okay?"

"Yeah . . . okay," Vera said, her voice not much more than a croaking sob.

Jeff hung up the phone, then quickly dialed his home phone number. After three rings, Sally picked up. Considering everything he had been through today and the two beers he'd already had, Jeff was really feeling his exhaustion, so he didn't spend much time talking with her. He still couldn't dispel the gnawing worry that something bad was going to happen to them while he was away, so he made sure that Sally wrote down Judy's telephone number so she wouldn't have to search for it if she had to reach him. Sally told him that Robin was taking a bath and offered to get her. As much as he missed his daughter, he told her not to bother her, but just to give her a big hug and kiss from him. He told Sally how much he loved her and gave her a kiss over the phone. As soon as he had hung up, he couldn't help but feel dejected and terribly lonely, just knowing that his family was so faraway.

Taking a deep breath, he looked around the kitchen, listening to the utter silence of the house. It was almost palpable—a cold, dark, pressing presence. He toyed with the idea that—somehow—the little boy he had once been was still somewhere here in the house, hiding from him maybe in one of the dark rooms upstairs or in the attic . . . or, he thought with a bone-deep chill, possibly in the cellar.

Jeff knew, if only for the sake of a good night's sleep, that he ought to sleep in one of the beds upstairs instead of on the couch, but he couldn't decide which bed to use—his own, if it was still up there, or his sister's. Neither prospect seemed all that inviting.

Before he took his luggage upstairs, though, he decided to have one more beer, just to help cut the edge, he told himself; it might help him get a decent night's sleep. Besides, he sure as hell didn't want his mind to get carried away with a whole host of depressing thoughts, so he got his third bottle of beer from the refrigerator, opened it, and walked back into the living room. He sat down heavily on the couch, leaned his head back, and began to drink. After a few slugs, he sighed deeply and placed the beer bottle on the end table. Closing his eyes, he concentrated simply on breathing slowly and deeply, letting himself relax and letting his mind wander freely.

"What the hell," he said aloud, his voice lazy and slurred. "What's done is done, right? There's nothing I can do about it now, anyway, so there's no point in worrying about it. No point at all . . ."

Chapter Ten

Conversation in a Dark Room: #3

"Hey, wasn't she looking foxy tonight, huh?"

The voice, speaking so suddenly in the darkness, startles me.

Shifting my feet forward, I peer into the blackness that swirls in front of my eyes, but I can distinguish nothing. I think I see the shimmering dull glow of the night sky through a single, small window, but whenever I try to focus on it, it shifts away and melts into the surrounding darkness.

"Who's that?" I say, noticing the dry, sleepy tone in my voice.

"Why, Katherine, of course, you fucking idiot!" the voice says. "Don't you think she was looking good tonight?"

"No, I mean who are *you?*" I say sleepily.

I vaguely sense that I should be a little bit nervous and on my guard, but I tell myself that I'm safe as long as I'm in the dark room.

"Well, it *has* been a while since we've talked, hasn't it?" the voice says.

I don't respond. Looking around the room, I am
sure I can see the dark shape of a person, either sitting
or standing in front of me. The shape is black against
black, and seems to swell in the darkness.

"But I've been keeping my eye on you, Jeff. Oh,
yeah. Not much slips past me."

"It's you, Sammy, isn't it?"

"Very good . . . *very* good," Sammy replies, punctuating his words with a sarcastic laugh. "I'm happy to
see that you don't forget your old friends."

"Hey, what can I say?" I reply. "I mean, it's almost
like you're a . . . a part of me, wouldn't you say?"

I can't help but laugh at my little joke and wonder
if this is a sign that I am truly getting better, if I can
joke about my previous psychological problems. I
wish Doctor Ingalls were here so I could ask him.

"You still haven't answered my question, though,"
Sammy says, his voice taking on a subtle but dangerous edge.

"Huh? . . . What question?"

"Jesus! About *Katherine,* you asshole! I asked if you
thought she looked good tonight."

"Well—yeah. Sure she did," I reply, swallowing
with difficulty. "It was . . . nice to see her."

"Nice to see her! Is that the best you can do? *Nice
to see her?* Come on, man, didn't you think she looked
like one hell of a piece of ass? I'll bet you wanted to
fuck her right there on the spot, didn't you? Too bad
she's married, huh? But then again, you're too
chicken-shit to do anything about it, anyway. Am I
right?"

"Well, not exactly," I answer. I can feel myself
blushing. "I mean, don't forget—I'm married, too."

"Oh, come *on,* Jeff! You can admit it, at least to me.
You know, that's been your only goddamned problem
all along—that you can't *admit* some of the things you

know you want to do. You can't tell me you didn't think she looked grade-A fuckable!"

"Well . . . I mean, it's not like that," I reply.

Of everyone I have ever met here in the dark room, Sammy is the person I enjoy talking to least. He is brash and verbally abusive. Although I have never seen him, I have a sense that Sammy is stuck in some preadolescent sexuality. He sure as hell talks that way.

"It's not like that! It's not like that!" Sammy says in a high, mocking tone. "Bull*shit* it's not like that! I know, as much as you wanted to do it back in high school, you never tagged her. You can't tell me you didn't think about it tonight while you were talking to her."

"Well . . . yeah, I might have a little, but I—"

"But *nothing!* You wanted to do it, but just like everything else you ever wanted to do, you didn't because you're chicken-shit!"

"Oh, really? And how do you know so much about what I want to do but don't dare to?" I snap, realizing I have to take the offensive to keep control over Sammy; otherwise, he'll just keep shooting off his mouth until he gets tired of talking and decides to leave.

"I know plenty, believe me," Sammy says, not sounding at all cowed.

"Well then, tell me something," I say, bristling with the challenge. "Tell me something about me that I don't already know."

The soft chuffing sound of Sammy's laughter fills the dark room, setting my nerves on edge.

"You don't know what you're asking for, bub," he says. Then he makes a growling sound in his throat as if he's about to spit.

I swallow hard, feeling a sudden fear that Sammy might be right. There must still be things from my past that I don't know and might not be able to handle.

Why else would I need to come into a room like this?

"Well, for starters, how about what you did to Judy?" Sammy says archly. "You want to start with that?"

"Wha-what do you mean?" My voice almost breaks. "I don't want to talk about what we did as . . . as kids. I've worked all of that out in my mind already, and I can see now that we were . . . we were victims. We can't be blamed for anything we did."

"For *anything?*" Sammy says with a snicker. "Shit, man, you don't even know the half of it, do you?"

Again, I swallow, my throat making a loud gulping sound. I feel sweat break out on my scalp.

"Well if *you* do," I say, trying hard to keep my voice from losing its resolve, "then why don't you tell me about it?"

"Because you wouldn't be able to handle it, that's why, asshole!" Sammy snaps.

The darkness in the room seems to shift, and I have the uncomfortable feeling that Sammy has moved closer to me—very close. I can hear his slow, steady breathing, and feel the warm stirring of his breath against my face. I want to reach out and grab him by the collar and shake him.

"Tell me one thing, then," I finally say, with only a small measure of control. "Last week, just before I left to go back to Colorado, did I—"

"Nope," Sammy says, cutting me off sharply. "No fucking way! I'm not gonna talk about that."

"Wait a second. You don't even know what I was going to ask."

"Oh yes I do," Sammy replies snidely. "You were going to ask me if I thought you came back to the house on Friday night and killed your sister, and then set it up to look like a suicide. Am I right?"

"No, I—"

"Cut the shit with me, okay? I know that you're

afraid—you're practically shitting your undies, wondering if one of us might have taken over and done something that you might have been too chicken-shit to do yourself. Am I right? Huh? Tell me. *Am I right?*"

"I . . . maybe . . . I don't know! Shit, you've got me so confused now, I don't even remember what we were talking about."

"We were talking about Katherine, and how fucking good she looked," Sammy says. The leering tone of his voice bothers me, but I've lost control of this conversation, and now Sammy's going to run with it.

"It's okay, Jeff. Honest. You can talk to me about it. I'm more than willing to listen. That's why I'm here. I don't mind at *all* talking about how much you want to fuck her! Hell, I wouldn't mind going along for the ride."

"First you tell me about last Friday night, and then I'll tell you what I thought about Katherine."

"No deal."

Sammy's burst of laughter explodes like a peal of thunder in the dark room.

"You actually think last Friday night is all that important? You see? That just proves how little you really know. You've got so much shit you've gotta uncover . . . Christ! Even if you *did* kill your sister—and I'm not saying one way or another—that's fucking *nothing* compared to some of the other shit you're gonna have to deal with."

"Then why won't you tell me about it?" I say, trying—and failing—to keep the desperate pleading out of my voice.

" 'Cause I ain't fucking interested in any of it, that's why!" Sammy says. "Hey, here's a quarter. Call someone who gives a shit."

"Well, then, if you're not going to help me out, why don't you just leave?" I say, hoping to gain a small measure of control over this situation. "I sure as hell am *not* going to talk to you about what I thought about Katherine."

"Hey, that's all right with me, man," Sammy says, snickering with hollow laughter. "I already know. But I *will* tell you one thing. You think you have me put in my place, don't you?"

I don't answer him.

"Well, I know you do, but I'll guarantee you this; if I ever get control again, the first thing I'm gonna do is drive over to Katherine's house. She told you where she lives, like she was asking for it, you know. And I don't give a shit whether it's day or night, I'm gonna knock on her door, go inside, and then I'm gonna fuck her brains out right there on the spot. Trust me on this. I know you'll enjoy it."

"You're full of shit, you know that?" I say, my voice crackling with anger. "There's no way you're ever going to be calling the shots again. You got that? Never!"

"Oh, yeah? Well, we'll see about that," Sammy says.

He laughs again, low and dark, then snorts and spits in the darkness. I hear the glob of spit hit the wall or floor with a dull *plop*.

"You think about things real hard, and maybe . . . just *maybe* you might start remembering some more of the shit that went down. I sure as shit can't spoon-feed it to you. In the meantime, I think I just might stick around so's I can keep reminding you about what you really ought to do with good ole Katherine. Know what I mean?" He starts to laugh again, this time a deep belly laugh.

I can think of nothing to say, so I just sit there, staring into the darkness and listening to the sound of Sammy's rising laughter as it spirals higher and higher until it becomes nothing but an irritating, mosquito-like buzz. As the sound reaches frequencies too high for me to hear, I suddenly lurch forward with a roaring intake of breath and jump to my feet.

"Jesus Christ!" Jeff shouted as his eyes snapped open. He was staggered by the sudden brightness of the room. Crying out, he covered his eyes with both hands.

After the span of several frantic heartbeats, he peeked out between his fingers at the room, but for a long time his vision was nothing but a stinging, watery blur that swirled and blended his surroundings into an incomprehensible mess. Clenching his fists tightly, he rubbed his eyes, pressing against his closed eyelids so hard he saw spinning circles of white-and-yellow light. Feeling a sudden sense of danger, he quickly opened his eyes again and looked around the room. His arm and leg muscles were tensed, wire-tight as though he expected to be attacked from his blind side at any moment. Cold sweat stood out on his brow, and his breath came in fast, burning gulps that rattled in his throat.

After another few seconds of confusion, he realized that he was standing in the middle of his sister's living room, and that every light in the room was on.

"Jesus Christ," he muttered again, softer.

Wiping his sweaty forehead with the back of his arm, he groaned as he dropped back down onto the couch and exhaled loudly. His insides were shaking like Jell-O, and hot, shooting pains stabbed his back from the sudden wrenching it had taken because he had stood up so fast. After a few moments, once he was starting to calm down, he realized that it was his left hand that hurt the most. His eyes still stung from the brightness of the room as he raised his clenched fist up to eye level and stared at it. Something sharp was digging into his palm like a knife blade. Ever so slowly, he opened up his fingers.

"Oh, *shit,*" he whispered when he looked into the center of his palm and saw what he was holding.

It was a shiny, new quarter.

Sighing, he leaned his head back against the couch, closed his eyes to hold back the tears he felt threatening, and in a low, shattered voice whispered, "Yeah . . . maybe I should call someone who gives a shit . . ."

Chapter Eleven

3:08

Someone's downstairs!

The thought was as clear as if someone had whispered it into his ear.

Jeff sat bolt upright in the bed. He held himself back from shouting a challenge as he looked at the bedroom door, which he had left slightly ajar. The hallway light was still on, and a thin wedge of lemon light angled across the floor and the bottom of the bed. Most of the room was cast in soft, gray shadows, making everything look unfamiliar, but it took him only a moment or two to remember where he was. After some intense mental debate, he had chosen to sleep in his sister's bedroom—at least for this first night—rather than face going into what used to be his old bedroom. Nervous about the memories that might be stirred up if he slept there, he had decided to wait at least until morning before he tried to face that particular challenge.

But now, something had awakened him.

What the hell had it been?

He glanced at the pale green numerals of the alarm clock on the table beside the bed.

3:08.

Pulling his legs up to his chest and hugging them tightly, he sat hunched forward as he stared at the partially opened door, straining to hear again what it was that had disturbed his sleep. The house was perfectly quiet, now, but he felt a winding nervousness as his gaze darted back and forth, jumping at every unfamiliar object he saw out of the corner of his eye. An expectant hush filled the room. Outside, the night seemed to press up against the bedroom windows like an animal, trying to find its way in.

I know I heard something—someone downstairs!

Moving as quietly as he could, he slid out from under the covers and placed his feet on the floor. As soon as his toes touched the bare wood, a spike of cold shot up the back of his legs. Before he shifted his weight to stand up, though, he heard the long, creaking sound of an old floorboard. In the stillness of the house, it seemed almost as loud as a gunshot.

A bracing chill raced up Jeff's back.

The sound had definitely come from downstairs!

He looked frantically around the bedroom but had no idea what to do. Had that just been the sound of the house settling, the floorboards reacting to the autumn chill that was in the air; or was there really someone snooping around downstairs?

For long, tense minutes, he sat there on the edge of the bed, listening tensely to the hollow silence of the house. Once or twice, he noticed the sound of traffic passing by in the distance, no doubt out on Route 77.

Shivering, he looked over at the alarm clock again. 3:12.

He'd been exhausted from his trip and had gone to bed just around midnight. He didn't remember having much trouble drifting off to sleep but he didn't feel at all rested. He didn't remember any dreams, and he certainly hadn't had any more "conversations" with anyone, but he sure as hell didn't feel as though he had been asleep, either. So where *had* he been? What had he been doing? The thought crossed his mind that maybe he—or one of his alter personalities—had been downstairs, poking around in Judy's things, but he dismissed it. He certainly couldn't be upstairs in bed and downstairs at the same time.

While he was staring at the clock, it switched to 3:13.

His bladder was filled with a dull pressure, and he was just about to get out of bed and go to the bathroom to relieve himself when another sound intruded on the night. It was subtle, just at the edge of hearing, but he immediately recognized it—it was the sound of someone opening a door downstairs. First there was a soft *click* of a door latch, then the faint, squeaking sound of old door hinges, complaining as they opened.

A jolt of fear splashed Jeff like a dousing of ice water.

Jesus Christ . . . there is someone down there!

He looked over at the telephone on the bed stand, considering for a moment calling the police, but he decided against it. He knew he was going to have to talk with the police soon, if only to get all the facts on Judy's death. But he thought he might look like a damned fool if he called them out here now and had to explain who he was and why he was here.

No, he decided, he would deal with whoever was down there on his own terms. After all, this was *his* house, now. He glanced again at the clock and saw that it was 3:17.

Resolved to do something, to go downstairs and confront whoever this was, Jeff slowly stood up, clenching his fists tightly at his sides. He hadn't even taken a single step, though, when he heard the light tread of footsteps on the stairs. Every step creaked in succession.

Jesus, they're coming upstairs!

Jeff's throat went desert dry. The pressure building in his bladder became painful. He wanted to turn on the light beside the bed and see if he could find something to use as a weapon to defend himself if he had to, but he was frozen where he stood. He didn't dare to move. Every muscle was locked in place.

Maybe, he thought, what he should do is make a sound or something. If it was a burglar, breaking in because he had heard Judy had died, he should warn him that the house wasn't empty. Maybe that would be enough to scare him away.

But mounting terror sealed his throat. His withheld breath was burning, trapped inside his chest. His legs felt suddenly rubbery, and he dropped back down onto the bed, his eyes riveted to the narrow opening of the doorway.

He waited, hardly daring to breathe, as he listened to the soft, steady tread of feet coming up the stairs. He almost cried out when he saw a faint, gauzy, gray shadow shift across the wall in the hall, blocking out the angled beam of light coming through the door.

Jesus, just go away! he thought desperately. His body was gripped by fear. *Please, go away! Just leave me alone!*

But the sounds of someone walking in the hallway grew steadily louder, coming down the hallway to the bedroom. As he sat there, staring at the doorway, he saw a shape—a black, backlit silhouette—appear in the entrance.

Cold, squeezing fingers tightened around Jeff's throat, making it impossible for him to take a breath. He watched in mute horror as, ever so slowly, the figure raised one hand and pushed open the door. The hinges squeaked like the long, slow pull of fingernails, raking across a chalkboard. The sudden wash of light from behind the figure erased any details of the face, but after a throbbing heartbeat or two, Jeff realized that it was a woman, framed in the doorway. She was wearing a long, flowing nightgown that glowed a hazy yellow from the light that was shining behind her. Her dark hair hung to her shoulders, framing her face, but even as she moved closer to him, he couldn't make out any facial details. For an instant, the thought flashed through his mind that it might be Katherine, coming to him in the night . . . coming to him to consummate a relationship they had broken off more than twenty years ago.

No, that was impossible!

As far as he knew, Katherine was now happily married, and he had made it clear—hadn't he?—that he was married and had a child. Besides, he had made sure to lock all the doors downstairs. It couldn't be Katherine!

Jeff's mind felt like it was going to overload.

He couldn't move, couldn't speak as he watched the figure move closer toward him with a silent, shifting glide. A long, black tongue of shadow rippled like dark water across the floor and then up onto the bed. Jeff felt its winter chill when it swept across him like a dark stain.

No, this can't be happening! his mind screamed crazily. *This can't be real!*

In a slow, fluid motion, with a soft whisper of silk or satin, the figure raised its arms, extending them forward and then letting them drop out to the sides. For a fleeting instant, it looked like a benevolent Christ figure, blessing a crowd; but then the light behind the woman shifted, and an eerie blue glow underlit the features of her face as she came closer to the bed.

Jeff wasn't sure if he gave vent to the sound or not, but inside his mind, he started screaming when he realized he was looking up into the cold, dead eyes of his sister, Judy!

No! Jesus! God! No! . . . This isn't happening!

The blue glow of light from the foot of the bed grew steadily stronger. It illuminated the high points of Judy's face and cast deep, black shadows into the hollows of her cheeks and eyes. Her thin, pale lips were set in a straight, unsmiling line. The points of her pearly teeth dimpled her lower lip.

The gauzy nightgown—Jeff recognized it as the one he had bought her while she was in the hospital—hissed like a snake with every motion she made.

Frantic with fear, Jeff cowered back against the bed's headboard, his hands grasping and squeezing his face as if he could somehow force away this vision. He watched in mute horror as Judy held her arms out to him. She looked as though she wanted to embrace him, but she stopped at the foot of the bed and just stood there, staring silently at him.

When he first noticed the dark splotches on each of her wrists, he thought they were stains of some kind on the sleeves of her nightgown. Then, with a sudden, numbing jolt, he realized that they were on her wrists. Jagged, white wedges of skin flapped open, exposing the dull gray and pink cylinders of bone, tendons, and muscles. Blood as black as India ink seeped slowly out of the opened wounds and dripped onto the floor with a dull, echoing *plop-plop* sound.

As he stared up at her, Jeff also noticed a dark stain that was spreading across the lap of Judy's nightgown. It looked like a dark flower, slowly opening in time-lapse photography.

Blood! his mind screamed. *Jesus Christ, there's blood everywhere!*

He looked again at his sister's dead face and thought for a moment that he saw himself reflected in her dark, glassy eyes. The glowing blue light swelled and pulsated with every hammering beat of his heart. Sharp pains shot up the back of his neck and down his arms. He was bathed in clammy sweat, and his lungs felt like they were about to explode.

Jesus, he thought, feeling a desperation he had never experienced before. *I'm going to have a heart attack!*

". . . Why? . . ."

The single word filled the room, hurting his ears as it echoed like the roll of distant thunder. Jeff licked his lips furiously, but had no idea what he could possibly say.

". . . Why, Jeff? . . . How could you do it? . . ."

Judy's voice had a dull, hollow reverberation that seemed to last much longer than it actually did. Jeff's ears hummed and thumped with every syllable.

"Do . . . do what?" he finally managed to say timidly. He was surprised how distant his own voice sounded to him. It had a high-pitched, nasal squeal that reminded him of a cat, yowling.

". . . How . . . how could you let something like this happen . . . to me? . . ."

"I—Jesus!—What are—I didn't!"

The expression on Judy's face remained absolutely fixed, blank and staring as though she were looking through him, staring in the darkest corners of his soul. No emotion, no spark of life flickered behind her eyes. Jeff wasn't even sure he saw her lips move when she spoke. Her voice seemed to be coming from all around him . . . or else it was inside his own head, like so many of the other voices that had been there in the past.

". . . I thought . . . I thought you loved me . . . ," Judy said, her voice still low and hollow sounding, but also gaining strength. "I thought . . . I trusted you . . . not to let something . . . like this . . . happen . . . to me . . ."

Jeff fought for control of his voice. "No, I—Jesus! Honest to God, Jude, I tried . . . I really did! You have to believe me! I tried like hell!"

". . . Look at this! . . . *Look!* . . ."

With a sudden rustling of satin, Judy thrust her arms forward, her wrists extended upward so Jeff could see into the gaping wounds. For a shattering instant, he thought he saw the flaps of dead, white skin open up and curl like lipless mouths that were uttering her words.

". . . Why did you let this happen to me . . ."

"I didn't! I didn't want to! I wanted you to live!" Jeff wailed, his words tearing at his throat like razor-edged blades. He pressed himself back against the headboard and frantically imagined that he could somehow push himself through the wall to get away from her . . . away from her cold, dead, accusing stare.

Judy didn't move any closer to him, but her body seemed to swell, blocking out all of the light coming from the hallway. The hellish underglow of blue light intensified, making every line, every wrinkle in her face look like deep, bloodless wounds. Her eyes looked as flat and hard as polished, black marble.

"Please," Jeff said in a shattered whisper. "Please, Judy! Just leave me alone. I didn't want you to die! Honest! I tried to help you!"

". . . Why? . . ."

Jeff was aware that the blue glow of light had begun to dim, and with it her voice began to fade. It still had an odd, dual reverberation that once again made Jeff think it wasn't her mouth, but the gaping wounds in her wrists that were talking.

"Just . . . just leave me alone!" he gasped. "Please. I did everything I could. You have to believe that."

Her dead eyes still held his gaze, fixing him with a hypnotic stare. He felt himself being drawn into their swirling black depths, but with a sudden surge of panic, he leaned forward.

"No!" he yelled, the shout bursting out of him like a deafening shotgun blast. "Go away! Leave me alone!"

He waved his arms wildly in front of himself as if she were a curtain of smoke he could make dissipate. He half-expected to make contact with something, but he swung his fists through thin air. With a sudden roaring *whoosh,* the blue light faded, and the figure disappeared.

Gasping, Jeff shook his head and stared at where, only a second before, his dead sister had been standing. He saw only emptiness. The bedroom door was still only slightly ajar, not wide open, and the warm glow of the hallway light shone in onto the floor and across the bottom corner of the bed.

"Jesus, no way," he gasped as he wiped his hands over his sweat-stained face. His breathing came in hot, fast gulps that hurt his chest. The tingling pain in his neck and arms began to subside. He was trembling all over as he stood up again. Momentarily disoriented, he had to lean against the side of the bed to help gain his balance.

Judy was gone.

"Christ," Jeff whispered, bracing his shoulders and standing up straight. He knew it had to have been a dream, but it had seemed so real, and he thought it odd that there hadn't been some kind of transition between dreaming and wakefulness. He couldn't shake the eerie impression that his dead sister had never been there . . . or else she still was, and he simply could no longer see her.

Moving to the foot of the bed, he looked at the spot where she had been standing, but there was no indication that anyone had been there. He let out a low groan when he looked at the bed and saw a single splotch of something dark, about the size of a quarter—

It could be blood!

—on the edge of the bedspread.

He tried to remember if he had noticed it there

before, while he was getting ready for bed, but he couldn't recall. Finally, only because the implications otherwise were too scary to contemplate, he convinced himself that it *had* to have been there before and he just hadn't noticed it. Yes, and he had dreamed seeing Judy. That's what it had to be. His fatigue, his grief, and his nervousness about being back home had all combined to give him one *hell* of a nightmare.

That's all there was to it.

He considered going downstairs and making sure once again that all the doors were locked, but he decided against it. Taking a shuddering breath, he cautiously walked out into the hallway.

His body was tensed, and he kept glancing around as though he expected at any second to see his dead sister again as he made his way slowly down to the bathroom where he relieved himself. When he was finished, he got a drink of water and then went back to the bedroom, being mindful to close the door halfway, as it had been before. As he lowered himself onto the bed, his body felt as wrung out as if he had just jogged several miles. Every nerve and muscle was burning with fatigue. He still felt wound up as he eased himself back under the bedcovers. Propping his hands under his head, he closed his eyes, but he knew it was going to be a long time before he calmed down enough to drift back off to sleep.

As he settled his head into the pillow, he opened his eyes and glanced over at the alarm clock beside the bed.

The time was 3:08 . . .

Chapter Twelve
Suspicious Minds

Morning light was streaming in through the bedroom window that faced east, looking out past a line of trees and the rooftops of a few houses to the distant ocean. Jeff groaned as he slit his eyes open and stared out at the view. He could just make out the dark shape of an oil tanker, creeping slowly along the horizon. Closer to shore, several fishing and lobster boats bobbed up and down on the wind-ruffled water. A cloudless blue sky faded to haze where it met the ocean. High above the water, several seagulls wheeled in slow, spiraling circles, bright white specks against the blue. Scores of small rocky islands, looking brown and drab in autumn's grip, dotted the inner bay.

What a beautiful day to start planning a funeral, Jeff thought as he shifted in bed. Just thinking about getting up gave him a sour sinking sensation in his gut.

He glanced over at the clock beside the bed and saw that it was already after nine o'clock. He had set the alarm for eight o'clock but, if it had gone off at all, he hadn't heard it. Thinking that Judy's alarm clock might be broken, he half expected to see that he had misread the time, and it was still 3:08; but he rubbed his eyes and clearly saw that it was 9:18.

Maybe, he thought with a subtle shiver, *3:08 was the time when Judy . . . did it.* He tried—again—but couldn't quite grasp the fact that his sister was truly dead.

A rectangle of sunlight fell across the bed, warming his legs and feet, almost too hot to be comfortable. Not feeling at all rested, Jeff tossed aside the bedcovers and stood up. A tremor raced through his body when he stretched his arms over his head and yawned.

"Ahh . . . *shit,"* he said with a deep gasp as he rubbed his face vigorously with the flats of his hands.

He knew he had a lot of things to do today, but he didn't feel at all up to the task. The nightmare he'd had last night still lingered uncomfortably in his thoughts. He couldn't dispel the feeling that, as much as he tried to convince himself that it had been nothing but a horrible nightmare, in some real sense he felt as though Judy *was* still here in the house . . . somewhere. Who could tell how long her uneasy spirit might continue to haunt the place where she had lived for so long and, ultimately, had taken her own life.

With uneasy thoughts like this swirling around in his head, Jeff walked down the hallway to the bathroom, shucked off the underwear and T-shirt he had slept in, quickly shaved, and then turned on the shower and stepped into its prickly, bracing spray. The water stung his eyes as if he were crying.

After breakfast, his first order of business would have to be to contact the funeral director at Marcigliano's, and then the minister, whoever it was now, at the Congregational Church. He was sure it couldn't be the same man—Reverend Livingstone? Yeah, that was it. He couldn't possibly still be there after all these years, so Jeff knew he would have to look up the name in the phone book. After that—well, he had promised

Judy's friend, Vera, that he would call her and give her all the details. Maybe he should even make arrangements to meet with her. It might help both of them deal with their grief if they shared memories of Judy. Then, all he had to do was wait until the funeral, which he expected wouldn't be until Thursday. He certainly had no intention of meeting with Judy's lawyer or a real estate agent to start the process of selling the old family homestead until after his sister was buried. Maybe he would take some time to go through the house top to bottom, to see what—if anything—was worth saving and what should be donated to Goodwill or whatever. Maybe Vera would want to do that with him.

He was still feeling on edge as he stepped out of the shower, towel-dried, and walked back to the bedroom to get dressed for the day. Before he got dressed, he leaned down and once again inspected the dark splotch on the bedspread. It was brick red, about the size of a quarter, and did indeed look like dried blood; but in the bar of morning sunlight, it looked faded— an old stain that Judy had apparently tried to wash out once or twice before. He couldn't quite bring himself to touch it to see if it was fresh. The image from his horrible dream last night, of his sister, standing there at the foot of the bed and shaking her slashed and bleeding wrists, sent a chill through him.

"How could you let this happen to me?"

Her voice was a papery whisper in his memory—a whisper he knew would never fade because, deep down, he *did* feel guilty, as though there *was* something else he could have done to help her.

And it was too late now!

Shaking inside, Jeff quickly dressed, putting on a clean, blue, button-down shirt and the same pants he had worn the day before. He felt wound up—"as tight as a tick," as his mother used to say—when he started downstairs. Every step on the stairs creaked beneath his weight, setting his teeth on edge. He couldn't stop thinking about the things he had heard—and seen—last night. He was trying desperately to dismiss it all as just a nightmare, so he wasn't prepared for what he saw when he walked into the kitchen.

Someone *had* been in the house last night.

The side door was wide open, shifting back and forth in the strong gusts of cold wind that swirled into the kitchen. A strong chill zipped like a razor up Jeff's back. Nearly every drawer and cupboard door was open or thrown onto the floor. Kitchen utensils—silverware, pots and pans, dishtowels, boxes of cereal, crackers, and other food supplies—were scattered everywhere. The kitchen table had been moved over in front of the stove, and all of the chairs were scattered about on the floor as if they had been knocked over by someone in a fit of anger.

Jeff stood there for several heartbeats, absolutely dumbfounded.

Tiptoeing through the rubble, he made his way out into the breezeway where he checked the side door. It was still locked, so whoever had done this, had at least been conscientious enough to lock the door behind him on his way out.

Christ, what consideration! Jeff thought, sniffing with dark laughter. *But how could this much destruction have occurred without waking me up?*

True, last night he had heard what had sounded like a door being opened downstairs, and then he had heard the heavy tread of footsteps coming up the stairs, but how could *this* much damage have been done without it sounding like the whole goddamned house was exploding? Was that what had awakened him at 3:08, the sound of the door latch as the culprit left? Or had all of this happened before—or maybe after—that? And who would do something like this in the first place?

The first person he thought of was Judy's friend, Vera. He had no idea who the hell she was. Maybe she had come over to the house during the night, after her phone call to him, and done this. Perhaps she had been looking for something—Judy's will or some other important papers, or maybe a key to a safety deposit box or a secret stash of money she knew Judy kept hidden somewhere in the house.

It was possible, but not very likely.

His heart was racing fast as he stood there in the doorway and scanned the destruction. At least none of the food packages had broken open. Whoever had ransacked the place had casually tossed things aside while they were searching for . . . something. Other than the general mess, there was very little real damage. The sense he got was that the person hadn't done this to make a mess; it had been to find something.

Jeff considered leaving things just as they were and calling the police, but since nothing appeared to be broken and—as far as he could tell—missing, he decided against it.

Frowning deeply, he searched through the debris until he found the jar of instant coffee he had bought last night. After filling the dented aluminum teakettle and putting it on the burner to boil, he set to work, straightening up the mess.

As he worked, he couldn't stop thinking that it looked as though the kitchen had been ransacked because someone had been looking for something. He couldn't stop wondering if they had found whatever it was they were looking for. But even if the intent had been simply to make a mess, the question remained: *Who would have done something like this?*

Jeff worked at cleaning things up until the teakettle began to whistle; then he made a cup of coffee, black, the way he liked it, and sipped at it while he finished picking up the mess. All in all, it took less than half an hour to get everything back in place and do a quick sweep of the floor. He didn't notice any muddy footprints on the floor, nothing that would help him figure out who might have been in the house last night. He supposed, if he decided to call the police, they could dust the place for fingerprints; but now that he had touched everything, he had probably smeared whatever fingerprints there might have been.

By the time he was finished, his stomach was in such a turmoil that he didn't feel much like eating, but he poured a small amount of cold cereal into a bowl, sprinkled on some sugar and added milk, got a spoon from the silverware drawer, and sat down to eat. When he pulled a napkin from the dispenser on the table, a piece of folded paper came out with it and landed on the table in front of him.

Jeff instantly recognized the page as one that had been torn from the notebook Judy kept on the counter near the wall phone. He could see that something was written on the inside in ink. Large, block letters had been gone over so many times they almost tore through the paper in several places.

Jeff's hand was trembling as he picked up the paper and unfolded it. He scanned the jagged, childish-looking penmanship and read the words silently, unable to believe what he was seeing.

LEAVE THIS HOUSE RIGHT NOW!
BEFORE WHAT HAPPENED TO JUDY
—HAPPENS TO YOU!!!

Exhaling loudly and feeling a cold clutching in his chest, Jeff sat back in the chair and rubbed the back of his neck, unable to believe what he was seeing as he repeated the words out loud.

"Leave this house right now before what happened
to Judy happens to you . . . *Jesus!*"

This is fucking crazy! whispered a voice in his head.
It doesn't make a goddamned bit of sense!

Why would someone break into the house, trash the
kitchen, and then leave a warning like this? It had
obviously been written sometime since Judy's death.
Jeff was positive it hadn't been there yesterday and
had no doubt that it had been left by the person who
had trashed the kitchen last night. It clearly indicated
that Judy's death *hadn't* been suicide.

What if his sister had been murdered, and this note
was a warning from her killer?

"This is serious shit!" he muttered, rubbing his chin
and trying to fight back his nervousness.

He had to think clearly.

For one thing, he realized that he should have contacted the police as soon as he had seen that the house
had been broken into. He regretted now that he hadn't
left the kitchen the way he had first found it. No
doubt, by cleaning up the mess, he had already de-
stroyed any evidence they might have found.

A chill skittered up Jeff's back, and he looked over
his shoulder. He had the sudden, intense feeling that
there was someone nearby, unseen, watching him.

Where?

In the doorway? Outside, looking in?

Forgetting all about his bowl of cereal, he stood up
and walked over to the kitchen window. Leaning over
the sink and gripping the edges with both hands, he
looked out at the yard. The lawn was a tufted mat of
uncut green and yellowing grass, littered with fallen
leaves and, in the shadows, silvered with morning dew.

Could there be footprints outside, maybe on the
doorstep or behind the house? If he or the police
searched carefully, would they find anything other

than his own tracks, where he had walked out back
last night and taken the key from its hiding place?

The cold, clutching sensation took a firmer hold on
his chest, making it impossible for him to take a deep
breath. He scanned the thin screen of trees that bordered the backyard, separating it from the neighbor's
property. Bright morning sunlight cast deep shadows
beneath the stand of pine trees. The morning breeze
coming in off the ocean made the boughs and their
deep shadows dance and sway. He knew, from playing
out there as a boy, that anyone could be hiding anywhere in those deep, green shadows. They could be
watching him right now through the window.

But what if you did it?

The thought popped into Jeff's mind as clearly as if
someone in the room had spoken. With a shout of
surprise, he spun around, fully expecting to see someone standing there in the doorway, staring at him. He
felt only a slight measure of relief to see that he was
alone.

I mean it, the voice went on, ringing like hammered
metal in his ears. *What if you—or some part of you—
did it all? What if you trashed the kitchen last night and
aren't even aware of it? And what if you left this note
here yourself . . . as a warning . . . a warning that
you—like Judy—might end up committing suicide if you
stay here too long?*

"No," Jeff said, his voice a shattered whimper, but
the other voice, the one speaking in his mind went on
uninterrupted.

*Or maybe . . . what if you were right before, that you
killed Judy and made it look like she had committed
suicide? And you don't even remember doing it! What if
this note is a warning TO yourself . . . ABOUT yourself?*

"No . . . no way," Jeff whispered harshly as he
shook his head emphatically. "That—that's *crazy!*"

Clenching his fists tightly, he pressed them against

the sides of his head as though trying to contain a gathering explosion.

Yeah, the voice went on, *probably not, but you have to admit you COULD have done it! Or maybe someone like Sammy, or even Karl might have done this last night without you knowing a thing about it . . . except for that small part of your mind that's trying to warn you.*

"No!" Jeff said, more forcefully as he ground his fists against his head. "I don't believe it! There— there's no *way* that I could have! I-I'm doing a lot better now! I've been better for a long time, now!"

Oh, sure, you think so . . . but maybe you're not, the voice went on with a teasing, lilting tone that irritated Jeff and made him cringe. *Maybe the pressure of everything that's happened lately has made you slip a cog or two. Lose some ground. It could happen, you know. You'd better at least consider it.*

"*No,* I'm all *right* I tell you!" Jeff shouted, shaking his fists with every other word. "I *swear* to *Christ* I *am!*"

He started pacing back and forth across the kitchen floor in long, purposeful strides. When he turned and looked toward the kitchen sink, a lance of sunlight reflecting off the faucet stung his eyes, bringing tears to them. White-hot pain jabbed through his head, forcing a tiny whimper from him.

Hey, I'm not saying you did it or anything, the voice went on. *I mean, I certainly can't tell you one way or another. All I'm saying is, you ought to at least consider it, don't you think?*

"No! I don't *want* to consider it!" Jeff shouted. The pain behind his eyes snapped and crackled like an overheating wire. "It doesn't make any fucking sense! I *know* I didn't do any of that! There's no *way* I could have!"

If you say so, but where does that leave you? the voice said, softer now, almost gentle.

Jeff felt as though he were gaining a measure of control as he continued to stride back and forth across the floor, punching his fist into his open hand; but every time he turned toward the sink, the reflected sunlight hurt his eyes, driving the pain in his head even higher. He knew, if he was going to function at all today and handle the things he had to take care of, that he should take a couple of aspirin right now, before the pain got any worse; but he couldn't stop wondering, if *he* hadn't done it, who had?

Who would have left a note like that for him to find?

It had obviously been left in the napkin holder for him to find, but how could it have gotten there? And who wouldn't want him here in Judy's house? Whoever it was, did this person have some idea how Judy had died? Was it a threat of murder? That was just as bad as contemplating the idea that some part of him was getting out of control.

Either way, he might be in danger!

He continued pacing back and forth, unable to stop as he turned each time from looking at the sunlight, gleaming like white fire from the kitchen faucet. His headache was blossoming behind his eyes, throbbing with a sharp, steadily rising pressure. He was just about to go look for a bottle of aspirin in the bathroom when, through the window, he saw a car pull up into the driveway.

"Oh, *shit*," he muttered, moving quickly to the window and looking out.

He wanted to see who it was, then go into the living room and pretend he wasn't home when the person started knocking on the door. Cold tension flooded his body when he looked out and saw that a two-tone blue police cruiser had stopped at the top of the driveway, parking right behind his rented car. He had the presence of mind to pick the note up off the table where he'd dropped it, crumple it into a tight ball, and slide it into his pants pocket as he started for the door.

The man standing on the doorstep held up his wallet which displayed a shield that identified him as Ray Foster, a detective with the Cape Higgins Police Department. Jeff told him who he was as they shook hands.

"Please, come on in," Jeff said, stepping aside and holding the door open for him. "Would you like a cup of coffee or something? I—umm, I'm sorry, but all I have is instant."

Detective Foster slipped his identification back into the inside pocket of his sports coat and nodded. "Instant will be just fine," he said in a low, serious-sounding voice. He had narrow, blue eyes that looked like slivers of ice, and his mouth was set in a grim, straight line. Jeff's instant analysis was that this man didn't have a shred of humor in him.

Jeff led him into the kitchen, thankful, now, that he had already cleaned everything up. He cringed, thinking about how it would have looked if Detective Foster had seen the mess that had been here this morning. The pounding pressure behind his eyes made him wince when he banged the teakettle against the faucet as he filled it, then placed it on one of the stove's burners. Every sound, every motion he made seemed to jack the pain in his head up another notch.

"I—ahh, you'll have to excuse me for a moment," Jeff said, squinting as he turned to face the detective who was standing beside the table, apparently waiting for Jeff to invite him to sit down. He looked as though he didn't trust the situation enough to let his guard down.

He probably never does, Jeff thought.

"You see, I just flew in from Denver last night, and

I didn't sleep all that well last night. 'S been a rough couple of days."

"Yes, I can imagine," Detective Foster said tonelessly. "I'm truly sorry about what happened to your sister."

Jeff raised his hand to his forehead and pressed hard against his eyebrows. "Umm, thanks," he said, taking a deep breath. "I've got one *helluva* headache."

Detective Foster nodded understandingly, but his face remained perfectly impassive.

"Do you mind if I sit down?" Foster asked.

"No, not at all," Jeff replied, wincing with pain. "Make yourself comfortable."

Taking hold of the chair back, Foster slid the chair away from the table. The chair's feet scraped loudly on the linoleum floor.

"If you'll excuse me for a moment," Jeff said, "I want to check the bathroom for some aspirin. I'll be right back." He could hear the tightness in his own voice and wondered if the detective had noticed it.

Of course he noticed it, whispered a different voice inside Jeff's mind. *It's his goddamned job to notice shit like that!*

"Go right ahead," Detective Foster said with another abrupt nod of his head.

Jeff walked quickly down the hall to the downstairs bathroom. The whole way, he ran his hand along the wall to help him keep his balance. Shimmering curtains of white light were shifting at the edges of his vision. He was mildly surprised to discover that the bathroom had not been trashed as the kitchen had been. Opening the medicine cabinet, he fumbled around until he found a bottle of Bayer aspirin, snapped off the safety cap, shook two tablets out into his hand, and hurriedly washed them down with a few gulps of water. He knew it would take a while for the aspirin to kick in, but he forced himself to smile as he walked back into the kitchen.

"There," he said, with a heavy sigh as he walked over to the cupboard and took down two clean coffee cups.

When Detective Foster didn't say anything right away, Jeff kept himself busy, getting things ready. Over his shoulder, trying to sound casual, he said, "So, what can I do for you? I assume you're here on official business."

He couldn't help but wonder if one of the neighbors had noticed the unusual activity at the house last night and had reported it, as Vera almost had. Or maybe someone else in the neighborhood had had a similar break-in, and the police were just going around, checking to make sure everything was okay.

"Oh, nothing official," Detective Foster said flatly. "I'd heard that you were in town, staying here at the house. I thought I might drop by to . . . well, to answer any questions you might have."

"About my sister's death, you mean?" Jeff said. He couldn't help but wonder who would have informed the police that he was back in town.

Foster regarded him with a slow, steady stare. Jeff noticed that the man hardly ever blinked his flinty eyes. The more he thought about it, the more Foster reminded him of a lizard.

Just then the teakettle began to whistle. The sound pierced Jeff's ears, making him wince again, but he gritted his teeth and busied himself with spooning instant into each cup and pouring the hot water. He carried the two cups over to the table and slid one over in front of Detective Foster; then he got the sugar bowl and a jug of whole milk from the refrigerator before sitting down across the table from the officer. He hoped the detective didn't notice how much his hand was shaking when he raised his cup to his mouth, blew on it, and took a slurping sip.

"I—umm, well, I've heard pretty much most of what happened—who found her and all," Jeff said, wincing as he swallowed, "but to tell you the truth, I was wondering if there was a—well, I don't quite know how to put this exactly." He put his cup down and shifted uncomfortably on his chair. "But I was wondering if you thought there might be—you know, evidence of any foul play. I mean in my sister's death, that is."

Foster frowned, and one of his eyebrows shot up questioningly, but he said nothing as he regarded Jeff with his hard, steady stare.

"What I mean is," Jeff went on, knowing that he was only making things worse by stumbling over his words. "I've been told that she—she killed herself, but—you know, the thought has crossed my mind a few times that—well, what if she had been murdered?"

"Do you have any reason to suspect anything like that?" Foster said, his voice barely modulating at all. "Is there something you know that you're not telling me?"

This was it, Jeff thought; this was his chance to tell him about how last night the house had been broken into and trashed. There still might be some evidence the police could find if they looked hard enough. Also, there was the note he had found in the napkin holder.

If *that* wasn't a threat, what was? Reaching under the table, Jeff rubbed his hand over the bulge of the crumpled note in his pants pocket and thought about showing it to Foster. It was a tangible piece of evidence that very well could indicate that Judy had been murdered. The police should know about it. He should file a report just in case something else happened.

Biting down on his lower lip, Jeff considered for a moment, then shook his head vigorously. The motion sent a white-hot bolt of pain into the center of his head even as that faint, irritating voice started whispering in the back of his mind.

Probably a smart move, it said. *You don't want to raise the possibility that you might have done it just before you flew back to Denver, now, do you?*

"Uh—no," Jeff said, shaking his head more decisively in spite of the blossoming pain. "I mean, I didn't see my sister all that much. We didn't stay in very good touch, what with me and my family living in Colorado and all."

"You're married and have one child, isn't that correct?" Foster said.

Jeff nodded. "Yes, and—well, you see, I certainly didn't know any of my sister's business or personal situation or anything. I know she's been divorced twice, but I think both times it was her husband who wanted the divorce at least as much as she did. But you see, I just thought . . . you know, as a standard thing or whatever, that you wouldn't rule out the possibility that she had been killed."

Foster's expression darkened slightly as he nodded once, quickly.

"You're absolutely right," he said emotionlessly. "We don't rule out anything, and in the instance of an unattended death, we make absolutely no assumptions until we've checked out all possibilities."

"And—umm, well, how about with Judy?" Jeff said with a noticeable tremor in his voice. Every muscle in his body was tensed. He wanted to take another sip of coffee but was afraid that his hand would start shaking so badly he would splash it all over himself. His pulse was thudding like muffled hammer blows in his ears, and each pulse beat made his head throb painfully. A ring of sweat lined his neck like a tight-fitting collar.

Foster cocked his head to one side and stared at him steadily, looking like an inquisitive owl.

"All the evidence seems to indicate that she was responsible for her own death," Foster said in his flat voice. Jeff noticed that he didn't use the word *suicide*. "Especially considering what had happened the previous week."

"You mean with her going to the hospital."

"Right," Foster said. "So as far as we're concerned—officially, that is, the situation is a closed book . . . that is, unless you have some reason to suspect otherwise."

"Oh, no—no, I don't," Jeff said, perhaps a bit too hastily. He almost reached for his coffee cup again but quickly drew back his hand. "I was—it was just something I had been . . . you know, been worrying about. That's all."

"Well you can stop your worrying because I feel confident that we've covered every angle," Foster said. After stirring sugar and milk into his coffee, he picked up his cup and took a deep gulp. Jeff couldn't think of a thing to say, so he just sat there, wondering how to make small talk with the police detective who had come over to his house to discuss his sister's suicide. The silence in the room lengthened uncomfortably until, at last, Foster took another sip and then slid the cup, still more than half-full, away from him. He got up from the chair and straightened his shoulders.

"Well, Mr. Wagner—" he said.

"Jeff. Call me Jeff."

"Fine . . . Jeff."

Reaching across the table, Foster held out his hand so they could shake. Jeff was aware of how cold and clammy his own hand must have felt.

"If there's nothing else, then, I won't take any more of your time. I'm sure you have a lot of things to attend to today."

Foster slid his hand into the pocket of his sports jacket and pulled out a business card that had his name, phone number, and the town seal printed on it.

"If you do have any questions, or even if you want to talk to someone, you can always give me a call down at the station. If I'm not there, you can leave a message."

"Thanks," Jeff said, nodding. He took the card, glanced at it briefly, then placed it on the table beside his coffee cup. Inside his head, the voice was shouting at him to say something if only to get it off his chest—express his concerns that *he* might have done something; admit that *he* had been in town the night Judy had died—or been killed—and that *he* was afraid he or one of his alters might have done it!

Instead, though, he said simply, "Thanks for stopping by. I appreciate your willingness to help."

"Just doing my job," Foster said with a curt nod. "I'm sorry we had to meet under circumstance such as this." His flat, toneless voice didn't sound at all sympathetic; he was simply doing his job, step by step, by the book, and that was it.

Jeff walked the detective to the door and held it open for him as he stepped outside. The morning air had a bracing snap to it. Standing in the doorway, Jeff watched as Foster got into the cruiser, started it up, and backed down the driveway to the street. After closing the door and making sure it was locked, he went to the kitchen window. Bending over and bracing his hands on the windowsill, he watched until the cruiser had disappeared around the bend. Then he straightened up stiffly and released the breath that he had been holding.

"Jesus," he whispered, closing his eyes for a moment and rubbing his forehead.

Well, said the familiar-sounding voice inside his head, *I guess you did it.*

"Did *what?*" Jeff said aloud, his voice growling between clenched teeth. He opened his eyes, but the bright daylight made his headache spike.

You got him out of here without making him suspicious, said the voice. It sounded casual, now, not at all mocking, but Jeff thought there was an accusative edge to it all the same.

"That's because there's nothing to be suspicious about," he said sharply.

Oh, yeah, but if you did do anything—and I'm not saying you did, but IF you did do anything . . . to Judy, I mean, well, the cops certainly haven't got a clue about it, so it sure as shit looks like you're gonna get away with it!

Jeff squeezed his eyes shut tightly, choking back the panic and tears that raged inside him.

"But I didn't do *anything,*" he said in a high, shattered voice that broke on nearly every syllable. His shoulders sagged forward, and he sobbed so hard it hurt his throat. "I swear to God, I-I didn't do *anything!*"

Chapter Thirteen

The Fetch

"I miss you, honey."

"Yeah, I miss you, too."

Jeff paused and took a sip of beer, the sound of it bubbling in his ear through the receiver. When he swallowed, his throat made a loud gulping noise that made him laugh out loud in spite of himself.

"Sorry," he said, chuckling tightly. "Just having a little sip of barley soda."

"So, how are things going out there?"

Jeff sighed heavily. He could easily visualize his wife, sitting at the table in their small kitchen back home in Denver. He got such a sharp mental image of the room—its pale blue walls, the maple table and chairs, and the refrigerator covered with Robin's artwork—that a sharp pang of homesickness filled him. He got so choked up, he almost couldn't speak.

"Well, I guess it's going about as good as could be expected. It's been a rough couple of days, though."

"Yeah, I can imagine," Sally said.

It was early evening, Wednesday—two days after he had come back to Cape Higgins. He was sitting in the living room, drinking beer as he held the phone to his

ear and stared out the picture window at the backyard.
The sun had just set, and beyond the line of pine trees,
finger-shaped bands of purple clouds striped across a
darkening cobalt blue sky. Fitful gusts of wind rattled
fallen leaves against the windows like frantic hands,
trying to claw their way into the house.

"Yeah, I guess I have everything taken care of for
the funeral. Man, I'll tell you, though, the toughest
part had to be picking out the . . . the coffin yesterday.
It—"

A sudden burning filled his eyes, and his voice
caught in his throat, but he forced himself to keep
talking.

"—it really drives it home, you know? Realizing
that Judy . . . that she's really . . ."

His voice trailed off to nothing, and he squeezed his
eyes tightly shut, trying to regain a measure of control
over his tortured emotions.

"Yeah . . . I know," Sally said in a sympathetic
whisper. "It's gotta be *real* tough. I just wish you had
wanted me and Robin to come out there with you."

"No, wait a second! It's not that I didn't *want* you
guys to come with me," Jeff said, perhaps a bit too
hastily. "But I'm—I had my reasons. I thought you
understood that."

"I do, but I also understand that I wanted to be
there to help you with everything."

"I'm handling everything okay. Honest, I am. I'm
coping. I've made sure the people at the cemetery
know we need to have a new grave dug in the family
plot."

"Yeah, you told me about that last night when you
called. Did you finally get in touch with that minister
you were trying to see?"

"Uh-huh. I talked to him this afternoon, got him all
lined up. You won't believe it, but it's Reverend Liv-

ingstone, the same guy who was minister at the Congregational Church back when I was a kid."

"Really? That long ago?" Sally said with a soft snigger. "Why, he must be as old as God."

"At least," Jeff said. In spite of the tension he felt, he couldn't help but laugh along with her. "He seemed almost senile, but he remembered me—at least he said he did. I'm surprised he hasn't retired yet, but he said it'd be no problem; he'll do the funeral service. It's all set for tomorrow morning, eleven o'clock, rain or shine."

"So how's the weather been out there?"

"Really cold for this time of year, and I forgot how being near the ocean makes it feel so raw. God, the wind cuts right through you. They're predicting rain for tomorrow." He leaned forward and scanned the rectangle of sky he could see through the window. "I hope not, but it looks like it's clouding up already."

"Umm, that's too bad," Sally said, her voice lowering. "But about this minister. . . . Did you get a chance to talk to him?"

"Yeah, sure I did. I just—"

"No, I mean *really* talk to him. You know what I mean." Her voice had an edge to it. "You know, to let out some of your feelings."

Jeff took a shuddering breath and held it for a moment as he slumped back onto the couch. "Well, yeah—sure I did . . . I mean—some, anyway."

"Remember, Jeff," Sally said sharply. "I *know* you. I know that you have this—ah, *tendency,* shall we say, to bottle things up inside you because you think you can handle everything on your own by not talking about it."

"No—seriously, we talked."

Jeff laughed, but it was a tight, nervous laugh. Sally didn't say anything, but her silence was accusatory.

"Come on, we talked, okay? And . . . okay—yeah,

maybe he helped me out . . . a little, I guess." He took another quick sip of beer.

"You know, that's what I've been telling you all these years, Jeff. That people go to church for a reason. It's because we all *need* religion for times like this, to help us cope."

"Well . . . yeah, but it's not like I'm your gung ho churchgoing kind of guy, you know? To tell you the truth, I found it a little irritating to listen to his religious angle about everything."

Especially after all the shit good old Aunt Mildred and Uncle Kirby put you through, right?

The voice sounded clear and close to Jeff's ear. He jumped and glanced around to see if there might be someone behind the couch, but, of course, there was no one else in the room. The air around him felt suddenly several degrees colder, and a wave of prickles went up the back of his neck to the base of his skull.

"So—umm, are you and Robin still getting along without me around?"

"Oh, sure. We're doing great," Sally said. "Things around here are going along as usual—you know, school and work. We're doing just fine."

"Well, I hope you're not spoiling her rotten while I'm away."

"Oh," Sally said with a laugh, "we're treating ourselves to a few things. We had girls' night out last night—went out for supper and then caught an early movie."

"On a school night?"

"We're struggling along without you as best we can." Then, lowering her voice to a more serious tone, she added, "She really misses her daddy, you know . . . and so do I."

"Yeah," Jeff said.

He felt a slight choking sensation and took another sip of beer, letting the carbonation explode in his mouth before swallowing it, but the feeling didn't go away. He shifted his gaze back and forth, looking at the darkening room and wondering if there was anything lurking there in the deepening shadows.

"Have you done anything about selling the house and taking care of that end of things?"

"Well, a little bit. At least I got the ball rolling. This afternoon, after I saw Reverend Livingstone, I had an appointment with—damn! What was his name? I can't remember it off hand. Nichols . . . yeah, Mark Nichols. Judy's lawyer. I had a brief meeting with him and— Oh, shit, yeah! That reminds me. I have to call Vera."

"Vera?" Sally said. "Who's Vera?"

There was just enough of an edge of suspicion in Sally's voice to make Jeff immediately think guiltily of Katherine. He didn't know why, but he knew that he shouldn't mention anything about seeing her again. He wasn't even sure if he had ever mentioned her to Sally before, but there was no point in making her suspicious now. It wasn't an issue for him. For a moment, his mind went blank; then he shook his head.

"Uhh . . . Vera . . . yeah, she's a—umm, a friend of Judy's," he said finally. "I'll probably just get things started—you know, take care of what I can. I was thinking of asking her if she'd mind taking care of the rest of it once I got back home."

"Do you think you can trust her?" Sally said with a shade of suspicion in her voice. "I mean, who is she?"

Jeff shrugged. "She was Judy's best friend. She worked with her at UNUM. I'm not going to give her power of attorney or anything. I was just thinking it'd be a good thing to have someone here who can show the house and keep things in motion if it looks like the house is gonna sell. I can probably take care of all the paperwork by fax once I'm back home."

"And just when do you think that might be?" Sally asked.

Again, Jeff thought he caught a suspicious edge in her voice, and once again he immediately thought about Katherine. He was positive he hadn't mentioned anything about seeing her.

Had he? Shit, he had blanked out for a moment, there, so maybe he—or one of his other personalities—had said something about her.

And even if he had, so what? Katherine—like all the rest of Cape Higgins—was a part of his life that he had locked away in his past. But now, once again, he felt a strong wave of guilt wash over him. He hadn't seen or called Kat since that first night at the Shop 'n Save, but he had to admit that over the last couple of days, there had been a few times when he had been just lonely enough so he had thought about giving her a call . . . just to see what she was up to.

Scratching the back of his neck, he thought if he had his way, he'd leave for Colorado tomorrow afternoon, right after the funeral. That wasn't practical, he knew, and he couldn't deny—at least to himself—that he had been thinking about calling Katherine after the funeral if only to take her up on that offer of a home-cooked meal.

"Jeff? . . . I asked you when you thought you might be coming home."

"I . . . ah, I dunno for sure," Jeff said, shaking his head. "It probably won't be for another few days, at least. Maybe a week, tops."

"Well, I certainly hope it's soon," Sally said, still sounding edgy. "You know, what with paying for the substitute teachers for your classes and all, I don't want to drain our bank account dry."

Jeff had the distinct impression that money wasn't the issue here . . . no, not at all, but he decided to play along with her if only to hide what he had been thinking about Katherine.

"Yeah, but, you gotta remember that eventually there's gonna be some money—quite a bit, I think, from the sale of the house . . . that is, unless we get hit with a few surprises and find out that Judy had one hell of a lot of debts. Her lawyer is going through everything now. I've been trying to settle up her hospital bill with the insurance company but unfortunately, because this was a . . . a suicide—"

He almost choked on the word and took another sip of beer before continuing.

"—there's a good chance we won't get any of the money from her life insurance policy. We'll have to see about that, but I'm listed as the sole beneficiary."

And you're positive you didn't come back and kill her, right? said a voice in his mind. *You're sure you didn't kill her for the money or anything . . .*

Sally was silent for a moment, and Jeff couldn't help but wonder if he had said something that he shouldn't have—something that he didn't even remember saying. Then Sally sighed softly and said, "Well, as long as you think you're handling everything okay. I just don't want to have to worry about you."

Jeff thought he still detected a note of—of what? Not worry. No, it was suspicion that edged her voice. Trying his best to sound totally casual, he said, "You don't have to worry, hon. Really, I'm coping fine here . . . just fine. To tell you the truth, the first night here was pretty rough. I had quite a bit of trouble falling asleep and all, but I slept like a baby last night, and this will all be over before we know it."

Even though Judy's going to be dead forever! said the voice in his mind.

Jeff shifted his gaze nervously around the living room and then to the window again. He shivered when he saw how dark it was outside and realized that it was still daylight back home in Denver. The pang of homesickness—and guilt—got worse.

He could admit to himself that what he had just told Sally wasn't true at all. Although there hadn't been another instance of anything like what had happened the first night, last night he had lain awake in bed for hours unable to fall asleep. Whenever he would start to drift off to sleep, even the tiniest sounds inside or outside the house would startle him awake. Memories of that nightmare—and he had to keep telling himself that's all it was; a nightmare that had its source in the emotional turmoil of what he was dealing with—sent rippling chills up and down his back. He made a mental note to make sure—again—that all the doors to the house were locked before he went upstairs to bed.

"Well, you just make damned sure you take care of yourself, okay?" Sally said. "And promise me you won't forget to call tomorrow."

"I promise," Jeff said, his voice catching slightly. "In fact, I'll probably call you at work right after the funeral. That'll be around noon, my time."

"I'll be waiting," Sally said before making the loud smacking sound of a kiss into the receiver. "And *you* just remember that there are two women here in Denver who really love and miss you, all right?"

"Don't worry. I will," Jeff said softly. The words came hard because of the subtle pressure that was still gripping his throat. "Make sure to give Robin a big hug and kiss for me, all right? I wish I hadn't called while she was over at a friend's house."

"Well, don't worry about it. I'll tell her you called. It'll be the first thing she asks when she gets home, anyway."

Sally paused, and Jeff heard her take a deep, slow breath.

"I love you, Jeff," she said.

He wished it didn't sound like she was close to tears.

"I know," he replied. "And I love you, too, Sal."

He closed his eyes tightly, thinking just how much he meant it.

Jesus, with every ounce of his being, he *meant* it!

One hour and two beers later, Jeff was upstairs, standing outside the closed door of what used to be his old bedroom. His hand was poised in the air, inches from the doorknob. His breath came in ragged gasps as he moved his face close to the door, almost pressing it against the polished wood as though, before he opened the door, he wanted to eavesdrop on a secret conversation that was going on inside the room.

His eyes were wide open and staring, his gaze riveted by the swirling wood-grain pattern of the door. He realized that it had to be a trick of his eyes, no doubt aided by the more than usual amount he'd had to drink this evening, but the wood-grain pattern sure as hell seemed to be moving, shifting subtly back and forth like dark clumps of seaweed, swaying in the ocean current.

He had vivid memories of this door and its wood-grain pattern. He shivered, recalling how he used to imagine that within its pattern, he could see distorted, melting faces trapped inside the wood. Dark, deep-set, sightless eyes stared back at him; gaping mouths screamed silently. In later life, he associated these images with the famous painting by Edvard Munch, *The Scream.*

Forget about the door. What do you think is trapped inside that room? said a tiny voice in the back of his mind.

Chills skittered up and down Jeff's spine, and he drew his hand back quickly as though some subtle electrical charge had tickled him. Casting a fearful glance over his shoulder, he saw that there wasn't anyone in the hallway besides him. Nevertheless, he felt a cold, unseen presence, lurking just out of sight somewhere nearby.

Last night for at least half an hour, he had stood outside this door, but he ultimately had not been able to summon up the courage he needed to twist the doorknob and enter his old bedroom. He wondered if he would find the courage now, but he was afraid—no, afraid was too mild a word; he was *terrified* of what he might discover inside there. The silent mouths in the wood grain seemed to be screaming loud enough for at least some part of his subconscious mind to hear. The dark, dead eyes—looking so much like Judy's eyes had in his nightmare—stared back at him, tearing into the darkest corners of his heart. A high, nervous pulse fluttered like bellows in his ears, making him feel dizzy.

The clearest, most mind-numbing image he had was that if he pushed the door open, the hinges would squeal like the long, tortuous pull of rusty nails from old wood; and in the soft glow of the hallway light shining over his shoulder, he would see his old bed over against the wall by the closet door, right where it had always been.

And lying on the bed in the darkness he would see a figure, its face and form indistinct.

Indistinct, yes—but threatening.

Terrifyingly threatening!

Against his will, he imagined that he would enter the room, gliding irresistibly forward as though he were sliding across a greased floor. And as his vision resolved, he would see in the darkness that the person on the bed was himself. Maybe it would be the scared, trembling ten-year-old boy he remembered being, huddled and shivering beneath his bedcovers . . .

Frightened? Frightened of what? he wondered even as a shiver passed through him like an icy blade.

Or perhaps it would be an image of himself at his present age—the adult he might have become if he had

never gotten out of Maine, if he had lived his whole life
to adulthood in this house.

No, Jeff! A tiny, scared-sounding voice spoke inside
his mind. *Maybe it's . . . your fetch!*

This wasn't the same voice Jeff was used to hearing
inside his head. This one sounded much higher and
tight, like that of a terrified child.

"Jesus, the *fetch!*," Jeff said. His voice was low and
tremulous. The words rang in his ears and sent numbing chills through his body.

Suddenly, he remembered when he and his sister
were young, how they used to scare each other by
reading ghost stories out loud to each other. For the
first time in a long time, he recalled one particular
story titled "The Fetch."

"Oh, Jesus," he muttered as the memory came rushing back at him.

He couldn't remember the author's name, and
something about his memory of it made him wonder
if it had been a real story at all. Maybe he had made
it up or dreamed it, but as he remembered it, the story
concerned a man—a doctor in Victorian England—
who was responsible for something horrible that had
happened. The details were lost to him now, but he
thought it might have had something to do with a
young woman whom the doctor had gotten pregnant
and had refused to marry or even acknowledge.

While walking home from the theater one night, the
doctor saw someone who looked exactly like himself
walk up the steps to his house, unlock the front door,
and go inside. At first he hesitated outside in the shadows, thinking he should go alert the police; but then he
decided that this must in fact be a burglar who, in the
darkness, had merely *looked* like him; so he stealthily
followed the figure into the house. Downstairs, he lit
a candle, which glowed with an eerie blue light, and
went upstairs to his bedroom where—to his horror—

212 *Rick Hautala*

he was confronted by a shimmering translucent mirror image of himself.

Reaching out for him with thin, bony hands, the ghastly apparition spoke in low, sonorous tones, informing the doctor that he was his *Doppelgänger*—his invisible twin who had been born the same time as the doctor's birth. Because the young woman whom the doctor had refused to marry had killed herself and, therefore, her unborn baby, the apparition had been sent by her restless spirit to *fetch* him, to bring him to the land of the dead.

Terrified, the doctor turned and ran, but at the top of the stairs he slipped and fell down the entire flight of steps, landing at the bottom with a broken back and a cracked skull. As he lay there at the foot of the stairs, unable to move but certain that he was dying, he looked up in mute horror as the ghostly double of himself shifted silently down the stairway. It held both of its skeletal hands out to him and told him there was no escape.

And then the doctor died . . . of pure fright.

"Is *that* why I'm afraid?" Jeff whispered. His throat was raw, and his voice sounded like the soft, dragging scrape of feet on the floor behind him. "My *fetch* . . . After all these years, am I afraid that my *fetch* is in that room—that it's been there all along, just waiting for me to come back home?"

His hand was trembling uncontrollably as he moved it closer to the door, his fingers curling to conform to the shape of the doorknob. Cold sweat broke out on his forehead and ran in thin streams down his face and neck. His stomach and shoulder muscles were tensed. The heavy, rapid slamming of his pulse in his ears sounded like distant, gathering thunder.

Go on! commanded another, sterner-sounding voice inside his head. *What the fuck are you waiting for, anyway? Are you chicken-shit or something? You know there's nothing in there! Hell, Judy probably didn't even keep any of your old furniture! More than likely, she threw all of it out ages ago. So go on! Open the goddamned door! You'll see! There's nothing in there to be afraid of! Not a goddamned thing!*

"But what if there is?" Jeff said in a low, shattered whisper. "What if there really *is?*"

He couldn't push aside the thought that, as soon as he opened the door, he would see a ghostly image of himself in the room—the same self that had trashed the kitchen the first night he had spent in the house . . . the same self that had come back to the house last Friday night, before he left for Colorado, and killed Judy . . . the same self that had written that note he had found, warning him that murder—*or suicide!*—waited for him if he stayed much longer in this old house.

His fetch!

With a sudden groan deep in his chest, Jeff turned away from the door and started back down the hall. His throat was parched, and he told himself that all he wanted to do was go downstairs and get another beer. He needed to calm down a little, and maybe then he would go back up and check the room. It took effort for him not to break out in a run. Halfway down the hall, he hesitated and, turning around, cast a fearful glance at the bedroom door. He more than half-expected to see the doorknob move as someone on the other side turned it. He waited with baited breath, watching for a narrow, dark opening to appear, and a ghastly, death white face to lean out into the hallway and look at him.

"Jesus," he whispered, fighting hard against the feeling that this, too, was just part of a bad dream. The sound of his own voice didn't lend him an ounce of courage.

Once he was at the top of the stairs, his hand securely gripping the railing, he paused and looked back again at his bedroom door.

Had the door opened? . . . Just a crack?

It sure looked it, at least from this angle.

Jeff wanted desperately to convince himself that it was just the shadow, cast by the hall light.

That's all it was!

That's all it *could* be!

Sliding his hand along the stairway railing, he started down the stairs, trying his best not to imagine that this was the same railing, the same stairway in the house that had belonged to that fictional doctor. His stomach went cold when he imagined himself, lying at the foot of the stairs with a broken neck, unable to move as the ghostly double image of himself shifted down the stairs and reached out to take him to the land of the dead.

Fear was winding up inside him like a burring saw blade. As he walked down the hallway and into the kitchen, he kept glancing over his shoulder, fearful that he would be confronted by a vision of his *fetch,* but the house appeared to be empty. Shaking horribly, he went over to the refrigerator and grabbed a bottle of beer—his third this evening. After popping off the bottle cap, he leaned his head back and gulped down almost half of the beer before pausing long enough to take a deep breath. He groaned like a man with a fever as he rolled the cold bottle back and forth over his forehead.

"Jesus Christ, come on . . . Come *on!* Get a god-damned grip, will ya?" he whispered heatedly.

He wiped his mouth with the back of his hand as his eyes darted back and forth, trying to catch a glimpse of whatever might be lurking in the corners of the room. The silence of the house was palpable. It seemed to press in all around him, squeezing him with an ever mounting pressure. A gust of wind sent a sudden flurry of dead leaves against the window, making him jump.

Leave this house right now!

The words of the note rang like metal against metal in his memory. Had that been his own handwriting? Or someone else's?

Clutching the beer bottle, he backed up until he was wedged in a corner of the room. His body was so tense, the muscles were aching.

Leave this house right now! Before what happened to Judy happens to you!

"No," he said in a tight, controlled voice. "I *won't* leave!"

Narrowing his eyes, he drained the bottle of beer and then, squeezing it so tightly his knuckles went bone white, he looked around the kitchen, his eyes twitching wildly. His ears were ringing in the utter silence, and for a moment or two, even the voices inside his head were silent. When he caught sight of his own reflection in the window, he jumped and squealed with surprise.

"Jesus," he said through gritted teeth. "Calm down, will ya? Just calm the fuck down! Everything's all right. There's no one out there."

He earnestly wanted to believe that, but as he stood there in the corner, all he was aware of was the cold, silent night that was pressing in against the house. It seemed to be clawing its way under the door and through the windows, and winding its chilly fingers around his heart. And no matter what he tried to tell himself, all he could think was that there *was* someone either inside the house or outside, looking in. He had no idea whether it was some twisted double of himself or the ghost of his dead sister or something else; but he could *feel* its presence, and he knew that it had been responsible for the warning.

Leave this house right now! Before what happened to Judy happens to you!

Chapter Fourteen

Dark Day

For once, the weather forecaster was right. On Thursday morning, the sky was dark, and it was raining hard.

A perfect day for a funeral, Jeff thought as he rolled his head to one side and stared out the bedroom window.

He couldn't see the ocean through the shifting gray curtains of mist, but he could easily imagine its gray, storm-tossed surface, veined with white foam and black tangles of seaweed as it crashed in towering waves against the rocks. Beneath a lowering sky of twisting clouds, the trees and houses were lashed by the cold rain. Hammer-fisted gusts of wind buffeted against the house and whistled under the eaves, wavering up and down as if someone were blowing into the tops of a soda bottle.

Jeff yawned, scrubbed his face with both hands, and sighed heavily.

He hadn't slept well last night. He felt wrung out, exhausted, but was thankful—at least—that there hadn't been a recurrence of the nightmare he'd had his first night in the house. Groaning loudly, he swung his legs out from under the covers and stood up. The motion was a bit too sudden and made him feel light-headed. He held out his hands for a moment until he regained his balance. His stomach was sour from the beer he had consumed last night. How many had it been—three, four? Well, at least he didn't have a hang-over.

Glancing at the clock beside the bed, he saw that it was a little after seven o'clock. Judy's funeral wasn't until eleven o'clock, so he had plenty of time to get ready.

Too much time, he thought.

After a warm shower, he got dressed, putting on the dark suit and black tie he had brought with him. It was still only a quarter to eight, and he was ready to go. He had at least another hour or two to kill before he should show up at the funeral home.

He came down the stairs slowly, his head cocked to one side so he could listen as he moved toward the kitchen. As he came around the corner, he let out a sigh of relief when he saw no evidence that anyone had broken into the house overnight. Nevertheless, he went out into the breezeway and checked to make sure the side door was still locked.

"Well, maybe things are finally beginning to settle down," he said to himself as he walked back into the kitchen, took two slices of bread from the plastic bag, and dropped them into the toaster. He filled the tea-kettle at the sink and put it on to boil, then poured himself a glass of orange juice.

He shivered wildly as he leaned back against the counter and sipped his juice. Outside, the hissing rattle of rain beating against the house sounded like a scat-tershot of tiny pebbles. The cold wind seemed to have found its way into the house through at least a dozen different cracks. Even with the furnace running—Jeff could hear it rumbling away like a friendly beast down

in the cellar—chilly drafts curled around him like unseen hands, tugging at his feet and back. He jumped
when his toast popped, but chose to ignore it and just
stood there, staring with an unfocused gaze down at
the worn pattern of the linoleum floor. He didn't move
until the teakettle began to whistle shrilly.

Turning slowly, as if he were drugged or in a dream,
he turned off the burner and made a cup of instant
coffee. He stopped himself just before he added milk
and sugar.

*What the hell's wrong with me? I never use milk and
sugar!*

Trembling slightly, he put the rapidly cooling slices
of toast onto a plate, spread a thin coating of jelly over
them, and sat down at the kitchen table. A cold, hard
knot was tightening in his stomach, dulling whatever
appetite he might have had, but he forced himself to
take a bite of the toast, knowing he probably wouldn't
eat again until some time in the afternoon . . . not until
after the funeral.

As he chewed, the sound of toast crunching loudly
in his ears, he kept shifting his eyes back and forth,
looking around the room and out the windows at the
rain-soaked driveway and beyond, where the slick,
black ribbon of road disappeared around the curve.
The view filled him with somber memories of his childhood—of all the times he had walked, run, or ridden
his bike down that road, off to school or to meet up
with his friends. The fleeting memories seemed so
vague, so distant they felt like they were from another
lifetime. He acknowledged that they probably were.
He knew he certainly wasn't the same person who had
lived that life. If he could somehow go back in time
and encounter himself as he had been while growing
up in this house, he probably wouldn't even recognize
himself. He had lived so long in Colorado that he was

positive he no longer had a single thing in common
with the person he had once been.

Now that Judy was dead, his last link with his childhood here in Maine was gone, too. Whoever he had
once been, and anything he might have felt or done or
thought, was just as dead and gone as she was.

He sighed, trying not to think of the more recent
times spent in this house after his parents had died, of
the times he had never witnessed when Judy was living
here, either alone or with one of her two husbands who
were God-only-knows-where now. He couldn't even
begin to get a grasp on what Judy's life must have been
like—her hopes, her dreams, her frustrations, and her
fears. But now, any opportunity to share any of that
with her had slipped away and was gone . . .

Forever.

The rain and lowering clouds set a perfect mood. A
cold, lonely ache filled Jeff's chest when he tried once
again to grasp the fact that his sister was gone . . . truly
gone . . .

Forever!

Jeff shivered and hugged his shoulders.

She's gone, that is, whispered a tiny voice inside his
head, *unless she's still lurking around here somewhere in
the house. Maybe it was her ghost that trashed the
kitchen and left that note for you?*

Jeff was so absorbed by his own musings that he
hardly responded to the intruding thought. It was
there; he considered it; and then he let it go.

Yes, said a voice which he recognized as his own,
*that's all it is; that's all they ever are—just intruding
thoughts. I can pretend all I want that they sound like
someone else, like different voices talking inside my
head, but after eight years of therapy, I finally know the
truth . . . I know they're just different aspects of my own
mind, my own personality, trying to assert themselves.*

Realizing he had been lost in thought, he took a sip

of his cooling coffee, wincing at its bitterness. Maybe milk and sugar would have made it better today. After one more bite of toast, he dumped what was left of his breakfast into the sink and ran the water to flush it down the garbage disposal. Then he rinsed out his cup and juice glass, stacked them in the dish drainer beside the sink, and went upstairs to finish getting ready. He went to the bathroom, combed his hair, and brushed his teeth, then came back downstairs.

Glancing at his watch, he knew if he left for the funeral home now, he would still arrive much too early, but there was nothing else to do. Maybe on the way to South Portland he could stop at the Quik-Pik Store where Cove Variety used to be and buy a morning newspaper. He could wait in the parking lot a while and read, at least until the minister showed up. He laughed softly to himself, wondering if Reverend Livingstone might be so senile he would forget all about the funeral today and decide that it didn't really matter. Jeff realized he was nervous about facing the service and burial, but he braced himself, knowing that whatever happened, he would have to see it through to the end. Within a few hours, after Judy was buried, he would simply have to get on with doing whatever else he had to do to settle her affairs as soon as possible so he could get back home.

Back home . . .

The thought made the lonely ache inside him grow even worse. Checking his watch, he guessed that Sally was already at work and Robin was at school, but then he realized that it was still only around seven o'clock back home. They were probably just getting up, fixing breakfast, and getting dressed for the day.

Lucky them, he thought. After all, they didn't have to face a funeral today!

"Jesus," Jeff muttered, shivering as he shrugged his arms into his overcoat. He patted his hip pocket to make sure his wallet was there, then walked out into the breezeway, shutting the side door behind him. He jiggled the doorknob several times to make sure it was locked. Then, gripping his keys tightly in one hand and pulling his collar up around his neck with the other, he hunched over and ran out into the storm and down to his rental car. Cold needles of rain stung his face, and he was soaking wet by the time he got the car door unlocked and slid in behind the steering wheel. He looked in the rearview mirror and stared at his hair, plastered against his pale forehead. Too bad he had forgotten to check for an umbrella in Judy's house, he thought, but he wasn't going back now.

After he had started up the car, before he shifted it into gear, he suddenly froze.

There was a . . . a *feeling* about the car, something about it that bothered him. His eyes shifted back and forth. His ears echoed with the drumming of the rain on the roof. It was almost like he could sense another presence in the car with him.

He turned quickly and looked into the backseat, but it was empty. A shiver gripped the back of his neck. He glanced at the door on the passenger's side and realized that it was unlocked.

How could he be so careless? he wondered, but then his gaze shifted downward, and he saw something else. There was a wet spot on the floor in front of the passenger's seat. Dirt and dead leaves floated in the small puddle of water, and the longer Jeff stared at it, the more it looked like a footprint—a fresh footprint, as though someone who had just been out in the rain had been sitting in the seat beside him.

"Jesus," Jeff whispered. His grip tightened on the steering wheel until it hurt.

He looked at the wet spot again, trying to convince himself that there was just a leak on that side of the car; that it only *looked* like a footprint. Who would be out here, sitting in his car just for the hell of it on a day like this?

It was crazy.

Forcing any such speculations out of his mind, he shifted into gear and started backing down the driveway.

Driving more slowly than usual, his gaze shifting now and then to the wet spot on the floor, he headed down Long Shore Drive toward the center of town and turned right onto Main Street.

Other than a passing town police cruiser, gleaming black and slick-looking in the rain, and a battered, rust-bucket pickup truck that was parked outside of Donut-Haven, the town was deserted. The windows of the local businesses were all dark, their shades drawn, and there wasn't a single person on the street. Of course, who would be out walking around on a day like this?

For some reason, seeing the town this way made Jeff think about taking the long way around to the funeral home in South Portland. He had plenty of time to kill, so why not? What better day would there be to drive around the old neighborhood and stir up more memories of his childhood? After today, as far as he was concerned, he was leaving all of this behind forever.

But when the choice was there, either to turn right onto Pleasant Hill Road or left on Route 77 and head out to Scarborough and Prout's Neck, he turned right onto Pleasant Hill Road, forgetting all about his plan to pick up a morning newspaper at the Quik-Pik. He drove straight to Marcigliano's and pulled into the parking lot a little bit after nine o'clock.

The smell of flowers almost overwhelmed Jeff as soon as he stepped into the entryway of the funeral home. John Marcigliano, the undertaker, must have seen him pull into the driveway because he met Jeff at the door, opening it for him before he had a chance to ring the doorbell. John was a tall, rather gaunt man with thinning white hair which he combed straight back. His sparkling blue eyes and wide smile seemed a little bit out of character for an undertaker. He was wearing a dark blue, pin-striped suit with a small white carnation pinned to the left lapel. His grip felt soft and dry as he and Jeff shook hands.

"Good morning, Mr. Wagner," John said, bowing slightly.

He held the door open for Jeff as he hustled in out of the rain.

"Actually, it's quite a terrible morning," Jeff said. Stamping his feet and shaking his head as he shrugged out of his dripping overcoat, he turned to put it on a hanger in the closet. With a hand gesture and a nod of his head, John indicated the guest book on the small wooden stand by the door.

"If you would like," he said softly, "you can sign the guest book."

After a moment's hesitation, Jeff signed his name on the top line. Remaining respectfully quiet, John directed Jeff down the carpeted hallway and into the main funeral parlor.

The instant he walked into the dimly lit room and saw Judy's casket at the far end, Jeff felt momentarily disoriented. His legs almost gave out on him, and for several seconds all he could do was stand there in the doorway, staring ahead and desperately trying to catch his breath.

He gripped one wrist tightly, holding his hands in front of him, and bowed his head slightly, but his gaze was drawn irresistibly to the open casket at the far end of the room. It was illuminated by a diffused glow of light through the curtained windows. At this distance, the light made Judy's face look as pale and hard as polished marble. He flashed on the image of Sleeping Beauty, asleep in her crystal casket.

Surrounding the coffin were bouquets and garlands of flowers, many of them, no doubt, from Judy's friends and coworkers at UNUM. Sally had told him that she and Robin were going to send flowers, too. Soft strains of organ music wafted from the small speakers that were strategically placed on the walls on both sides of the room. At times the music was almost drowned out by the hissing rattle of wind-driven rain against the windows. To one side of the casket stood a small, dark wooden podium.

Jeff glanced over at the undertaker, feeling a near desperate need to say something but having absolutely no idea what. After hesitating a moment or two and trying his best to absorb the reality of what he was looking at, he started walking slowly down the center aisle toward the casket. Pausing a few feet away from it, he locked his hands in a tight, prayerful grip and looked down at his sister's immobile face. Her slack, emotionless expression looked like a painted mask, but as he stared at her, he was almost positive that, once or twice, he saw her chest stir as she took a shallow breath. The illusion was terrifying.

Maybe she's not dead! whispered a grating voice inside his head. *Maybe she isn't dead at all, and this has all been a put-on, a huge, sick, practical joke . . . all at your expense!*

"No . . . ," Jeff whispered, his voice hitching in his chest.

He knew she couldn't still be alive. She was *dead*— really *dead!*

Tears welled up within him, stinging his eyes, and all he could think about as he stared down at his sister's frozen expression was how many times he had looked at her face while she was alive . . . how many times he had watched as she had laughed or cried or talked with him while they were growing up. She had been his older sister, two years older than he, so—sure, a lot of times when they were young they had made it a point to ignore each other—especially, Jeff thought with a guilty twisting in his gut, considering what they had *done* together. As they got older and were in high school, there had been conflicts, and they had both done and said things that had hurt the other. But as they entered adulthood, especially after losing their parents, there had always been a strong bond of love and trust between them. After all, when they were growing up and even as adults, more often than not they had been the only person either one of them ever had for love and trust and affection.

Cold, tightening pressure filled Jeff's gut as his mind churned, trying desperately to grasp the one basic, simple fact that he had to accept now.

Judy was dead.

Dead!

It was all over for her.

Never again would she smile or laugh or cry or talk or do *anything* with him or anyone else!

She was gone from his life . . . *forever!*

"She. . . . You did an excellent job," Jeff finally said in a halting, raw whisper as he turned toward John.

The undertaker was standing a respectful step or two behind Jeff, his hands clasped solemnly in front of him as though in prayer. It was impossible for Jeff to make eye contact with him, but he caught the man's acknowledging nod.

"Thank you very much," John said softly.

He paused, and the silence in the room was broken only by the faint music and the muffled sounds of the storm outside.

"It's still quite early yet, Mr. Wagner. If you would like, you can wait in the greeting room. I could bring you some coffee and a Danish."

Biting his lower lip, Jeff shook his head sharply.

"No . . . no, thank you. I . . ."

He glanced behind him at the rows of padded chairs, all lined up in a semicircle that faced the polished casket and podium.

"I . . . I think I'd just as soon sit here for a little while, if you don't mind. I-I'd appreciate some time alone with . . . her, if that's all right."

"Certainly, Mr. Wagner," the undertaker said, tactfully ignoring Jeff's tortured emotions.

As the undertaker turned and walked away, his shoes whispering on the thick-pile carpet, Jeff slid into the front-row aisle seat on the right-hand side. Clasping his hands together and leaning forward on his knees, he took a shuddering breath and stared wide-eyed at Judy's face. She looked asleep, not dead. After a while, Jeff closed his eyes tightly and tried desperately to focus his thoughts, but time and again, he couldn't stop himself from opening his eyes and looking at his sister.

"I can't believe it! I can't believe you're dead! You're really dead!" he repeated softly to himself, his voice punctuated by sniffles.

Once or twice, he had the brief impression again— *and that's all it is,* he told himself, *just an impression!*— that she was still breathing. He glanced at his watch and saw that it was still more than an hour before the funeral service was scheduled to begin, but he didn't know what else to do except sit there and think sad thoughts, stewing in his grief.

Yes, grief and regret . . . regrets that, in spite of how he tried to convince himself, he still could have done *something* more to help her. He should have been able to prevent her from doing what she had done.

That is, if she even really did it, the voice whispered close to his ear. He jerked in his chair and turned around to see if someone was standing beside him. Then he looked back at his sister's corpse.

After all, the voice continued, rustling like dry leaves in the gutter, *you don't know—for a fact—that she really killed herself, now, do you? . . . Well? Do you?*

No matter which direction Jeff looked, the voice seemed to whisper in his other ear.

"No," he said, "but I—yes! Yes, goddamn it, I *do!*"

Jeff kept his voice low and tight. He was fairly certain the undertaker had left the room and neither he nor anyone else was close enough to overhear him, but he turned around and looked at the back of the room just to be sure.

"That's what that detective, Ray Foster, told me," he said, turning back around. "She committed *suicide!* Do you hear me? So I know *she* did it!"

As he was talking, his gaze came back to Judy's face. He stared at her until the darkness on the fringe of his vision began to vibrate and telescope inward.

Oh, come on, man! I mean, stop kidding yourself, will you? said the voice. *You don't know that for a fact! I mean—Christ, think about that detective. He was just a kid! He was probably having his nose wiped and his diapers changed back when you were in high school, for Christ's sake. What the fuck would he know?*

Jeff squeezed his eyes tightly shut for a moment, forcing out tears that ran, warm and slick, down his face.

"She did it, okay?" he said under his breath, his voice trembling with repressed tension. He clenched his fists tightly and punched his thighs hard enough to sting. "Jesus Christ, she *did* it, and there's *nothing* anyone can do to change that, so just leave me the Christ alone!"

The cloying atmosphere of the room, the hissing of rain on the windows, and the sonorous organ music all worked to dull Jeff's overwrought senses. After three nights of lousy sleep and two days of running around town, making sure all the details for Judy's funeral were covered, he felt so emotionally and physically wrung out that he started to drift off to sleep. Slouching in his chair with his eyes closed, he lost all sense of his body as he floated on a soft, warm cushion of air. His mind shuffled lazily through many of the memories he had of his sister, but he felt so relaxed now that he didn't even react when faint, arguing voices began to whisper inside his head.

"Maybe you can finally admit it now, huh? What do you say?"

"Admit it? . . . Admit what?"

"Admit that you still wanted to fuck her, that you want to fuck Judy! Come on, Jeff, I mean, maybe you can even come around to admitting that you came back to Maine that first time because you thought, you were hoping you might get another chance to do it with her again! Ain't that so?"

"That's bullshit! I came back home because I—I wanted to help her."

"Oh, yeah, right. You really crack me up, you know that?"

"I'm serious. She needed help, and I wanted to help her. I *had* to help her, for Christ's sake! She was my sister!"

"She was more than a sister to you. Come on, man. Admit it. You know you wanted to—"

"That's bullshit, and you know it!"

"Hey, okay. Fine . . . fine. Go ahead and pretend all you want, but *I* know the truth. I know how much you wanted to put it to her just one more time. Hell, I even know that you're not even sure if you did it right the first time—you know, back when you were kids. I know you wanted to fuck her one more time, just to make sure."

"Why don't you just shut the fuck up?"

"Hey, there's no need to get all hostile about it, all right? I'm just trying to help you work this all out, okay? Trust me on this, Jeff. I know what I'm talking about."

"The hell you do! *I* happen to know that you're full of shit, so why don't you just fuck off and leave me alone?"

"Sure . . . fine. Hey, I know when I'm not wanted. No hard feelings, I hope."

"Go fuck yourself!"

"Well, if you won't or can't admit it even to yourself, how the hell am I supposed to help you? Huh? I just hope sometime later, you know, if things really turn to shit, you don't blame me for not trying."

"Don't worry, I won't! What the hell can happen that's worse than *this?*"

"I don't think you want to know. I don't think you could handle it."

"Handle what? Come on, tell me! . . . Hey, are you still here? Come on, answer me! If you know something, tell me! *Tell me!*"

A subtle sense of motion behind him drew Jeff's attention back.

For an instant, he felt as though he were falling backwards, his body spinning head over heels. With a strangled shout, he sat up straight in his chair, his body scrambling as though he were trying to keep his balance.

His eyes snapped open, but it took a heartbeat or two for him to remember where he was. Glancing at his wristwatch, he was shocked to see that—somehow—more than an hour had slipped by. Gasping

with surprise, he turned in his chair and looked toward
the back of the room where a small crowd of people,
all of them dressed in dark suits and dresses, was mill-
ing about. He recognized none of them. When a few
entered the funeral parlor, they moved with a shy
skittishness that reminded Jeff of the way wary deer
approach an open glade.

Jeff sat half-turned in his seat, watching the people
from the corner of his eye. He figured they must be
friends of Judy's whom he had never met, portions of
her life he would never know. He was unsure whether
or not he should get up and go introduce himself to
any of them. He wondered if Vera was among them,
but he realized that he wouldn't recognize her if she
was.

Why hadn't he made arrangements to meet with her
some time before the funeral? he wondered. He had
thought of it quite a few times. He hadn't, using the
excuse that he wanted to keep his own grief private,
but now he wasn't so sure.

Sighing, he started to stand, but then saw John Marcigliano step forward and greet each of the guests with
a formal handshake. He seemed to know one or two of
them. With a graceful arm gesture, he indicated that
they could seat themselves wherever they pleased.
Jeff's neck was prickling with heat as he turned back
around, his gaze locking on the face of his dead sister.

"Jesus," he sighed and closed his eyes again, fer-
vently wishing that all of this would be over soon. One
thing he was glad of now was that he had arranged for
a private burial in Pine Grove Cemetery in South Portland after the service—just him, the minister, the undertaker . . . and Judy.

Jeff lost track of the time as he sat there, staring
sightlessly ahead and only dimly aware of the activity
that shifted around him. He sensed that the room was
slowly filling up with people as they shuffled down the

aisle and chose where to sit after drifting like phantoms past the coffin and gazing down at Judy. A few of the visitors made brief eye contact with him and, obviously guessing that he must be her brother, bowed their heads in sympathy, but he spoke to no one until he felt a light tap on his shoulder.

He was expecting to see either John Marcigliano or the minister when he turned around. When he found himself face-to-face with someone else, he let out a surprised gasp that echoed in the restrained silence of the room. A few people looked over at him in surprise.

"Oh my God!" Jeff said, unable to contain his sudden shout as a knife-edged shiver ran up his back. "Aunt Mildred . . . Uncle Kirby."

Jeff could see right away that both his aunt and uncle had aged a great deal since he had last seen them, Kirby in particular, but he immediately recognized both of them. The instant familiarity sent a tremor of fear through him.

Kirby was wearing a tattered gray herringbone jacket, baggy dark pants, an ill-knotted black necktie, and what had once been a white dress shirt but which now had an aged, yellowish tinge to it. His white hair was combed to one side, the thin wisps barely covering the peeling, sunburned top of his bald head. Mildred was wearing a slouchy, dark blue dress that was decades out of style. She clutched her purse to her side as though expecting someone to try to snatch it.

While Kirby looked to be about the same build as Jeff remembered, Mildred seemed to have gained quite a bit of weight. Her dark hair, which had once been as black as a raven's wing, was now shot through with white highlights. It was done up in a tight bun that made her look like a schoolmarm. Their seamed faces looked weathered and cracked with age. A quick calculation made Jeff realize he was taller than either of them, but there was something about them, their presence that made him feel much smaller, like he was still a ten-year-old boy looking up at them.

Jeff also realized one other thing. He was terrified of both of them!

Kirby smiled at him, exposing a row of brown-stained, crooked teeth. His breath reeked of onions and stale tobacco.

"Well, young fella," he said in a grating whisper. "I certainly am surprised as all get-out to see *you* here. I hadn't heard anythin' 'bout you bein' back in town."

For only a moment, he held his hand out for Jeff to shake, but Jeff didn't turn around far enough in his chair to grab hold of it, so Kirby let it drop to his side. Jeff merely nodded, hoping that his surprise didn't register *too* much on his face.

"I—umm, no, I just got in the other night," Jeff said, horribly aware of how forced his voice sounded. "I've been so damned busy, I haven't really even had a chance to call you yet."

"Watch your language there, boy," Kirby snapped. His face darkened so suddenly it sent a ripple of fear racing through Jeff.

"Sorry," Jeff said, not even sure what offensive word he had used. What difference did it make to Kirby, anyway? It was *his* sister they were here to bury, so he could use whatever language he wanted.

"It's so terribly sad that we have to meet on an occasion like this," Mildred said, lowering her eyes for a moment. Her voice sounded respectful, but Jeff instantly detected its hard edge, which, as he remembered, always lurked just below the surface as if what she *really* wanted to do was scold him for not being in touch. He was glad she didn't lean forward, expecting a hug and a kiss from him.

Jeff's eyes danced from side to side as he looked back and forth between his aunt and uncle. He tried to speak, but words failed him entirely. He couldn't stop

the numbing rushes of chills that were wiggling like
tiny snakes up his backbone. He suddenly realized that
he had been holding his breath, so he let it out in a
long, slow whoosh.

"It's not the *Lord's* work, I can tell you *that* much,"
Kirby said, staring ahead at Judy and shaking his
head. "What she did, it was a sin in the eyes of the
Lord. It's a terrible shame when family can't be laid to
rest with a proper service in a church."

His voice was low, but it rang with an angry author-
ity that buzzed like a whirring saw blade in Jeff's ears
and made him cringe.

No, it sure as hell wasn't the Lord's work, Jeff wanted
to say. *She did it all on her own, and no God—of yours
or anyone else's—is going to judge her for what she did!*

Instead, he bit down on his lower lip and remained
silent.

Funerals were supposed to be a time of healing, for
a family to pull together. Jeff knew that he should
invite Kirby and Mildred—Judy's only other surviv-
ing relatives—to sit in the front row with him, but
there was no way he wanted to sit beside either one of
them. Although he felt a bit guilty that he hadn't
contacted them as soon as he had arrived in Cape
Higgins, the truth was, he had hardly even thought
about them. When he did, he wanted to push the
memory back into a dark corner of his mind. The
shock of seeing them now, so unexpectedly, had almost been too much for him. Just hearing the stern,
angry tone of Kirby's voice stirred long-buried memories in Jeff . . . things he didn't even want to think
about.

Yeah, maybe I should have called them, he thought,
but he knew there was no way he ever would have!

Just like everything else about Cape Higgins, Aunt
Mildred and Uncle Kirby were something else that he

wanted to push out of his mind and forget about
. . . *forever!*

He twisted back around in his seat and faced the
front of the room, but it still felt as though Kirby's
piercing stare was fixed on the back of his head. He
suspected that his aunt and uncle were wondering why
he didn't ask them to sit with him, but he didn't care.

*Hell, they should know why you don't want to see
them, shouldn't they?* said a clear voice inside his head.
*Even if you don't want to think about it . . . I mean, if
ANYONE should know, THEY should, don't you think?*

"Do you mind if we sit next to you?"

The soft tone of a woman's voice—certainly not
Mildred's—rang like a bell in Jeff's ears, making him
jump. Turning around quickly and looking up, he
couldn't disguise the flood of relief he felt when he saw
Katherine and Danny standing in the aisle beside his
chair.

"Yes . . . sure . . . please do," Jeff said, half-standing
as they walked in front of him and sat down in the
seats next to him, Judy beside him and Danny next to
her.

Well, Jeff thought, feeling a small measure of gloating satisfaction. *I guess that takes care of worrying
about Kirby and Mildred for now!*

He thought Katherine looked absolutely stunning,
dressed as she was in a somber, dark gray outfit. Her
hair hung loosely to her shoulders, framing her narrow
face. She had used only a small amount of makeup—
nothing dramatic or overdone, just a light blush of
color on her cheeks and lips, and a tasteful hint of eye
shadow that looked completely natural in the dim
light of the room.

Danny, on the other hand, looked like toothpaste
being squeezed out of a tube. His suit coat was at least
one size too small for him. It showed an inch or two
of skinny wrist at each cuff. He was wearing high-

water pants and a red-and-blue polka-dotted clip-on tie that made his shirt collar look like it was strangling him. His face was several shades paler than Jeff remembered it from the other night. Maybe this was his first funeral.

"I—uh . . . Gee, I wasn't expecting to see you here," Jeff said. He unconsciously reached out and took hold of her hand, giving it a gentle squeeze. His first impulse was to give her a kiss on the cheek, but he quickly checked that urge.

Katherine smiled at him, but a lingering trace of sadness clouded her eyes as she squared her shoulders and smoothed her dress. She shivered when she glanced over at Judy in the open casket.

"I . . . I hadn't planned to come, but I thought I would . . . in case you needed some support," she whispered, leaning so close to Jeff that he could feel the warm wash of her breath against his cheek. "It was just something I felt I *had* to do."

A whiff of floral perfume tickled Jeff's nostrils. He tried to control his reaction but felt himself getting an erection in spite of himself.

"Yeah, thanks," he said, shifting uncomfortably in his seat, "but I don't think Danny should have to miss any time at school just to be here." He leaned forward and regarded the boy for a moment, struck by how much he reminded him of himself at that age. "He doesn't look like a happy camper."

It was obvious that, given the choice, Danny would have chosen school over a funeral.

"Well," Katherine said, still whispering and leaning closer to Jeff, "you know, ever since Doug left us, we've had to be each other's mutual support system."

"Doug?" Jeff said, thinking he sounded completely stupid.

"Yeah, Doug. My husband," Katherine replied. *"Ex*-husband, I should say. The son of a bitch left us high and dry about two years ago. Took off with some little underaged bimbo he'd met in some bar somewhere."

"I see," Jeff said, nodding his head and still thinking he sounded absolutely foolish.

Why, he wondered, did this piece of information make him feel a sudden rush of hopefulness? It wasn't as though he was looking for or even thinking that he had any kind of possibility of rekindling his romance with her. That had been ages ago. Besides, he didn't even *want* to start something with her. He was a happily married man with a daughter of his own back home in Denver. What the hell was he even thinking?

He had his hand on his leg, and Katherine slipped her hand under it. He automatically gave her another reassuring squeeze that sent a warm thrill racing through him. He couldn't get over how comfortable it was to have her here beside him. It was dizzying how completely natural it felt to be holding her hand again, as though the twenty or so years since he had last touched her had never happened. In some deep, undeniable way, he felt as though maybe they *did* still belong together.

And what if everything—absolutely *everything*—he had done with his life since high school had all been a big mistake?

He realized that what he was feeling was no doubt a result of the sadness and grief generated from his sister's funeral. But, he told himself, one thing he would never forget was that Katherine had been there for him when he had needed *someone* and there had been no one else around that he could trust.

"So tell me, Jeff. 'S this your wife? I don't believe we've ever met."

The grating tone of Kirby's voice from behind him sent another shiver racing through Jeff. Turning halfway around again, he looked at his uncle and shook his head in firm denial.

"No, this is a good friend of mine. Katherine—ah, Katherine Foster."

Jeff realized with a sudden panic that he didn't know Katherine's married name, but he decided not to worry about it—she probably decided to use her maiden name after the breakup. He was positive Kirby must have met her at some time or other back when they were high-school sweethearts, or he certainly must have seen her around town at some point. It seemed unlikely that they had never met, but he appeared not to recognize her face or name.

"Katherine, this is my uncle, Kirby Wagner, and his wife, Mildred. This is Katherine's son, Danny."

"I'm pleased to meet you . . . both of you," Katherine said, smiling brightly as she shook hands with Kirby and nodded a greeting to Mildred. Danny looked shyly at the two people sitting behind him and then quickly looked away.

Both Mildred and Kirby regarded Katherine with steady, unfriendly stares.

"So then, your wife didn't come back East with ya, huh?" Kirby said, gripping the back of Jeff's chair and leaning forward as though he were hard of hearing. For a moment, the stale smell of his breath overpowered the redolent aroma of the flowers and Katherine's perfume.

"Uh, no," Jeff said, shaking his head and pulling back from his uncle. "She—ah, she had to stay at home because of her job."

It wasn't exactly the truth, but what did he care?

"I see, I see," Kirby replied, nodding his head and making no attempt to hide the glimmer of suspicion in his narrowed eyes. Realizing that Kirby was no doubt suspicious of exactly what he had been thinking a moment ago, Jeff blushed and shifted uneasily in his

chair again. A rush of movement beside him drew his
attention. He looked to his left just as Reverend Livingstone was walking up the aisle toward him.

Jeff stood up and shook hands with the minister.
After speaking with him briefly, Reverend Livingstone
walked up to the podium, opened a hymnal, and
began the funeral service. In keeping with Jeff's understanding that Judy hadn't been an active church mem-
ber, the service was brief. A woman from the Congregational Church choir sang "Nearer My God to
Thee," and then, after a brief eulogy, Reverend Livingstone offered a prayer and then asked the gathering
to recite with him Psalm 23 and the Lord's Prayer.

Throughout the service, Jeff tried to keep his mind
focused on everything that was being said, but the
whole time he could sense, he could *feel* Kirby's piercing gaze, boring like a white-hot drill into the back of
his head. He felt extremely uncomfortable, and several
times Katherine, mistaking his reaction for a flood of
overwhelming emotion, took his hand and gave it a
reassuring squeeze. Every time, her touch sent a warm,
shimmering thrill of heat through Jeff.

Against his will, he found himself actually fantasiz-
ing that Katherine *was* his wife, and that Danny was
his son; that he had never moved away from Cape
Higgins to go to college; and that for the last however
many years, the three of them had lived happily, going
about their lives in this quiet, quaint Maine seacoast
town. Comforting thoughts like this almost compen-
sated for the withering glances he knew were being
directed at him behind his back from his uncle and, no
doubt, his aunt.

All it did was give him another reason to hope to
God that this would all be over soon.

*   *   *

The rain had started to let up and was not much more than a light drizzle when Jeff drove into the Pine Grove Cemetery. He parked his car several feet behind the hearse, leaving enough room so they could get the back door of the hearse open. Reverend Livingstone pulled up and parked a little too close behind Jeff, making him feel uncomfortable, boxed in. The exhaust from the idling hearse's tailpipe spiraled into the air like a miniature tornado. Thin fingers of mist drifted like smoke between the gravestones and under the surrounding trees.

Sighing heavily, Jeff turned off the engine and sat there for a few seconds, trying to collect himself. His grip tightened painfully on the steering wheel, and his breath came in fast, shallow gulps that sent sharp twinges of pain through his chest. He'd been running the car's heater, but as soon as the engine was turned off, a damp, bone-deep chill started working its way into the car. It grabbed him by the back of the neck and sent shivers down to the base of his spine. Moisture collected on the windshield and ran down in thin streams. He looked over at the floor in front of the passenger's seat, but was no longer sure exactly what he was looking for.

Well, Jeff thought, *I guess this is it!*

The thought was like a ball of ice that was slowly expanding in the center of his head and steadily building up pressure. He felt too numb to do anything more than just sit there and watch in stunned silence as the pallbearers from the funeral home hefted Judy's casket out of the back of the hearse and carried it over to the canopied graveside. John Marcigliano and one of his helpers quickly shuttled back and forth, carrying wreaths and bouquets which they laid beside the open grave. Outside in the cold and damp, the flowers already looked wilted, their colors drab and fading.

As soon as he was as collected as he thought he

would ever be, Jeff snapped open the car door and walked slowly over to the graveside. His gaze shifted to the white marble tombstone that marked his mother's and father's graves.

JOHN HARRISON WAGNER August 11, 1932–
May 5, 1978
MARGARET HOLDER WAGNER September 2,
1937–May 5, 1978

Standing with folded hands, Jeff shifted his gaze and stared blankly at the dark, polished wood of Judy's coffin. Moisture was collecting on it, beading up like tiny silver drops of spilled mercury. Jeff caught a glimpse down into the cement-lined crypt and shivered when he tried to imagine the impenetrable cold and darkness that was waiting for Judy down there.

And what's she looking at now, huh? whispered a taunting voice deep within his mind. *What's it like for her, lying there in her coffin, staring up at that solid wall of eternal blackness? Christ, just imagine that cold . . . the darkness . . . the silence!*

So lost was he in his own thoughts that he didn't even notice that Reverend Livingstone had walked up beside him until the minister spoke.

"Would you like me to say a prayer now?" he asked, his voice sounding almost strangled by age and the raw weather.

The voice speaking so suddenly beside him startled Jeff and made him jump. He turned and looked at the minister, then shook his head.

"No, I—uh, I think just a moment of silence . . . for now," he said softly.

"Whatever you'd like," Reverend Livingstone said, looking slightly disappointed. He nodded and took a respectful step away from Jeff.

While Jeff stood there, staring into his sister's grave,

the clouds overhead shifted and darkened once again. After a few seconds, a heavy rain began to fall with a loud patter. It bounced like bullets off the top of the coffin. Jeff thought he heard a faint squeak of brakes as a car pulled to a stop somewhere nearby, but he didn't turn to look. The rain hissed as it swept in a gray sheet across the gently rolling expanse of the cemetery, but Jeff paid no heed to it. He just stood there, feeling and listening to the soft splatter of rain on his head and shoulders, and feeling a cold twisting of misery in the pit of his stomach. Cold streams of water ran down his neck, making him shiver, but he made no move to go back to his car to get out of the rain.

What did it matter how long he stood here? This was it. This was the end of the line for Judy.

And why am I still alive? he wondered. *Why can I still feel the rain on my face and the cold wind blowing at my back, but Judy can't?*

She can't, and she never will again! Jeff thought, not even sure if it was his own mental voice or someone else's.

He was almost sick with grief and guilt and he couldn't help but think—again—that there must have been *something* he could have done to prevent all of this.

If only he had known what!

But then again, whispered a voice inside his head, *maybe there was nothing you could do! Maybe this was fated ever since the two of you did what you did!*

Jeff shook his head from side to side, feeling a salty sting in his eyes. He sensed a shifting of motion beside him and heard the squishy sound of footsteps on the soggy ground. He was surprised when the rain was suddenly cut off as someone held an umbrella over his head. Wiping raindrops and tears from his face with the flats of his hands, he turned and looked to one side.

He was expecting to see either John Marcigliano or else the minister, and was surprised to see Katherine standing there, holding an umbrella over his head. Glancing down at the cars, he saw Danny's face, as pale as a full moon, staring up at him from the parked car.

"I . . . ," He started to say, but his throat closed off with a sharp click, and he let whatever he had been about to say fade away.

He raised one hand slowly and took hold of the shaft of the umbrella, the side of his hand pressing against Katherine's hand. The tingling warmth he felt from her living hand spread like a brushfire up his arm and into his chest. He took a deep, shuddering breath and looked at her again. With tears streaming down his face, he forced himself to smile.

"Thanks," he said, his voice no more than a raw croak that sounded like a dying man, gasping for his last breath.

"Thanks for . . . being here."

Chapter Fifteen
Graffiti

As much as he would have liked to go, Jeff declined Katherine's offer for him to come over to her house for lunch. He seriously considered it, and she repeated the offer enough times so he knew she really meant it, but he felt so drained by the morning's events that all he wanted to do was go back to Judy's house, take another shower and a couple of aspirin, and lie down for a while. He didn't have a bad headache—not yet, but he could feel one coming on, building up strength like a thunderstorm just below the horizon.

The minister and undertaker each expressed their condolences to Jeff before leaving, but Jeff and Katherine stayed behind at the cemetery, huddling beneath her umbrella as the rain beat down on them. Danny waited in the car, his pale face looking wraithlike through the misted car window.

Jeff and Katherine said very little as they both stared thoughtfully at the flower-covered grave. Finally, once he thought he was ready to leave, Jeff turned to Katherine and gave her a bracing hug.

"Thanks . . . again," he said, speaking loud to be

heard above the snapping sound of rain on the umbrella. "For . . . for being here."

Katherine looked at him, smiled weakly, and nodded.

After an awkward moment staring at each other, Jeff leaned forward and gave her a lingering kiss, full on the lips. He knew damned well that both of them had been through a lot of changes over the years, too many changes for either of them to have any clue about the other, but he couldn't help but think how good, how natural it felt to be holding her in his arms once again. She felt so . . . so *different* from Sally, and as much as he didn't want it to happen, he felt himself getting an erection just by touching her. He tried not to imagine what might happen if he *did* take her up on her offer to go back to her house.

Go ahead, whispered a teasing voice in the back of his mind. *You know you want to . . . and who the hell's ever going to know, huh?*

After saying goodbye and repeating his vague promise that they would get together before he went back to Colorado, he got into his car and drove back to Cape Higgins alone. He knew it would take a long time—maybe the rest of his life—for the reality of everything he had just been through to sink in, but he also knew that he just had to keep moving ahead and try to accept it.

Judy was dead . . . dead and buried, and there wasn't a damned thing he could do about it!

There was a cold emptiness in his life; and he knew no matter what else ever happened to him, that emptiness would *never* be entirely filled.

Tears were running from his eyes, blurring his vision as he drove back through town and turned onto Long Shore Drive. The hollow, lonely ache in his gut got even worse when he pulled into the driveway and parked his car at the top of the driveway, close to the garage door. The rain was still coming down hard, its huge drops sounding almost like hail as they ricocheted off the car's roof and hood. He turned off the ignition and was about to get out and make a dash for the house, but he slumped back in his seat for a moment and, closing his eyes, listened to the voice in his head.

You're a goddamned fool for not going back to her house with her!

No, it wasn't like that . . . I didn't want to do anything! Besides, even if we both—you know, both wanted to . . to do something, how could we with her kid around?

No, I don't mean that, for Christ's sake! I mean just to have time to spend with someone! Shit, it's not good, you spending all your time alone like this!

I don't mind . . . Honest, I can handle it.

Yeah, right!

When Jeff opened his eyes and glanced up at the house, he felt a cold shock when he saw that the side door was hanging open. Fitful gusts of rain-laden wind were swinging it slowly back and forth, slamming it against the house. Although he couldn't hear it, he could easily imagine the steady teeth-grinding creak made by the rusted hinges and the gunshot loud bang.

"Oh, shit," Jeff muttered, unable to move for several seconds as he wiped the tears from his eyes and stared long and hard at the door. He glanced quickly at his watch, wondering how long he had been sitting out here.

He was absolutely positive he had locked the door on his way out this morning. He had even checked it a few times before leaving.

Hadn't he?

Now he wasn't so sure.

Maybe because the sills were swollen from the rain, the door hadn't locked behind him but had only gotten stuck. Maybe he had left the house just *thinking* he had locked the door, and while he was gone, the wind had blown it open.

That was most likely what had happened, but seeing the door open made him feel inexplicably nervous. His body tingled with tension as he stepped out of the car, slammed the car door shut, and slowly, unmindful of the steady downpour, started up the walkway toward the side door. He clenched his fists so tightly at his sides that the palms of his hands hurt all the way up to his elbows. Leaning cautiously forward into the breezeway, he peered into the house. His nostrils flared as though sniffing the air for danger.

"Shit," he muttered when he saw that the other door was open, too. Looking down at the floor, he saw muddy footprints leading into the kitchen.

"Oh, *Jesus!*"

He glanced around inside the breezeway, hoping to find something—anything—he could use as a weapon in case the intruder was still inside the house, but there was nothing. Gripping his key ring so two keys protruded from between his knuckles, he leaned cautiously into the house, keeping his back against the wall. Every muscle in his body was tensed and ready to respond at the slightest indication of danger.

What he saw in the kitchen sent a hot bolt of fear sizzling through him.

The kitchen hadn't been trashed as it had been a few days before, but on the far wall by the door that led into the dining room, positioned so he could see it easily from the doorway, was a splash of bright red paint. It was smeared and runny, and looked like a gory spray of . . .

Blood!

It took Jeff a heartbeat or two to realize that it wasn't just a random splash of paint.

No, there were odd-looking symbols scrawled on

the kitchen wall—a crude upside-down cross inside a circle, something that looked like a trident with two large, outward curling horns, and a single word. The letters were almost indecipherable because of the running drips, but Jeff could make them out.

DEAD!

For a long time, he just stood there, panting heavily and shivering as rainwater dripped down the inside of his coat collar. He couldn't believe what he was seeing, that this vandalism could have really happened while he was out. He closed his eyes and shook his head, half-hoping it wouldn't be there when he looked again.

But it was.

Who would have done something like this, he wondered. *And why? Maybe this is another dream!*

But he shook his head and knew that he was awake. As bizarre as this was, it didn't have that odd sense of dislocation a dream has.

It took him a few minutes to compose himself enough so he dared to enter the kitchen. Moving like an automaton, he walked over to the wall, staring intently at the graffiti, studying it. The symbols looked vaguely familiar, but he couldn't think of where he might have seen anything like them before. Reaching out with a trembling hand, he lightly touched the paint, not surprised in the least to discover that it was still tacky. Over in the corner beside the refrigerator, he saw an overturned bucket of red paint and a discarded paintbrush. There was a red smear on the linoleum where the culprit had apparently stepped into the wet paint and skidded.

"Okay . . . okay, now don't touch anything this time," he cautioned himself, but he looked back and saw that he had already smudged the footprints in the doorway with his own.

Moving stealthily, he went over to the wall phone, picked up the receiver, and hurriedly dialed the number for the police, which was on a preprinted sticker on the base of the telephone. When he got the police dispatcher on the line, he hurriedly explained what had happened and that he wanted someone to come over right away to check it out. Hoping he didn't sound too rattled, he kept his voice low . . . just in case the intruder was still in the house.

"Don't you worry, Mr. Wagner," the dispatcher said. "I'll have a unit out there in less than five minutes. Just stay where you are and don't do anything until an officer gets there, all right? If you'd feel safer, you might want to go back and wait in your car until the officers arrive."

"No, I'm not going anywhere. Just hurry up," Jeff said before hanging up the phone.

He found it difficult to take a deep enough breath as he leaned back against the wall and stared at the graffiti. Once again, he was struck by the vague familiarity of the symbols, but he still couldn't place them. The only impression he got was that they looked somehow . . . evil, like the symbols a black magic or Satanic cult might use.

He wanted desperately to go through the rest of the house and see if anything else had been damaged, but he knew he had to wait until the police arrived. It didn't seem likely that whoever had done this would still be in the house, but he wasn't about to take that chance. Maybe the person didn't have time to get out and was trapped somewhere in the house?

It felt like a lot longer, but in less than two minutes, according to Jeff's wristwatch, a blue-and-black police cruiser pulled to a stop in the driveway. Jeff hurried outside to meet the officers.

"I thought I might bump into you before long," one of the officers said as they came up the walkway. The rain made loud popping sounds on the long, black slickers and clear plastic hat covers they were both wearing.

It took Jeff a moment to realize that the man who had spoken was Eddie Dearborn, his old high-school buddy. He saw right away that Eddie had changed quite a bit over the years, having gained a bit of heft since their high-school days. His face was lined and puffy, and he now sported a bushy mustache, but he still had that same wise-guy twinkle in his eyes, and beneath that mustache was that same silly, crooked half-smile of his.

"Jesus Christ, Eddie!" Jeff said, caught completely off guard. He held his hand out for him to shake. "I thought I'd heard something about you being a town cop now. How the hell have you been?"

"Oh, I'm getting by," Eddie said. "Still married to Dianne, if you can believe it. We've got a couple of kids and live over in Cape Elizabeth. Nice house. Good neighborhood. Been there for *years,* now." He paused, then lowered his gaze a moment and added, "Awfully sorry to hear what happened to Judy."

"Umm, yeah . . . thanks," Jeff said, glancing down at the ground. He took a shuddering breath and shivered. "I . . . just got back from the funeral."

Eddie regarded Jeff with a lingering look as though he wasn't quite able to believe that this was his best friend from high school, but then Eddie's features dropped into a neutral, businesslike expression as he indicated his partner. "This here's Frank Hamilton. So, what seems to be the problem? You reported a break-in."

Jeff nodded. "Yeah. Christ, let's get in out of the rain, huh?" He led the two men through the breezeway and into the kitchen, unmindful now of ruining the footprints that had been there. Eddie whistled between his teeth as soon as he saw the smears of red paint on the wall.

"Christ's mother!" he said, shaking his head and cocking one eyebrow as he turned to Hamilton. "I ain't never seen nothing like *that* before, have you, Ham?"

Hamilton was silent as he shook his head and looked at the graffiti. Without a word, he took out a small pad of paper and started jotting down notes.

"Are you sure the person who did this isn't still in the house?" Eddie asked.

Jeff shrugged and shook his head. "I have no idea. I didn't think it'd be all that smart to go check. I was waiting for you guys to show up."

"Good thinking," Eddie said. "Why don't you stay here while I take a look around?"

He slipped his service revolver from his holster, snapped off the safety, and holding it up by his face—just like the cops do in movies—moved into the dining room.

Jeff heard him pass through the dining room and into the living room, then start up the stairs. The steps creaked beneath his weight, adding to the hushed tension that filled the house. The whole time, Hamilton was staring silently at the symbols on the wall as if he were trying to decipher them. Jeff pointed out the spilled bucket of paint and the paintbrush in the corner.

"I hope you didn't touch anything," he said, nodding sagely as he checked the smudged footprint on the floor. "We'll have to dust the brush and that paint can for fingerprints. Might even be able to get something from where he stepped in the paint. Maybe tell what kind of shoe or sneaker he was wearing."

Jeff watched silently as Hamilton looked around. A few minutes later, Eddie came back into the kitchen, his revolver back in his holster and a relaxed expression on his face.

"Well, everything looks undisturbed upstairs. No evidence of any damage up there. Looks like he confined himself to the kitchen. I don't think he even went up there, but you'll want to check through your belongings carefully, just to make sure nothing's missing."

Jeff nodded as Eddie glanced at the wall again and scratched his head. He went over to it and touched it, lightly fingering the tacky paint.

"Whoever it was must've split just before you got here, judging by how fresh this paint is. I wonder if he brought the paint with him, or if he found it here."

Jeff shrugged. "Maybe he got it from down in the cellar."

For the next fifteen or twenty minutes, Jeff and Eddie sat at the kitchen table. He answered Eddie's questions while Eddie painstakingly filled in the complaint report. Meanwhile, Hamilton got a camera from the cruiser and went around snapping photographs from several angles of the graffiti and the smudge of red paint on the floor. He took two plastic evidence bags and carefully placed the paintbrush and paint can into them, then sealed and marked them.

Jeff answered most of Eddie's questions without hesitation, giving as complete and accurate an account of his activities as he could remember. He had checked the time so often throughout the morning that he had no trouble detailing everything he had done—when he had left the house, where he had gone, when he had arrived at the funeral home, when the service began and ended, who he had been with, and what he had done right up until the time he had pulled into the driveway. A few times he faltered, a bit reluctant to mention that he had spent any time with Katherine—after all, he and Katherine used to double-date with

Eddie and Dianne—but Eddie just wrote everything down without batting an eye.

Jeff's tension only increased, though, because a voice inside his head kept asking him questions . . . questions he didn't even want to think about.

How can you be really sure where you were and what you did this morning?

How do you know one of us didn't do something without you knowing about it?

Do you have any idea how long you sat out there in the driveway before you came inside?

And how about that muddy footprint you saw on your car floor this morning, the one on the passenger's side? What about that?

"I—uh, I don't think this is the first time someone's broken into the house, either," Jeff said once Eddie had finished with the report and closed his folder. Eddie looked at him, eyebrows raised. "I mean, not even since I got here."

"Oh?"

Jeff shifted uncomfortably in his chair and took a deep breath.

"Yeah, well, you see, a few days ago—the first morning I was here, in fact, I think someone might have broken into the house during the night. The kitchen was messed up a bit. You know, emptied out a few drawers and stuff. Like maybe someone was looking for something."

"Like what?" Eddie asked.

Jeff shrugged. "I have no idea. I don't know if Judy—" He almost choked on her name but kept talking. "—had anything valuable hidden around here."

"So why didn't you report it?" Eddie asked.

Before he could answer, a voice inside Jeff's head whispered, *Because maybe you were convinced one of US had done it . . . Right?*

Jeff shrugged as though helpless. "Well . . . nothing

was broken or stolen, at least as far as I could tell, so I . . . I just let it slip, I guess."

"This was when?" Eddie said. He reopened his file folder, his pen poised above it.

"Uh—on Tuesday . . . last Tuesday morning."

For the next five minutes or so, Jeff detailed what had happened and what he had done about it. He tried to make light of it by dismissing it as nothing serious, but it was obvious to him that Eddie and his partner didn't think so. Two acts of vandalism in the same week, in the same house obviously didn't match with their opinion of what life was supposed to be like in their little Maine seacoast town. After almost an hour, they were preparing to leave.

"Well," Eddie said as he adjusted his hat and rain-coat, "we'll file the report, but to tell you the truth, there's not a whole hell of a lot we can do. I'm sure we'll be assigning a patrol car to drive by the house several times over the next few days and nights. If I was you, I'd change the door locks and make sure all the windows and the cellar bulkhead are secure."

"Yeah, I will," Jeff said, nodding.

After an awkward pause, Eddie asked, "So when are you heading back?"

Hamilton had already taken the evidence bags and camera back out to the cruiser. He was now standing in the doorway, obviously anxious to get going. In his hand was a portable radio that kept squawking, but Jeff couldn't make out anything that was being said.

"Uh, just another couple of days," Jeff replied with a shrug. "I want to get the house cleaned out, take care of most of Judy's stuff, and then put the house on the market. No sense keeping the place now."

"What, you mean you're not planning on moving back to Cape Higgins?"

Jeff wasn't sure if his old friend was kidding or not, but he gave him a half-smile and shook his head. "No, you're not getting me out of Colorado unless it's six friends, carrying me in a box."

Eddie considered for a moment, then said, "Well, you know, I'm off duty at eight o'clock tonight. Maybe we could get together for a beer or two. Might do you some good to get out. It'd be great to talk about old times and catch up with each other." He gasped and shook his head. "Christ, what's it been? More than twenty years now?"

"Yeah," Jeff said. "Time sure does fly."

He didn't respond to Eddie's request right away because he was wondering if, either now or later, he dared to talk to Eddie—off the record—about the psychological problems he'd been having and about how he was afraid that some part of himself might have been responsible for what had happened . . . and maybe worse!

No, you don't want to tell him about us, said a rasping voice inside his head.

Why not?

Just because . . . How do you know someone like him would even understand? He's a cop, for Christ's sake! How do you know he wouldn't turn right around and use something like that against you?

But he used to be my best friend.

Used to be! That's the operative phrase, isn't it? USED to be! He isn't any more. He'd probably just act like a cop and use it against you.

"So, what do you say?"

"Huh? About what?" Jeff said, shaking his head in an attempt to snap his attention back.

"About getting together later tonight for a couple of cold ones. I can give you a call once I'm done with my shift. There's a couple of nice places in-town we could hit."

"Yeah, sure," Jeff said, still distracted. "Why not?"

But you can't tell him about us! Don't even think about it!

"You know, if I was you, I'd slap a couple of coats of paint over that shit," Eddie said, indicating the dripping graffiti. "We got enough photographs of it, and you sure as hell aren't gonna get any buyers interested in this place if they see something like *that.*"

"Yeah, you're right," Jeff replied absently. "I-I'll check around. Maybe Judy's still got some extra paint of the same color down in the cellar."

He was wishing—almost desperately—that he felt comfortable about talking to Eddie about what he was thinking, but at the same time he was regretting having made plans to see him later.

"Maybe a touch-up will do it," Eddie said. "It'd sure as hell be better than having to paint the whole friggin' room."

Eddie paused, then held his hand out to Jeff, and they shook hands firmly.

"Sorry again about what happened," he said. "You know, if you're really concerned about it, you might want to check into a motel for a couple of nights. See if things settle down."

Eddie's expression of concern seemed genuine, and it touched Jeff, but he shook his head. "No . . . I'll be fine, 'specially if I change the locks."

"Well then, I wouldn't worry too much about this," Eddie said. "Probably just some asshole prank, anyway."

"Yeah, thanks," Jeff said, knowing there wasn't much else he could say.

"But—shit, it's *great* to see you again, Jeff." Eddie clapped him roughly on the shoulder. "You know, for as long as it's been, you haven't changed all that much."

"Oh, I've changed, all right," Jeff said weakly. "Believe me, I've changed."

After another handshake, Eddie followed Hamilton out into the downpour. Jeff watched from the kitchen window as the two cops got into the cruiser, started it up, and drove away. As soon as the cruiser had disappeared around the bend in the road, Jeff was hit—hard—by how lonely and foreboding Judy's house felt. The steady patter of rain drumming against the house and windows, cold drafts snaking across the floor, and radiators and floorboards creaking and snapping all contributed to the effect. Worst of all, though, was the feeling that there was an unseen presence, lurking in the house . . . a presence that, at least at times, could make itself known.

Yeah, Jeff thought, fighting back a wild shiver as he stared out at the pouring rain, *living in a lonely old house like this, it's no fucking wonder Judy wanted to kill herself!*

"Jeez, you don't sound so good," Sally said.

Jeff couldn't believe how good it was just to hear the sound of his wife's voice. Standing in the kitchen with a half-empty beer bottle in the other hand, he was unable to tear his gaze away from the bright splash of paint on the wall.

DEAD!

What the hell did that mean? Was it a warning, or a statement of fact? And who was it for? Judy . . . or him?

"No, I . . . ," he said shakily. "I don't feel so good, either. The funeral was . . . pretty tough."

"Yeah, I'll bet, but you got through it."

"Just barely."

"But you *did* it."

"Uh-huh."

"And you're feeling okay . . . I mean, considering?"

"Yeah . . . considering, but—I don't know. Yeah, I guess so."

Jeff was barely paying attention to what he was saying because he was mentally debating whether or not he should tell Sally about the break-in, the graffiti on the wall, and everything else that had been happening. He wanted desperately to talk to *someone* about it, but he didn't want her to be worried any more than she already was.

"You know," Sally said softly, "I don't want to keep hassling you about this, but I still wish we'd made plans for all of us to be out there."

"Yeah . . . I know."

Jeff couldn't stop himself from wondering how different things would have been if Sally and Robin had come to Maine with him.

Maybe *none* of this would have happened.

Maybe—especially if one of his alters was doing these things—having Sally around would have prevented it.

But no matter who was responsible, whether it was him or someone else, things sure as hell seemed to be escalating. What had happened today was certainly a lot more serious than someone simply breaking into the kitchen and messing things up a little. The message on the wall, for instance—*DEAD!*

Was that a statement of fact?

Or a threat?

"So what are your plans for tonight?" Sally asked.

"Well, I met one of my old buddies from high school. A guy named Eddie Dearborn. We were thinking about going out for a few drinks."

"Uh-huh. Sounds like fun."

"Yeah, but I have to pai—to, uh, to get a few things done around the house, first, so it looks presentable."

"I see."

Was that a trace of suspicion in her voice? Jeff wondered. Why, as soon as he had mentioned Eddie, did he immediately think about doing something with Katherine, instead?

"Yeah, then sometime in the morning, the real estate agent's coming over so I can sign the contract. By tomorrow afternoon, I figure there should be a big FOR SALE out on the front lawn. I . . . uh . . ."

Again, he considered mentioning the break-in but didn't.

"Like I said, there's a few little things I want to do around the house. You know, to make it presentable. And in a day or two, once I've had a chance to look everything over, I want to give Goodwill a call and have them come and pick up the furniture . . . most of it, anyway."

"Is there anything worth hanging on to, like family heirlooms or something?"

Jeff almost laughed aloud at the suggestion but said simply, "No, I don't think so. If there's anything I want to keep, I can always put it in storage here or ship it back home. I don't really feel like renting a U-Haul and driving it all the way to Colorado. We've got everything we need."

"Umm . . . and it's probably not a good idea to take any more time away from teaching than you have to."

"Boy, have you got *that* right!" Jeff said, but he couldn't help but think Sally was pushing him a bit too fast.

Shit, maybe Katherine would be a bit more understanding about things, huh?

The voice speaking in his mind was so clear and so distinct that Jeff jerked the receiver away from his ear and stared at it, convinced that the voice had come over the phone. He heard the buzzing of Sally's voice and quickly put the receiver back to his ear.

"Sorry, what did you say?"

"No, I was just saying how it's really busy here at

the office, and I probably shouldn't tie up the line much longer."

"Yeah, well . . . okay," Jeff replied.

There, see what I mean? She's not even listening to anything you're saying! I swear to Christ, she doesn't even give a shit!

Jeff tried not to, but once again he found himself imagining what it would be like if this were Katherine he was talking to, not Sally. How different would that be? Again, he felt himself getting an erection just thinking about Katherine . . . and the way she had held onto him when he had hugged her . . . and how it had felt when he kissed her . . . the trembling eagerness he had sensed seething inside her.

"You'll give me a call then tomorrow night, won't you, honey?" Sally asked.

"Yeah, sure I will," Jeff said. "Talk to you then."

"Bye-bye, hon. I love you."

His ear rang with the loud smacking sound of a kiss, but he couldn't help but think that she didn't mean it . . . Not one bit!

"Love you, too," he said, his own voice sounding flat and mechanical through the receiver.

It wasn't until he had hung up that he realized he hadn't even asked Sally to give Robin a hug and a kiss for him. Leaning back against the counter, he stared blankly ahead at the red splashes of paint on the wall. Then, tipping his head back, he finished off his beer with a couple of deep gulps.

"Dead!" he said aloud as he reached blindly behind himself and placed the empty bottle on the counter.

His voice seemed to echo oddly in the kitchen, and he couldn't help but shiver wildly. Outside, the rain continued to beat against the house, and from somewhere upstairs, Jeff heard the loud snap of a floorboard.

Chapter Sixteen
The Cellar Door

Jeff tried to stop his hand from shaking as he undid
the hook-and-eye lock on the cellar door, opened it,
and reached into the stairwell. He fumbled around
blindly until he found the light switch and clicked it
on, but he didn't feel any better when the soft wash of
yellow light spilled out onto the hall floor and down
the stairs. A choking, musty smell of damp earth, old
cement, and rotting wood chimneyed up the stairway
in a chilly draft that made him shiver. The smell was
instantly familiar and brought back a swirl of memories about the many times he had played down here in
the cellar when he was a boy.

But now, for some reason, he felt unaccountably
nervous.

He told himself, all he had to do was go down there
and see if Judy had any leftover paint that was the
same bright yellow as the kitchen walls. That was it.
What could be simpler? He had checked everywhere he
could think of upstairs, through all the cupboards and
closets, and hadn't found anything. She might have
stored any painting supplies out in the barn, but it was
too damp and cold to go out there now. Besides, it was

getting dark. If he didn't find what he needed down in
the cellar, he decided he would just wait until morning.
The last thing he wanted to do on a cold, rainy evening
was drive into town to the hardware store just to buy
a gallon of paint, a paintbrush, and a paint roller.

But now he was beginning to think that might not
be half as bad as having to face going down into the
cellar. If he drove to town, he could also pick up some
new locks for the doors.

On a deep, subconscious level, alarm bells were
going off like crazy. He didn't think it was just because
he was nervous about going down into *this* cellar. He
knew that wasn't what was bothering him.

No, this cellar reminded him of something else
. . . something that he knew was there, he could *sense*
it, but it was buried so deeply within his mind that, no
matter how hard he tried, he couldn't quite grasp it.

He felt deeply threatened, just thinking about going
down there, and suspected that it had little—if anything—to do with thinking that the intruder might be
hiding down there.

No, it was worse . . . much scarier than that.

He stood at the top of the stairs for what seemed like
several minutes, breathing heavily and poised, ready
to descend, but he was unable to make his legs move.
He was paralyzed with fear.

No, it wasn't fear.

It was deeper than that!

It was something he knew he didn't want to have to
face . . .

Ever!

"Come *on!* Jesus *Christ,* get a *grip!"* he whispered in
an attempt to bolster his courage; but looking down
the stairway into the cellar made him feel weak and
disoriented. For a dizzying instant, the stairs seemed
to telescope in and out, and he grabbed at the wall for
support. The feeble glow of the stairway lightbulb

barely cut the darkness below. Thick, black clots of cobwebs hung from the shadowed rafters and walls, swaying like clumps of seaweed in the updraft.

Jeff tried to take a deep breath, but the clammy air washing up over him was as thick as fetid water. It choked him and made him gag. A tiny whimper escaped from him when he backed away from the doorway and wiped the cold sweat from his forehead with the back of his arm.

"Jesus Christ," he whispered.

Suddenly, he turned and, moving as fast as if someone were charging up the stairs at him, went back into the kitchen where he rifled through the drawers until he found a thick-bladed carving knife. Clutching the knife in one hand, he walked back to the cellar door and looked down the stairs. Inhaling what he tried not to think might be his last breath of decent air, he started cautiously down the steps.

Ancient wood creaked as rusted nails pulled beneath his weight. The cold, dank air of the cellar swirled around him and blew into his face like the rancid breath of some foul monster. With every step down, he had the distinct impression that he was sinking deeper and deeper into slimy swamp water. His skin was clammy with sweat that made his clothes cling to his body. His stomach was tensed, and he felt his testicles shrivel. He wanted desperately to take another deep breath, but he didn't relish the thought of that closed, fetid air entering his lungs.

When he was halfway down the stairs, he heard a faint rustling sound from the darkness somewhere off to one side. Freezing in mid-step, the carving knife poised and ready to strike, he watched and waited for several heartbeats, but the sound wasn't repeated. He told himself it must have been a mouse or a rat, scurrying for cover, and not to allow his imagination to play it up into anything larger or more dangerous.

At the foot of the stairs, Jeff paused a moment to look around, surprised how clearly the cellar had been implanted in his memory. The fading gray light of day barely made it through the dirt-encrusted windows, and two grime-covered lightbulbs hanging from the ceiling, one at each end of the cellar, gave off a feeble yellow glow that seemed to be swallowed by the surrounding gloom. Their light certainly wasn't strong enough to push aside the shadows in the dark, cobweb-filled corners. The cellar walls were constructed of thick blocks of granite. White streaks of lime from deteriorating mortar veined the walls and stained the dusty floor. The ceiling was so low that Jeff had to tilt his head forward so he wouldn't bang into the rafters.

Everything was exactly as he had remembered it, and the instant familiarity of the cellar stunned Jeff. He shivered, remembering the times he used to come down here with his friends to play hide-'n-seek or moon-'n-stars. Later, once he was older, he used to stash his stolen copies of *Playboy* down here and, whenever he had the chance, come down and masturbate. He looked guiltily over at the doorway to the small storage room behind the furnace where he used to kneel down on the cement floor and, holding a flashlight in one hand, his penis in the other, stare at pictures of naked women until he was rock hard.

Rock hard! . . . You mean the way you felt when you were with Katherine today, right?

Jeff narrowed his eyes as he tried to push the intruding thought out of his mind. He resisted the impulse to turn and look to see who had spoken to him.

Yes, by Jesus! he told himself as he squeezed the handle of the knife even tighter. *That's all it is—just another thought. There's no one else down here except me!*

As his gaze danced nervously around the rock-enclosed space, he couldn't dispel the impression that the granite walls were steadily, imperceptibly sliding inward to crush him. He even imagined the sound of his footsteps on the cement floor was really the sound of the ceiling and floor, subtly closing together, narrowing . . . squeezing down on him.

All right, there's no need to panic! he told himself, but his breath came in fast and shallow gulps regardless. *You've been down here dozens, probably hundreds of times before! Don't let yourself get so goddamned worked up!*

But he didn't listen to his own inner voice. There were other voices, soft but gathering in strength, telling him other things.

Tension and fear were building up inside him like the irresistible pressure of a steadily tightening spring. He felt an impulse to cry out, to scream if only to break the winding tension inside him, but instead he took a few cautious steps forward toward the workbench, where he saw several cans of paint stacked among the scattering of rusted tools and assorted junk. They seemed to have a thinner coating of dust than the rest of the junk down here.

Look, just get your ass over there, check them over, take one if it looks like the right color, and get the hell out of here, okay?

But he couldn't stop himself from jumping at the slightest sound. When the furnace clicked on and started to run, he shouted and wheeled around, tensed and ready to strike. Feeling suddenly foolish, as if someone might be watching him, he took a deep breath, braced his shoulders, and walked boldly over to the workbench.

Just about everything on the bench was old and rusted, tools and assorted junk that were practically useless. He knew he would no doubt be carting most of this off to the dump—that is, if he didn't leave it for whoever bought the house to deal with. He looked at the four paint cans that were stacked on one corner of the workbench. They looked relatively new, and one of them was ringed with drips of bright yellow paint. It was impossible to tell in the lousy lighting of the cellar, but it very well might be the exact color of the kitchen. Also among the mess he found other painting supplies, including several sizes of clean, black bristle paintbrushes, a well-used rolling pan, and a paint roller and pad that was crusty with dried paint. He rolled it back and forth over his hand, satisfied that it was still serviceable.

"Aw'right," Jeff said to himself, but as he was reaching for the can of paint, his hand suddenly froze. The brand name on the label was almost obscured by the yellow drips, but he could see that it was a Sherwin-Williams paint, the same brand as the can of red paint that had been used on the wall upstairs.

. . . DEAD! . . .

Whoever had painted those symbols and that word on the kitchen wall might very well have come down here to get it!

Jeff shivered and tensed as he glanced around the cellar. The furnace was still running, so he couldn't hear anything else, not even his own pulse, slamming in his ears. He was frustrated that the lighting wasn't very good. In every dark corner, he thought he saw faint flutters of motion. When he looked over at the doorway to the small storage room, he was almost positive he saw a hint of motion that looked like someone ducking back inside the darkness of the doorway.

Squeezing the knife handle tightly, Jeff cleared his throat and called out, "Hey! Is anyone there?"

He waited a few seconds but, of course, didn't expect a reply. Even if someone *was* there—possibly the intruder—he'd be a damned fool to reveal himself if he didn't have to. Jeff wondered if he had the courage to force the issue.

"I have a gun, you know," Jeff shouted, feeling a sudden jolt of courage as he took a few steps toward the doorway. "You'd better show yourself now before something happens."

He strained to see into the thick darkness of the storage room, but he couldn't quite bring himself to move any closer to it. If he had a flashlight, he told himself, he might feel a little more confident about checking this out. As it was, he was trembling wildly, fearful that someone was going to burst out of the darkness and attack him.

"I'm warning you! I mean it!" Jeff yelled. His voice wavered even though he put as much force as he could into it. "I know you're down here. I've already called the police. They're on their way. If you—if you're the asshole who did that little paint job upstairs in the kitchen. . . . I'm warning you—you're in deep shit."

He strained to hear, but the steady rumble of the furnace still blocked out every other sound. Again, the darkness inside the doorway seemed to shift, and he thought he saw someone moving about, but no one came forward.

"I swear to God, the police are on their way!"

He waited.

Still nothing.

Jeff felt suddenly very foolish. He knew he couldn't very well stand here for hours, waiting for something to happen; but he didn't quite dare to move forward to confront anyone if they were hiding in that room, either. Finally, he decided that he must be letting his imagination get carried away, so he went back to the workbench, picked up the can of yellow paint, and gave it a hearty shake. Paint sloshed inside. The can felt like it was maybe half-full. Taking the roller and rolling pan and two different size brushes, and still gripping his knife, he turned and started back toward the stairs.

With every other step he cast a nervous glance over his shoulder at the darkened doorway of the storage room. He had to fight back the impulse to break into a run as gut-tightening shivers raced through him. He wondered why the hell he was so nervous about being down here.

Hey, bad things happen in dark places, whispered a voice inside his head. *You should know that as well as anyone else . . . maybe better.*

But seriously, he asked himself, what were the chances that whoever had broken into the house and painted all that shit on the wall would stick around? Like Eddie had said, it was probably just a prank by someone who had heard that Judy was dead and thought the house was empty.

That is . . . unless YOU did it, said a voice inside his head. *You still don't know for sure that you didn't!*

Again, Jeff was shaken by the thought that it wasn't *this* cellar . . . or anything down in it . . . that he was afraid of. This place was reminding him of something else.

But what? . . .

When he reached the foot of the stairs, he looked up. The brightly lit hallway looked as clear and distant as the shimmering surface of the water to a drowning man. Suddenly aware that he hadn't taken a deep breath in a long time, Jeff inhaled, trying to fill his lungs, but he ended up choking on the dust-laden air of the cellar. With a sudden burst of speed, he ran up the stairs, taking them two at a time. At the top of the stairs, he slapped the light switch off, then turned and slammed the door shut behind him.

"Jesus," he whispered as he leaned back against the door, trying to catch his breath. His chest was heaving, and his face was slick with sweat.

He braced himself, pressing his back hard against the wooden door, and waited to hear the heavy clomp of footsteps on the stairs . . . and then the angry pounding of *someone* who wanted to get out.

But no sounds issued from the cellar. At some point, the furnace had stopped running, and now an eerie, pressing silence filled the house. Jeff could hear the thick whooshing of his pulse in his ears and feel the heavy slamming in his neck.

"Jesus, just calm down," he whispered.

Taking another deep breath, he leaned forward and carefully placed his painting supplies on the floor. With the carving knife still in one hand, he turned and slipped the hook-and-eye lock back into place. He knew that didn't provide any real security. If there was someone on the other side of the door, even a moderate push would tear the screws out of the wood; but at least it was something.

Jeff carried his supplies into the kitchen, pried off the lid of the paint can, and mixed up the paint. Once everything was ready, he started applying a first coat over the bright red graffiti. Using a paintbrush, he did a few practice strokes. He could tell right away that it was going to take at least two coats, possibly three to completely obliterate the markings; but he figured if he put one on now, it might dry fast enough so he could apply a second coat before going to bed. He got himself a beer and, as the sky darkened outside, set to work.

It had obviously been quite a while since Judy had painted the kitchen. The fresh coat of paint Jeff applied didn't come close to blending in with the rest of the wall. He knew he was going to have to go over the whole surface at least two more times, but he trimmed the edges with a brush and covered the wide areas using the roller. He finished the first coat just about the time he finished his third beer and stood back to admire his work. While he waited for it to dry, he sat in the living room and watched a bit of TV. He had just started to drift off to sleep when the telephone rang, startling him awake.

"Hello," he said, grabbing the phone. His voice was thick with sleep and one too many beers. All he could think was that this must be Sally, calling to see how he was doing.

"So, Jeffy-boy, you still feel like doing something in a little while?"

Jeff was silent for a moment, unable to place the man's voice on the other end of the line. No one had called him "Jeffy" since high school. He glanced at his watch and saw that it was almost eight o'clock, then remembered that Eddie had said he was going to call.

"Ohh . . . hey, Eddie." A thick, sour taste filled his mouth. " 'S been one hell of a day." He smacked his lips loudly. "Yeah, hi. Thanks for calling."

"Sounds like I woke you up, man."

"Uhh—yeah . . . yeah, I guess I must've drifted off," Jeff said. He sighed loudly.

"Sounds it. Well, hey, I'm off duty in a half hour. You still wanna go out for a few drinks?"

Jeff rubbed his eyes vigorously and shook his head, trying to clear it.

"I—uh, gee, Eddie . . . I'm not so sure it's such a good idea tonight."

"Ohh?"

"Yeah, I . . . I just finished painting over all that graffiti, and to tell you the truth, I'm beat to hell."

"I see."

"Maybe we ought to take a rain check on that. I'll be around for another couple of days, until the middle of next week, at least."

There was a long pause where neither of them said anything. Jeff could tell that his friend was disappointed, but he honestly didn't care. What, after all,

did he owe Eddie Dearborn? Sure, they had been best
friends in high school, but that had been a long time
ago. Since then, they had lost touch so that for the past
ten years they hadn't even exchanged Christmas cards.
There wasn't any true friendship between them. Besides, it was still raining. Why would he want to leave
a nice, warm house on a night like this? It'd be much
better to slap another coat of paint on the wall and
then go to bed early. Maybe—now that the funeral
was over—he could get a half-decent night's sleep.

"Maybe we can make plans this weekend," Jeff said.
"I've got some business I have to take care of tomorrow morning—to get the house on the market, you
know, but after that maybe we could do something."

"Ahh, you see, I'm working a double shift this
weekend," Eddie said. "I probably won't have any
time off until Monday afternoon."

"Well then—Monday would be fine . . . I should still
be around."

"Yeah . . . okay. You want me to give you a call?"

"Sure. Give me a buzz on Sunday afternoon, and
we'll figure out where we're going," Jeff said.

"Okay . . . cool."

Jeff could hear the disappointment in Eddie's voice,
but he didn't care. Looking at the jewellike splatters of
rain on the window, he told himself that it would be
foolish to go out tonight.

"Talk to you later, then," Jeff said.

As he replaced the receiver, he realized that he had
absolutely no intention of going out drinking with
Eddie, on Monday afternoon or any other day. After
he signed the real estate contracts tomorrow, he was
going to give the house a quick once-over, pack his
bags, and head back to Colorado. As far as he was
concerned, he wouldn't stay in Cape Higgins even if
Katherine gave him a call right now and told him he
could come over and do whatever he wanted with her.

But isn't that what you want? whispered a voice.

He shook his head firmly as he walked back out into the kitchen and inspected the work he had done. The symbols and the single word *DEAD!* were still visible through the first coat of paint, so he grabbed the roller, rolled it back and forth in the tray until it was coated, nice and thick, then rolled it over the word several times. Each stroke made the graffiti disappear a little bit more, but it was still visible, like something seen through a fog.

When he was done, he washed out the roller and pan at the sink. Looking back at his work, he was positive that, even with a second coat, the graffiti would still be visible when he came down for breakfast in the morning. He wondered if he would *ever* be able to make it disappear.

"Dead," he whispered, shaking his head as he left the kitchen and went upstairs.

A loud bang—as loud as a shotgun blast—split the night.

Torn from his sleep, Jeff uttered a strangled scream and sat bolt-upright in bed. His eyes were instantly wide open and staring at the half-opened bedroom door. The light was on in the hallway, casting a faint yellow glow that spilled into his room and angled up over the foot of his bed.

Was that just part of a dream? he wondered.

His heart was slamming hard against his rib cage, and his throat felt dry and raw.

Or did I really hear something?

He shifted his gaze nervously around the bedroom, his body tensed as he waited to hear the soft shuffle of footsteps on the creaking stairs . . . or to see a gauzy gray shadow flitter down the hallway, but the house was now perfectly silent.

Too silent, he thought.

He found himself wondering—again—if Judy's house might be haunted. The thought had certainly crossed his mind before, and he wondered now if maybe that's what had driven his sister to suicide. Maybe there was something in the house—something evil that was strong enough so it could even do things . . . things like tear the kitchen apart, open and close doors, and paint graffiti on the kitchen wall.

A rational corner of his mind told him that such things were impossible, that *someone* had to be doing them, but how else could he explain some of the strange things that had happened to him since he had gotten here. If weird stuff like this had been happening to Judy, maybe it *had* gotten to her—over the years— making her unstable until it finally drove her crazy . . . and to suicide.

"No . . . no way," Jeff whispered, shaking his head decisively. "That can't be it!"

Yeah, said a soft voice inside his head, *but if that's not it, what IS it? Someone's gotta be doing it!*

Maybe it's you, said another voice.

No, it . . . it had to be just part of a dream, Jeff thought, but he couldn't repress a shiver because he couldn't dispel the feeling that the sound that had awakened him had been real . . . something inside the house.

He shifted his feet to the floor and stood up, cringing at the loud squeak the floorboards made beneath his weight. He was trembling as he walked over to the bedroom door.

The hallway was empty and quiet. At the far end, almost lost in shadow, was the dark rectangle of the door to his old bedroom. Jeff's body tingled with rising panic as he wondered if the sound might have come from in there.

What if that's where he's hiding . . . the same person

who painted all that shit on the kitchen wall? whispered a voice inside his head. *Hey, for all you know, there could be someone living in there! . . . It might even be the same person who killed Judy and made it look like a suicide!*

Jeff shivered at the thought, but he knew he would never dare go in there and check. He'd been back in Maine for four days, now, and he still hadn't dared to look inside his own bedroom. As far as he was concerned, he never would. No doubt he would eventually have to glance in there to see if there was anything of value before he sold the house, but he had been seriously considering asking Vera Becker, Judy's friend, if she would check in there for him. He regretted not asking Eddie if he had looked in there when he had checked around upstairs. He knew it was foolish, cowardly, in fact, to avoid a room like this, but he doubted that he could bring himself even to open the door, much less go inside.

What the hell are you so afraid of?

Jeff shook his head as though replying to the thought. He didn't care what he or anyone else thought—he knew absolutely that he wasn't going to go into that room!

Ever!

When he stepped out into the hallway, he felt a cold draft—much colder than there should be with the furnace running—sweeping up the stairway. Taking tiny breaths and wishing that his racing pulse would slow down, he started down the stairs, taking them slowly, a step at a time. The wood was cold to his bare feet and creaked with every step. If there was anyone down there, he was sure he wasn't going to be able to sneak up on him. He wished now that he had kept the carving knife handy, or that he had something else he could use as a weapon.

Turning on the lights in each room as he went, he

walked through the living room and dining room and into the kitchen. His gaze was immediately drawn to the wall beside the refrigerator where the graffiti had been. He was glad to see that once the second coat had dried, it had pretty much covered up everything. Only by looking at it very carefully could he see faint traces of the red paint beneath.

Dead!

The single word echoed in his mind with an odd reverberation.

He told himself that after a final coat of paint in the morning, it would look just fine, and he could forget all about it. Any prospective buyer who came to look at the house wouldn't have to know a thing about it.

But what the hell could have made such a loud noise . . . loud enough to wake me up?

Still wire-tight with tension, he went out into the breezeway and checked to make sure the side door was still locked. It was, but for some reason he didn't feel at all reassured. He checked the floor for fresh footprints but didn't notice any.

Coming back into the kitchen, he walked over to the sink and leaned over to look out the window at the backyard. He was happy to see that the storm had finally passed. Puffy steel gray clouds were being pushed by a brisk wind coming in off the ocean. They shifted fast across the face of the moon, their ink-black shadows wavering over the backyard with an odd strobe-light effect. Against the star-filled sky, the pine trees that lined the property looked like fragile black lace cutouts.

Jeff shivered, imagining for a moment that he saw a hint of movement—someone running across the yard and into the woods. He knew it had to be just the shifting shadows and his own overwrought imagination, but suddenly the woods behind the house seemed to be full of subtly shifting motion, as though dozens of people were lurking there.

Jesus, it had to be just the wind, banging something—a branch or something—against the side of the house, he told himself as he straightened up and looked around at the kitchen again. Taking a deep breath and telling himself that he had to calm down, he walked out into the hallway. When he looked over at the cellar door, he stopped dead in his tracks and gasped.

The door was hanging wide open, and the dim light from the bulb in the cellar stairway was on, illuminating a small rectangle of the hall floor. Glancing down, Jeff saw the hook-eye lock where it had fallen on the floor.

"Jesus Christ," he whispered, taking a step back.

Every nerve in his body was tingling as he cautiously approached the open doorway. Obviously, this was the source of the cold draft he had felt on the stairway. After scanning all around, trying to see if anyone were lurking nearby, he bent down and picked up the hook lock. It was twisted out of shape from the impact that had yanked it out of the door. Looking behind the door, he could see a fresh gouge in the plaster wall where the doorknob had banged into it. A small coating of plaster dust, like a sprinkling of sugar, had filtered down to the floor.

Jeff stared down at the cellar light for a moment, trying hard to remember everything he had done earlier that evening. He was absolutely positive he had turned off the light and locked the door behind him after coming up from the cellar with the paint and supplies. He was sure of it, and he knew he hadn't gone anywhere near the cellar door since then.

Gripping the edge of the door, he swung it partway shut and felt the splinters where the lock had been torn out of the wood. The damage was fresh.

"Christ," he said, shaking his head as he tossed the twisted lock back and forth from one hand to the other, "it's gotta be one of two things. Either there really was someone hiding down there in the cellar all along . . . or else I—"

His throat made a loud gulping noise when he swallowed.

"Or else I did it and don't even realize it."

He covered his mouth with his hand, holding back the terrified scream he could feel building up inside him.

Either way, it's pretty scary, huh? said a voice in his mind.

Jeff swallowed again and squeezed the lock so tightly it dug painfully into the palm of his hand.

"Yeah," he said, his voice so raw and twisted that he hardly recognized it as his own. "But more important—what the fuck are you going to *do* about it?"

Chapter Seventeen

Twilight Lover

Jeff found Judy's diary on Friday morning while he was cleaning up the house in preparation for the arrival of Merilee Bryant, the real estate agent from Century 21 who was going to be handling the sale of the house. The small, black, leather-bound book was almost two-inches thick, and was wedged between the mattress and headboard of Judy's bed. Jeff was surprised that he hadn't noticed it there before, and he felt a wave of guilty interest as he sat down on the edge of the bed and idly flipped through the pages. Every page of the first two-thirds of the book was covered on both sides with Judy's distinctive script. The entries were written in a variety of colors of ink, mostly black, and were all dated. The last entry had been written on October 9, about two weeks before Judy's first suicide attempt. It ended in mid-sentence.

". . . and if he ever comes back here again, I swear to God I'll—"

Jeff snapped the diary closed, suddenly ashamed to be reading it; but after a moment, his curiosity got the better of him, and he opened it again at random. Scanning the entries, he caught a few words and phrases here and there, but he still told himself that he shouldn't read any of it. These were his sister's private thoughts, and no doubt the secrets and revelations inside should die and be buried along with her. Jeff regretted that he hadn't found the book before Judy's funeral. He would have put it inside the casket with her. What he should do right now, he knew, was go down to the living room, open up the fireplace, and burn the book—page by page, if he had to—in order to make sure that no one ever read any of it.

But then he had another thought.

Other than a scrapbook full of old photographs and a few home movies, this was the only personal trace he had of Judy's life. If he read it, the things she expressed in the privacy of her diary might make him feel somehow closer to his dead sister; they might help ease the pain of his loss. It certainly would help him remember her in a more intimate way than he could manage otherwise.

Settling back on the bed, he opened to another page at random and started to read. This passage, dated almost three years ago, was about how much Judy disliked her new boss, Larry Wilson. She went on for almost two pages about what an "obnoxious little cocksucker" he was, always making the people in his department feel as though their contributions and ideas didn't count for shit, and taking all the credit whenever anyone of them came up with anything good.

Jeff scanned several more pages but found little of interest until he moved toward the last few parts of the book. There he found an entry which, upon first reading, stunned him.

May 11—
He's back! My "twilight lover" is back! I saw him last night, outside the house, in the backyard. At

least I think I saw him. I was looking out the
bedroom window just before dark. It's been such
a long time, I was beginning to think—no, I was
positive I had made up all of it. That he wasn't
real. How could he be? It couldn't possibly be
who I think it is! Jeff lives in Colorado. There's
no way he could be hanging around here, too.
But I swear to God, this person—whoever he
is—looks just like Jeff. Same size, same build,
maybe a bit smaller, but the same color hair and
facial structure, at least as far as I can tell at a
distance. I've only seen him maybe seven or eight
times all together, always at twilight, always
standing out there in the shadows behind the
house. "Twilight Time." Wasn't there an old
rock song, from the fifties, by that name? And
why always just at twilight? I've only seen him
from my bedroom window, so I don't know how
many times he might have been out there when I
didn't see him. He usually takes off before I can
get a good look at him, but once or twice he's
stayed there, looking up at me as though he
didn't know—or care—that I could see him. I
called the police the first time he was there. They
checked around but never found anything, no
evidence that anyone had even been there, so
maybe he's not even real. I dunno. There's a
scary thought. Maybe he's a ghost who haunts
the house and yard. God! That thought gives me
the shivers! I don't want anyone to think I'm
crazy or imagining things. But even the way he
walks reminds me so much of the way my brother
moves . . . and when I think about him—oh
God!—I just want to

Judy had lined out the next few words so heavily
that, even by angling the diary so the morning sunlight

shone obliquely across the page, Jeff couldn't make
out what she had written. He flipped the page and
looked at the back of it, hoping there would still be an
impression of the crossed-out words, but Judy had
written an entry on that side, too, so there was no way
he could make out anything. Below the crossed-out
passage, undated, was a short, obviously hurriedly
written passage.

Same night—
No. I can't even write about it yet. Maybe later
. . . maybe a lot later . . . maybe never!

Trembling, Jeff skimmed the next few entries, all of
which had different dates, until he came to another
section that caught his interest.

June 21—
He hasn't been around lately, but I think about
him . . . a lot. Not just about him, either because
he reminds me so much of my brother and some
of the—God! It's so hard to write about this stuff
sometimes. I've tried to work it all out in my
mind, but I still can't quite believe that we did
what we did. I know we were just kids at the time,
and we were scared and probably just fooling
around, experimenting sexually, but—I don't
know. How many other kids have played around
like that with their brother or sister? Is it wrong?
Is it sick or unnatural? I don't really think we'll
go to hell for it, like they say. We were just kids.
What—ten and twelve years old? Who isn't starting to be interested in sex at that age? I was just
starting to feel like a . . . woman. I hadn't started
my period yet, but I knew all about it from talking with my friends at school. I certainly couldn't
count on my mother to help me figure out the

things I was feeling, how I was feeling so different about myself. And Aunt Mildred! Good <u>God</u>, no! Who would <u>ever</u> trust her about <u>anything</u> after some of the mean things she did to us kids? Already at twelve years old, I was starting to get breasts, and I had tiny wisps of pubic hairs between my legs. I had no idea what was happening to me! Maybe . . . Just maybe I thought Jeff could help me figure it all out. I don't know! I still feel so guilty about it all. Jeff was so sweet, so innocent. He had no idea that his little "wee-wee" was for anything except peeing. It almost makes me laugh, but I feel more like crying. But I <u>do</u> know this—I wish we had never done what we did, and I wish, even after I was married, whenever I made love to a man, I wish to God I didn't imagine more than half the time, if only for a moment, that the man I was with was my brother! Tell me how—how can I stop myself from thinking like that? The man I see in the backyard sometimes— and always from my bedroom window . . . My "twilight lover"! Who can tell me if he's even real at all? I certainly don't know! And why—<u>why</u> do I fantasize that he's my <u>brother</u>?!!!

Jeff was twisting with guilt before he finished reading this passage. Closing the book on his finger to mark his place, he heaved a deep sigh and collapsed back on the bed.

There, see?

The voice was clear and sharp in the silence of the room. It made Jeff jump and look around, but there was no one there. Dazzling sunlight filled the room and cast thin blue shadows across the floor.

You see that? It says so, right there! She wrote it! Look at the date. It was written just a couple of months

*ago! She said she still wanted to fuck you, Jeff, just like
I know you still wanted to fuck her!*

"That's not what it said!" Jeff said between clenched
teeth. "That's not what it said at *all!*"

The voice inside his head fell suddenly silent. There
was an odd vacuum in the room, as though someone
had quickly left. Jeff sat up and looked around. A
subtle tingling went through him when his gaze shifted
to the window that looked out over the backyard.

Right out there! he thought, feeling a rising rush of
panic in his chest. *That's where he was!*

And what was worse, he thought, was that this same
person, his sister's "twilight lover"—whoever the hell
he was—just might be the same person who had broken into the house and messed things up in the
kitchen, the same person who painted graffiti on the
walls, the same person who had been locked inside and
who had broken out of the cellar!

It must have been him!

Jeff wanted to believe this wasn't all just his imagination. He desperately needed to believe that the
strange things that had been happening around the
house weren't the results of some aspect of his own
personality, acting without his knowledge or consent.

No, maybe it was Judy's "twilight lover"!

It *had* to be!

But who the hell was he?

Jeff opened the book again and skimmed the passages he had just read. They were loaded with implications that sent shivers rippling through him. Worst of
all was Judy's admission—right there in her own
handwriting for him or anyone else to read—that
when she was making love to a man—even to her own
husband!—she had been thinking about *him!*

Tears welled up in Jeff's eyes, blurring his vision as
he turned page after page of the diary and scanned the
entries. Near the back of the book, almost the very last

entry, he read something that, even before he was finished with it, made him tremble violently.

July 16—
He's real! Oh, my God, he's back and he's <u>real</u> . . . either that, or else I've really lost my mind! Last night, just before evening, at twilight, I looked out my bedroom window and saw him in the backyard again. I can't help but wonder why I only see him from this window, but he was standing in the shade of the pines, on the edge of the lawn, looking up at the house. The shadows of trees reached out like fingers across the lawn, right up to the foundation of the house. I imagined they <u>were</u> fingers, and I could hear them scratching on the side of the house, trying to get in. It had been a scorcher of a day, and I had to work late. I had just gotten home and taken a shower when I happened to look outside, and there he was! I moved to the window and opened it, not for a second daring to take my eyes off him for fear that he would disappear. I remember how cool, how thrilling the ocean breeze was through the window. It stirred the curtains, making them billow like sails. I was wearing nothing but my bathrobe, and the evening breeze made my nipples hard. As I gazed out the window at him, I did something I never thought I would ever do . . . I don't know what came over me. Maybe I <u>am</u> crazy. I know I was to do what I did, but I opened the collar of my bathrobe and exposed my breasts to him. The sun was shining into the window. There was no way he couldn't have seen me or known that I saw him. I let the robe slide off my shoulders and fall to the floor and was standing there stark naked, the cool breeze caressing me like gentle fingers. I raised

one hand and beckoned to him. Everything seemed to be moving slow, like I was in a dream . . . or maybe my mind had been taken over by someone else who was using my body and watching while I did things I normally never would have done. In some ways, I felt like I was a spectator, just watching all of this happen to someone else who just happened to look like me. It was weird! After waving to him, and knowing that he would come to me, I went to the bed, pulled the covers down and lay down—naked, trembling, waiting . . .

The entry stopped at the bottom of the page. Jeff couldn't control the shaking in his hand as he turned the page and continued to read. The entry was written with a different color ink, and the penmanship looked different, almost like someone else's writing.

Next morning—July 17
He came to me later that evening—my "twilight lover." As I lay there on the bed, I heard the front door open and close, and then I heard his footsteps on the stairs. I was trembling all over with fear and excitement. I knew he could just as easily be a killer who would murder me as a man who would want to make love to me, but there was a part of me that no longer cared. What did it matter if I died? I have two ex-husbands who never speak to me, who don't even live in the state anymore . . . I have a brother who was always saying how much he loved me—loves me!—but who hardly ever writes or calls and never visits me! What did it matter if I died? The room was thick with gloom. I purposely left all the lights off, knowing that he preferred the darkness, the shadows. Then—after what seemed like

forever—he was standing in the doorway. He just stood there for the longest time, framed by the light from the hallway. His hands were at his sides as he stared at me. I could hardly breathe as I watched him, no longer certain or even caring if he was real or imaginary. The thought crossed my mind even then that I might have completely lost my mind, gone crazy and was hallucinating him, but I didn't care. When I could no longer bare the silence and the expectation, I held my arms out to him and said, "I've been waiting for you all my life." God, now it sounds like something out of a crappy romance novel, but he moved slowly toward me. I closed my eyes, not wanting to see up close just how much he looked like my brother. He made love to me. Soft, gentle, tender, passionate. I lost all sense of time as he took me to places, made me feel things I'd never felt before. Afterwards, once I knew he was gone, I got up. I must have slept because when I looked at the clock, it was well past midnight. For more than an hour, I sat by the open window, looking out on the backyard and wishing and wondering if he was real and if he would ever come back to me . . .

Jeff sat back, unable to believe what he had just read.

Squeezing his eyes tightly shut, he shook his head and tried like hell to remove the image of his sister, lying naked on her bed—on *this* bed!—and making love to a complete stranger . . . her "twilight lover." A man, so she wrote, who looked very much like him!

Against his will, Jeff felt himself getting aroused. He stood up and began pacing back and forth across the bedroom floor, Judy's diary clenched in one hand. With each turn, his gaze would go to the window that looked out on the backyard. It was a beautiful autumn day with a brilliant blue sky and a bright wash of sunlight, but as he stared out at the line of pine trees behind the house, he couldn't help but ask himself— *Was he real? . . . And is he still out there?*

He wanted to believe that these diary entries were merely Judy's sexually frustrated fantasies, that they had no more substance than that, but over the past few days, he'd had more than ample proof that there was *someone* lurking about the house.

Who the hell could he be?

"Jesus . . . Jesus . . . *Jesus!*"

With every step, he smacked the flat of his hand against the diary as if he could somehow magically alter the words that were written within. A cold, hollow tension filled him like a fat snake, coiling in his stomach. Pressure was building up behind his eyes, making it feel like his head was about to explode. His whole body was trembling and clammy with sweat.

With a sudden, pained shout, he turned and grabbed the telephone from beside the bed. His hand was shaking wildly as he dialed a telephone number from memory. He couldn't swallow; he could hardly breathe as he waited for the long-distance connection to be made. After what seemed like much too long, just as he was about to hang up and try again, the phone at the other end of the line began to ring, its irritating buzz drilling into his ear.

Once . . . twice . . . three times, the phone rang.

Then there was a soft click, and a recorded message began to play.

"Hello, you've reached the office of Doctor Walter Ingalls. I'm sorry I can't take your call right now, but if you leave your name and number, and the time you called, I'll return your call as soon as I can. Thank you, and have a nice day."

Jeff looked at his watch and quickly calculated that

it was only seven-thirty back home. He didn't even wait to hear the *beep* before he slammed the receiver down hard enough to make the phone ring once. Wiping his hand across his forehead, he let his gaze shift back to the bedroom window.

He's real, and he's out there! . . . Somewhere . . . Right now! If you find him, then you'll know who broke into the house . . . and maybe even who really killed Judy!

Wave after wave of tension swept through Jeff, making him shiver. He clenched his fists and ground them hard against the sides of his head. The steady throb of pain behind his eyes was getting more intense.

"You've *got* to handle it! You've *got* to handle it!" he whispered harshly to himself. "You can't let bull-shit like this throw you now. You've done really well so far, hanging in there. Don't slip! Don't crack now!"

He let out a surprised shout when, from downstairs, he heard the doorbell ring.

It took him a moment to remember that it must be the real estate agent at the door. After slipping Judy's diary under his pillow, he glanced in the bureau mirror to make sure he looked all right before going downstairs. He thought his face looked a little pale, and his eyes were puffy from crying, but he knew there wasn't much he could do about it as he walked downstairs and greeted Merilee at the front door.

Merilee was at the house for more than two hours, and in all that time Jeff was trying to ignore his pounding headache. He gave her a guided tour of the house from the cellar, where he felt more than a little nervous, up to the second floor. When Merilee was approaching the closed door to his old bedroom, Jeff excused himself, saying that he had to go to the bathroom and telling her she could check the room out by herself. He got a couple of aspirin from the medicine cabinet, and washed them down with several gulps of water while he waited to hear her leave his old bedroom. He listened to make sure she closed the door behind her before rejoining her in the hall.

They took a quick tour of the attic, checking carefully for any evidence of condensation or rot, then went back downstairs to the kitchen. Jeff put the teakettle on to heat up water for instant coffee. Sitting across from each other at the kitchen table, they made casual conversation until the water was hot. Jeff made them each a cup of coffee, and they sipped at it while they nailed down terms of the contract. They quickly agreed upon what Jeff thought seemed like a fair price for the house, considering the current real estate market. Merilee filled out the necessary papers, and Jeff signed them without hesitation. She told him that someone from the office would be out to place a FOR SALE sign on the front lawn within a day or two.

It was almost noon by the time Merilee left. As he watched her drive away, Jeff was filled with a wave of almost overwhelming exhaustion. The aspirin had dulled but certainly not eliminated his headache. Touring the house had made him realize once again just how much work he still had ahead of him. There was a lifetime's accumulation of possessions here to sort through and either haul off to the dump or give to Goodwill. Jeff knew it would be impossible for him to get everything done within a week. Once again, he reminded himself that he had to contact Vera and ask if she would be willing to take over once he left for Colorado.

For now, though, his head was throbbing, and all he wanted to do was lie down. Taking a cold beer from the refrigerator, he walked into the living room and flopped down onto the couch. He looked over at the phone and considered trying to call his therapist again, or maybe Sally, but he decided not to. He still needed someone to talk to, but at least the immediate panic was over. If he could just get through this last stretch, in a couple of days he'd be out of Cape Higgins and Maine for the rest of his life.

Chapter Eighteen

Conversation in a Dark Room: #4

"Are you sure the door's locked?"

The voice rustles like silk in the pressing darkness.

"Yeah, I'm sure," I say. "Hey, this is Sammy, isn't it?"

"Of course it's me. Who do you think you are, fucking Sherlock Holmes?"

"No, I-I thought I recognized your voice."

I take a deep breath, lean my head against the wall, and roll it slowly back and forth with my eyes closed. The depth of darkness doesn't change a bit. The wall is soft and yielding, which surprises me. Usually whenever I'm in the dark room, the walls are as hard as stone. I wonder why the room seems different now.

Is it the same place?

Am I still safe here?

Has something changed inside me to alter the room?

A subtle current of tension winds through me, but I take another deep breath, squeeze my eyes even more tightly shut, and try to force myself to relax.

"So tell me, Sammy," I say, purposely drawling my

voice to help myself calm down. "How the hell have
you been?"

"Believe me, I've been keeping an eye on you, Jeffy-
boy, and everything you've been doing." Sammy's
voice is laced with sarcasm, but I try my best to ignore
it. "Man, I swear to Christ, I can't fucking believe you
sometimes!"

"Oh, is that so?"

"Yeah."

"Give me a for instance?" I say; but even as I say it,
I sense that I'll regret it.

"Shit, man, where do you want me to start? There's
so much."

"Try anything."

"Okay, how about when you were with Katherine?"

"What, do you mean at the funeral yesterday? Or
back when we were dating in high school?"

"Yesterday . . . at the funeral."

"Yeah? . . . What about her?"

I realize I'm holding my fists tightly clenched and
force myself to ease back and loosen them.

"Well, yesterday when she asked you over to her
place after the funeral. *Jesus,* man! Why the hell didn't
you go? I couldn't fucking believe it when you didn't
go with her!"

"Why should I have?"

"Why? Do you mean you really don't know?"

"Well, I—" I take a shuddering breath and sigh
heavily. "I . . . I just wanted to be alone."

"Bullshit!"

Sammy's voice snaps at me like a bullwhip from the
dark.

"You were afraid of her! You were scared shitless!
You knew damned well what she was looking for, and
you didn't have the balls to go do it."

"Uh, excuse me, Sammy, but you don't seem to
remember that I'm a married man?"

"Yeah? So what? Why would you let something like *that* stop you? You had your chance, man, just like you had your chance with Judy."

"All right, you can stop it right there," I say. "This has nothing to do with Judy!"

Again, I clench my fists. Opening my eyes, I shift forward and am about to stand up, but I decide that I don't want to start stumbling around in the dark. Instead, I take another deep breath and press my head back against the cushioned wall. A dull throbbing in the center of my head begins to radiate lightly.

After a moment, in as mild a voice as I can muster, I say, "It's been you all along, hasn't it?"

"What do you mean, *me?*"

Sammy's voice is edged with hostility.

"All along, it's been you."

"I don't know what the fuck you're talking about, Jeff?"

"Oh, is that so? I think I figured it out. You're the one who's been taunting me, telling me how much Katherine and Judy wanted to have sex with me. Haven't you?"

"Hmm . . . could be."

"Well I want you to stop it, starting right now."

"Come on! You've got to admit that Kat was looking pretty damned good yesterday. I'm talking prime table-grade, here. What? Don't you agree? And she's divorced, too. Don't tell me you didn't pick up on that! I'm telling you, man, she's looking for it. Shit, she probably hasn't had her ashes hauled in many moons. She's hot for your ass, Jeffy-boy."

"I think you're full of shit," I say, "and stop calling me Jeffy-boy."

Sammy snickers in the dark. The sound makes me cringe.

"Yeah," Sammy says after a lengthening pause. "You know how sometimes women pretend they don't

need sex—that they don't even think about it! I'm
telling you, man, ninety-nine times out of a hundred,
they really *want* it. They want it *bad!* Why, she's horny
as all hell. You can't tell me you didn't think she
looked downright fuckable."

"Well—yeah, I mean, it was good to see her again,
and I appreciated that she came to the funeral and all,
but I sure as hell didn't mean—"

"So why don't you get your ass in gear and give her
a call, for Christ's sake? Why the fuck are you sitting
around the house here, snooping in your sister's diary,
drinking too much goddamned beer, and feeling so
goddamned sorry for yourself? Goddamn it, man,
you're acting like you have a perpetual hard-on for
your sister or something. Look, your sister's dead—
dead and buried. Get it? So you might as well—"

"Shut up!" The words burst out of me like a shotgun blast. "Just shut the fuck up! In case you didn't
realize it, I happen to love my wife very much."

I lean forward and squeeze my fists together tightly.
In the darkness, I can hear Sammy's breathing. He's
taking deep breaths and letting them out with a slow,
whistling hiss, like wind blowing through a hollow
cave.

"Okay, okay," Sammy says at last. "I'll drop it if
you want. You'll probably never see her again, anyway, so what's it fucking matter?"

"It matters plenty," I say, still feeling a burning rush
of anger at Sammy. "I love my wife and family, and
I'm sure as hell not going to do anything stupid to
jeopardize that relationship. And I don't need you
hounding me about it, either, if you don't mind."

"Okay, but you mean to tell me that if Katherine
came over here tonight, dropped her pants, and asked
if she could sit on your face and wiggle, you'd send her
away? Is that right?"

"Look, if that's how you're going to talk, I don't

even want you around, all right? So why don't you just leave?"

"Yeah, why don't you just leave."

This new voice, sounding almost like an echo, comes so suddenly from the dark that it makes me jump. My ears are still ringing with the sound of it as I try to place the voice, but whoever it was spoke so fast I was caught completely off guard. I look around as if I could somehow pierce the surrounding darkness, but it's so thick I can't even tell if my eyes are open or shut.

"Who was that?" I say, my voice trembling.

"Don't worry. It's just me. Karl. I think Alexander and a couple of the others might stop by in a while, too."

"What's the occasion?" I ask, feeling more nervous.

In the past, I always spoke to only one person at a time in the dark room. That was one of the conditions: that whoever talked to me here would be assured he was talking in complete privacy. When I first enter the room, one of the first things I do is mentally lock and bar the door. On a few rare occasions, I've spoken to two people at the same time in the room, but never more than that. How had Karl gained entry? Had he been here all along, keeping quiet in the corner and listening?

"I don't know as there's any *occasion,*" Karl says, "but I wanted to talk something over with you. I'm not gonna talk about it with Sammy here, though."

"Sammy?" I call out. "Are you still here?"

Karl and I wait quietly for several seconds, but there is no reply—just thick, impenetrable silence.

"I think he's gone," I say finally. The thought makes me relax, at least a little bit, so I lean back against the soft wall again and take a deep breath.

"No," Karl says after a moment. "I know he's still here. He's just staying quiet because he wants to hear what we have to say. You know how he is. Hey,

Sammy? You'd better get your ass out of here now, or else you'll be in trouble. You know what the rules are here. You don't want Alexander getting mad at you, do you?"

"All right, all right," Sammy says, sounding like a scolded child. "I'm going . . ."

His footsteps echo loudly as he walks out of the room and shuts the door behind him. From outside the room, Sammy speaks again, his voice echoing from a great distance.

"But don't you forget what I told you, Jeff," he says. "She wants you, man! She wants you *bad!* And I think you're a goddamned fool not to jump at the chance."

His voice fades into the darkness, reverberating from all sides at once, and then is gone.

"Okay, he's not here," I say. "So tell me. What do you want to talk about?"

"What's *really* going on, that's what," Karl says in his crisp, clipped voice. No nonsense, as usual.

"Well then, exactly what *is* going on?"

Even before he's finished his question, I feel a tingling rush of expectation blossom in my stomach. Of all my alters, Karl generally is the most practical, the most direct and honest, even more so than Alexander. Through years of therapy, I've learned that I can generally trust whatever Karl tells me, even though I might not always like what he has to say.

"I think you're missing the whole point here," he says. "This has absolutely nothing to do with Katherine. It has *everything* to do with Mildred and Kirby."

"It does?"

A cold, prickling rush spreads out into my arms and legs. Suddenly it's almost impossible for me to take a deep enough breath. It feels like something has me by the throat and is squeezing steadily tighter . . . tighter.

"You're damned right it does," Karl says, his voice

soft yet demanding. "And I think I've got it all scoped out for you."

"Can you tell me about it?"

"Sure I can. What do you want to know? I know a lot of things I've never told you because—well, frankly I'm not so sure you're ready to hear them."

"Try me," I say, my voice catching in my throat.

"Okay. How's this for starters? I know that you've been wondering if Judy might have not committed suicide, that you think you or one of us might have had a little more to do with her death than you remember."

"Well, yeah . . . I-I've been wondering about it . . . you know . . . trying to think of alternatives. I sure as hell don't like the idea that I might have—"

"Or one of us!"

"Yeah, or one of you might have done something without me knowing about it."

"Well then, try this on for size. What do you think about the idea that maybe Mildred and Kirby had a bit more to do with Judy's death than you might expect?"

I suck in my breath and shake my head as the thought registers.

"What the—? You don't mean you think they . . . killed her?"

"Oh, no, no, no. Not outright, anyway, but . . . Look, do you remember a while ago we were talking about how they used to abuse you kids?"

"Uh-huh."

"Have you managed to dredge up any more memories about any of that?"

I close my eyes and try to block out the sudden rush of thoughts and images that fill my mind. I *can* remember more—a lot more, and the memories send spiked chills through me.

"Well . . . yeah . . . a little. Now that you mention

it, I remember one time when I-I hadn't memorized a Bible passage Mildred wanted me to learn, so she had Kirby take me down into the cellar—"

As soon as I say the word *cellar,* my throat makes a loud clicking sound and chokes off. I swallow once, then continue in a broken voice.

"I remember he put me inside one of those big metal oil barrels."

"The oil drum! Ah-hah, so it *is* coming back to you. No one else told you about this, did they?"

"No—" I swallow again with difficulty. My spit feels like liquid fire in my throat as painful memories sharpen in my mind, making me want to cry out loud. "I remembered this on my own."

"So tell me about it."

"Well, I . . . I remember that he started banging on the side of the oil drum with his fist or a hammer or something. A steady banging. Boom! Boom! *Boom!"*

With each word, I smack my fist into the palm of my hand in a slow, steady cadence.

"And the whole time, he was reciting the passage I'd been trying to memorize. Shouting it! Screaming it at me! Before long, he was banging in time on the oil drum with a heavy beat. Banging hard! My ears were ringing. After a while, it was so loud I couldn't even hear him. I couldn't hear anything else, not even my own thoughts."

The terrifying memory comes rushing over me, fast and strong, gripping me and swirling around me like a tornado. A small cry escapes me as I squeeze my eyes shut and cup my hands over my ears, trying to block out the sound, but my head continues to vibrate with a steadily rising *Boom! Boom! Boom!* that matches the rapid hammering of my pulse in my ears and throat.

"And tell me this," Karl goes on, his voice almost—but not quite—drowned out by my memory of the sound. "Do you remember what Bible verse it was?"

"No . . . I, uh, not really."

"Tell me this, then. How many times did Kirby do this to you? How many times did you get put into the oil drum. Do you remember?"

I shrug and shake my head frantically. The sound is reverberating in my ears, in my mind, in my soul. It is deafening and rising steadily louder.

"I-I'm not sure. I—Once . . . maybe twice. I don't know! *I don't know!*"

I clap my hands over my ears to try to shut out the sound, but it does no good. Kicking my feet out in front of me, I thrash from side to side as the memory of being curled up in a fetal position inside that metal oil drum rips through me like lightning. I want to scream, but my voice is lost to me.

"Really? Once or twice you say?" Karl says, almost laughing. "Hey—what's that sound?"

"Make it stop!" I cry in a tortured voice that rips my throat. The metallic reverberating beat—*Boom! Boom!*—rises louder and louder. "Please! . . . Make it stop!"

"You're the only one who can do that," Karl says calmly. "Just calm down. Let the memory pass over you, through you. Don't hang on to it. Don't let it have any more power over you."

For another few frantic seconds—or minutes—I listen to the heavy hammering beat inside my head, but then, imperceptibly, it begins to fade. After a while, as I sit there on the floor trembling, my face bathed with sweat, the sound recedes into the darkness, fading like muffled hoofbeats.

"Do you want to talk about it?" Karl asks once the room is tomb quiet again, and I am breathing deeply and evenly.

Unable to speak, I grunt and wipe my forehead with the flats of my hands.

"Pretty scary, isn't it?"

I grunt again.

Karl waits another moment, then says, "Look, Jeff, I don't want to push you too hard on this, okay, but that bit with the oil drum—it was more like twenty or thirty times."

There is no trace of malice or pleasure at my expense in his voice, but I shiver nonetheless and feel a sudden rush of anger directed at him.

"You have to be making that up!" I say in a voice that is still strangled and raw. "How could it have been that many times?"

"Trust me on this, okay, Jeff? I know what I'm talking about. I was there, too. You may not have known it at the time, but I was there. I saw and heard *everything.*"

"I . . . No! I don't believe you. I mean, we didn't spend all that much time with Kirby and Mildred. And even if we did, even if Kirby and Mildred were doing all sorts of stuff like that to us, our parents would have done something to stop it."

"Oh? And how do you know that? How do you know they didn't know all about it? What if they did, and they didn't care?"

"I . . . No, I can't accept that."

The air and darkness inside the room seem to be building up pressure, squeezing in on me from all sides at once. I cringe, waiting to hear the rising sound of the drumbeat start again.

"What if they even knew about what you and Judy had been doing?" Karl asks almost teasingly. "And what if they thought that might be the best way to beat it out of you?"

"No! They wouldn't have let that happen! They were our parents, for Christ's sake! They would have stopped anyone from hurting us if they had known about it!"

"Calm down and just think about it for a minute. As

far as your mother and father were concerned, you kids were a pain in the ass, right? Don't you remember how it was? You guys used to talk about it all the time. You knew you were an encumbrance to your parents' life-style, to what they wanted to do. They pawned you off on your aunt and uncle whenever they could, several weekends a year and most of the summers for two or three years. From the sound of things, you don't even remember how much time you spent there, but believe me, it was a lot!"

"Twenty or thirty times in the oil drum?" I say, my voice weak and trembling with incredulity.

"At *least* that many."

"No way," I say, shaking my head. "I-I still don't believe you."

I cringe, hearing the strong edge of denial in my own voice. The memories that had been stirred up are getting stronger, becoming clearer, and they fill me with white-hot flashes of terror.

"Well, then, you see? You just proved me right," Karl says mildly.

"About what?"

"I told you I knew a lot of things, but you probably didn't even want to hear them. Didn't I say that? . . . Didn't I? I'll bet you don't even remember how many times Kirby said he was going to beat the Devil out of you, do you?"

"Beat the Devil—" I echo, and a numbing chill takes hold of me. I feel compelled to say more, but something catches in the back of my throat, making my voice cut off sharply.

"You bet your ass," Karl says, so casually he almost sounds cruel. "That's what he *always* said he was going to do, wasn't it? He was going to *beat the living Devil out of you!*"

Part Three

It is not the mountain we conquer but ourselves.
—Sir Edmund Hillary

There are times when even justice brings harm with it.
—Sophocles

Chapter Nineteen
The Past Repeats

Jeff spent the rest of Friday afternoon going from room to room, sorting out things and making decisions as to what to keep and what to get rid of. At one point he tried to call Vera to ask if she would come over and help him sort through Judy's clothes and personal effects, but she wasn't home so he left a message on her machine, asking if she would call or stop by later tonight or tomorrow. Everything else in the house—the TV, stereo, CDs and books, furniture, and kitchen utensils—was easier to deal with because they didn't seem quite as personal. He briefly considered calling up Kat to ask if she would like to help him. Maybe he could offer her Judy's twenty-three-inch Sony Trinatron or something, but he realized that calling her would be a mistake even before Sammy's voice hissed inside his mind.

Come on, man! Go for it now! Call her up! You know she wants your ass!

Whenever he went upstairs, he would pause outside the door to his old bedroom and stare at it, sometimes for so long that he would shake his head and mutter to himself in order to snap his attention back on what

he was supposed to be doing. One time he had actually
reached out, put his hand on the doorknob, and had
been about to twist it, but he hadn't found quite
enough courage to open the door.

*Jesus Christ! What do you think might be in there,
anyway?*

He wasn't sure if the faint voice whispering inside
his mind was his own thoughts or one of his alters
talking.

*Come on! You can talk to me about it! What the hell
are you so afraid of, anyway?*

But Jeff ignored the voice, whoever it was, pretending that he didn't hear it as he went about his business.
How could he even think about looking into that
room? No, it would be much better just to leave it the
way it was, closed and locked forever.

That's avoidance, pure and simple, the voice in his
mind said, but he ignored that comment, too.

His plan was simply to collect everything he didn't
want to keep, which was just about all of Judy's
possessions, and store them in the garage until he
could hold a yard sale. He could probably do that in
a day or two. If the weather held, Sunday afternoon
would be perfect. The summer tourist season was over,
but no doubt there would still be plenty of people
driving around, looking at the scenery. He could probably get rid of most of this stuff, as long as he put a
reasonable price tag on everything. Then he could call
and have Goodwill haul away whatever was left, including whatever clothes he didn't sell. With luck, the
house would be empty by Monday or Tuesday at the
latest.

But come on, man, the voice inside his head kept
saying, nudging him. *Don't you want to go into your old
bedroom and have one last look around? You never know
what you might find in there. You've got a lot of memories associated with that room.*

Thoughts like this kept intruding into his mind, growing louder and more insistent as he worked around the house, even when he was downstairs. Soon enough, it became the predominant thought in his mind. He tried to drown it out by cranking up some loud music on the stereo, but even that didn't help much. Now and then, he would cringe, just waiting to hear a faint reverberation—the echo of someone beating on the sides of a metal oil drum.

Boom! Boom! BOOM!

After he finished sorting things downstairs, Jeff headed upstairs to check out the attic when he paused and looked down the hallway at the closed bedroom door again.

Come on, Jeff. Who knows what's behind that door? Maybe you have a houseguest living there . . . Maybe that's where Judy's twilight lover has been staying all this time.

"Cut it out," Jeff whispered, his gaze riveted by the doorknob. His vision blurred, and for a moment the swirling wood-grain pattern on the door seemed to take the shape of a face, bulging from the wood. He shook his head to clear away the illusion, but the voice in his head continued.

Or what if there's another part of you that's still living in that room . . . Maybe the little boy you used to be has been living there all these years . . . living alone . . . in the silence . . . in the dark . . . afraid . . .

"No! Stop it right *now!*" Jeff shouted. His voice was ragged and sounded like tearing paper.

He tensed and looked around, suddenly fearful that someone might be lurking nearby, watching everything he did, listening to everything he said. After a moment, he went to the attic door, opened it, and ran up the stairs.

The attic had collected a small amount of heat from the day and was actually quite comfortable. Jeff was thankful that none of this had happened during the summer, when he would have had to come up here in sweltering July or August heat, but soon enough his face was slick with sweat as he set to work, sorting through piles of boxes and assorted junk.

Through the attic window, he noticed that the sun was setting. Long shadows reached out across the attic floor from under the eaves like soft, gray arms. He moved over to the window and looked out at the backyard, mildly surprised that he didn't see a shadowy figure, lurking on the margin of the woods. He started whistling a tune under his breath, then caught himself when he realized that it was the old rock 'n' roll song, "Twilight Time."

Forcing himself to stay focused on the work he had to do, he started sorting through boxes filled with old books. Some contained Judy's texts and notebooks from college, and he found several old best-sellers, including some early Stephen King novels which he thought might be worth keeping; but after a moment's thought, he put everything back into the boxes and closed the flaps. He sure as hell didn't want to have to rent a U-Haul to bring all this stuff back to Denver. It would probably be better to lug them all down to the garage and see if he could get a dollar or two per book in the yard sale. The rest he could donate to the local library.

The attic gradually darkened as daylight seeped from the sky. Jeff was just thinking about turning on the overhead light when the telephone started ringing downstairs. For a moment, he considered ignoring it, but then, guessing that it might be Sally or else Vera, just getting home from work, he ran downstairs to Judy's bedroom and snatched up the receiver.

"Yeah—hello," he said breathlessly.

A sudden coldness took hold of him when he heard a frantic voice on the other end of the line.

"Jeff. Oh, Jesus, Jeff! I don't know what to do! You have to help me!"

"Kat?" Jeff said, instantly recognizing her voice. "What is it? What the hell's going on?"

"I can't find him anywhere! He's gone!" She sounded as out of breath as he was. "I've been waiting for him since two o'clock this afternoon. He had a dentist's appointment at two-thirty today, but he still hasn't shown up."

"Whoa, there. Slow down a second. Take a breath and tell me what's happened. Who didn't show up?"

"Danny!" Katherine said, obviously fighting hard to control herself. "He never came home from school today."

As soon as Katherine said this, Jeff glanced out the bedroom window. The night sky was a deep Prussian blue, bleeding gradually into black. The fringe of trees in the backyard stood out like tangled black claws against the darkening sky.

It's twilight time.

The voice whispered inside Jeff's head, and he was sure that following it he also heard a teasing ripple of laughter. A deep tremor shook his shoulders as he wiped his hand across his forehead, surprised by how slick with sweat his face was. Glancing at his watch, he saw that it was already past four-thirty, almost a quarter to five.

"Well, you don't think he might have forgotten, about the dentist appointment, do you? I mean, maybe he forgot and just went over to a friend's house after school."

"No. I made sure to remind him when he left for school this morning. Besides, I've already checked around. I've called most of his friends, and none of them have seen him since he started home from school this afternoon."

Jeff could hear the frantic edge in Katherine's voice, winding up higher.

"Well I'm sure there's some reasonable explanation behind it all," he said, but he cringed at the lack of conviction he heard in his own voice. "It hasn't been that long. He probably—you know, just forgot and is off somewhere, playing or whatever. You know how kids are."

"But it isn't like Danny to forget," Katherine said. Her voice broke as she burst into tears. "I-I reminded him, and he—and he told me he'd come home right—right after school."

"Well then, have you notified the police?" Jeff said, trying to remain calm and think this through.

The suggestion sent a spike of cold through him, although he wasn't quite sure why. He gripped the receiver so tightly his palm started to throb. He was shaking like a man with a fever.

I told you. Just like last time, huh?

The voice was whispering so softly inside his head, Jeff hardly noticed it.

"I was so nervous I called," Katherine said. "I talked to Eddie . . . Eddie Dearborn. He came right over, but he said they can't do anything like file a—what the hell did he call it? A missing persons report until twenty-four hours from now. Jesus, Jeff. I just don't know what to do! I'm worried sick that something's happened to him. Something bad. He's never done anything like this before!"

"You and he didn't have an argument or anything, did you? Something that might make him want to run away or hide out for a while just to scare you."

"No. We get along just fine most of the time. That's why I'm so worried! He'd never do something like this! He wouldn't just take off and not let me know where he was going!"

"Do you want me to come over?" Jeff said.

He was unable to disguise the tension in his voice when he said it, but Katherine seemed to be so wound up she didn't notice.

"Yes, could you? I-I didn't want to bother you, but I—until the police can do something, I don't want to be alone."

Jeff considered asking if she had any other friends she could call, but he was flattered that she would think to call him first.

"Look, I've been working around the house, here, and I'll bet I smell like an old gym sock. Give me fifteen minutes to take a shower and change, and then I'll be right over, okay?"

"Yeah . . . thanks," Katherine replied shakily. "I'd really appreciate it. I live over on Wescott Street, number eighteen. It's the small gray house on the right, just after the curve. The number's painted on the mailbox out front."

She sounded like she was starting to calm down, at least a little bit, but Jeff could tell that she was still very close to cracking.

"I'll be over in a few minutes," he said.

"I'll leave the lights on, too," Katherine said. She took a breath, then added, "Thanks a lot, Jeff. I really appreciate you being so willing to help."

"Hey, what are friends for anyway, huh?" he said, and then he depressed the cutoff button with his thumb and hung up the receiver.

Staring blankly into a middle distance, his gaze shifted back to the window and focused on the jagged black line of trees against the sky. The night was thick, now, with only a faint scattering of stars. Jeff imagined that a cold wind was blowing in off the ocean, stirring the trees and the thicker shadows beneath them.

Maybe he's still out there!

Jeff nodded, as if in answer to the voice as he wiped his hand across his sweat-slick face. When he tried to swallow, his throat made a funny gulping sound. He wasn't sure why, but he wished to hell that hearing about Danny's disappearance hadn't unnerved him so badly. The first thought that entered his mind was that, maybe earlier today, either just before or just after he'd had that conversation with Sammy and Karl, he—or one of his alters—had gone out and *done* something to Danny.

That was a distinct possibility, he thought, especially if he gave any credence to the possibility that he or one of his alters might have started it all by coming back to the house last week and killing Judy.

What if one of his alters was out of control?

Maybe every time he went to have a conversation in the dark room, one of his personalities took advantage of the situation, and went out and did things that Jeff wouldn't ordinarily dare do.

He hoped something like this was impossible. Doctor Ingalls had told him as much, but the more he thought about it, the more he realized that he had absolutely no way of knowing for certain.

The second possibility that presented itself was just as scary, if not worse.

What if Judy's "twilight lover" was real?

What if he had been stalking Judy all along, and now that she was dead, he was after Jeff?

He could have been the one who had broken into the house and messed up things in the kitchen. What if, now, he had done something to Danny, just to get back at Jeff?

"Stop it!" Jeff said, moaning softly as he ground his fists against the sides of his head. "Jesus! Stop it right now!"

He knew, instead of torturing himself with such thoughts, that he should focus on the need to help Katherine. She was a friend who needed assistance. But even when he tried to ignore Sammy's whispered proddings, Jeff couldn't deny that he still felt a faint spark of affection for her, and he couldn't help but wonder if there might still be a flame, lingering in the ashes.

She wants you, man! Go for it!

Jeff suddenly lurched up off the bed, but a wave of dizziness swept over him, and he was barely able to stand. Shaking his head and still feeling numbed by Katherine's news, he walked stiff-leggedly down the hallway to the bathroom. Moving slowly, like an automaton, he stripped off his clothes, turned on the water, and stepped into the needle-sharp spray. But even when he turned the water up as hot as he could tolerate, it didn't begin to relax the knotted tension in his body. All he could think was, whatever the situation ultimately proved to be, he was worried as hell for Danny's safety.

And time after time, a voice so faint that he could barely hear it above the hiss of the shower was whispering in the back of his mind.

This is just like last time, isn't it, Jeff?

From the road, Katherine's house on Wescott Street looked modest but nice, a white-trimmed Cape that was weathered gray from the brisk ocean winds. The front yard was small but apparently well-tended, with numerous flower gardens now trimmed back and covered over for the winter. Somehow, it didn't surprise him at all that Katherine would choose to live in such a well-kept, modest house. He recalled that back in high school, when they had been dating, Katherine's family had lived in a large, run-down rambling old farmhouse out on Spring Brook Road, a dirt road off Pleasant Hill Road. He wondered if her family still lived there, but in the time since he had been back in Cape Higgins, he hadn't bothered to drive out past it.

He didn't see any point in tormenting himself with any more "might-have-beens?"

He shivered as he pulled to a stop at the top of the driveway, got out of the car, and started up the cement walkway to the front steps where the outside light was on. The night pressed in close around him. A chilling breeze—a taste of the coming winter—scattered dead leaves across the walkway. He paused halfway to the door and looked around, suddenly fearful that someone might be lurking in the darkness, but he saw and heard nothing except the whistling gusts of wind and the hiss of a car, passing in the distance.

Katherine met him at the door, holding it open for him as he stepped into the small, homey kitchen and shrugged out of his jacket. With a quick glance around, he saw that everything was neat and orderly—just as he had imagined it would be, knowing Katherine. The only chaos seemed to be on the refrigerator, where drawings, graded homework papers, and school announcements were held in place by an assortment of decorative magnets. Seeing the artwork and realizing that it had been done by a boy who had now been missing for several hours sent a cold pang through Jeff.

"I hurried over as fast as I could," he said.

Without a word, and with absolutely no hesitation, Katherine came over to him and practically collapsed into his arms. It took Jeff only a moment to loosen up enough to wind his arms around her and squeeze her to him. The first thing he noticed was how she didn't feel at all like how Sally felt when he hugged her; but there was also an instant sense of familiarity, and he automatically slid one hand up to cup the back of her head. When she looked up at him, her eyes glazed with tears and worry, he had to fight back an almost overwhelming impulse to kiss her full on the lips.

"I-I can't believe how scared I am," Katherine said in a raw voice that broke on nearly every syllable.

"Have you heard anything else, from Danny or the police?"

"Nothing at all," Katherine replied, shaking her head and biting down on her lower lip. With a downcast gaze, she eased out of his embrace.

"Not a damned thing. A couple of his friends' parents called back to see if he'd come home yet, but nobody's seen him since around two o'clock today."

Jeff could see that Katherine was trying hard to maintain a strong front, but her expression suddenly melted. He stepped forward and hugged her tightly once again.

"I-I just don't know what to do," she said, her voice muffled against his shoulder. "I'm so scared, Jeff. I'm really scared that something bad's happened to him!"

"Well I'm sure everything will be all right," Jeff said softly. "Really, I do."

He couldn't understand the dark worry that was gnawing away inside of him, but his own eyes were beginning to fill with tears. Telling himself that he had to be strong, if only so he could help Katherine, he hugged her tightly and let her sob against his chest, all the while whispering, "There, there, Kat . . . Just let it all out . . . There, there."

After several minutes, once Katherine had seemed to gain a measure of control over herself, she wiped her eyes with both hands and stepped away from him. He noticed that her eyes were bloodshot and glazed. They danced nervously around the room, and she seemed to wince no matter where she looked, as though everything she saw only reminded her of her missing son.

"What do you say we go sit in the living room," Jeff said mildly. "You can tell me all about it."

Hand in hand, they walked into the living room and sat down close together on the couch. As if it were entirely natural, Jeff cupped her hands with both of his and gave them a reassuring squeeze. Katherine was so choked up with emotion that it took her nearly ten minutes, but eventually she told him everything she knew.

It wasn't very much.

Jeff listened patiently, trying to fight back his own rising sense of nervousness as he wondered if it were possible that he or one of his alters might have been involved in any of this.

"How about his father?" Jeff finally asked. "Where's he living now?"

"In Massachusetts."

"Do you think Danny might have taken off with him?"

"I don't think so," Katherine said. "The police already asked me that, too. Doug—that's his father—is a trucker. Who knows where he could be right now? Out on the road somewhere, I suppose. Danny wasn't even in touch with him all that much, so I don't see how he could have—"

"But you told the police about him. Your ex-husband, I mean. They've put out a bulletin, looking for him, right?"

"Oh, yeah, I'm sure of it—at least Eddie said they will after twenty-four hours. That's when they send out a missing persons report. I just don't see how . . . if Danny was going to run away or whatever, I don't see how he would have even gotten in touch with his dad. They weren't very close even before the divorce."

Jeff took a deep breath and let it out slowly.

Play it nice and smooth, now, whispered the voice inside his head, but Jeff tried to ignore it. He gritted his teeth and shook his head to help him concentrate.

"You know, I'll still bet you ten to one that Danny's off someplace, involved doing something with a friend, and he's just lost track of the time," Jeff said. He

hoped to hell that he sounded at least half-convincing.
"It's still only been a couple of hours. I'm sure he's
going to show up before too long."

"It's already *been* too long," Katherine said.

She looked Jeff straight in the eye, and he was almost bowled over by the intensity of her pain and
worry. The light from the table lamp beside her reflected in her eyes just right, making them glisten with
an icy blue fire. He remembered all those days and
nights—a lifetime ago—when he had stared into those
eyes, thinking that this was the person he would marry
and love for the rest of his life. Shifting closer to her,
he slid his one hand around behind her back. Once
again, the impulse to kiss her was almost overwhelming.

"Let's talk about something else, okay?" he said
softly, rubbing his hand up and down, gently massag-
ing the small of her back. "I mean, you've done everything you can for now, so just try not to think about
it."

"How can I not think about it!"

Jeff shrugged. "You have to trust that he's all right,
and that the police will find him if there's been any
trouble."

Biting her lower lip, Katherine looked at him and
nodded tightly. Her lips parted as though she were
about to say something else, but Jeff suddenly leaned
forward and covered her mouth with his own. Even as
he did this, he was mentally chastising himself, but as
the kiss lengthened and grew more passionate, he felt
Katherine's stiffness loosen in his embrace. The tip of
her tongue began to probe between his lips. She
moaned, and he felt her arms encircle him, clinging to
him almost desperately. Her fingers, like claws,
hooked into his back and pulled him roughly to her.
They shifted around on the couch until they were facing each other squarely. As Jeff felt the rising heat of

their passion, he felt himself getting an erection and thrust his hips forward, pressing his body against hers. Another soft moan, either of desire or near desperation, escaped from her, and it inflamed Jeff all the more. His erection stiffened almost painfully.

Do it, man! Go for it now! Jesus Christ, she wants you!

But the voice, speaking so suddenly inside his head, was loud enough to break the magic of the moment. Feeling suddenly embarrassed, Jeff broke off the kiss. Twisting away from Katherine, he sat back on the couch, suddenly flustered. His arms dropped uselessly to his side, and for a long, awkward moment, they simply stared silently at each other.

Jeff sensed that Katherine—like he—was frantically trying to balance what she felt she wanted with what she knew she needed. An expression of confusion and lingering sadness crossed her face as she slid her hand up behind his neck and then down across his chest. Her hand felt hot and dry as she took hold of his hand and gave it a squeeze.

"I know," she said in a soft, broken whisper. Her grip on his hand tightened. "I know. You're married, and you think this is all wrong." She took a breath and let it out in a soft sigh before sniffing back her tears. "And . . . and it *is* wrong."

Anything Jeff might have wanted to say was caught in his throat. He gazed into her eyes, nearly overwhelmed by the powerful and contradictory feelings he had for her right now; but he knew that she was right. Even if this was the right thing, for them to be together again, this wasn't the time. Not when she was caught in a moment of such utter weakness and despair.

"Yeah," Jeff finally managed to say, feeling a terrible loss deep inside, "it . . . is."

Katherine nodded as she stared straight at him.

Tears spilled from her eyes as she took another shuddering breath, and then, uttering a low moan, pressed her face against his chest and hugged him tightly. She was trembling like a frightened child. As he rubbed her back and looked around the living room over her shoulder, tears filled Jeff's eyes. When she spoke again, her voice was so constricted and thick with emotion that, for a flickering instant, Jeff wasn't entirely sure if it had been Katherine speaking or one of his own inner voices. As what she said gradually registered, an icy panic gripped him, making his whole body go numb.

"God, this is so much like what happened to you and your family, remember?" Katherine said.

Emotion strangled her voice past the point of recognition. Jeff started shaking his head as though he hadn't quite heard or understood her.

"Back when we were kids," Katherine went on, "when your baby brother, Jeremy, disappeared."

Jeff suddenly jerked back as though he'd been given an electric shock. He looked at Katherine, absolutely dumbfounded. When he tried to say something, the only sound that would come out of him was a strangled, meaningless stutter. He could make no sense out of the explosion of voices that were shouting and screaming for attention inside his head.

"I still remember how scary that was for everyone, how terrible it all was," Katherine said in a tight, halting voice as she gripped his hand tightly and shook it. "The whole town was in such an uproar for weeks— months afterwards with people wondering if he had run away or been kidnapped or killed by some maniac. God, Jeff, I pray . . . I pray to God that the same thing hasn't happened to Danny. I-I don't think I could take it!"

Chapter Twenty

Conversation in a Dark Room: #5

"You have to calm yourself down, Jeff. You're not going to be any help to her if you lose control now!"

"Alexander? Is that you?"

"Yeah, it's me," Alexander replies.

His voice is low and soothing. I find it actually quite calming in spite of how upset I am. Over the years, I've always looked to Alexander to be my best steadying influence.

"Jesus *Christ,* Alexander! You have to tell me what the fuck's going on!"

I open my eyes wide and look all around, but I see nothing except impenetrable darkness. I take a deep, shuddering breath and hold it until my lungs begin to hurt.

Far off in the distance, I can hear a low, muffled rhythmic beat that seems to be getting gradually louder. At first I think it's my pulse; but as it gets louder, it reverberates with a ringing metallic sound, like someone banging against the side of a metal barrel. It can't possibly be the sound of my own heartbeat.

I'm not sure why, but the sound makes me feel extremely uncomfortable.

"I think, deep down inside, you already know what's going on, Jeff," Alexander says mildly. "Haven't you known, or at least guessed at it all along?"

I shake my head, trying to clear my mind, but a chorus of thoughts, memories, and other, fainter voices are exploding inside my head. I can't cut through the confusion to make much sense of anything . . . except one thing.

I used to have a younger brother. A brother named Jeremy who had died.

No, not died.

That was never proven. .

Jeremy disappeared when he was six years old and I was ten. He was never seen again, and his body was never found, but he must have been dead, now, for more than twenty-five years.

"And you think you were to blame for it, don't you?" one of the other voices in my head asks. It speaks so fast that I don't recognize who it is. I shake my head violently and, with tears stinging my eyes, whisper, "No, it wasn't my fault. Honest to God, it wasn't!"

"Oh, I believe you all right," Alexander says. "But the real question is, do *you* believe yourself?"

"Of course I do, but I—no, I don't know. I mean, I'm not sure of anything anymore."

"But you were supposed to be watching him, remember?"

This time, I recognize the voice. It's Sammy. Yeah, leave it to good ole Sammy to want to start causing trouble.

"No, I was—"

"You were down by the river, remember?" Sammy

says sharply. "Your parents were away on a trip, this time to Niagara Falls, wasn't it?"

"I can't remember."

"Anyway, the three of you were staying with your aunt and uncle again. Don't you remember what a hot day it was? It was the last week of August. Think about it for a minute. Remember listening to the crickets, buzzing in the tall grass? The sound was so loud, almost deafening."

"I . . . never liked that sound," I say in a voice that catches and almost breaks.

"I can certainly understand why," Sammy says, "but on that particular day, Mildred had asked you to keep an eye on Jeremy while she went to town for groceries. You were playing in the woods, out behind the house, when a couple of your friends showed up. Come on! You can't tell me you don't remember any of this."

I close my eyes and rub them vigorously. For a moment, I watch the swelling explosions of bright lights inside my head. The pounding sound inside my head is getting steadily louder. I can feel it, pulsing with throbbing red waves behind my eyes as it steadily builds up pressure.

The oil drum, I think but can't say.

Remembering the source of the sound blunts, for just a moment, the cold razor's edge of my rising panic.

"Yes," I finally said, my voice dragging like the slow, sludgy pull of warm taffy. "I . . . I think I do remember."

"You told Jeremy to stay where he was, to play on the rope swing. And you told him not to—"

"Not to go down by the river," I finish for him. "Yeah, I do remember that. Eddie and Hank. That's who showed up. I had told them I was going to be staying with Kirby and Mildred for the week, so they rode their bikes out to the farm to see me."

"And you went off with them because they wanted to show you the dead woodchuck they'd found on the road, remember?"

"That's right," I say, trembling as the memory of that afternoon becomes even sharper. "I remember that I specifically told Jeremy not to go down near the river, that I would take him wading after I got back. I only thought I'd be gone five or ten minutes, but when I—when I got back, he was—"

My voice suddenly chokes off, leaving a terrible sour taste in my mouth.

"Gone," Sammy says, "and neither you nor anyone else ever saw him again."

"Jesus Christ!"

I slouch back, feeling my shoulders drop. A cold pressure tightens around my chest, and the steady, echoing drumbeat rises even louder inside my head, keeping time now with my rapid heartbeat. Wave after wave of burning pain shoots through my body.

"And they never found him," Sammy says softly.

I can't help but notice the hint of satisfaction in Sammy's voice, and wonder why he takes such morbid pleasure in the pain this memory stirs up for me.

"How . . . how long have you known about this?" I finally manage to ask after a long silence.

"Who, me?" asks Sammy, sounding all innocent. "Why, I think a couple of us, quite a few, actually, have known about it all along. I know for sure that Alexander's known about it. We've been arguing for years over whether or not we should talk to you about it. I wanted to tell you a long time ago, but—well . . . hell, you know Alexander. He always wants to protect you until he thinks you're ready."

"Do you really think he's ready now, Sammy?"

Alexander asks, his voice clipped with barely suppressed anger.

"There really wasn't much choice, now, was there, Alex?" Sammy says. "I mean, none of us had any control over whether or not *she* would mention it to him, now, did we?"

"I'm not so sure about that," Alexander replies, letting his voice drawl as though he's suspicious. "You know, Sammy, it kinda makes me wonder why you've been pushing so hard for Jeff to get in touch with Katherine. Maybe you did it all because—eventually—you knew she *would* mention it."

"Hey, wait just a goddamned second here!" I shout in spite of the burning pain that is blossoming like a slow-motion explosion behind my eyes. "I don't exactly appreciate it that you guys are talking about me like I'm not even here! I mean, whose fucking memories *are* these, anyway?"

"Why, they're yours, of course," Alexander says. "We're just here to—"

"Hold it!" I snap. "I don't see where you or anyone else has a right to control what I do or don't remember. That's not exactly fair."

"Boy, you still don't get it, yet, do you?" Alexander says, punctuating his comment with a light laugh.

"Get what?"

"Get that you *need* us for exactly that reason. We're here to remember the things that you can't handle. And as far as I'm concerned, that's how it's gonna stay until I think you *can* handle them."

I can feel my anger rising, bubbling up like molten lava. I am filled with a sudden impulse to get up, run to the door of the dark room, unbolt it, and throw it wide open so the light from the outside world will come pouring in. If I could reach out and grab Alexander, or even better, that smart-ass Sammy or any other of my alters, I would throttle them but good! Who the fuck do they think they are, keeping things from me, holding back memories that are mine?

I force myself to take a calming breath and let it out slowly, whistling between my teeth. The thundering rhythm inside my head is almost unbearably loud now. Each beat echoes with a deafening reverberation that hasn't even begun to fade before the next one comes, thundering even louder. The pain is like a red-hot drill that is piercing from one side of my head to the other.

"But who? . . ."

My voice trails off, and I almost scream in pain, but I force myself to keep talking. "But how the hell does any of this help with anything? Why'd you bring up this memory now? How's it going to help Katherine?"

"I'm sorry, Jeff," Alexander says softly, "but I only know the past. I can't predict the future."

". . . Jeff? . . ."

This is a woman's voice, calling out to me. It is faint, and almost lost below the other voices and the steady, echoing reverberations inside my head, but I can hear the sharp edge of panic in it. For a flickering instant, I think I recognize who it is, but then it is lost beneath the roaring rush of sound that fills my head.

". . . Can you hear me, Jeff? . . ."

"You let your baby brother die, Jeff," Sammy says simply. "Can you live with that thought?"

I think Sammy is laughing at me and wonder, if I could see Sammy's expression right now, would he be leering, gloating at my agony?

"It was your responsibility to keep an eye on him, and you let him die," Sammy continues, pushing hard. *"That's* why Mildred and Kirby wanted to punish you by putting you into the metal drum. The Bible passage was about Cain and Abel. Remember now? They wanted you to *feel* the guilt and shame of letting your brother die. They wanted you to ask—No! They wanted you to *beg* God for forgiveness, but instead, you tucked all of it far back into a dark corner of your mind where you thought you could ignore it. Well, Jeffy-boy. I'm here to tell you that you can't ignore it. Not anymore, and certainly not forever!"

"You did it, Sammy, didn't you?"

My voice is low and trembling with intensity.

"What, killed Jeremy? No way!"

"I don't believe you. I think you made all of this happen, that you did it all against my will!"

"I have no idea what you're talking about," Sammy says, snickering softly. "You know, you're really starting to sound pretty paranoid."

"No, I'm not! I think you might be the one who did it all—who killed Jeremy and Judy, who messed around in the house. I think you might even have kidnapped Danny just so you could force me to remember what happened to Jeremy. Come on, admit it, you son of a bitch! Tell me the truth for once! Where's Danny? Where did you take him? *Tell me, goddamn it! Where!"*

Rippling sheets of red light sweep like lightning across my vision with every heavy, thundering drumbeat, but still, below that sound, so faint that it sounds like someone is shouting to me from several rooms away, I hear a woman's voice, calling to me. I'm pretty sure I don't have any female alters, but maybe this is someone new—someone I've created recently to help me cope with everything that's been happening.

". . . Jeff! . . . Come on, stop it! . . . Please, Jeff! . . . Talk to me! . . . You're scaring the shit out of me!"

"Katherine?"

Jeff shook his head with great effort, wincing at the pain that gripped his neck and shot through every muscle and nerve of his body. He cleared his throat, took a deep breath, and shouted as loud as he could.

"Katherine!"

"Jesus Christ, Jeff!"

Katherine's voice rang harsh and clear in his ears as he snapped his eyes open and, blinking wildly, looked at her. Her face loomed close to him, horribly large and utterly frightening.

"Jesus, Jeff," she said in a tight, twisted voice that had a slight measure of relief. "What the hell's the matter with you?"

Chapter Twenty-one
Closer to the Edge

"Jesus Christ, Jeff! What's the matter with you?"

Jeff's eyes snapped open. Katherine's words were echoing in his mind, overpowering the hollow metallic reverberation that was rapidly fading away into silence. The light from the table lamp beside her wasn't very bright, but the glow stung Jeff's eyes enough to hurt them and make them water. Feeling both confused and embarrassed, he couldn't stop blinking as he looked at Katherine's expression. It was an odd blend of worry, fear, and utter bewilderment.

"Wha—what do you mean?" he said, shaking his head and vigorously rubbing his forehead. There was a cold, hollow center of numbness behind his eyes that felt about the size of a golf ball.

"What the hell just happened to you?" Katherine asked, her voice high-pitched and edged with worry. "You were—we were just sitting here talking, and all of a sudden . . . it was like you—you just passed out or something. Are you feeling all right?"

He knew it was a lie, but he nodded and said, "Yeah, sure I am."

He sucked in a quick breath as he continued to rub

his forehead. He was surprised that he didn't already have a blinding headache, but the shifting red light and the pounding pressure had begun to subside the instant he opened his eyes. Maybe there was hope for him after all.

"I just—that's a particularly painful memory for me, even after all these years. It's something I know I'm never going to get over, and I—umm . . . look, I didn't say or do anything weird just now, did I?"

Katherine was holding her left hand up to her mouth and gnawing on the knuckle, all the while staring wide-eyed at Jeff as though she couldn't quite believe what she was looking at.

"No," she said after a moment, sounding completely drained and defeated. "But I think I know what you mean. You still feel the way I know I'm going to if . . . if—" Her voice almost broke, but she managed to go on. "—if something like that has happened to Danny. But, Jesus, Jeff! You were . . ." Tears glazed her eyes as she stared at him, unblinking. "You really had me scared. I thought you were having some kind of seizure or something."

"No, it's just that whenever I remember what happened back then—you know, with Jeremy and all, I guess I sort of lose it. That has to be the worst thing that ever happened to me in my life."

"Yeah, I . . . I can imagine," Katherine said, her voice hitching with sobs. "But it was really scary. You just sat there, sort of blanked out, and . . . and—"

She cut off what she had been about to say, but Jeff picked up on it. Raising his eyebrows, he said, "And *what?*"

Katherine lowered her gaze as though suddenly embarrassed for him.

"You were mumbling to yourself," she said, "and at times you . . . you—"

"I *what?*" Jeff said, trying hard to keep himself from

shouting. He leaned forward, both wanting to hear
what she was going to say and dreading it.

"It sounded like you were talking to yourself . . . but
you were using different voices."

Even as she was saying this, a chill zipped through
Jeff, but he managed to force a smile and say, "Oh,
don't worry about that. I was just—you know, thinking things through out loud. I do that all the time.
What did I say?"

"Nothing . . . nothing I could understand, anyway,
but you. . . . It was kind of creepy, Jeff. Your whole
expression seemed to change. Your body went limp,
your eyes closed, and you started muttering under
your breath."

Jeff suddenly stiffened when the voice started whispering inside his mind again.

*Jesus, don't tell her about us, Jeff! She probably
wouldn't believe you in the first place, but there's no
reason to get her all worried, is there?*

"Yeah, you're probably right," Jeff said, nodding.

"Huh?" Katherine replied.

A cloud of concern drifted across Katherine's face.
She slid away from him as though he were suddenly
too dangerous to be near.

Jeff forced himself to smile wider.

"Don't worry about it, okay?" he said as mildly as
he could in spite of the panic rising inside him. "Right
now I don't think we need to talk about what happened with Jeremy. Why don't we just see if we can
figure out if there's anything else we can do about
Danny, okay?"

Katherine opened her mouth and was about to say
something, but her expression suddenly dropped.
With a sobbing moan, she leaned forward, planted her
elbows on her knees, covered her face with both hands,
and began to cry, raw and braying.

Feeling absolutely helpless, Jeff shifted closer to her

and was about to hug her, but he suddenly drew back, sensing that there was nothing he could say or do that was going to help. There probably wasn't anything *anyone* could do for her right now, short of bringing Danny home, safe and sound.

Close to tears himself and trembling inside, Jeff stood up and began pacing back and forth across the living-room floor, all the while twining his fingers together and cracking his knuckles.

I know what I should do, he thought. *I should go down to the police station right now and turn myself in.*

Mild electrical currents tingled through his body like teasing fingers.

Even if I don't consciously know anything about what's happened, chances are pretty damned good someone, probably Sammy, has taken over and done something to Danny. He's probably kidnapped him and stashed him away somewhere like up in—

"Up in my old bedroom," Jeff said aloud.

His voice wasn't much more than a breathy whisper, but it drew Katherine's attention.

"What did you say?" she asked, looking at him fearfully.

Completely flustered, Jeff ground his teeth and shook his head.

"No. Nothing. I was just thinking out loud again," he said shakily. His legs felt suddenly rubbery as a wave of dizziness washed over him.

He and Katherine locked eyes and stared at each other intensely for a lengthening moment. In that moment, something—some kind of message seemed to pass silently between them, but Jeff wasn't exactly sure what it was. He thought—at least he wanted to think—that she was trying to communicate to him just how much she still cared for him and needed him, still loved him, just as he thought—and feared—that deep in his heart, he still loved her . . . maybe even more than he loved his wife.

"I think . . . maybe you'd better go now," Katherine said after the silence had lengthened uncomfortably long. Her voice was faint and halting, and not at all convincing.

Jeff started toward her, his arms raised to embrace her, but then he jerked to a stop and let his arms fall to his sides. His body went suddenly cold as he stared at Katherine's grief-stricken face and saw, even through her misery, how beautiful she was. In that instant, he knew there was no way in hell he could give Katherine what she needed right now.

He wasn't strong enough.

Maybe he had never been strong enough. Maybe that's why they had broken up back in high school, because he hadn't been able to give her the strength and love she needed and deserved.

"Yeah," he said softly, sighing as he gazed down at the floor. "I guess I'd better go."

He patted his pants pocket, feeling for his car keys, but still didn't move toward the door. As he stared at the floor, a sudden hot flush burned the back of his neck. He could feel Katherine's gaze boring into him, but he didn't dare look up at her. He was afraid of the longing, the need he might see in her eyes.

Jesus, man! Don't get chicken-shit now! What the fuck are you waiting for, a written invitation?

"I can't," Jeff whispered.

Shit, man, Sally will never know about it if you do something! And you know sure as shit that's what Kat wants. She wants you now!

This voice and others buzzed inside Jeff's head, but he squeezed his eyes tightly shut for a moment and willed them all to be silent. He took a shuddering breath, and when he finally dared to look at Katherine again, he forced himself to smile.

"Just promise me you'll call if you need someone, okay?" he said.

Katherine's eyes were glistening as she stared at him. Biting her lower lip, she nodded slowly.

"Yeah," she said in a low, broken rasp. "I promise."

Jeff nodded. Without another word, he turned and walked to the front door, and went outside. The night air was cold, and he shivered. Tears blurred his vision as he walked down to his car, got in, and started it up. But as he backed out onto the road, heading back to town, he realized that he had no intention of heading straight back to Judy's house.

No, first he had some business to attend to downtown at the police station.

When Jeff entered the police station, Eddie Dearborn was in the dispatcher's office, behind a wired-glass window partition. He was sitting with one leg up on the desk as he joked with the dispatcher and two other policemen. All four of them looked up as the heavy glass door slammed shut behind him.

"Yo, Jeff," Eddie said, looking surprised as he waved and started around to unlock the partition door. He walked out into the reception area, holding his hand out for Jeff to shake.

"I thought we'd canceled until Sunday night," Eddie said.

"Yeah. We did," Jeff replied.

He found it almost impossible to look Eddie straight in the eyes. His gaze kept drifting nervously around the police station. It was a lot smaller than he remembered it but, except for a fresh coat of paint— the same industrial green he recalled it had always been—it looked exactly the same. In the reception area, there was a line of folding metal chairs. Above the dispatcher's window was a brightly painted town emblem. On the wall was a bulletin board that was covered with FBI "Most Wanted" posters and community safety announcements.

Jeff didn't recognize any of the other policemen, but he nodded a silent greeting to them. He didn't say anything more, and Eddie apparently caught on that there was something bothering him.

"Did you want to see me about something?" Eddie asked.

Biting his lower lip, Jeff nodded.

"Well then, let's go down to my office."

Jeff followed Eddie through a set of doors and down a short corridor to a small room. Eddie indicated for Jeff to sit in the chair beside a paper-cluttered desk as he eased the door shut and walked over to sit behind the desk.

"You look pretty worked up about something," Eddie said, immediately adopting a bit of a detached, professional tone of voice. "Is there something I can do for you?"

Jeff licked his lips as he glanced around the room. The walls seemed to telescope inward at odd, distorted angles.

"Probably," he said.

He tried to put some force into his voice, but just saying that single word took a great deal of effort. A chilling wave of dizziness swept over him. His eyes fluttered as he blinked back the gathering tears. So many different voices were chattering so loudly inside his head that he couldn't register anything any of them were saying. He had an inordinate amount of trouble trying to remember what—if anything—he had said aloud.

"Do you have a watercooler or something around here?" Jeff asked. "My throat's parched."

"Sure thing," Eddie replied. "Hold on a sec. I'll get you something."

Eddie left the office, allowing Jeff a moment to settle himself in his chair, to take a calming breath, and to look around. As far as he could tell, it was a typical policeman's office, with paperwork scattered everywhere and sheaves of notices taped to the wall and tacked to the large bulletin board. The only modern touch was a computer terminal on the side of the desk. The wastebasket, Jeff noticed, needed to be emptied.

The office door suddenly swung open, and Eddie reentered.

"Here ya go," he said, handing Jeff a conical paper cup that was filled almost to the brim with water.

Jeff nodded his thanks and took a sip, the water so cold it was numbing.

Walking over and sitting behind his desk again, Eddie cleared enough of a space so he could rest his elbows on the edge. He leaned forward and folded his hands in front of his face.

"So," he said, sounding serious, "tell me what brings you down here at this time of night."

Jeff glanced up at the wall clock and saw that it was already almost eight o'clock.

"It's about that missing kid," Jeff said. His voice almost shattered.

"You mean the Foster kid?" Eddie said, narrowing his gaze. "What about him?"

Jeff took another sip of water. When he swallowed, his throat made a loud gulp. He laughed nervously, then raked his fingers through his hair and stared at his old high-school buddy's face for a moment. He couldn't quite absorb the fact that this really was his old friend, Eddie Dearborn, wearing a town cop's uniform. He had an odd dissociated feeling that he and Eddie were still just kids, playing some weird kind of game.

"It's—ah, really kind of complicated," Jeff said after a moment.

"Go ahead. I'm listening."

Jeff looked straight into his friend's eyes, hoping he could find the courage to continue. He realized now that it might have been a big mistake to come down to the station without thinking all of this through, but it was too late now to reconsider. There was no way he could leave without looking suspicious as all hell.

"I-I realize that we haven't kept in very good touch since high school," Jeff began.

He spoke haltingly, trying to choose his words carefully, but it seemed as though at least four or five voices were shouting inside his head, all demanding his attention, all suggesting things he could say. One voice in particular—Sammy's, he thought—kept repeating, *This was a big mistake, Jeffy-boy! A big fucking mistake!*

Eddie snickered.

"Hell, I didn't even get a Christmas card from you for the past however many years, but, hey, I understand. People lose touch over the years. It happens."

"Yeah, I guess so," Jeff said. "I feel really bad about it, but you see—" He took a deep breath and let it out between his teeth slowly. "I-I've been having some problems of my own lately."

Eddie still had his elbows resting on the edge of the desk as he listened attentively. He seemed not even to blink his eyes as he stared at Jeff.

"What kind of problems?" Eddie asked, his voice sounding low and detached.

Jeff tipped his head back and took a big gulp of water, emptying the small cup. Then he crumpled it up in his hand and squeezed it tightly, staring at his knuckles until they went bone-white.

"Psychological problems," he said.

His voice was almost a whisper, but the tone sounded odd, as if not he, but someone else had spoken. He felt compelled to glance over his shoulder to see if anyone else was in the room with them, but he maintained eye contact with Eddie.

"I'm sorry to hear that," Eddie said, sounding sincere but with little emotion.

Jeff looked at him intensely for a moment, silently wishing that he had never come down here. He must have been crazy to think that Eddie or anyone else would give a shit about his mental problems. He should have taken the time and thought this all through before acting.

"You see, I-I've been diagnosed as having multiple personalities," Jeff said after a pause. "Do you know what that is?"

Eddie regarded him silently for a moment; then he smiled and said, "Sure I do. My wife watches *Oprah.*"

"I'm serious, Eddie."

Jeff tried hard to keep the frantic edge out of his voice.

"I've been in therapy for the better part of the last eight years, trying to work this all out. Up until a few days ago, I thought I pretty much had it conquered, but I still have . . . I have voices inside my head."

"Voices?"

"Yeah, voices . . . voices that don't feel or sound anything like my own thoughts. Do you have any idea what that must be like?" Jeff asked. His voice was trembling as it rose higher than normal.

Eddie's smile slowly melted as the two former friends stared at each other.

"No, I can't say as I do," Eddie replied, apparently realizing just how serious Jeff was.

"You see," Jeff went on, "I thought I had them— the other personalities inside me—under control, but now—especially ever since my sister died . . . ever since she *killed* herself, I-I'm not so sure."

Eddie leaned back in his chair and sighed, staring for a moment at the ceiling. The blood rushing inside

Jeff's ears made a loud whooshing sound that kept time with his rapid pulse.

"You said you wanted to talk to me about the missing Foster kid," Eddie said, still using his calm, professionally detached voice. "What's all this got to do with that situation?"

Jeff bit down on his lower lip until it began to hurt. Then, closing his eyes for a moment, he took another rattling breath and said, "I think . . . I'm afraid one of my personalities might have done something to him, to Danny."

He wasn't sure what he expected to see when he opened his eyes and looked at Eddie, but he was relieved to see that his former friend didn't look at all amused or skeptical about this suggestion. Eddie was frowning deeply and staring at Jeff so intensely that he shifted nervously in his chair.

"I-I know it sounds really wacko," Jeff said, looking down and wishing he could find something to do with his hands besides squeeze the crumpled paper cup. "I mean, if I was you, and I was hearing this, I'd probably be on the telephone right now, calling for the little men in white coats to come and cart me away to a rubber room or something."

"No," Eddie said, scratching the back of his neck. "I don't think I'll be calling the little men in the white coats just yet. Go on. Tell me more."

"There's not much else to tell, really," Jeff said. "I haven't mentioned this—my suspicions about what happened to Danny, to anyone else, not even to my therapist or wife."

Jeff found that Eddie's marginal acceptance gave him the confidence to continue.

"I've been wrestling with this problem for a long time, Eddie—a *very* long time, and now I'm worried that some part of me, a part that maybe still can't accept some of the shit that happened to me back when I was a little kid, is . . . is out of control and is *doing* things. I'm afraid this part of me might have done something to get back at Katherine because we broke up."

"Do you have any proof of this?" Eddie asked. "I mean, it sounds intriguing, but with your sister's funeral and all, and that break-in at your house, I figure you've got to be under a hell of a lot of pressure. I'm not a shrink. I need some concrete evidence. If you know, then tell me where the hell this kid is."

Jeff shook his head.

"I-I don't know, at least not consciously," he said.

Again, his voice sounded much higher than normal, almost like one of the other voices inside his head.

"But I think I . . . I have a pretty good idea."

Eddie's eyebrows shot up.

"Is that so?"

Jeff nodded.

"Yeah," he said.

He took a deep breath as he listened for the voices inside his head to start up, but they were all silent.

"I want you to come out to my sister's house with me and check one of the rooms . . . my old bedroom."

Eddie almost cracked a smile, but then he nodded very slowly.

"And why's that?"

"Because I think one of the voices inside my head is trying to tell me that Danny Foster might be in there, but I—"

His voice broke for a moment, but he cleared his throat and forced himself to continue.

"I'm just not sure if he's alive or . . . or dead."

Jeff drove in his car, and Eddie followed in the police cruiser. As he pulled to a stop in the driveway and got out of his car, Jeff was positive that never in his life had he felt more nervous. He was almost numb with fear and was afraid he was going to throw up. Even all the worries and concerns he'd experienced when Sally was giving birth to Robin paled beside this. At least with the birth of a child, there is always a strong element of happiness and joy and hope. As far as he could see, what he was facing now didn't have the slightest possibility of hope.

None, except that—finally, after many days . . . a whole lifetime of avoiding it, he was going to face whatever terrors he thought might be shut up in that room. He kept frantically trying to think of some excuse so he could avoid going up there with Eddie, but his mind was a roaring white blank. He knew he had to be there to see if he or some part of him had brought Danny there.

And to find out if Danny was alive or dead!

The moon was lost behind a high overcast, and a biting wind was blowing in off the ocean as they walked up to the side door. Jeff thought he could hear the hiss of crashing surf in the distance. As he unlocked and opened the door, he noticed that Eddie had unsnapped the strap of his holster. They entered the house, and he led the way through the living room to the stairway, turning on the lights as they went. By the time they started up the stairs, he saw that Eddie had his revolver drawn.

Their combined weight made every step creak horribly loudly as they went upstairs. Jeff was wishing he had mentioned Judy's "twilight lover" to Eddie before now, but he didn't think this was the right time. Eddie seemed to be taking all of this very seriously, and Jeff had to admit that there seemed to be something strange or brooding about the house. There was an eerie atmosphere to it, a foreboding silence that demanded caution. Eddie knew which room had been Jeff's and, without any hesitation, he walked down the

hallway to the closed bedroom door. Jeff had no
choice but to follow.

"In here?" Eddie asked, cocking one eyebrow as he
looked at the closed door.

Jeff grunted and nodded as he took a wary step
backwards. He was thinking about all the hours he
and Eddie had spent up in his bedroom, listening to
music, laughing, and talking about everything, mostly
baseball and girls. He wished like hell he could put on
a brave front, but he felt completely disoriented and
almost fainted as he sucked in his breath and watched
Eddie reach out for the doorknob, grip it, and begin to
twist it. A cold choking sensation clutched at Jeff's
throat and started to squeeze so tightly he saw tiny
spinning dots of white light shoot across his vision. A
high, fast pattering sound filled his ears, and he
cringed, just waiting to hear the voices begin to shout
inside his mind.

Everything he thought, saw, and heard seemed to be
magnified and happening in torturous slow motion.

The door latch clicked loudly, sounding like someone had banged a hammer once against a hollow,
metal drum.

The oil drum!

Eddie pushed the door inward. The hinges squealed
like tires, skidding out on wet pavement. An expanding wedge of light from the hallway spilled into the
room, but the interior was filled with a dense, velvety
darkness that seemed to pulsate with an ominous life
of its own as Eddie took a cautious step into the room.
The smell of a closed room—stale, stifling air and a
hint of mothballs—wafted out into the hallway, almost choking Jeff as he took an involuntary step forward.

As Eddie reached into the room and felt around for
the wall switch, Jeff was filled with a sudden, terrible
certainty that any second now, something horrible was

going to materialize out of the darkness, reach out, and grab him.

It seemed to take forever, but—finally—he heard a soft *click* as warm, yellow light filled the small room. Jeff choked back the shout that had been threatening to burst out of him as he looked over Eddie's shoulder into what had once been his bedroom.

It looked just as he had left it, nearly twenty years ago.

The walls were still painted a light, sky blue. The same pictures were hanging on the walls: a sunset scene over the mountains, two photographs of race cars, and Jeff's framed high-school diploma. The ceiling light was covered by the same blue glass globe, but it was now coated thick with dust that diffused the light. Over Eddie's shoulder, Jeff could see a corner of what had once been his bed and the faded brown Roy Rogers bedspread he had used since he was eight years old. Throughout high school, he had been embarrassed that he still had a "little kid's" bedspread, and had begged his parents to buy him a new one, but they never did. In the corner of the room, between the window and the closed closet door, he saw the battered pine bureau he had used right up through high school. It was still covered with all the stickers and decals he had put on it, mostly baseball and football team emblems. Right in the middle of the top drawer was his favorite, a fading picture of Rat Fink, drawn by Big Daddy Roth.

"Jesus Christ," Jeff whispered almost reverentially as he shook his head.

Eddie glanced at him over his shoulder, then looked back into the room. The floor was coated with a thin glaze of dust.

"Well," Eddie said at last, "it sure as hell looks like no one's been in here in quite some time."

"Yeah, I . . . I think so," Jeff said simply.

He was sure he caught an edge of sarcasm in his friend's voice, and he felt terribly embarrassed. Hanging back in the hall, he leaned against the wall for support as Eddie walked into the room. He went over to the closet door and opened it, but both of them could see that it was empty except for a few old, battered suitcases.

Eddie snapped the safety on his revolver, slipped it back into his holster, and strapped it. Placing his hands on his hips, he nodded as he surveyed the empty room.

You goddamned idiot!

The voice inside Jeff's mind was so loud and sudden he couldn't help but jump.

This isn't where he would be! Come on! Use your fucking brain!

"You say something?" Eddie asked, raising his eyebrows as he turned to look at Jeff again.

Jeff shook his head and tried to reply, but his throat felt like it was packed with sand, sealed shut. The blood drained from his face, and a cold pressure spread from his stomach and into his chest and legs.

"Hey, man," Eddie said, frowning deeply as he looked at Jeff. "You sure you're all right?"

"Yeah . . . sure," Jeff managed to say, but he felt as though his legs were going to give out from under him any second now.

He was mildly surprised that his mind wasn't filled with a chorus of shouting, demanding voices, but even the voice he had just heard had fallen silent. All he was aware of was a single, clear thought that was spoken in his normal mental voice.

So THIS is what you were afraid of, huh?

Chapter Twenty-two
Together Again

Now I'm the twilight lover, Jeff thought as he stood in the shadows at the foot of Katherine's driveway.

It was a little past midnight, and the air was cold enough to turn his breath to mist. Eddie had left the house more than three hours ago, and Jeff had decided to go for a drive to help clear his mind. But he didn't drive around aimlessly. He had gone straight to Katherine's house and parked his car a little way down the road, out of sight from the house.

Now he was standing on the roadside, shivering as he gazed up at the house. The lights were on in the kitchen and living room, so he knew that Katherine was still awake. Several times during the half hour he had been standing here, he had seen her shadow shift across the drawn window shades as she paced through the house, no doubt thinking the absolute worst had happened to her son. She was unable to sleep because she was dreading the next phone call from the police, the one that would begin, "I'm sorry to have to tell you this, ma'am . . ."

Jeff wished desperately that there was something he could do for her, but he felt absolutely helpless. Even

though he and Eddie had found nothing at the house,
he couldn't shake the feeling that, on some deep, subconscious level, he knew exactly what had happened to
Danny. The problem was, he had no idea how to find
out for certain. All of the voices in his head had fallen
curiously silent, but he didn't take this as a good sign.
He couldn't help but think their silence presaged some
horrible event, or there was something that some part
of himself wanted to keep him from discovering.

He wanted to do something, but he had no idea
where to turn. He already felt foolish for having involved Eddie as much as he had. He was certain, now,
that he never should have gone to the police station
and asked Eddie to come out to the house with him,
but—Jesus!—he had been positive that the closed
room had something to do with what was happening.
How could he have been so foolish?

As he stood there, shivering in the shadows and
watching Katherine's silhouette ripple across the
drawn shades, he tried to make sense of everything
that had happened recently, but his mind was tormented by confused thoughts and impulses.

Nothing made sense anymore.

For weeks now he had been holding one thought at
bay, but now it shot into his mind with the shattering
impact of an exploding bomb.

Maybe Judy had the right idea!

Maybe he should just say fuck it all and kill himself.

That certainly would put an end to all the misery,
confusion, and doubt, so why not? If Judy had the
courage to try it, why couldn't he?

*Come on! You know damned well what you want to
do!*

The raw voice spoke so suddenly and so loudly in
his mind that it seemed to come at him out of the
darkness from all directions at once.

What you gotta do is get your ass up there to the door,

ring the goddamned doorbell, and go inside. You know that's what she wants.

She needs you, Jeff, said a different, fainter voice, *but not like that.*

Soon, other voices were whispering in his mind—or in the surrounding darkness—but they were too faint for him to catch more than fragments.

"Shut up! Shut the fuck up, all of you!" Jeff growled between chattering teeth.

He looked up at the nearly three-quarter moon that was riding high in the sky. It cast thin, blue shadows across the lawn, which was silvered with early frost. Once or twice, far off in the distance, he heard the sound of a passing car, but other than that and the gentle sighing of the wind in the branches overhead, the night was absolutely still.

So still, in fact, that Jeff could hear his racing heart-beat, pounding like a hammer in his ears.

He tried to deny the strong feelings he still had for Katherine by convincing himself that his desperation and vulnerability were making him read things into the situation—things that just weren't there.

How could he even think that he still loved Katherine?

What they had shared was all in the past, and nothing they could do would resurrect it. They weren't the same people they had been back then.

Hey, you're missing the whole point, buddy. She wants you now. You know she does.

But even if he wasn't imagining things, he told himself, it wouldn't be right to go to her now, thinking that anything he could offer would help her. In spite of the one voice that kept prompting him, he certainly didn't want to take advantage of Katherine at the worst possible moment.

"No," he whispered, surprised by the intensity of his voice. "I can't do it!"

Oh, yes you can, the low voice whispered from out of the cold darkness. *You'll be back in Colorado soon. This is probably your last chance! Don't let it slip by you!*

Jeff tried to deny it, but he couldn't stop himself from getting an erection as he thought about Katherine. Vivid, erotic fantasies played through his mind, and he kept repeating a single, burning question to himself.

What would be so wrong about it, if Katherine and I were to make love? Where's the harm in it?

Sure, he was married, and he had no doubt that he still loved Sally. He would never do anything to hurt her or Robin, but right now, he and Katherine were wounded people. Why should they be denied a chance to be together, if only to give each other a slight measure of solace?

Go on up to the fucking door and knock! the voice said, rasping so loudly in the night that it made Jeff's ears ring. *You don't have to do anything. Just go up there and talk to her . . . feel out the situation . . . see what happens.*

Feeling as though he were moving in a dream, Jeff started up across the lawn. His feet made hushed, crinkling sounds as they dragged through the frosted grass. The cold night air burned his throat and lungs, and he was breathing heavily by the time he reached the foot of the steps.

Forget about it, said another voice, speaking faintly inside his mind. *Go back to Judy's house. Think about everything you have back home in Colorado. Don't let yourself be pushed into doing anything you don't want to do.*

"I'm not being pushed," Jeff whispered.

He watched the misty ball of his breath disperse like smoke on the night wind. Then, taking a deep breath, he mounted the steps. Clenching his hand into a tight fist, he watched in amazement, as though he wasn't quite in control of his own actions, as he raised his hand to knock on the front door.

Go on! Do it! Don't kid yourself. This is what both of you have been waiting for and wanting all along! Jesus, just do it! I swear to God you won't regret it!

Jeff squeezed his fist so forcefully it began to hurt. He cast a nervous glance over his shoulder, unable to get rid of the eerie feeling that someone or maybe several people were lurking in the darkness, lost in the shadows as they eagerly watched him. He turned and looked, expecting to see the cold fire of their eyes in the shadows under the trees as they stared back at him.

Shivering, he sucked in a breath and held it until his lungs began to hurt. In quick succession, he rapped on the door three times. His hand was cold, and the impact stung his knuckles. The knock sounded hollow, and a loose pane of glass vibrated.

Stepping back, Jeff coiled with tension as he waited, wondering if Katherine had heard him.

Go on! hissed the loudest voice inside his head. *Knock again! Harder!*

Jeff was just raising his hand when a distorted shadow shifted across the drawn shade of the door. The outside light winked on, so suddenly and brightly it stung his eyes. He had to shield his face with his hand.

The door lock clicked, and the door edged open a crack. A narrow wedge of yellow light widened until an eye peered out at him through the narrow opening. Then, with a sudden *whoosh,* the door flew wide open, and Katherine rushed out at him.

"Jeff! Oh, Jesus! Jeff!" she cried in a high, warbling voice.

Jeff took one step forward but was almost knocked over as Katherine threw herself into his arms, wrapping her arms around him and squeezing tightly. She felt warm and trembling in his grasp, like a frightened bird. Jeff was stunned, speechless. Tears filled his eyes as he hugged her close. He tried to say something but ended up stammering. He couldn't help but notice how natural they felt together as his hand went to the back of her head and stroked her hair, twining it between his fingers.

After a moment, Katherine pulled back and looked at him with red-rimmed eyes, glassy with grief. Jeff started to say something, but she cut him off by pulling his face down to hers and giving him a long, passionate kiss on the mouth. The warm tip of her tongue gently probed between his lips, sending excited chills through him. When they parted for a moment, both of them gasping for breath, Katherine stepped back and smiled weakly.

"I knew you'd come," she said in a deep, throaty whisper.

Taking him by the hand, she guided him into the house and shut the door, locking it against the night. Jeff shivered, thinking momentarily of the eyes he had sensed outside, observing him. He knew they were still out there, watching.

Clutching his hand almost desperately, Katherine led him up the stairs and down the hallway to her bedroom. Jeff couldn't dispel the intense sensation that all of this was a dream as, without another word, Katherine guided him over to her bed and eased him down onto it. Then she sat down beside him and curled into his embrace.

Slowly and lovingly, they hugged and kissed, their passion increasing as they tasted each other. Jeff wasn't sure who started it, but before long their hands were running eagerly, almost desperately up and down each other's body, grabbing and probing. Their soft sighs and deeper moans filled the room as they began to undress each other. Lips and hands rubbed against smooth skin as clothes peeled away. The hallway light, which had been left on, illuminated the room with a gauzy, lemon glow.

Jeff's mind was spinning. He felt almost drunk as he closed his eyes, amazed by how familiar Katherine felt when he kissed her lips and face, and cupped her breasts with his hands.

All these years, this is how it should have been, he thought as his lips moved along the line of her jaw and then, after he unbuttoned her blouse and unsnapped her bra, started nibbling down to her neck and shoulders. He groaned when Katherine's hand slid down his chest, rubbed his belly, and then slipped into his pants. She grabbed him and began to rub him up and down.

Jesus, it's like we've never been apart, he thought. *Like I'm the key, and she's the lock.*

As soon as they were naked, Katherine slipped from Jeff's embrace, rolled over onto her back and, holding her arms out to him, sighed softly as she pulled him down on top of her. She let out a low, passionate groan as he nudged her legs apart with his knees and then entered her.

Even through his closed lids, morning sunlight stung Jeff's eyes. He awoke with a startled yelp and found himself face-to-face with Katherine, who was staring at him.

"Good morning," she said.

A weak smile played at the corners of her mouth, but a sad, tearful gleam sparkled in her eyes. Jeff saw the pain and worried tension in her expression, and it cast an instant gloom over his memory of the night before and the things they had done to and for each other.

Licking his upper lip, he cleared his throat and managed to say, "Hi."

Suddenly embarrassed, he turned away from her and closed his eyes. Cupping his hands over his face, he took a deep breath, the air whistled between his fingers. He jumped when he felt Katherine's fingertips brush across his bare shoulder.

"Hey, are you all right?"

Jeff grunted in reply but didn't quite dare to look at her. He could feel the gentle wash of her breath on his skin. In spite of himself, he found the sensation pleasurable and started to grow hard. Opening his eyes, he looked at her again, then shook his head.

"No . . . not really," he said, surprised by the twisted sound of his own voice. "I think I . . . well, you have to admit that last night was probably a . . . a—"

He cut himself off, but Katherine finished the sentence for him.

"A big mistake, right?"

Biting his lower lip, Jeff looked away for a moment and nodded.

"Yeah." He took a deep breath. "Don't you think so?"

He had no idea what he wanted her to say. It pained him to see the misery in her eyes, but Katherine shook her head and whispered, "No, I don't think so at all."

Jeff swallowed with difficulty and cleared his throat again.

"But I—" he started to say.

Katherine hushed him by placing her forefinger across his mouth.

"I know . . . I know," she said. "You're married. You love your wife, and you feel guilty as hell about this." Her hand brushed up and down on his arm, leaving hot, tingling tracks. "Don't worry, okay, Jeff? I promise you this was it. I won't make any more demands on you from now on, okay?"

Hot tears stung Jeff's eyes as he gazed into the swirling depths of Katherine's and tried to measure her pain against his own. Although it remained unspoken, he knew that the utmost thought in her mind was concern for her son and her fear that he might already be dead. He shivered, recalling the depth of his own anguish when his brother, Jeremy, had disappeared so many years ago.

"But I did want to do it, too," he finally said in a high, strangled voice. "Ever since I first saw you . . . that night in the grocery store . . . I've been thinking about you a lot, and how we . . . how maybe we never should have broken up."

Katherine smiled wanly, fluttering her eyes to blink back the tears. Turning away from him, she dropped her head into the well of the pillow and stared blankly up at the ceiling.

"Umm . . . yeah," she said, in a low, feeble voice. "Over the years, I have to admit that I've kinda thought about that, too."

Jeff shifted around. Supporting his weight on his elbow, he reached out and cupped her face, touching her cheek with his thumb to wipe away the tear that was rolling down toward her chin.

"But I . . . I just don't think that last night can change everything that's happened, you know?" he said. His voice was struggling for control. "We both know that, don't we?"

Blinking her eyes rapidly, Katherine nodded. "Yeah . . . I guess so," she whispered.

She pressed her hand against his hand, forcing it flat against her face.

"But last night—" She took a deep breath. "Last night was everything I'd ever hoped and imagined it would be."

"Yeah," Jeff said after a long pause. "For me, too."

His first impulse was to make love to her again, but they both remained silent for a long time as Jeff lay there, staring at her profile and wondering how different his life would have been if he had married Katherine and settled down in Cape Higgins. Finally, after telling himself that he would go crazy worrying about such things, he threw the bedcovers aside, picked up his clothes where he had tossed them in the darkness, and hurriedly dressed. The whole time, Katherine lay there silently on the bed, staring up at the ceiling.

Jeff knew what was on her mind, and as he dressed, he kept glancing over at her, feeling absolutely helpless to say or do anything more to help. What they had done last night had been selfish, almost desperate on his part, no matter what she said she felt or thought about it.

Once he was dressed, he leaned over the bed and kissed her lightly on the cheek. He slid his hand from her face to her throat, thrilled by the feel of her skin. It was cold to the touch, but a subtle electrical current seemed to pass between them. Fresh tears glistened in her eyes.

"You know I can't stay," he said. He got up from the bed and walked to the bedroom door.

His hand was poised to push the door open, but he was reluctant to leave. A strong, almost overpowering urge to go back to her took hold of him. He wanted to hug her; make violent, passionate love to her again; but the voice that had been speaking inside his head last night, urging him on, was now curiously silent.

"You know where I'm staying," he finally said, standing in the doorway and looking at her.

For a shattering moment, he saw no signs of life, not even the faint stirring of her breath, but then Katherine's eyelids fluttered. She shifted her head to look at him.

"Yeah," she said, then she turned away from him again and closed her eyes.

"I mean it, Kat," Jeff said, still torn between wanting to stay or leave. "I'll be there at least until the end

of next week, and I promise you one thing. I'm going
to do everything I can to help find Danny. You have
my phone number, so, please, any time, day or night,
call me if you need someone, even if it's just to talk,
okay?"

Katherine took a deep breath and held it.

"Please, Kat."

Even to his own ears, his voice sounded shattered.

"Promise me you'll call."

"I will," she finally said, but her voice was so soft
and raspy that Jeff had the impression that she hadn't
really spoken at all—that he had imagined her reply.

Without another word, he left the room. He walked
down the stairs and out the front door. Morning sunlight slanted across the lawn, making the autumn-
brown grass glow like molten gold. His insides were
twisting with guilt as he closed the front door gently
behind him and started down the road to where he had
left his car. No matter what else happened to him, he
told himself, last night would be burned into his brain
until the day he died.

"So where were you last night?"

Sally's voice sounded faint and tinny over the telephone. Jeff closed his eyes so tightly he saw spinning
wheels of light.

"I was—ah, out pretty late," he said, cringing with
guilt. He was positive Sally could hear the betrayal in
his voice.

"Doing what?" she asked archly.

"I—ah, I hooked up with an old friend from high
school. Eddie Dearborn. He's a town cop. We went
out and hit a few bars in Portland after he got off duty.
I didn't get home until—God, it must've been a little
after midnight."

"I tried calling you at one o'clock your time," Sally

said a bit snappishly. "You didn't have the message machine on. The phone must've rung at least ten times."

Jeff sighed and rubbed his forehead.

"Hmm. I never even heard it," he said, flinching inwardly. "I was pretty drunk by the time I got back. Probably slept right through it. God, I'm still pretty hungover."

He was definitely beginning to get a headache, but it had nothing to do with drinking last night.

"Jeez, Jeff. That's not like you, to go out drinking, I mean," Sally said. She still sounded suspicious. "I'm not sure that was a very good idea, considering the stress you've been under lately and all."

"Believe me. I needed it," Jeff replied, blushing with guilt.

Unbidden, his mind filled with the memory of how Katherine had felt as they made love, her body twisting and thrusting eagerly beneath him. He tried to stop himself, but he couldn't help but compare her with Sally.

"You know, since I got back here, something else has happened."

"What's that?"

"One of the local kids has disappeared."

"Oh, dear."

"Yeah. He never came home from school yesterday. Actually, he's the son of a high-school friend of mine. Not the cop. Someone else."

Careful, now, whispered a voice inside his head. *You don't want to give away too much.*

"The whole town's in an uproar," Jeff said. "In fact, I thought I saw him and reported it to the police, but it—it turned out to be a . . . a mistake."

"I see," Sally said.

There was a short pause, but it was long enough for Jeff to wonder if he should tell Sally about last night.

Should he blurt it out now and admit his mistake, or should he wait until he was home? Or maybe this was something he was going to have to hide from her for the rest of his life, and hope that—eventually—he forgot about it.

"So how are things going with getting the house cleaned out and all?" Sally asked at last.

Jeff thought he could still hear suspicion tinging her voice, but he decided not even to hint about what he had done, at least not until he was home. Then he would prove to her that his one night with Katherine had been just that—a one-nighter, nothing more.

"Oh, I'm getting there," he said, wondering how convincing he sounded. "There's still a shitload of stuff to go through, but I should have everything done in another day or two. I was thinking about getting a flight for Friday."

"Oh, that'd be great!" Sally said, for the first time sounding genuinely enthused. "It'll be good to see you. Robin and I have missed you something terrible, you know."

"I know. I miss you, too," Jeff replied. "I love you."

He thought his voice sounded flat, and he couldn't stop wondering just how much he really meant those three words—if at all. Lasting relationships were built on love and trust. Had last night done irreparable damage to his marriage? How could he ever expect Sally to trust him if he couldn't even trust himself?

"Hey, you take care of yourself, now, you hear?" Sally said.

His ear filled with the loud, smacking sound of her kiss.

"Yeah," Jeff whispered. "Bye."

"Call me tomorrow," Sally said.

"I sure will."

An overwhelming wave of grief swept through him

as he hung up the phone. He closed his eyes and leaned against the wall, wondering how in the hell he could ever be the same person with his wife—or anyone else—ever again.

Chapter Twenty-three

Billy

It was late afternoon, slipping toward evening. Wide bands of purple clouds streaked the pale sky like fingers that were dragging the sun down below the horizon.

Gravel spun up from the tires and rattled against the underside of his car as Jeff turned right onto Bridge Road, a single-lane dirt road about two miles out of town. The steering wheel played loosely in his hands as orange sunlight flickered through the pine trees that lined the roadside, creating an odd strobe-like effect. Jeff glanced into his rearview mirror and saw the plume of yellow dust and dead leaves that swirled in his wake. His car started to drift, and he quickly corrected his steering and focused on the road ahead.

The farther he drove down the road, the more he was surprised by a powerful feeling of familiarity. He seemed to recognize every curve, every rise, every bump as if he had been driving through here every day of his life for the last twenty years. If it had been any other road, he no doubt would have found the drive relaxing, the view pleasant, but a cold clutching gripped his heart and wouldn't let go. A mile or so down the road, he pulled over and stopped. Breathing shallowly, he watched in the rearview mirror as yellow dust, glittering like powdered gold in the slanting sunlight, settled behind him.

Turning to look straight ahead, he focused on the left-hand turn onto a narrow, deep-rutted dirt-and-gravel driveway. The driveway was flanked on both sides by dried, head-high weeds and grass. The head of the turn was marked by a rusty, battered mailbox, which was stuck onto a rotting post that angled out toward the road. Long ago, the number sixteen had been painted in white on the front of the mailbox, but the number was now yellowed and peeling, almost invisible.

Jeff cringed, knowing that no more than a hundred yards down that driveway, hidden behind a screen of thick brush and pines, was the farmhouse that belonged to his aunt and uncle, Mildred and Kirby Wagner.

He had an immediate and remarkably clear mental image of the Cape-style house with its narrow windows, sagging porch, and gray weathered shingles. Even without closing his eyes, he could see in his mind the ancient barn with its swaybacked roofline and cavernous, double-doored maw. He remembered with a shiver how, whenever he worked up in the hayloft with his uncle, he would imagine that the rough-cut, gray roof beams overhead were the ribs of a whale that had swallowed him whole, like Jonah in the Bible story his aunt and uncle had once made him read.

He rolled the window down and took a deep breath. The air was heavy with the scent of pine and rotting leaves, a peculiar quality that further stirred his memories. He could almost taste the dust in the house's weed-choked dooryard. He could almost smell the dark, fresh-turned soil of the vegetable garden out behind the house. And beyond that, behind the house, he could almost see the wide, stone-strewn fields that rolled down to the narrow, tree-lined course of the Scarborough River, which emptied into the ocean south of Prout's Neck. He shivered, remembering that this was the river where, so many years ago, his brother, Jeremy, had drowned.

Jeff didn't like it that his memory of his aunt and uncle's house seemed sharper than his memory of his own family home.

"Jesus Christ," he said in a raw whisper.

He wiped his hand across his face and, slouching low in his seat, stared at the mailbox until his vision began to blur. He fought hard against the dizzying rush of memories, and couldn't help but notice that none of them were very pleasant. His grip on the steering wheel tightened until the heels of his hands began to throb.

He had no idea why he had driven out here today, especially now, with evening fast approaching. He was exhausted after spending the better part of the day cleaning the house and lugging things down to the garage to store them until the yard sale, which he still planned for Sunday afternoon. He knew what he should have done was take a long, hot shower, have something to eat, and then settle down in the living room and knock off a beer or two while reading or watching TV. He knew he also should have called Katherine to see if she had heard anything from the police; but right now, he knew what he needed more than anything else was a little R&R to get his mind off all of his—and Katherine's—problems.

But all day as he worked, even with some Jethro Tull cranked up loud on Judy's stereo, he couldn't stop thinking about the things that had happened over the past week or two. He felt incredibly guilty about what he and Katherine had done last night, and he couldn't stop wondering if he had given in too easily

to Sammy's pushing him to go over there. He had
hoped to lose himself in work all day but, instead, it
had simply given him more time to dwell on things
. . . too much time.

One thought in particular kept cropping up in his
mind. He wasn't even sure where it had come from.
There was no whispering voice inside his head, at least
none that he was consciously aware of, but *something*
had been prompting him to take a drive out to Mildred
and Kirby's house.

Today.

Just to have a look around, he thought, as his gaze
tracked down the shadowy curve of the driveway. *Just
to see the old place one last time.*

But now that he was here, there was no way he
wanted to drive down and actually see the house, no
way he wanted to chance seeing his aunt and uncle
again. They, like the rest of this town, were something
he wanted to keep locked in the past—especially now
that he was beginning to remember some of the things
they had done to him.

He looked up and grunted with surprise when he
noticed his reflection in the rearview mirror. The angled rays of the setting sun brightly lit one side of his
face and cast the other side into deep, purple shadow.
When he smiled at himself, he had a strong, almost
overpowering sensation of dissociation, as if he were
staring into someone else's eyes. He moaned softly as
he stared at himself, wondering just who the hell he
was!

Do you think we could talk now?

The voice inside his head was as clear and sharp as
a roll of thunder.

Startled, Jeff looked over at the passenger's seat,
more than half-expecting to see someone sitting there.
A dry, tight pressure took hold of his throat. The air
inside the car suddenly felt too dense to breathe, so he

stuck his head out the window and inhaled deeply. The cold breeze made him shiver, but after a moment, he felt at least marginally better.

Leaning his head back against the headrest, he closed his eyes, swallowed, and said softly, "Yeah. I don't see why we can't talk now. What do you want to talk about? Who are you, anyway?"

I'm Billy. Don't you even remember me?

The voice was high and whiny. It sounded like a little boy who was either extremely irritated or else excited about something.

"Yeah," Jeff said, rolling his head back and forth against the headrest. "Of course I remember you, but we haven't talked in quite a while. How old are you now, Billy?"

I'm ten, going on eleven.

"Is that so? When will you be eleven?"

On my birthday, silly, Billy replied.

"Oh, I see. And where have you been all this time? Why haven't I been able to talk to you?"

Oh, I've been here and there, Billy replied. *You could've talked to me any time if you wanted to.*

Jeff noticed the high edge in the boy's voice, tight and trembling, as if he had something else to say but didn't quite dare to.

I have no idea why we haven't been talking, Billy went on. *Maybe you just never asked me to come around. I have been kinda lonely.*

"What have you been doing?"

Oh . . . just stuff.

"So why do you want to talk now?" Jeff asked, his body prickling with anticipation. "It's been so long, I thought maybe you had grown up and gone away."

No, I've always been here, Billy replied. *It's just that, now that you've come out here—you know, out where a lot of this stuff happened, I thought maybe I'd better remind you of a couple other things.*

"Oh, really?" Jeff said.

He noticed that his own voice sounded drowsy in spite of the subtle current of apprehension that was winding around him like a cold river. He shifted in his seat, acutely aware that he and Billy weren't in the dark room. He didn't feel very safe, talking to anyone outside of the safe room; but if Billy wanted to, he assumed that it was all right to talk to him now.

Well, Billy said, his voice shaking and sliding up and down the scale. *It's just that . . . now that I'm here, I . . . I'm not so sure I want to talk.*

Jeff was convinced now that the boy was afraid of something, but he knew he couldn't pressure him. That never worked.

Heck, I don't even know if they will let me talk to you about this stuff.

"What's it to them, whoever the hell they are?" Jeff said.

Yeah, but I-I don't want them to be mad at me. They could hurt me. They're a lot bigger than me, you know.

"Who? You mean Alexander and Sammy?"

Umm . . . Yeah . . . Them and some of the others.

"How many others?" Jeff asked, mildly curious to know how many of his alters Billy was aware of.

Oh, there's lots of 'em. Do I have to tell you everyone who's around?

"Not if you don't want to, but if you've got something to say, why not just come right out and say it?"

"I-I can't. I mean—well, I'm not sure that I should. They might get really mad at me, and besides, I . . . No! I don't even want to think about it.

"Why not?"

Because it scares me too much.

"What does?"

There was a long pause.

Jeff figured Billy didn't feel safe talking to him now because he wasn't in the dark room. He was conscious

of the hushed silence both inside and outside of the
car. He could feel the chilly air, swirling in through the
opened window. When he had first closed his eyes, one
side of his face had felt warm, heated by the sun; now
the darkness behind his eyes was deepening, and he
could tell the sun had slipped down behind the trees.
The wind moaned softly, sounding like an old person
in pain.

"Tell me what scares you, Billy?" Jeff said, trying to
sound patient and in control even though he was
gripped by a dark rush of fear. "You can tell me."

There was such a long pause and such a vacuous
silence that Jeff started to think that Billy might have
left, but then the boy spoke again in a low, rasping
whisper.

*"I . . . I don't like to talk about what they . . . what
they did to him, okay? I don't even want to think about
it.*

"What who did to who?" Jeff asked, shivering as
cold, bony fingers traveled up his spine, playing it like
a xylophone.

*You won't get mad at me for reminding you about this
stuff, will you?*

"Of course not," Jeff said, fighting back strong,
numbing rushes of apprehension. "You can say whatever you want. We're all in this together, you know."

*Yeah, but . . . you'll make sure they don't hurt me,
won't you?*

"I promise," Jeff said.

*Yeah—well, still, I just don't like to think about it
'cause it was . . . it was really scary, what they did to
you.*

"First you said 'him,' now you're saying 'you.' Do
you mean me? What who did to me?"

*Your aunt and uncle . . . Don't you even remember
what they did? How they used to bring you kids down*

*into the cellar for punishment whenever they thought
you were being bad?*

"So you mean me and Judy?"

Yeah, and Jeremy.

"Right . . . and Jeremy," Jeff said.

He swallowed, but the dry lump in his throat
wouldn't go down. Just saying his dead brother's
name aloud filled him with a cold, sinking dread. His
nervousness was growing steadily stronger. He considered stopping this conversation now. If it scared Billy
so much, maybe it was something he shouldn't talk
about or remember, either.

"Well," Jeff said, "I do remember the oil drum, and
how Kirby used to put me in it and bang on it. And I
remember that he used to make me work real hard
around the farm, and that he whipped us sometimes
with his belt, whenever he thought we were being—
what was the word he always used? *Recalcitrant.*
When we were recalcitrant and didn't memorize those
Bible passages he wanted us to learn."

Right, but nothing else?

"Look, Billy, if you know something, just tell me!"
Jeff said, trying hard not to shout. He could hear his
own voice tighten, rising higher until it sounded like a
frightened little boy's voice.

*You don't remember . . . what they made you do
. . . to Jeremy . . . down there in the cellar?*

Billy's voice was soft, sounding more distant, like he
was moving away from Jeff.

"No, I don't—" Jeff started to say, but then the
import of Billy's words hit him like a punch in the gut.
Another memory—sharp and terrifyingly clear—came
rushing back at him, the memory of a cold, dank,
nearly lightless and airless cellar.

Kirby and Mildred's cellar!

"Yeah," he said, gasping for breath. "I . . . I think
so."

He could taste the moist, moldy air on the back of his tongue. He cringed at the memory of seeing a little boy, buck naked and stretched out over a barrel. The metal oil drum. At first he thought it was himself, but then he realized, without seeing the boy's face, that it was Jeremy. His hands and feet were tied so he embraced the barrel, making his thin, white buttocks stick up into the air. Jeremy's entire body was trembling with tension and fear. His high, reedy voice was asking, begging to be let go, but Uncle Kirby growled as he handed Jeff an inch-wide leather belt and nodded at the bound boy.

"You know what to do, son."

The memory of Kirby's voice punched like a hot spike through Jeff's brain.

He *had* known what to do, and fearful that the same would happen to him if he didn't obey, he had taken the belt and used it to whip his younger brother because, as his uncle had said, he was being "recalcitrant." Jeff cringed and cried out as he remembered the *whoosh* sound the belt had made in the air as he brought it around, and then the loud *snap* as it connected with Jeremy's naked bottom.

"Harder!" Kirby shouted, his eyes gleaming like wet marbles in the dull light of the cellar. "Beat him harder! You have to whip the Devil out of your brother, boy! He's *filled* with evil, but you can save him! Only you can save him! Do it, son. Do it for Jesus' sake!"

Kirby's voice was ringing in Jeff's mind with such clarity that Jeff wondered if the man might have found him parked here on the roadside and was standing beside the car, shouting at him; but he squeezed his eyes tightly closed as he plummeted deeper into this terrifying, long-buried memory.

Jeff recalled how he had tried not to hit his brother very hard, but after a few feeble strokes, Kirby had stood behind him and taken his hand, squeezing it until it hurt as he swung the belt back for him and lashed the boy until thick, red welts appeared on his butt and thighs. After a few more strokes, with Jeremy wailing in such pain and fear his voice broke, thin trickles of blood ran down the backs of his legs. Dark splotches of blood colored the tan leather as it snapped in the air and connected again with flesh. A few drops of blood splattered Jeff's face, but he thought it was sweat until he wiped his face and saw the red smears on his hand.

There, you see? You do remember! Billy said, his voice high and frantic. *That's what I was talking about!*

Billy's voice cut through the terror of Jeff's memory and snapped him back to the present.

You're not mad at me, are you? Billy said, suddenly sounding meek. *I mean, you're not gonna hurt me or anything, are you?*

"No, I—don't worry, but I . . . I don't blame you for being afraid," Jeff said. He was furiously licking his lips, trying to compose himself, but he felt too shattered inside. After a moment, he said, "You were there, weren't you? You saw it all."

Yeah. Actually, that's the first memory I have. I think that might be when you first created me.

Billy said this so matter-of-factly Jeff realized he knew on some level that he wasn't a separate entity, but a part of Jeff.

"Billy, did you ever think that you might *be* me?" Jeff asked. "I mean, that you're the *me* who was there in the cellar, the little boy who had to do those terrible things to his brother and . . . and sister?"

I don't know about that, Billy said. *I don't think it's really for me to decide, but you must have realized how much your uncle enjoyed having someone under his control like that. Especially a scared, little kid. Both of them—your aunt and uncle—were sick, twisted people, Jeff. . . . They still are!*

Jeff was silent for a moment, and then a thought hit him hard enough to make him sit up straight and gasp.

"Jesus, do you think—"

He tried to continue, but the sudden choking pressure around his throat was almost intolerable. He took a deep, whistling breath and swallowed but still couldn't speak.

Do I think what? Billy said. *Do I think what you're thinking, that Kirby and Mildred might have kidnapped Danny and are keeping him out at their house?*

Jeff made a gagging sound that could have passed for anything.

Yeah, Billy said, sounding thoughtful and almost not scared, now that he had shared his secret fear. *That might be possible, and I think it might even be worse than that. I think if they do have Danny, they kidnapped him thinking that—well, either one of two things.*

"And what's that?" Jeff asked, surprised that he could speak at all.

I think they're either trying to frame you for it, you know, for kidnapping Danny, or else they want to drive you so fuckin' crazy that you end up killing yourself, just like your sister did.

"Jesus, do you really think—"

Maybe, for some reason, they want both Judy and you out of the way.

"You can't possibly—"

That was all Jeff could manage to say because he knew, as soon as he registered what Billy was saying, that it could very well be true. Now that he was back home, Mildred and Kirby might be afraid that he still hated them for the abuse he and his sister—and his dead brother!—had suffered at their hands. Maybe they were afraid that he would want to get revenge for what they had done. Or maybe they still thought that he and Judy—like Jeremy—were servants of Satan, filled with evil, and that they both deserved to die!

Trembling all over, Jeff opened his eyes and let out a startled yelp when he found himself staring straight ahead into a swirling wall of darkness. It took him several heartbeats to remember where he was. As his eyes gradually adjusted to the night, he saw a sprinkling of stars above the jagged black line of trees. Up ahead, the dirt road and rutted driveway were nothing but indistinct blurs, almost completely lost in the surrounding darkness.

"Jesus," Jeff whispered, shivering wildly as he rolled up the car window.

He didn't dare close his eyes again as he rubbed his sweat-slick forehead. As soon as he felt as though he had regained a slight measure of control, he reached for the ignition, started up the car, snapped on the headlights, and shifted the car into gear. Pulling into the driveway, he backed around, almost bumping into the mailbox, and then started back toward the main road.

As he drove, he had to fight a mad impulse to stomp on the gas and speed away from the old farmhouse. His insides felt like jelly, and his mind was flooded with a confusion of terrifying thoughts and memories. One thing, however, stuck out clearly in his mind. He was positive now that he knew why he had been so afraid to go down into the cellar at Judy's house. It wasn't her cellar that he was afraid of.

Not at all.

It was Kirby and Mildred's cellar.

That was the real source of his fear, and he realized now that it hadn't been at all irrational. The things Kirby and Mildred had done to him, his brother, and his sister in their cellar had scarred him for life . . . and maybe even forced Judy to commit suicide.

If Kirby and Mildred were afraid that now, as an adult, he still hated them and might want to retaliate, they certainly might have done something as desperate as kidnap Danny in an attempt to get at Jeff. It was entirely possible and, in a certain paranoid way, it made perfect sense.

But Jeff couldn't figure out one thing. Why would they choose Danny as the way to strike at him? How would they even have known about him?

Then he remembered.

His aunt and uncle had sat behind him, Katherine, and Danny at Judy's funeral.

"You bastards!" Jeff said as he glanced into the rearview mirror at the impenetrable wall of darkness closing in behind him. "You lousy, rotten bastards!"

But then, as he was approaching the stop sign at the end of the road, another thought struck him. He let out a pained groan, and his foot went to the brake, pressing down so hard the car went into a drifting skid. The tires sounded like ripping cloth as they tore at the loose dirt, and for a sickening instant, the tail end of the car started to swing around. Jeff spun the steering wheel hard to the right and regained control, stopping only a few feet from the turn onto Route 77. His breath made a high whistling sound as he sat there squeezing the steering wheel and staring blankly ahead.

Or what if I brought him out there?

The thought sent a cold spike of panic through him.

What if one of my alters, one who can't accept what happened to us back then, has taken Danny back to Kirby and Mildred's house and is keeping him down in their cellar, using him to reenact what happened to me?

The thought was too frightening to contemplate.

Whimpering softly, Jeff leaned over the steering wheel, covered his face with both hands, and began to cry. A lifetime of fear, tension, and anxiety boiled out of him in one long, anguished wail.

As soon as he got home, Jeff went upstairs to get ready for bed even though it was only a little after six o'clock. He lay down in bed, his hands laced behind his head, and shivered with gathering dread as he stared at the ceiling. He knew there was no way he was going to fall asleep—now or at midnight. He wanted desperately to talk to someone, but he had no idea who.

His first thought was to call his wife, but he knew he couldn't unload any of this shit onto her. He already felt guilty enough because of what he and Katherine had done last night. Once he was back home in Denver, he knew he was going to have to confess everything to Sally simply because he wouldn't be able to live with himself otherwise. Guilt and remorse twisted inside his belly like a cold blade, and an aching dread gripped him as he wondered if Sally would be as patient and understanding as she had always been, or if this would—finally—be too much for her and lead them into divorce.

But whatever happened once he got home, he knew he couldn't call her now.

But he didn't feel like calling Doctor Ingalls, either.

Even though his therapist had told him to call any time, day or night, if he was having trouble, Jeff wasn't convinced that he could trust Doctor Ingalls. After all, wasn't he the one who had convinced him that he had successfully reintegrated all of his alter personalities?

Well, shit—if he had done that, then why had the stress of Judy's death and everything else brought his alters back out—stronger, if anything? So strong, in fact, that Jeff still considered the possibility that all along one or more of them might have been doing things that he wasn't even aware of.

Like kidnapping Danny . . . or killing Judy . . .

And as much as Jeff would have liked to right now, Jeff didn't dare call or go over to see Katherine. He wanted to know if the police had found her son, but he didn't dare talk to her even over the phone because of the feelings he knew he still had for her, and his fear of what he might blurt out as soon as he heard her voice. He couldn't stop wondering how different his life would have turned out if he had married her and remained in Cape Higgins. As much as he had hated his hometown and had wanted to get out of it as fast as he could after high school, maybe all of his psychological problems were because he had run away instead of staying here and facing them.

Or maybe they're all still here!

Maybe they're still out there in the house on Bridge Road!

For almost an hour, he lay in bed, staring at the window and trying to let himself be lulled by the gentle whistling of the wind in the eaves. Every time he started to drift off to sleep, though, confused and unnerving thoughts—or dreams—would swirl through his mind. Suddenly a frightening image popped into his head and made him sit up in bed with a startled yelp. The skin on the back of his neck crawled as goose bumps washed down his arms. For a moment, he thought the pale, thin figure that was lashed over an oil drum was in the room. The air filled with the sound of a leather strap slapping flesh. Thick gouts of blood splattered white skin, and then came the dull plopping sound of blood, dripping onto the floor. Even after Jeff had opened his eyes, the dark bedroom echoed with fading, frantic cries for help.

Knowing that he wasn't going to get to sleep, Jeff finally realized what he had to do. In spite of his previous embarrassment, he was going to have to go to the police and tell them what he suspected about his aunt and uncle. Maybe, if he could talk to Eddie Dearborn off the record, he could convince him to go out to Kirby and Mildred's farm and have a look around . . . just to see if Danny was out there.

It was crazy, he knew, probably another wild-goose chase, but the chorus of whispering voices, either inside his mind or emerging from the darkness, eventually convinced him that was what he had to do.

Now!

One voice in particular whispered in his ear, as faint as the flutter of a moth's wings, unseen in the dark.

That's a darn good idea, Jeff, the voice said.

Jeff couldn't be sure, but he thought it sounded like Billy's voice—frightened and in pain.

Do it, Jeff! Do it right now!

Chapter Twenty-four
Doppelgänger

"Well, they sure are one strange couple, I'll grant you that much."

Eddie Dearborn's words came out as a floating white ball of mist in the cold air as he opened the cruiser door and, huffing, slid in behind the steering wheel. The car seat sagged beneath his weight as he settled into position. Jeff had been sitting in darkness for nearly half an hour, so the glow of the dome light, as faint as it was when it came on, stung his eyes and made them water.

Eddie was shaking his head in wonderment.

"I mean, I see both of them around town from time to time, but I probably haven't spoken to either one of them since—hell, since back when we were kids and used to come out here to swim or fish in the river or whatever."

Jesus, that's right! Jeff thought. *Eddie . . . Eddie and Hank were out here that day Jeremy disappeared! They wanted to show me that dead woodchuck!*

A sudden, bone-deep chill gripped him. He had a brief mental image of the dead woodchuck they had found, squashed flat in the middle of the dirt road.

Before it faded from his mind, the animal's face seemed to blend into that of a five-year-old boy.

Jeremy's face!

Jeff shivered as he glanced over at his friend. He was tempted to ask him what he remembered about that day, but then he shifted his gaze past Eddie and focused on his aunt and uncle's house. A single light was shining in the living-room window, casting a dusty, yellow glow out into the front yard. The rising moon was still low in the sky, almost behind the house. It reflected like a big, distorted blue eye in the polished black hood of the cruiser. Dead leaves, sounding like a horde of clicking insects, skittered in the driveway in a fitful gust of wind.

Sitting at the top of a gentle rise, the house and attached barn were silhouetted against the star-filled sky. Every line and angle was edged with a dull, blue fire. The bare branches of the maple trees out behind the house reached up into the sky like gnarled, skeletal fingers that swayed gently in the breeze. Other than seeming perhaps a bit smaller than he remembered it—especially the front yard—Jeff was amazed how clearly the place had been etched in his memory.

"Yeah," he said after a long moment. His breath came in a fast gulp that caught in his chest and almost choked him. "You sure as hell got *that* one right."

The longer he stared up at the house, the louder and more insistent the voices inside his head became. Soon, all of them were yelling so loudly he couldn't distinguish what any of them were saying, but the wailing chorus of voices stirred more painful memories of the abuse he and his sister—and his brother—had suffered in that house . . . and what they had done with each other to find solace. The pain, edged with stinging guilt, was sharper than any remembered pain; it was fresh and immediate, an open wound. Jeff felt so twisted up inside, he was sure he would have started crying or screaming if he had been out here alone.

"I'll tell you one thing, though," Eddie said, snickering softly to himself. "I've never seen a house filled up with so much religious shit. I mean, hell, I'm pretty sure I believe in God, and I go to church now and then with my wife and kid, but . . . shit! They've got religious sayings and pictures of Jesus hanging up all over the place like he . . . like he was fuckin' Elvis or something. You should see it."

"I have," Jeff said.

His voice hissed between his teeth as he wondered if he would ever find the courage to enter that house after all these years. It had been difficult enough just asking Eddie to come out here tonight; he knew there was no way he would have been able to go inside, with or without him; but his memory of the inside of that house was as clear as if he had been in it just this morning.

"You mean they were always like that?" Eddie asked, not sounding all that surprised.

"You don't know the half of it," Jeff replied, chuckling darkly and shaking his head.

After a moment of uncomfortable silence, he said, "So tell me how it went in there." He couldn't help but notice how badly his voice was shaking, and not just from the cold.

Eddie looked at him and was silent for a moment as he drummed his fingers on the steering wheel; then he cleared his throat.

"You know, Jeff, I hope you realize just how far out of line I went just bringing you out here with me," he said. "By all rights, I should have turned this over to the investigating detectives."

"Yeah, I know, but we agreed that this was unofficial, right?" Jeff said, forcing a smile he wasn't even sure Eddie could see in the dark. "You were just following up on a lead."

"Uh-huh, and that's exactly what I told your aunt and uncle."

"So what happened? What did they say?"

"Well, first off, they told me how sorry they were that they had only seen you at your sister's funeral, and how they wished they'd had you out to the house for a home-cooked meal."

Jeff snorted and rolled his eyes as Eddie continued.

"They said they figured you were too busy, taking care of everything else. Anyway, I elaborated a little bit on the story we'd made up. I told them someone driving by on Route 77 yesterday was pretty sure they had seen a kid who fit Danny's description walking along the side of the road. I asked if they had seen anyone out around here either last night or today."

"And they said no."

Eddie nodded. "Of course they said no."

The car seat creaked like the slow pull of rusty nails as Eddie turned, propped his arm on the back of the seat, and faced Jeff.

"Look, Jeff," he said mildly. "I don't want you to get all upset about this, but I think this is—umm . . . this might be—"

"—just like what happened when we checked out my old bedroom, right?" Jeff finished for him.

The only sound Eddie made was a long, slow inhalation. His silhouette against the moonlit night looked dark and foreboding. For a moment, Jeff had the unnerving impression that Eddie was someone else, someone he didn't even know—someone he couldn't trust.

"Is *that* what you're thinking?" Jeff asked, surprised by the strength he heard in his own voice.

Slowly, almost imperceptibly in the dark, Eddie nodded.

"Yeah, that's right," he said. "Look, I think you have to trust me on this, okay, Jeff? I don't know what kind of psychological problems you've been having, but my gut instinct tells me that your aunt and uncle are a perfectly harmless old couple. Sure, they may be a little on the fanatical side with their religion and all, but I honestly didn't get any feeling that they would hurt anyone."

"But you don't—"

Jeff was going to say, *know what they did to us,* but his voice faded away.

Stroking his chin, he looked up at the house, staring straight at the light that was shining in the living-room window until it became a watery smear. Then he sighed, closed his eyes, and massaged the bridge of his nose as his mind filled with memories of the small rooms in that curiously airless house. He remembered how, whenever he stayed there, he always felt like there wasn't enough air in the house, that he was suffocating. He took a breath now, and his breath remained painfully in his chest.

And that room with the light on is right above the cellar, a faint voice—was it Billy's?—whispered harshly. *The cellar, Jeff! THAT'S where you couldn't breathe because you were so fucking scared! You thought—no, you KNEW you were going to die down there!*

Jeff shifted and looked at Eddie again, wondering how much he could really trust him. After all, although they had been friends long ago, they hadn't been in touch in years. Why should he think he could trust this man—policeman or not—with any of his deepest fears and worries?

"You were going to say something?" Eddie said in the growing pause.

Jeff grunted and shook his head.

"No, I—uh, I was just going to ask if you got a chance to look down in the—in the cellar."

"And just how was I supposed to do that?" Eddie snapped. "I don't have a goddamned search warrant, and there sure as hell is no probable cause, so I don't think any judge is going to give me one, not based on just a . . . just a 'hunch.' "

"Well, that's *my* hunch," Jeff said. He was trying his best to sound casual, but he could feel himself getting defensive. "What about *your* hunch? You seem to expect me to go along with your instant assessment that my aunt and uncle are just a couple of crazy old coots who wouldn't harm a fly."

"Uh-huh. That's pretty much it."

"And what if you're wrong? What if they're *not* so fucking harmless?"

"Well, then I'd say they're damned good actors," Eddie replied. "I'm not a detective or anything, I'm just a patrolman, but ninety-nine times out of a hundred, I think I can spot it if someone's trying to hide something."

Again, Jeff almost blurted out to Eddie about the mental and physical abuse he and his sister and brother had suffered at Mildred and Kirby's hands, but he was suddenly positive that he couldn't trust Eddie, even though they used to be best friends.

Used to be, a voice whispered close to his ear in the darkness. *That's the operative phrase: 'used to be.' But who CAN you trust?*

Times change . . . people change, Jeff thought. He and Eddie weren't anything like the people they used to be. He certainly didn't suspect that Eddie was in collusion with his aunt and uncle, but it upset him that his former friend seemed so reluctant to give any credibility to something he was so convinced was true.

You're absolutely right! whispered the voice, so close to Jeff's ear it made him jump. *I'll bet Danny's up there right now! I swear to Christ they have him locked up in the cellar, where they used to keep you!*

Jeff let his gaze track up the hill to the lighted living-room window again. He stiffened when he sensed more than saw a dark shadow shift against the night sky and then duck back around the corner of the house. It moved too quickly for him to really register it, and he was already telling himself that it had simply been a trick of his eye, but the immediate impression was that a person had been squatting low to the ground, hiding behind the yew bush that grew in front of the house, and watching them in the cruiser. Jeff almost said something to Eddie but decided to let it drop.

Yeah, the voice said, grating in his ear. *You know what you're gonna have to do anyway, don't you?*

Jeff cringed when he glanced at Eddie to see if he had noticed his reaction, but apparently he hadn't. Grunting softly, Jeff shook his head and thought savagely, *No . . . there's no fucking way!*

Oh, yes there is, the voice said, rattling like dead leaves in the darkness. *You know you can't trust this guy, so you're gonna have to go up there by yourself and check it out.*

Jeff wanted to protest, but as the mental voice faded away, his mind filled with raging panic. As much as he wanted to deny it, he knew that the mental voice, whether it was his own or someone else's, was absolutely right.

From here on out, it was up to him to go up there, face his fear, and find out the truth.

He had just one question—one word that burned like a cheery-red coal in the center of his mind.

When?

* * *

Eddie started up the cruiser, backed around, and headed back to town. Neither he nor Jeff had much to say until Eddie pulled into Judy's driveway and slipped the shift into park. Jeff opened the door, and the dome light came on. Wincing in the light, he turned to Eddie and held his hand out to him. When they shook hands, he noticed that Eddie's grip was firm and dry. He couldn't help but wonder if his own hand felt like a dead fish to Eddie.

"Well, anyway, thanks for trying to help me out with this," Jeff said.

His face was flushed with embarrassment, and he still found it difficult to take a deep enough breath.

"Hey, no problem. What are friends for, anyway?"

Eddie sure as hell sounded concerned, but Jeff thought he could detect a ringing note of falseness.

"Yeah, right," Jeff said, and for a heartbeat or two, a dull silence filled the car.

"I hope you keep in touch," Eddie said. "Are our plans still on for tomorrow night?"

"Yeah—sure," Jeff said. But even as he said it, he knew he would have to come up with some kind of excuse to get out of it.

With a quick nod, he stepped out into the night and swung the cruiser door shut. For some reason—maybe it was the slamming sound the door made, or the way the moonlight reflected off the shiny door panel—he had the distinct impression that he was closing a coffin lid.

Jeff took a few steps up the walkway, then stood and waved as Eddie backed the cruiser down to the road. The headlights shone full on Jeff, so bright they hurt his eyes, but he forced himself to smile. His smile quickly melted as he watched Eddie drive down the road and soon disappear around the bend.

Jeff stood there, listening to the fading sound of the car, and then the night closed down around him like a muffling blanket. A cold breeze hissed in the trees that lined the road. The sound made him shiver as he stared at the dark curve of the road until it was swallowed in darkness. Jeff was filled with a cold, hollow sense of loss. The darkness seemed to swell and pulsate with a subtle energy, and he imagined he saw thin, glowing faces and dark shapes shifting in the moonlit shadows. A tickling chill went up his back. He shifted his gaze across the yard to the solid black line of trees that edged the night sky, which was dusty with stars.

Even without the whispering voices inside his head to remind him, he had one clear thought as he started up the walkway to the front door.

When the fuck would I ever dare go back out there to my aunt and uncle's house?

It was well past midnight, almost one o'clock in the morning when Jeff first heard the laughter—at least when he first became consciously aware of the laughter. As soon as he was jolted awake, having dozed off on the couch while watching TV after knocking back four beers, he realized that he had been hearing it for . . .

How long?

He wasn't sure.

It seemed like a long time.

His first thought was that it might have been something on TV, but the volume was down low, and he could see that there was a news report on about the spate of forest fires out in Montana and Wyoming. No one was going to be laughing about that! The remote control was still in his hand, so he thumbed the TV off and sat perfectly motionless until he heard another short burst of laughter.

It was faint, but it seemed to be coming from right here in the living room—a light, muffled sound that ran quickly up and down the scale as though whoever was laughing was trying out different laughs to see which one suited him best.

Jeff's eyes were wide open and staring as he looked around, but he didn't get up off the couch.

Maybe there IS a ghost in the house!

That was his next thought. Even though he knew it was irrational, after all the things that had happened lately, he had to consider it.

Maybe Judy's ghost was haunting her old residence . . . or maybe the restless spirits of his mother and father had returned to where they had spent much of their lives. Or what if it were Jeremy?

Jeff shivered, imagining how there could be many unseen presences lurking in the house, all of them watching him; but he also felt a small measure of comfort or hope at the possibility that his sister and parents might not be entirely gone, that some part of them might still be here in the house where they had lived . . . and where Judy had died.

Holding his breath and moving so slowly he could feel every muscle in his body tensing and stretching, he shifted forward and got up from the couch. He was still a little woozy from the beer and had to catch his balance. The only light on in the house was the table lamp in the living room. It was on the lowest setting of its three-way bulb. Shifting his gaze back and forth, Jeff reached out, pinched the switch between his thumb and forefinger, and rolled it fast enough so it clicked three times. The light got brighter, brighter again, and then snapped out.

The sudden plunge into darkness was dizzying. Jeff sucked in his breath and leaned his hands against the end table for support as he listened to the dense silence of the dark room.

No laughter . . . not even an echo of it.

I must've been dreaming, he thought as he squared his shoulders. *That's probably all it was.*

Now that he was ready to hear—and possibly see—whatever might have been there, he was convinced it wouldn't be repeated; but after a moment, with his pulse ruffling lightly in his ears, the burst of laughter came again with a stark suddenness that made him jump. It was low and rumbling, like the drumroll of distant thunder.

That's a man's laugh! Jeff thought.

Frowning, he looked around, straining to see in the darkness, but his vision flickered with a subtle strobe effect. He held his breath, waiting patiently for his eyesight to adjust to the dark, then he tiptoed over to the dining-room doorway. He paused every few steps, straining to hear if the sound had come from the kitchen, or maybe from the doorway that led down into the cellar.

He was almost to the kitchen when the laughter came again, but it seemed more distant, so he turned and walked back through the living room and into the hall. He was looking up the stairway when the sound came once again, but still, it seemed to be farther away.

It can't be upstairs. Maybe it's coming from down in the cellar! he thought.

He shivered as he walked unsteadily back into the living room and stood beside the couch. No matter where he stood, when he heard the sound again, faint and echoing, he couldn't get a fix on its direction. It had a muffled quality and seemed to be all around him in the darkness, reverberating through every room in the house.

Maybe it's all in my head, he thought as a stronger shiver gripped him.

After a while, though, once his senses were fully adjusted to the darkness, when the laughter came again, he realized that it must be coming from outside.

Suddenly it rose higher, like a strong gust of wind, and then abruptly cut off.

Jeff moved over toward the living-room picture window. He was unable to shake the sensation that there were dozens of unseen eyes in the room, all staring coldly at him. Flattening himself against the wall, he took a deep breath, then reached out and took hold of the curtain. Squeezing it tightly, he lifted the lacy edge a few inches as he shifted around and peeked around the window frame.

A nearly full moon was riding high in the sky, lighting up the yard almost as bright as midday. The lawn stretched back about fifty feet to the dark line of trees that bordered the property. The grass looked like it was glazed with a thin coating of snow that glowed eerily blue in the night. The trees swayed in the gentle wind that was blowing in off the ocean. The moonlight was strong enough to make him squint.

Jeff lifted the lacy curtain a bit higher as he leaned forward and scanned the patches of light and shadow in the backyard. He tried to ignore the steadily strengthening sensation he had that there was someone standing behind him, unseen but sensed in the darkness . . . someone who was moving stealthily closer.

His nerves were singing like hot wires. When he finally couldn't take the tension any longer, he turned around and looked. Everything in the living room was lost in thick darkness, but none of the shadows shifted. Then, louder and sharper this time, almost braying, the laughter came again, filling the night.

Jeff's eyes widened as he shifted his gaze back outside. He gasped when he realized there was a figure, standing out on the edge of the lawn. It was motionless, a darker-than-night shape just within the thick shadows of the trees. It seemed to melt away whenever he looked directly at it. Jeff honestly couldn't say whether or not it had been there the first time he had looked out, but his throat went suddenly dry. His body was paralyzed with fear as he watched the dark, vaguely human-shaped blot glide silently forward until it was out in the full glow of moonlight.

It was a person!

A man!

Jeff's heart gave a sudden, hard punch against his ribs. He heard a low whimper but didn't realize that he had made the sound as he stared at the person in the backyard. Moonlight glinted off the man's face, making his skin look like polished white marble that was lined with deep shadows. His eye sockets were two bottomless black holes that seemed to drain the darkness from night as he stared up at the living-room window.

At me! Jeff thought with a numbing chill.

Even at this distance, he felt a tingling rush of recognition as he watched the figure shift closer to the house. As it did so, the man leaned his head back, and a winding howl of laughter, sounding like a warbling coyote's howl, filled the night, loud enough to make Jeff's ears throb.

No! This is crazy!

The thought screamed in Jeff's mind, but the sound of laughter outside the house rose higher and higher until it became a whining buzz that drowned out all of the voices inside Jeff's head.

He wanted to cry out, but a cold, tightening pressure was squeezing his chest and throat, choking off his air. His pulse was racing with a high, frantic patter. Darts of numbing white pain shot out from the center of his chest into his neck, arms, and legs.

This can't be happening! It can't be happening!

Still leaning his head back and laughing as he stared up at the moon, the figure moved steadily closer to the house. He seemed not to take steps but to glide effortlessly across the frost-glazed lawn. The sound of his laughter rippled like a curtain through the night. Wave after dizzying wave of panic crashed over Jeff as every ounce of energy drained from him. He stared out the window in amazement a moment longer, then turned and slumped back against the wall.

Frantic with panic, he looked around the darkened living room until his gaze came to rest on the dim outline of the telephone on the end table.

That's what he should do. Call the police. If they got here fast enough, they might be able to catch whoever this was. And even if the intruder took off now, there was frost on the lawn; he would have to leave footprints they could backtrack to find out where he had come from.

Jeff was panting furiously as he pressed his back against the wall. Every breath burned like fire in his lungs. His joints and muscles ached. He felt almost compelled to look out into the backyard again, but he couldn't force himself to move. His gaze was riveted to the misshapen rectangle of moonlight that fell through the window and across the carpet. It glowed a gauzy gray that removed all colors from the pattern on the carpet.

There's no one out there! he thought, panting heavily. *I just imagined it! I was dreaming. Maybe I'm still dreaming!*

As Jeff stood there in the dark, trembling and watching, something that moved like a slowly shifting storm cloud came between the moonlight and the window. A thick, black shadow, distorted by the folds of the thin curtain, angled across the floor, growing larger until it seemed to block more than half of the window. Jeff gasped when he saw first the head, then the shoulders of someone who came right up to the living-room window and, bending forward, leaned forward against the glass. The person raised his hands to his face, cupping them around his eyes so he could see into the living room.

Jesus! Jeff thought, pressing his back against the wall, afraid even to breathe. He realized the man was no more than arm's reach away from him. If the window were open, Jeff could easily have reached out and grabbed him!

Who the hell is it? Jeff thought as he frantically tried to focus his mind on what he should do next. *What the hell is he doing out there? What the fuck does he want?*

The shadow rippled across the floor as the person outside shifted back and forth, obviously trying to get a better view into the living room. Jeff held his breath and flattened himself against the wall.

Jesus, does he know I'm here? Did he see me? Can he sense me? He must have seen the living-room light go off. Does he think I went upstairs to bed and that it's safe to break into the house now, or does he know that I'm still here?

After an unbearable moment of winding tension, Jeff heard the man outside laugh again—snickering softly now, but still loud enough to vibrate the window. Jeff could imagine the man's heated breath, fogging up the windowpane. He squeezed his hands into fists, desperately wishing he had a gun or some other kind of weapon.

Go away! he shouted in his mind. *Go away! Just leave me the fuck alone!*

But the person remained there in the window, his shadow shifting silently back and forth across the windowsill and floor as though he knew damned well that Jeff was standing there. He was teasing him, taunting him, daring him to show himself.

Jeff looked over at the stairs and wondered if he could get to them without being seen. He might feel a lot safer if he was upstairs. He could lock the bedroom door and call the police from up there if he had to.

Or maybe he should stroll out into the kitchen just as casually as he could, pretending that he had come downstairs for a midnight snack and had absolutely no idea anyone was outside looking in. If this was a burglar trying to break into the house, he might take off as soon as he saw Jeff.

Or maybe, Jeff thought, maybe he should just dart out and confront this person face-to-face, with just the window separating them. Maybe he could give whoever this was one hell of a fright. Then he could either call the police or else go outside and beat the living shit out of whoever this was.

Jeff's stomach was knotted with tension. He could feel his arm and leg muscles winding up, tightening as he prepared to move.

Go ahead! whispered a voice inside his head. It sounded like Alexander, but he wasn't sure. *Face your fears! Isn't that what you and your therapist are always saying, that it's better to face your fears head on?*

Jeff let his breath out in a long, shuddering sigh, then sucked in another gulp of air. He started to move before he could change his mind. Grunting loudly, he wheeled around, dropping into a tight, defensive squat, and tore the curtain aside in one swift motion.

The person outside didn't even jump. He stayed right where he was, his face pressed against the glass mere inches from Jeff. With the moonlight behind him, his face was mostly lost in shadow, but Jeff was close enough, and there was enough ambient light so he could make out a few of the man's features.

Especially his eyes!

They glowed with a malicious glee that held Jeff entranced. A bolt of blinding white panic sizzled through him. He almost passed out right then when he realized he was staring straight into his own eyes!

"Jesus Christ!" he shouted, so loud his voice tore his throat.

For a tingling instant, he thought he must be seeing his own reflection in the dark glass, but his eyes had fully adjusted to the darkness by now, and he could clearly see the man, standing outside the window. He didn't move, didn't even flinch as Jeff, his mouth hanging open in shock, stared back at him.

Jesus, it's me!

The feeling of dissociation was dizzying. Jeff felt like he was tumbling head over heels in a spiraling, dark void. He couldn't tear his gaze away from the face that was leering at him through the glass. Then the man outside the house threw his head back and, his mouth moving almost spastically, roared with laughter so loud it vibrated the window. Jeff was afraid the glass was going to shatter. He had a brief, terrifying mental image of looking at himself sprawled on the living-room floor, his body lacerated with hundreds of gaping wounds and knife-shaped shards of broken glass sticking like quills out of his body. He was shaking uncontrollably, and tears were streaming down his face.

This was no reflection!

He was looking into the face of someone who looked exactly like him!

His *Doppelgänger!*

Nearly numb with terror, Jeff staggered backwards, feeling blindly behind him as he careened off furniture and almost fell. The dark silhouette in the window didn't move. It stayed right there, like a permanent stain on the glass.

A chorus of screaming, shouting voices suddenly filled Jeff's head as he struggled to keep his balance. He had no idea where he was or what he was doing. The darkness in the living room swelled up like a powerful tidal surge and then collapsed around him. Jeff felt himself being sucked into an airless, directionless vacuum. Bright white explosions of light zig-zagged like comets across his vision. The only sounds he heard were a high, keening wail of rising laughter . . . and a scream that might have been his own.

The last clear thought he had before he passed out was, *It's my fetch . . . and he's come to get me!*

Chapter Twenty-five
Seeing the Door

"Have you heard anything yet?"

Jeff thought his voice sounded reedy and strained over the phone, but not for the same reasons that Katherine might think. He was sitting at the kitchen table, leaning back with his feet up and the phone cradled between his chin and shoulder. Slanting morning sunlight poured in through the east-facing window and fell across the back of his neck, making it feel sweaty. He knew he should be enjoying the welcomed heat of the sun, but it didn't come close to dispelling the subtle chill that was wrapped around his heart. Yesterday's *Portland Press Herald,* the Saturday edition, was lying on the table in front of him, open to the page that listed the times of the local church services.

Katherine hesitated. Jeff could hear her take a shuddering breath before she spoke.

"Uh, no—nothing. They haven't found him . . . yet. Not a trace."

Her voice ended in a strangled whisper. Just hearing how miserable she sounded made Jeff's eyes sting with tears.

"The . . . uh, the state detectives came by again

yesterday afternoon," Katherine continued. "They were asking all sorts of questions. They said they've interviewed just about everyone in town, but nobody's seen Danny since school got out on Friday. They said they'd probably start an area search by tomorrow morning."

"Why are they waiting so long?"

Katherine sighed heavily, and Jeff thought he could feel at least a small measure of her worry and pain.

"They—"

Her voice caught, and she had to clear her throat before she could continue.

"They seem pretty much convinced that he's run away. They think he might have taken off with his father."

"Is that possible?"

"Sure it's possible, but not very likely," Katherine replied. "We—I mean . . . well, no family's perfect, and sure, Danny and I had our disagreements and stuff, but the police think he might have contacted his father and asked him to come and get him."

"Have they spoken with his father yet?" Jeff asked. He wiped the back of his neck, then looked at his sweat-slick fingers. "You mentioned that he was living in Massachusetts, right?"

"Yeah, but—well, there's sort of a problem there. You see, he's a trucker, and according to the dispatcher where he works, he's been on the road now for a couple of days, taking a delivery up to Caribou."

"Uh-huh. So it *is* possible that he stopped by on his way through and picked up Danny, right?"

Jeff knew this was a fragile hope to hold out to her, but it was considerably better than some of the alternatives he could think of.

Hey, don't try to kid yourself or her, whispered a hollow voice that made him shiver and look around.

*You know where he is! He's up there . . . in THEIR
house . . . right now!*

Katherine sighed again, and her voice shook when
she spoke.

"The time frame—that's the term they kept using—
the 'time frame,' like it's some goddamned game
they're playing, not my *son* they're talking about!
They say the time frame's about right, but—at least so
far—they haven't been able to locate Doug. They have
an APB out on him."

Jeff was silent for a moment, then added, "Would
Danny have taken off without telling you?"

"No, I mean . . . well. Jesus, I don't know! I suppose
he *could* have, but I—I just can't imagine it." Katherine's voice was twisted tight with frustration. "Like I
said, Danny and I might not have always seen eye to
eye on everything, but we got along pretty well, but I
don't think his dad would have . . ." She looked up at
the ceiling for a moment, her eyelids fluttering. "No,
no way! Danny and Doug weren't on very good terms,
you know, even before the divorce."

"Uh-huh."

Jeff shifted in his seat to get out of the warm wash
of sunlight. Realizing he was pressing the phone hard
against his ear, he moved it to the other one. He
glanced at the kitchen clock and saw that it was two or
three minutes after eight o'clock. For a moment, he
considered why he had called Katherine so early in the
morning and almost decided to let it drop, but then a
voice—was it Karl's this time?—whispered inside his
head, urging him on.

*Come on, Jeff! Jesus Christ, don't just sit there! If you
don't do it now, when the hell will you ever do it? You
know you can trust her, don't you?*

"I was—" He took a breath. "I just wish there was
something I could say or do," Jeff said.

He felt suddenly uncomfortable, afraid that she

might think he was referring to them making love the other night, but he didn't want to think about that now. He figured it would be best all the way around if they both just forgot about it.

"You've done everything you can, Jeff, . . . and more," Katherine said. Her voice caught, and he was sure now that she was crying.

Jeff racked his brain, trying to think how he could broach the reason for his call but finally decided that all he could do was blurt it out. After taking another deep breath, he said, "Look, Katherine, I know this is gonna sound really crazy to you, but I-I think I might know where Danny is."

There was a long pause at Katherine's end of the line, and then, very softly, she inhaled and said, "You do?"

"I . . . I don't want to talk about it, at least not until I can see you face-to-face." Jeff paused and furiously licked his lips. The words he wanted to say were all being shouted in several different voices that filled his head and momentarily confused him. "I was hoping I could come by and . . . and pick you up so we could go somewhere to talk . . . just talk. It'd probably be good for you to get out of the house."

He wanted to make it clear that he didn't expect them to make love again.

"Yeah, but I—maybe I should stick around . . . in case the police call."

"This is really important, Kat," Jeff said, hoping to cut off her protests.

After a moment's hesitation, Katherine finally said, "Sure. When?"

"How about right now, if you're ready?" Jeff spoke quickly, before he lost his nerve. He looked again at the clock. It was seven minutes past eight. "It's a long story, and I-I'm not even sure I know all of it myself, but I'll tell you what I *do* know on the drive out to my aunt and uncle's house."

"Your aunt and uncle's? Why are you—"

"I'll tell you when I see you, okay? Can you be ready in, say, ten minutes?"

Katherine paused. As he waited, Jeff listened to the hollow *whoosh* of blood sounding in his ear over the phone. For a fleeting instant, he saw spots of white light flitting like fireflies in front of his eyes. He took a deep breath, afraid that he was going to pass out, but then Katherine said, "Sure. I can be ready in ten minutes."

"Okay. See you then."

Jeff cut the connection and stood up so quickly the blood drained from his head, making him dizzy. He had to steady himself by grabbing at the table before going over and hanging up the phone. His hands were shaking, and he felt like he couldn't take a deep enough breath as he came back to the table and picked up the newspaper. His eyes began to water as he stared once again—as he had for nearly half an hour before his call to Katherine—at the announcement for the morning services at the First Baptist Church of Cape Elizabeth. This was the church Uncle Kirby and Aunt Mildred had attended back when Jeff was young, the same church they had made Jeff and Judy and Jeremy attend whenever they stayed with them. The first and only service of the day was scheduled to begin at nine o'clock. Jeff closed and rubbed his eyes, hoping to hell that Kirby and Mildred were still members of the church and would be attending today.

He dropped the newspaper to the table and, covering his mouth with both hands, sighed heavily. "Please . . . *please* let that give us the time we need," he whispered to himself.

* * *

Yellow dust swirled up around the car as Jeff drove past the turn into his aunt and uncle's driveway, stopped, backed around, then pulled off onto the shoulder of the dirt road and parked the car. He was careful to shield the car behind a screen of dense brush that afforded him a good view of the road ahead before he turned off the engine. He told himself he didn't need much of a view—just enough to see whether or not both Kirby and Mildred were in their truck when they drove off to church this morning. He certainly didn't want them to see him!

IF they drive off to church this morning! said a teasing voice.

Jeff shivered as a cold tendril of nervousness uncoiled inside his stomach, but he was betting that— Bible-thumpers that they were—Kirby and Mildred were still regular church-goers.

He glanced at his watch. It was almost eight-thirty. If Kirby and Mildred planned on being in Cape Elizabeth in time for the nine o'clock service, they would certainly have to leave soon . . . if they hadn't left already.

Jeff had decided that he would wait until nine-fifteen. If he hadn't seen them leave by then, he would have to go up and check to see if their truck was still in the driveway.

And if it isn't? a mental voice asked.

Yeah, another softer, goading voice whispered. *If it isn't, then what?*

Jeff grunted, closed his eyes for a moment, and shook his head. The swirling darkness behind his eyelids was dizzying. If his aunt and uncle were still there, then he had no idea what he'd do next; but he knew— somehow—he was going to have to find the courage to go up to the house and go down into the cellar to see if Danny was there.

He *had* to find out if the voices inside his head were right.

And if they weren't, then he would have to seriously consider that he might really be losing his mind.

You know damned well Danny's up there . . . in the cellar . . . and that he's just as afraid as you were!

Jeff squeezed his eyes tightly shut, willing the chattering voices inside his head to stop, but they didn't. Memories of what had happened to him in that cellar flooded his mind like raging torrents. He saw a terrified little boy who was tied by the hands and feet over an oil drum, but the face shifted and blended from Danny's to his own to Jeremy's and then back again to Danny's.

On the drive out to Bridge Road, he had told Katherine some—but certainly not all—of what he had been thinking. He told her how he thought Mildred and Kirby, in order to drive him crazy, maybe even to the brink of suicide—like they might have done to his sister—had kidnapped Danny and were keeping him in the cellar. When she asked why they would have done something like that, he said he wasn't sure. He thought maybe it was so they could reenact the abuse he and his siblings had suffered out there.

Maybe, he had told Katherine, they even *wanted* him to know Danny was out here so he would come looking for him.

Maybe it was all part of an elaborate setup.

Although he didn't tell her this, he wondered if maybe they had already killed Danny and were trying to lure him out to the house so they could pin the blame on him. If they didn't outright kill Jeff, or if he didn't go insane and kill himself, the situation might push him so far over the edge that no one would believe anything he said. They could use his history of mental illness as part of their case against him. He knew he was starting to look a little like "The Boy

Who Cried Wolf" after taking Eddie on two wild-goose chases already.

And maybe, Jeff thought with a shiver, but he hadn't told Katherine this, just maybe he would end up in jail, charged with kidnapping, child abuse, and possibly even murder!

He knew it was far-fetched, even paranoid thinking, but he told Katherine he was convinced that Mildred and Kirby were afraid of him, now that he was back in town; afraid that he wanted to expose them because of the abuse he had suffered at their hands as a child. Maybe they were afraid that he intended to have them take the blame for Jeremy's death. If that was the case, they might be desperate enough to try practically any-thing—including murder—to stop him from exposing them!

Just as he had expected, Katherine had reacted skeptically to all of this; but after listening to him, she had finally agreed to go out to the house with him.

One voice rattling inside Jeff's head kept telling him that she didn't believe him at all. She was simply hu-moring him and agreeing with his irrational thinking because she had realized on the short drive over just how crazy he really was—maybe even *dangerous!*—and that she would be in serious trouble if she tried to burst his paranoid fantasy.

And that's entirely possible, don't you think? one part of him asked archly. *What with all the pressure you've been under these past few weeks, your mind very well may have snapped! You may have lost your marbles entirely! The lights are on, but nobody's home!*

No! Jeff thought, gritting his teeth and shaking his head viciously. *Sure I've been under a lot of pressure, but I'm not crazy! I'm holding it together pretty fucking good, considering!*

Considering WHAT?

Jeff tried to comfort himself with the thought that

Katherine was with him. At least he could trust her
even more than he could trust Eddie Dearborn. Her
presence might give him the courage and strength he
lacked but would need if he was going to go into the
house and down into the cellar . . . to face the sum total
of all his childhood fears.

Are you sure of that? a hissing voice asked. It might
have been Alexander's, but Jeff couldn't be sure. *How
do you know you can trust ANYONE anymore?*

Jeff couldn't answer that, but even if the answer was
No one, it was already too late. The course was set, and
they were committed.

For long, dragging minutes, he and Katherine sat in
silence. Katherine kept wringing her hands and glancing over at Jeff as though she expected him to say
something reassuring. He knew, more than anything,
that she wanted to be home in case the state police
called.

Jeff rolled his window down. A brisk breeze blew in,
stirring his hair and cooling the sweat on the back of
his neck. His two-fisted grip on the steering wheel
tightened as he leaned forward and stared at the view
of the road ahead. Every few seconds he would glance
at his watch to note the sluggish passage of time. Minutes seemed to take forever to pass. It seemed like it
had been hours or even days ago that he had called
Katherine.

It was 8:42 A.M. by his watch when he first heard the
distant chug of an engine. From the direction of the
sound, he knew instantly that it was coming from the
driveway.

"It's gotta be them," Jeff said, craning forward so he
could get a good view through the dense brush of the
road ahead.

The truck's engine sputtered and backfired like exploding firecrackers in the chilly morning stillness as it
rattled over the ruts in the driveway. The sound grew

steadily louder, filling the woods. A blue jay started to squawk and then flew off into the woods. Jeff cringed when he heard the squeal of old brakes as the truck slowed for the stop before pulling out onto the dirt road. He leaned forward, staring at the wall of brush between them.

And then he saw it.

For just a fleeting instant, the rusty, slow-moving pickup truck appeared in the narrow gap between the bushes, looking ominously close. It stayed in sight just long enough for Jeff to get a clear view of who was in it. Sunlight shining in through the driver's window clearly illuminated Kirby's face in profile. The old man was sitting hunched in his seat, leaning forward so his chin almost touched the steering wheel as he corrected his steering. He was wearing the same dull gray suit coat he had worn to Judy's funeral. The same tie was knotted around his neck, and the loose, tanned skin of his neck, looking like the flesh of a newly plucked chicken, spilled out over his shirt collar. A stray reflection of sunlight caught the corner of Kirby's eye and made it appear to gleam wickedly like quicksilver. His big-knuckled hands gripped the truck's steering wheel, but all Jeff could think when he saw them was—*Those are the same goddamned hands that held the belt that whipped me and Judy . . . and made me whip Jeremy!*

Sitting beside Kirby on the passenger's side, seen only in dim silhouette, was Mildred. She was staring straight ahead at the road, her expression set and grim. She was wearing a heavy winter coat against the morning chill and a round straw hat that had a spray of small flowers on top.

"Jesus, I can't believe it," Jeff whispered, more to himself than to Katherine. For a moment, in fact, he had forgotten that she was sitting there beside him.

The truck appeared and a second later was out of sight, lost behind the dense brush, but Jeff stared at the dust that slowly settled in its wake. He realized he had been holding his breath, so he let it out slowly, then took a long inhalation before turning to Katherine.

"You ready?" he asked.

He could hear the high flutter in his voice, but he was heartened when Katherine, biting her lower lip, looked at him and nodded. "Yeah," she said. "Let's go."

I think she believes you! said a voice in his mind.

Jeff started up his car and shifted into gear, but he waited a few more seconds, just to be sure Kirby's truck was out of sight before he pulled out onto the dirt road. He couldn't stop wondering why Katherine had agreed to come along with him. He knew he wanted her to be here, but a part of him still couldn't quite accept that she believed him.

It doesn't really matter, does it? said a tiny voice, struggling to be heard above the roaring sound that filled Jeff's ears. *She's probably so goddamned desperate she'll believe anything if it means her son is all right and still alive. The point is, she's here with you now! You can do it, Jeff! You HAVE to do it!*

"Yeah . . . maybe I can," Jeff whispered.

He released his grip on the steering wheel and wiped his sweaty hands on his pants legs.

"What'd you say?" Katherine asked, looking at him questioningly.

For a moment Jeff thought her voice was one of the voices inside his head. Then he realized that she had spoken. He shook his head.

"Huh? Oh—no. Nothing," he said.

Then, before he lost his nerve, he pressed down on the accelerator, pulled out onto the dirt road, and took the turn into Kirby and Mildred's narrow, rutted driveway.

* * *

Jeff thought his hand looked death-white as he curled his fingers around the doorknob and gave it an easy twist. He wasn't sure if he was dreading—or hoping—that the door would be locked, but the latch clicked softly. With a chattering groan of ancient hinges, the door swung heavily inward.

Of course it would be unlocked, he thought. *This is small-town Maine. Everyone who lives here is honest and pure and trustworthy! We never need to lock our doors!*

A wave of dizziness swept through Jeff as he glanced over his shoulder at Katherine and then looked into the house.

So this is it, huh? said Alexander's serious-sounding voice inside Jeff's head. *This is what you've been dreading all along?*

The aroma that wafted out of the house, carried by a gentle draft of air, was instantly, almost frighteningly familiar. It was a curious mixture of smells: brewed coffee, old rope, dampness like the smell in the hayloft on rainy days, and something else . . . something indefinable. A numbing ripple of fear raced through Jeff, tingling his hands and face, as he tried to identify the smell. Then, forcing a smile, he took a deep breath and stepped across the threshold into the entryway as if he owned the place. Katherine was only a step or two behind.

"I-I'm not so sure we should be doing this," Katherine said hoarsely. Jeff couldn't help but notice the slight quaver in her voice. "I mean, what if they come back and find us here, or what if the police are—"

"It's not a problem," Jeff said, fighting to keep his own voice steady. "After all, this is my aunt and uncle's house. We're family. If anyone sees us and asks what we're doing here, all we have to say is we came out for a visit, but no one was home."

"Yeah, but . . . I dunno," Katherine said, shaking her head and looking not at all convinced.

All the while, Jeff's eyes were sliding back and forth, trying to take in the small, cluttered entryway that led into the living room on the left and the kitchen straight ahead. It all seemed so familiar, but it had an odd, distanced sort of familiarity, like a recurring dream. Standing beside the closed closet door on the right was a tarnished brass coatrack that held an assortment of jackets and moth-eaten wool sweaters. Below that, in the boot tray on the floor, was a pile of shoes and mud-crusted boots. The rug by the front door was so badly faded and worn the pattern was all but lost, but it looked as though there had once been a picture of some kind of flowering tree with several birds flying around it. The plaster walls were cracked with age and in desperate need of a fresh coat of paint. Up in the corners where the walls and ceiling met, filmy gray clots of cobwebs hung. They wafted lazily in the draft, like drifting kelp until Jeff swung the door shut. On two of the walls beside the doorways, there hung framed, fading pictures of Jesus, one of him on the cross, the other of him, arms extended, welcoming a group of little children.

"Hey, we'll be fine," Jeff said, wishing he believed it himself. He didn't miss the irony of the picture of a loving Jesus with children. "We'll just have a quick look around, then we're out of here, okay?"

"Yeah, okay," Katherine said, but she didn't look at all convinced.

Once again, Jeff couldn't help but wonder if she was here, not because she believed what he had told her, but because she was afraid of what he might do if she said she didn't believe him.

It really doesn't matter, does it? Jeff thought. *She's here with me now, and that's what counts!*

"So, what do we do?" Katherine asked.

Jeff tried to ignore the subtle feeling that she was patronizing him as he nodded in the direction of the kitchen.

"This way," he said. "The door down into the cellar is in the kitchen." Before he could say anything more, his voice cut off with a loud click.

Jeff smiled at Katherine before they started walking down the short corridor to the kitchen doorway. Katherine was one step behind him. With each step, Jeff could feel the walls of the entryway closing in on him, squeezing around him until he felt it almost impossible to take a deep enough breath. The curious smells inside the house were strong. They clawed like a wet cat at the back of his throat, making it feel raw. The hallway floorboards seemed uneven, warped with age and use. Jeff stumbled and almost fell when he first entered the small, dark kitchen.

His body felt all rubbery, drained almost entirely of strength as he stood there in the doorway and looked around. Dull lemon sunlight filtered through the curtained windows, but it did little to remove the thick, pressing gloom of the room. Muted squares of sunlight illuminated the worn countertop and cracked linoleum floor. Although he hadn't thought much—if at all—about this place throughout his adult life, the sense of recognition was immediate and almost overwhelming. He couldn't shake the sensation that this was all a dream, and that he would wake up in Judy's house . . . or maybe even back home in Denver.

His blank gaze shifted from the old-fashioned woodstove to the gray slate kitchen sink and counter. Sunlight gleamed dully off the tarnished faucets. In one corner of the room stood an antique Frigidaire refrigerator. Its motor was running with a low, irritating rattle. The enamel was no longer white, but looked like old bone showing through an accumulation of years of grime and wear. Next to the sink was an old-fashioned gas range, its burners black and crusty with grease. In the center of the room, two chairs stood at either end of a narrow table which was covered with a stained, pockmarked red-and-white checkered tablecloth. In the center of the table was a half-full napkin holder and a small pewter tray, which held a sugar bowl, salt and pepper shakers, and a few amber bottles of medications.

But it was the door leading into the cellar that immediately drew Jeff's gaze and held it like the metal jaws of a bear trap. The varnish on the door was cracked and yellowed, blackened in the corners of the panels. The brass doorknob looked almost green with age and use. A thumbtack in the middle of the door held a calendar with a picture of Jesus walking on a storm-tossed ocean, his white robe flowing like a pure cloud against the raging seas. Jeff was surprised to see that the calendar was for this year.

A sudden chorus of voices filled Jeff's head as he stood there, staring in amazement at the cellar door.

This is it! said one clear, sharp voice in his mind. Jeff knew how simple it should be to walk over to the door, open it, yank on the pull chain to turn on the light, and go down there to have a look around.

Easy! Absolutely nothing to it!

But Jeff remained frozen where he stood. He could hear a low groaning sound but didn't realize that he was the one making it as he staggered backwards. He reached blindly behind him, his hands clawing for the wall or something to support him.

Jeff saw Katherine look at him, her eyes suddenly widening with concern. She said something, but even when he stared at her moving lips, he couldn't make out what she was trying to say. Babbling voices filled his head. He felt as though he had suddenly found himself in a crowded room where everyone was talking, but he couldn't distinguish anything that was being said. His head—the whole room—filled with a swelling, unintelligible general murmur that rose and fell like churning, gushing swells of the ocean.

Get a fucking grip, Jeff! Go to the door now and open it!

The voice was stern, commanding, but it was immediately swallowed by the muttering rush of voices. Jeff kept back-pedalling, each step jarring his body like a hammer blow until he felt the back of his legs bump into something. He didn't know what it was or what he was doing when he grabbed the back of one of the chairs and pulled it away from the table. The chair feet clattered loudly on the floor.

Katherine's face was creased with deepening concern as she took a few steps closer to Jeff and reached out to him. Jeff's vision telescoped crazily in and out. Numb with terror, he watched as Katherine's arms and hands extended and magnified like a cartoon character's. She grabbed him by the shoulders, and he could feel her shake him, but it was distant and dull, almost as if it were happening to someone else.

A sudden chill gripped Jeff. Numbing tingles rippled up and down his body, unstringing his muscles. For a timeless, terrifying moment, he had the sensation that he had somehow snapped outside of his body and floated up to the dingy ceiling where he could look down at everything that was happening in the kitchen. The room was suffused with a dull, throbbing glow of light that seemed to keep pace with his rapid pulse.

Katherine said something to him, but her voice dragged, like a tape being played much too slowly. Jeff had no idea what she was saying. Her words melted and twisted together like taffy. As he watched from his vantage point on the ceiling, his body felt like it had been injected with a megadose of Novocain.

Numb . . . comfortably numb, he thought, distantly aware that the phrase mirrored a Pink Floyd song.

He saw more than felt Katherine push him back.
His knees buckled and folded up as he sat down heavily in the chair. The impact was hard, stunningly real.
A tearing *whoosh* filled his ears. Caught in an irresistible, reeling spin, he felt his consciousness being
sucked back into his body.

It was dizzying . . . terrifying!

But as a painfully hot, tingling sensation took hold
of him and seemed about to tear him apart, there came
another, louder rushing sound. This one was like a
slow, echoing peal of thunder that started to fade but
never quite disappeared, an echo beyond the horizon.
An inward-turning funnel of darkness surrounded
Jeff, tearing at him as it sucked him down into itself.
His mind was screaming, but he knew his throat was
paralyzed, and he wasn't making any sound. Besides
his own internal scream, the last thing he was aware of
before he was lost in the crashing roar of darkness was
three words . . .

Three words that growled like a landslide of boul-
ders that was burying him alive.

. . . *the dark room* . . .

Chapter Twenty-six

Conversation in a Dark Room: #6

I open my eyes to a wall of solid darkness and am momentarily afraid that I've gone blind. I can feel that I'm sitting down, maybe in a chair—a wooden chair with a hard, straight back; or else I'm on the floor, leaning against a stone wall. Whatever it is, it feels cold and unyielding against my back.

"Is there . . . anybody here?" I call out.

The nervous quaver in my voice fills the darkness like an unseen presence. When I take a breath, it feels as though a dozen knife blades have slid in between my ribs and are slicing into my lungs. The darkness pulsates, but there is absolutely no sensation of light. This is a darkness more pure and impenetrable than any I have ever experienced before, a darkness so dense it's like staring into . . .

Nothing . . .

Finally, after waiting for what seems like several minutes, a voice speaks up.

"Sure. . . . We're all still here. No one's gone anywhere."

I immediately recognize Alexander's voice and feel a flood of relief.

"Jesus Christ, Alexander! Where the hell am I?" I ask, but even before I've finished phrasing my question, I know the answer.

I'm in the safe room . . . the dark room!

Alexander doesn't answer; he doesn't have to. His silence fills the room with a hushed expectancy.

"Are you . . . all alone, Alexander?" I ask once I can no longer bear the silence. It might only be my imagination, but I think I hear or sense others, lurking in the darkness around me.

I think maybe I have regained a slight measure of control over my voice but know I'm not fooling anyone, not even myself. My face and hands are all prickly, and I have the distinct impression that, although I can't see a damned thing, several other people are in the room, and they can all see me easily.

"No, I'm not alone," Alexander says. "I haven't taken a roll call or anything, but I think pretty much everyone's here."

"Everyone? Why everyone?" I ask. "I thought our rule was only one person at a—"

I cut myself off when a sudden thought fills me with blinding panic.

Jesus, maybe I'm not in the dark room! Maybe I'm dying—or already dead and in my coffin!

Although it doesn't change anything I see, I squeeze my eyes tightly shut and stare into the swelling darkness which squeezes me like a gigantic fist. I try to remember what I was doing just before this, but I draw a complete blank. A sinking rush of panic fills me when I realize I have almost no memory of *anything*. I know who I am, but that's about it. I clear my throat, forcing myself to speak.

"So, why are you all here now?"

"We all have our reasons," Alexander replies. "Different ones, I suppose. I can't speak for anyone else, but I think—for me, at least—it's because this is where it all began."

"What are you? . . ." I say, but the question dies on my lips. I am suddenly quite certain that I don't want to know what Alexander's talking about.

"You're getting pretty close to it, Jeff," Alexander continues in a voice that is low and soothing, almost reassuring; but the thoughts that fill my mind are nearly paralyzing. "You're *very* close now."

"Close?" I croak, no longer able to disguise the rising panic in my voice. "Close . . . to *what?*"

"Close to finding out," Alexander says. "You must realize by now that you have to go through with this, don't you? I mean, you can't just avoid it, like you have in the past. You can't just throw up some more walls and try to lock the doors. That won't work any-more—not now that you're here."

But where is HERE? I want to ask but am unable.

Alexander takes a long breath that sounds like a rushing surge of surf. I can't get rid of the feeling that I am surrounded by a circle of people—personalities I've created—and they're all closing in on me, tighten-ing the circle.

"The doors are opening, Jeff," Alexander says in a mild, almost singsong voice. "You might have thought you were cured before now, but you weren't. You never were."

"But why—"

"I think you know why, Jeff."

Muffled silence fills the darkness.

"No, I . . . , I finally say after taking a shuddering breath. "I don't."

"Why did you hesitate just then?" Alexander asks. His voice stings like the snap of a whip in the dark.

I wince at the throb of pressure that is building up behind my sightless eyes. During the long stretch of silence that follows, my ears begin to ring with a high, buzzing hum. I desperately want to say something—anything—to break the intolerable silence, but my mind is lost in total turmoil.

"Shit, stop beating around the bush, will you? I'll tell him if you won't."

This new voice, speaking so loud and close behind me, surprises me. I think it sounds like Karl but can't be sure. I want to hear a few more words before I decide.

"Don't you think it's best if he figures this out for himself?" Alexander says.

The resonance in his voice gives me a slight measure of calmness and hope, but not much. I think I can hear the dull shuffle of feet on the stone floor as the crowd presses in around me in the darkness.

"We've never agreed to that, and you know it!"

I am sure, now, that it is Karl speaking. I wonder how many other people are there, moving closer . . . silently waiting.

Waiting for what?

"Well, I say if he's so fucking stupid or scared or whatever, then it's up to us to tell him," Karl suddenly shouts. He pauses a beat as his words reverberate in the dark room, then continues, "Things are getting pretty fucking serious, Jeff. You must realize that, now that you're *here!*"

Now that I'm where? I want to ask again, but I am unable to make a sound. A bone-shaking panic makes me want to cry out, to start screaming and never stop.

They don't need to tell me! I think through my blinding fear. *No one does! I know EXACTLY what he means!*

I realize I am panting heavily. I can feel the trickle of sweat running down my face and sides. The flesh at the back of my neck is crawling, sliding with a cold, clammy trickle.

I've known it all along, I think, *but I could never admit it—not to Sally, not to Doctor Ingalls, not even to myself!*

"You know it's not *this* door, the cellar door in the kitchen, don't you, Jeff?" Karl says.

His voice is low and menacing, like the quick jabs of an unseen knife in the dark that is slicing deeply. Although I can't see a thing, I twist my head back and forth and stare into the darkness as I frantically search for something to say.

"You *know* it's not the cellar door I'm talking about, don't you, Jeff?" Karl repeats, sounding like a teacher who is losing patience with a particularly slow student. He waits another moment, then says, "I said *don't you?*"

"No . . . no, it . . . it isn't," I stammer. The sound of my own voice surprises me.

"And exactly what door do I mean?" Karl asks. I can feel him pressing close to me in the dark. "Can you tell me *that,* Jeff?"

"I . . . I'm not sure," I say.

Every word I speak thunders painfully in my ears. I feel a sudden warm gush in both ears and think it will be a miracle if I'm not bleeding from the ears. "I'm really not sure."

"Oh, yeah—right," Karl says, tisking with disgust.

"I don't think this is the way to do it, Karl," Alexander says.

I turn my head in the direction of Alexander's voice, silently hoping that he will assert himself, as he always has, and make Karl keep quiet.

"It doesn't matter if it's right or wrong," Karl snaps, his voice sharp with command.

I am surprised that he is standing up to Alexander. That's not how things usually go in the dark room.

"Right and wrong have nothing to do with it," Karl

says. "We tried it your way . . . for much too long, and *that* certainly never worked!"

"I think it did," Alexander replies, but his voice sounds weak, almost defeated.

"Well even if it did, not anymore! Not now that he's back here!"

I cringe in the darkness, listening to this exchange and feeling the crackle of emotions. I feel impelled to jump in and say something, but I have no idea what I think or what I should say. On a soul-deep level, I have an inkling of what Alexander and Karl are arguing about, and it fills me with a sharp, twisting dread that I want to avoid at all costs.

"You know no matter what we say or do he's going down there, don't you?" Karl says evenly. "And he's gonna find . . . well, he'll find whatever's down there. At least now he knows *where* the door is."

"You're making a big mistake," Alexander says, but I'm not sure if he means me or Karl.

"You *do* know what I mean, don't you, Jeff?" Karl asks.

Yes . . . yes, I do? I think, but I can't say it. I shiver with a tingling rush of fear that won't seem to stop.

"There, you see?" Karl's voice barks in the solid darkness. "He knows it. He's just never told you that he did!"

There is a long, threatening pause. Again, I feel like I should say or do something, but my mind is a roaring chaos. At last, Alexander speaks.

"Is that true, Jeff? *Do* you know?"

I shake my head in denial, knowing that the motion is wasted in the darkness.

"No . . . no, I don't . . . I-I'm not sure," I say.

My voice is at least one octave too high. Karl lets fly a burst of derisive laughter.

"Oh, is that so?"

"Look, this isn't doing any good," Alexander says.

"It was a mistake for all of us to be here. I shouldn't have agreed to it. It's just not right to be pushing him so hard."

"That's bullshit!" Karl shouts. "He knows *exactly* what I'm talking about! He knows what he's looking for is down there! Shit, he's known it all along! He just won't admit it! Come on, Jeff. Admit it!"

"Yeah," I say, just a whisper.

The single word echoes in the darkness, but instead of fading, it rises higher and louder until it *becomes* the darkness. I hear Karl's voice. It is faint, as though he's shouting from someplace far away.

"So tell him! . . . Tell everyone what you know, Jeff!"

I lick my lips furiously and try to swallow the hot, dry lump that has formed in my throat. Words and thoughts cascade crazily in my mind, but I feel as though I'm floating high above them and looking down at the confused jumble they make.

"Yes," I say, my voice cracked and almost broken. "I know what the safe room is, and I know *where* it is. . . . It's behind that old hutch, down in Kirby and Mildred's cellar. There's a hidden door that leads into another room."

"Into the safe room!"

I have no idea who said that. The words hiss in the darkness like cold water being splashed onto a hot stove.

"Yes. There used to be a bigger house here, but it burned down years ago," I say. "When Mildred and Kirby rebuilt, they walled off part of the cellar, so the cellar is actually bigger than the house above it. And there's a . . . a way into that secret room behind one of the walls. That's where they used to put us when they—" My voice catches painfully in my throat as terrifying memories twist inside me like a tangle of snakes, but I force myself to continue. "When they were done with us . . . for the time being. That's where they kept us—Judy . . . and Jeremy . . . and me."

"And that's when you started calling it the 'safe room,' right? Because they never hurt you when you were in there?"

I am sure now that it is Karl who is speaking, but it doesn't matter because I realize this voice is asking the question for all of the personalities who silently surround me in the darkness. I sense that even Alexander is waiting expectantly for the answer.

"Yeah, they—they left us alone in there . . . sometimes for a real long time . . . in the dark . . . That's when we would . . . would talk to each other."

"The voices in the dark room," Karl says mildly, but his voice sounds funny, as though it's resonating with the tones and inflections of dozens of other voices.

"The *safe* room," I whisper, surprised that my voice doesn't choke off.

I slump back against the hard chair—or stone wall—and try to take a deep breath. I can still sense the circle of people gathered around me, but the sense of threat has diminished, at least a little.

"All along, I thought the room was just a . . . just something I created in my own mind, something I had made up," I continue. As I speak, my voice gains strength. The darkness pressing in around me seems to ease back a little.

"But it was real!" I say, wanting to shout but barely able to whisper. "It's down there in the cellar—the hidden door is behind the old hutch."

I feel a chilling rush of fear as I say these words out loud. A roaring sound fills my ears, echoing like thunder in the darkness; but then, very faintly at first, I hear something else. It seems like endless minutes before I realize what it is: then I recognize the soft, chuffing sound of someone laughing. Soon one, then two, then many other voices join in, and before long the room is resounding with rising squeals and howls of echoing laughter.

"I *do* know it!" I say, scarcely able to hear myself above the nearly deafening sound.

"Jesus Christ, I've known it all along! The dark room down there was where I always felt safe, where I could sit in the darkness and nobody would come to hurt me. I could talk to people . . . people I couldn't even see . . . and all along it was Judy . . . Judy and Jeremy. *They* were the first voices in the dark room! *They* were the ones who helped me get through it!" Tears sting my eyes, and the cold pressure inside my head seems about to explode. "We . . . we tried to help each other, but we couldn't . . . not really!"

I am trying hard to control myself, but I am filled with such a dizzying sense of elation that I'm not able to for long. Against my will, I join in and am soon laughing along with everyone else, laughing so hard my stomach knots up and I find it almost impossible to catch my breath. I cross my arms over my stomach and lean forward, laughing so hard tears carve hot tracks down my face.

But they are tears of happiness . . . tears of relief. I don't know if I am thinking or shouting the words out loud, but a single thought fills my mind, making me feel light-headed, almost insanely giddy.

I know where it is! After all this time, I remember where the dark room is!

Chapter Twenty-seven
Opening the Door

Jeff opened his eyes to see darkness surrounding him and funneling inward like a slow-turning kaleidoscope. His chest felt compressed, and it took several pounding heartbeats before he could remember where he was.

He sighed and, slumping forward in the chair, covered his face with both hands and let out a long, wavering groan. He sounded like someone who just didn't want to get out of bed in the morning. His body was wire-tight and trembling, as if a subtle electrical current was tickling through him. His stomach muscles were tight, and his shoulders were shaking, but he wasn't sure if it was from fear or an overwhelming sense of relief.

Probably both, he thought as he wedged his eyes open and looked between his fingers at Katherine.

She was standing midway between him and the cellar door. A narrow beam of sunlight sliced across the tips of her shoes. Her face looked ashen, almost ghostly in the shadowy kitchen as she stared at him. Her mouth was gaping open as though she had no idea whether to go to him or turn around and run for her life.

You're okay, whispered a voice deep within Jeff's head. *She's scared shitless, so tell her you're okay.*

Blinking his eyes like a mole suddenly caught out in the midday sun, Jeff straightened up and forced himself to smile at her as he licked his lips and said, "Hey, don't worry. I . . . I'm all right."

Katherine's mouth was moving soundlessly. Jeff had no idea what she might be trying to say because echoing voices from the conversation he'd just had in the dark room were still rippling in his mind, sounding just as vivid and real as his own voice. He struggled against the frightening thought that Katherine wasn't even real—that she was a creation of his imagination, or a ghost, who was haunting him, like so many other ghosts.

"Seriously," he said, his voice sounding shaky and raw as he rubbed his face. "I'm okay. I just . . . just needed a minute there."

"God, Jeff! You were . . . you were . . ."

Katherine's voice trailed away to nothing as she stared at him, her eyes round and bugging out.

"I'm sorry," Jeff said with a tight shrug.

Every bone and muscle in his body complained as he twisted around, clamped one hand on the back of the chair, braced himself, and then stood up. For a frightening instant, he thought his legs weren't strong enough to support him, but he locked his knees and pushed the chair away. It teetered for a moment and almost fell, then righted itself.

"I just . . ."

He took a shuddering breath.

"I just remembered something," he said.

He fought hard to maintain control of his voice and body as he raised his arms, holding his hands out to her, and took a single step forward.

Katherine suddenly stiffened. Her hands clenched into fists, and she backed one step away from him, keeping the same distance between them.

"You . . . you had me *really* scared!" she said, her voice high and whining. Her lower lip was pale and trembling, and he noticed that she kept glancing over at the nearest door out of the kitchen.

Say something! Jesus! She thinks you're dangerous, that you're going to hurt her!

"I said I was sorry," Jeff said, lowering his voice, "but I—"

"I can't *stand* it when you *do* that!" Katherine said, obviously trying hard to keep herself from shouting. "That's twice now that you just . . . just sort of blanked out like that and . . . and . . . Jesus, Jeff!"

"It's nothing to worry about, Kat. Honest." He paused and rubbed his face again, trying to snap himself back. "Did I—you know, say anything . . . out loud, I mean?"

He took another step forward, and Katherine backed away another step. She was almost to the cellar door, easily within arm's reach of it. The thought that she might turn around, open the door, and run down into the cellar—*into the dark room to get away from him!*—filled him with a cold, twisting dread.

"You were muttering to yourself . . . just like you did the other night at my house. God, Jeff! What the hell's wrong with you? It's like you . . . like you go into a trance or something."

"Yeah, that's sort of what happens," Jeff said, trying his best to sound dismissive, "but I was . . . Jesus, Kat, you have to understand that just being in this house after all these years is like—it's kind of overwhelming. But that's all it is. I just have to . . . to get my mind together."

Boy, ain't THAT the truth! a voice whispered close to his ear.

Jeff almost laughed out loud at the thought, but then his gaze shifted past Katherine, over her shoulder to the cellar door, and he froze. Even without the voices whispering inside his head, he knew—now, more than ever—that he was going to have to go down and look into the secret room.

The DARK room! . . . The SAFE room!

He knew this could all be just a product of his overactive imagination, a projection of his mental illness, but he knew he had to check to make sure Kirby and Mildred didn't have Danny down there.

Oh, he's there all right! You KNOW damned well they have him!

Shaking his head and straightening his shoulders, Jeff cleared his throat and said, "Look, I'm okay, Kat . . . Honest!" He glanced around the kitchen, then sighed and shook his head again. *"Shit!* We didn't think to bring a flashlight or anything, did we?"

By *anything* he meant a weapon, but Katherine didn't respond. She just stood there, staring blankly at him.

"Well," Jeff continued, as if everything was now perfectly under control, "let's see if we can find one around here someplace."

Without waiting for Katherine to say or do anything, he went over to the counter and started rummaging through the cupboards on either side of the sink. He found stacked dishes and cups, boxes of cereal, spices and other cooking ingredients, and an assortment of well-used kitchen items and tools, but no flashlight. He was careful not to move anything too much out of place as he peered into the back of the cupboards. The last thing he wanted was for Kirby and Mildred to know that someone had broken into the house and had been poking around.

After he'd gone through all of the upper level cupboards, he started on the lower ones, slamming each cupboard door shut harder than the last as his level of frustration rose. Before long, he was almost in a panic to find a flashlight. Without one, there was no way he was going down into the cellar, but he also knew this would be his only chance, and they didn't have much time as it was.

Finally, in the fifth cabinet, he found what he was looking for—a long-tubed emergency flashlight with a shiny metal barrel. It felt slippery in his sweaty hand as he picked it up and hefted it. He pointed it downward and thumbed the switch. A tight smile spread across his face when a bright oval of light appeared on the kitchen floor.

"All right. The batteries seem to be pretty good," he said as he clicked the flashlight off and shook it. He turned to Katherine. "You ready to go?"

Katherine hadn't moved an inch from where she had been standing. Her teeth were clenched, and Jeff could see her jaw muscles rapidly tensing and untensing. She still held her fists at belt level as she stared at him, her eyes wide with fear and deepening suspicion.

Jeff swallowed hard, then exhaled noisily as he raked his fingers through his hair.

"Jesus Christ! Come on, Kat. You have to back me up on this," he said. Even to his own ears, his voice didn't sound at all normal. "I know this has gotta seem a little bit crazy, but I—"

"A *little* bit?" Katherine echoed, frowning deeply. "Jesus, Jeff!"

"Yeah, I know," Jeff said, "but I *have* to go down there, and I want you to come with me."

"Why?" Katherine said, her voice snapping like a whip.

Jeff hesitated a moment. "Because I'm *sure* Danny's down there, and I—" He choked and swallowed, then took a deep breath before finishing in a shattered voice, "And because I don't think I dare to go down there alone."

Katherine's gaze never wavered from him for a second, but her expression darkened.

"And how do you *know* that?"

"I . . . I just do," Jeff said.

When he took another step closer to the cellar door, Katherine's fists crossed her chest defensively, and she dodged to one side, but Jeff kept his eyes focused straight ahead at the cellar door. His gaze was riveted by the swirling grain pattern in the wood. No matter how much he wanted to look away, he couldn't do it. All he could think was, *I'm going down there. With or without her, I have to go down there!*

With one hand he squeezed the tube of the flashlight, wishing to God it was some kind of weapon instead; with the other hand he reached out for the doorknob, gripped it, and slowly turned it. For a trembling instant, the latch stuck, but then, with enough pressure, it finally clicked. The sound made him wince. It sounded like a bullet, sliding into the chamber of a gun.

Jeff wanted to look back at Katherine, to see what she was doing, but he couldn't tear his gaze away from the door as he tightened his grip on the slick brass doorknob and slowly pulled the door open. The door swung smoothly, with no squeal of rusted hinges to set his teeth on edge.

As soon as the door was open a crack, a damp, fetid draft swirled out over Jeff like a wash of cold swamp water. Clammy sweat broke out on his face and arms as he stared into the steadily widening wedge of darkness that was opening up in front of him. He was swept up in a rush of dizziness, suddenly afraid that he was staring straight down into a black, bottomless pit. He uttered a low whimper when he imagined himself falling forward, tumbling head over heels. His grip on the doorknob tightened as if he were clinging to a lifeline.

He was distantly aware of the whisper of Katherine's shoes on the floor as she came up behind him and looked over his shoulder, down the cellar stairs. The moist stirring of her breath on the back of his neck made him shiver. He wanted desperately to say something reassuring to her, but his mind was a roaring blank. He knew everything that could be said had already been said.

Now it was time to *do* something!

He snapped on the flashlight and shone it down along the rough wooden steps. The halo of light rippled over the steps like a Slinky, climbing downstairs. The stairs were dirty, but the centers of the treads were worn smooth with use. Jeff swung the light around, barely noticing the grimy walls, clotted with knots of cobwebs and dirt, until he saw the string and connected pull chain that led to the light at the bottom of the stairs.

A quickening chill gripped him. It was just as he had remembered it.

He took hold of the string and gave it a quick tug. There was an instant of slack in the string, and then resistance and a muted *click* as the lightbulb winked on. The chain hit the lightbulb with a faint tinkle sound. The bulb was filmed with dirt, and cast a weak yellow glow over the stairs and cellar floor.

Jeff's feet felt like they were weighed down with lead as he placed one on the top step and started down. He shivered wildly in the cool draft and wrinkled his nose, fighting back the flood of memories the dank, earthy smell of the cellar awoke in him.

A voice nearly breaking with panic shrieked inside his mind. *This is the place! This is where it all started!*

Don't go down there, Jeff! shouted another voice. This one sounded like Billy. *Please don't go! You're not gonna like what you find, I promise you!*

No! shouted another voice, but Jeff was so panicked now he couldn't tell who it was. *You HAVE to go! Maybe you can end it all right here, right now! Wouldn't you like that, Jeff?*

With all of these voices and others demanding his attention, Jeff's head started to spin so badly he thought he was going to be sick. His stomach knotted up like a fist, and gut-deep convulsions shook him. His eyelids fluttered wildly, making the soft glow of light in the cellar flicker before his eyes. The stairwell seemed to telescope crazily in and out. He tried to take a step back, but he tripped and would have fallen if he hadn't caught hold of the thin wooden railing. Quickly regaining his balance, he whispered, more to himself than to Katherine, "Just take it easy now. Take it easy!"

Somehow—he had no idea how—he took one step, and then another step down. The stairs creaked beneath his weight, the slow pull of old nails sounding like someone groaning in the dark. With each step down, it felt like he was wading deeper and deeper into icy lake water that rose up, inch by inch over his groin and stomach to his chest, then to his throat, and finally over his mouth and nose.

All sounds, even the raw creaking of the old wooden stairs, were muffled by the rapid flutter of his pulse in his ears. He knew that Katherine was right there, a few steps behind him, but fearful of losing his balance again and falling, he didn't dare turn around. The air of the cellar, heavy with the smells of old mortar, damp earth, and something much worse—*fear!*—clung to the back of his throat like a rancid taste that wouldn't go away.

As soon as he was at the bottom of the steps, Jeff directed the pale circle of light from his flashlight over to the far end of the cellar. He felt dizzy and disoriented. The darkness seemed to swallow the light,

draining it of its power; but over against the wall, he
saw what he was looking for—the tall, wooden hutch.
It looked so old, rotting, and discolored it seemed to
be made out of stone instead of wood. Jeff tried hard
not to look at anything else, including the dark,
rounded shape he had seen only fleetingly over beside
the ancient furnace.

Jesus, it's the oil drum!

Rivers of ice ran through his veins.

"There, see?" Jeff said in a low, quavering voice as
he swept the beam of light across the length of the wall
and then brought it back to the hutch. He wanted to
stay focused on why they were here and not let his
memories of past abuses get the better of him.
"Doesn't the wall look like it's a lot closer than it
should be?"

Katherine grunted, and Jeff glanced quickly over his
shoulder at her, but he didn't like taking his eyes away
from the hutch, not even for a second if only because
he didn't want to chance seeing the oil drum again. He
remembered how scared he had been only a few days
ago when he had gone down into the cellar at Judy's
house, and he knew now that it had been *this* place
that he had been remembering—*this* cellar that had
held such stark terror for him. He trembled like a little
boy who had been caught doing something bad and
was going to be punished for it . . . *severely* punished
to beat the *evil* out of him!

It's all right here, Jeff! someone inside his head said
to him. *Inside the secret door . . . right behind that
hutch!*

The dark room!

*You were safe in there once, but you might not be
NOW!*

"You—ah, you probably wouldn't even notice it if
you weren't looking for it," Jeff said, still trying to
keep his mind focused on simple, concrete things and

not let any of his irrational fears carry him away. He was surprised that his voice sounded as steady as it did. "I'll bet, even if Eddie had checked down here, he wouldn't have found it."

Katherine said nothing, and after a short pause, Jeff filled his lungs with a deep breath of the moist air and walked over to the hutch. His feet made loud scraping noises on the cement floor. Directing his flashlight downward, he illuminated the deep, semicircular grooves that had been worn into the floor by the wheels on the feet of the hutch. Shifting to one side he shone the flashlight over the barely visible hinges that attached the right side of the hutch to the wooden frame that was embedded in the stone-and-cement wall. The hinges looked well-oiled and rust-free.

"See here?" Jeff said simply, pointing at them with the flashlight.

Katherine sucked in her breath with a sharp gasp, then let it out slowly.

"Yeah," she said weakly, "but still—that doesn't prove that Danny's—"

Her voice cut off sharply when Jeff moved to the other side of the hutch, gripped the edge with both hands, and pulled back. The hutch moved much easier than he had thought it would. There was a rough grinding sound of metal wheels on concrete as another, darker rectangle opened up in front of him. This darkness was as thick as a night with no stars. Like looking into . . .

Nothing.

"Oh, my God," Katherine whispered behind him once the opening was wide enough so either of them could have fit through.

Jeff was too frightened to speak as he bent forward, leaning his head into the opening. The air was thick and stifling, impossible to breathe. He shone the beam of light ahead of him, but it seemed to be much dim-

mer now. Jeff gave the flashlight a quick shake, but it
didn't do any good. Either the batteries, which had
seemed as good as new upstairs, were fading, or else
his eyesight was going. Jeff stared in stunned silence at
the narrow passageway. He knew that, about ten feet
up ahead, it opened up into a small, windowless room.
If his memory was correct, the room was no more than
twelve feet square with rough stone walls, dirt floor, no
windows, and other than this door, no way out.

Dark.

Silent.

Cold.

Jeff took a deep breath and thought he could hear
his ribs cracking.

It's not too late, Jeff! You can still turn back now!

Jeff started grinding his teeth as he shook his head,
denying the voice any influence. Reaching behind him,
he took Katherine's hand in his and then stepped
through the narrow doorway. No matter where he
directed his flashlight, the darkness surrounding him
seemed to close in like a living thing that was trying to
swallow them both whole. They moved forward
slowly, their feet scuffing loudly on the hard-packed
dirt floor.

Jeff was no more than five feet into the passageway,
and Katherine was a foot or two behind him, when the
back of his neck suddenly felt cold and prickly. In-
stinctively, he yanked Katherine to one side, forcing
her against the stone wall as he wheeled around in a
defensive crouch. But he knew it was already too late.
In the suffused glow of his flashlight, he saw a dark
shape materialize out of the darkness and move toward him with the silent swiftness of a shadow.

Jeff cried out and raised one arm to cover his face.
As he did, the flashlight beam swept around to reveal
a face, horribly underlit.

Jeff saw his own face, looming at him out of the darkness.

The fetch! screamed a voice that ended with rising, gibbering laughter.

Before Jeff could react, a fist lanced out of the darkness and connected solidly with his jaw, snapping his head back. He heard something in his neck crack, then Katherine's shrill scream filled the narrow passageway as Jeff staggered backwards. The thick, coppery taste of blood flooded his mouth, and white stars were spinning in out-of-control cartwheels across his vision. He staggered back and bounced off the stone wall but kept his feet.

Katherine was whimpering almost soundlessly behind him as she scrambled to get away from their attacker, but she moved farther down the passageway toward the small room. Jeff's head felt like it was going to explode from the pressure and pain, but he brought the flashlight up again and shone it squarely into the person's face. His mind was filled with the vision of what he had seen last night, outside the living-room window. He was hoping—crazily—that his first impression of seeing himself had been wrong. As he sucked a whistling breath through his teeth and told himself to calm down, to try to gain control, he realized that he had been right.

If he had been looking into a mirror, he couldn't have been looking at someone who looked any more like him!

"Well, now, what do you know about that?" the man said.

His face split with a wide grin as he took a step forward to block their way out through the secret door.

"Looks to me like I got myself one bitch of a problem to deal with now, don't it?"

Chapter Twenty-eight

Confrontation

Moving steadily toward them, his breath snuffing like a pig grubbing for roots, the man forced both Katherine and Jeff down the narrow passageway and into the dark room. The only source of light was the beam from Jeff's flashlight as it swung wildly back and forth, leaving trailing blue afterimages in Jeff's field of vision. Behind him, all around him, lost in the dense darkness of the room, he could hear the low murmur of voices and the faint, mocking laughter of unseen people.

Jeff's mind was clicking fast as he tried to calculate when he might be able to catch the man off guard. If he shone the flashlight into his eyes, he might blind him . . . at least long enough so he could get the drop on him. That would be his best chance, but he didn't see an opportune moment to strike. They would have to be much closer, and the man was keeping a safe distance, his dark bulk—solid and real—filling the doorway that led back out of the secret room.

Jeff tried hard to push aside his rising panic, but he couldn't stop thinking irrationally that this was Kirby who had come back to the house and found them down here, and was now—*finally!*—going to punish him once and for all for *everything* evil he had ever done or thought.

Kirby's words from years ago rolled like the hollow echo of thunder in Jeff's memory.

"I'm just gonna have to whip the Devil out of you, boy, however long it takes!"

Jeff and Katherine crossed the dirt floor to the opposite wall, backtracking and tripping over their own feet as they went. The man stayed where he was in the doorway, blocking any possibility of escape. From the time he had spent down here as a boy, Jeff knew there was only one way out.

After a tense, lengthening moment, during which all Jeff could hear was his own labored breathing, the man snorted with laughter as he shook his head and reached up for the old lantern that was hanging from a nail driven into one of the rafters. He fished a wooden match from his shirt pocket and, still chuckling, lit it with his thumbnail, raised the chimney glass of the lantern, and touched the match to the oily wick. The flame sputtered as a thin lick of sooty smoke curled upward like a snake. Then the harsh orange glow blossomed in the room, brightening when the man replaced the sooty glass globe and hung the lantern back up on the nail. The rough stone blocks of the walls and thick, age-blackened rafters overhead stood out in stark relief. Hard, black shadows stained the yellow dirt floor like splashes of dark water.

Suddenly, Katherine's screech filled the room, resounding like a gunshot off the stone walls. Jeff's body tingled with apprehension as he turned quickly and saw the reason.

Danny, pale and trembling, his eyes as wide as saucers and full of fear, was sitting on the dirt floor in the far corner. He was leaning against the rough stone wall, next to a tattered mattress. On the mattress was a woolen blanket, full of holes, and a blue-and-white striped pillow without a pillowcase. Another rusty oil lamp and a Bible, lying open, were on a rickety wooden crate beside the bed.

Danny's legs were pulled up in front of him, his wrists and ankles bound by several loops of thick rope. Highlighted by dark shadows, his face looked pale, almost skeletal, and much thinner than Jeff remembered it from the day of Judy's funeral. Dark circles ringed the boy's eyes, making him look like a frightened raccoon. His long, dark hair was matted and plastered in oily strands over his forehead. There were thick scratches on the side of his face that looked like they might be infected. He was shivering, his shoulders shaking and teeth chattering wildly as he looked up at his mother. His eyes glistened with welling tears that shimmered in the lantern light. When he opened his mouth to say something, the only sound that issued was a stuttering groan.

Katherine darted over to him and knelt down beside him. She made a low, comforting sound as she ran her hands over his face as though not quite able to believe that he was real . . . that he was alive. After a moment, she turned and glared over her shoulder at the man in the doorway. Her eyes were brimming with tears, and a savage, almost insane expression contorted her features.

"You *bastard!* If you've hurt him, I swear to *Christ* I'll kill you!" she shouted. "I'll rip your fucking lungs out with my bare hands!"

She started to rise but when Danny made a low whimpering sound, she knelt back down and focused all of her attention on him.

The man in the doorway regarded her with a steady, baleful gaze for a long moment. Then, clicking his tongue with disgust and shaking his head from side to side, he said, "You'd be wise not to take the name of the Lord in vain in my home, ma'am."

He spoke softly, but his words were laced with an icy threat, and Jeff was positive the man could deliver on that threat.

Struck speechless, Jeff just stood there and stared at the man facing them, absolutely unable to process or accept how much he looked like his own mirror image. The resemblance was staggering. Jeff shivered, remembering last night when he had looked into that same face outside the living-room window. It *had* to be the same man! For a heart-stopping instant, Jeff toyed with the idea that he had actually—somehow—dissociated into two separate people, that this was the manifestation of one of his alter personalities. This was a part of him, the part that had driven Judy to suicide and ransacked the house and kidnapped Danny!

But then another thought—one too terrible, too unbelievable to consider for very long—stirred in the back of his mind. He tried to push it away, but a chorus of voices suddenly filled his head, all of them demanding his attention.

Yes sir, by Jesus, that has to be who you think it is! shouted one of the voices, so loud and clear it seemed to be coming from all around him in the darkness. Jeff wondered crazily why Katherine or the man standing in the doorway couldn't hear it.

It's gotta be him! said another voice. *It's gotta be Jeremy!*

Remember? someone else whispered, sounding like a soft wind, blowing through dead grass. *They never found his body.*

All this time, all these years, he's been down here . . . living in the dark room!

Probably just been waiting for you to come back!

This was followed by a dry, sniffing laugh.

*And he knew you'd have to come back . . . eventually.
Didn't he?*

Oh, yeah . . . he's been waiting . . . for YOU!

"Jesus! . . . No!" Jeff muttered, shaking his head
tightly. His own voice was almost drowned out by the
disembodied voices that swirled around him, filling
him with a deep, quaking dread.

But there was no denying it.

This man looked so much like him they *had* to be
brothers!

What other explanation could there be?

This had to be Jeremy, his brother who had disappeared down by the river that day so many years ago
and who had been presumed dead . . . dead and forgotten for all these years.

But how can he still be alive and living here?

The idea almost completely unstrung Jeff's nerves as
he stared at the man, whose face was cast in thick
shadow from the light of the lantern overhead. His
skin looked pale, almost ghostly white except where it
was smudged with dirt and soot. His blond hair was
cut short and looked greasy, unwashed. He was wearing a dark green T-shirt under a frayed flannel shirt,
faded jeans, and scuffed, brown work boots. But what
caught and held Jeff's attention was the wild gleam in
the man's eyes. Jeff instantly recognized it. It was the
same gleam he had seen in his own eyes years back—
and not so long ago—when he thought he might be
going crazy. No, when he *knew* he was going crazy and
had stared long and hard at his own reflection in the
bathroom mirror.

THOSE ARE THE EYES OF A CRAZY MAN!

"Wh-who are you? What's your name?" Jeff finally
managed to say.

As the man shifted his gaze slowly over to Katherine
and Danny, then back to Jeff, his smile widened to
expose a row of upper teeth that looked brown with

rot in the lantern light. Jeff had a fleeting impression
of a cat that was getting ready to bite the head off a
mouse, but then the man—*Jesus, it had to be Jeremy!*
Who else could he be?—tilted his head back and let
loose a burst of high, keening laughter.

"What's my name? Is that *all* you have to say? After
all this time? *What's my fucking name?*"

Jeff's body was nearly numb with panic. In a sudden, cold rush, he felt all of his strength drain out of
him. He staggered back until he hit the wall. The flashlight slipped from his nerveless hand. When it hit the
floor, it sounded like the lens shattered, but he didn't
care. He couldn't tear his gaze away from the man—
away from Jeremy!—and the absolutely insane fire
that lit up his eyes.

Jesus, he's crazy! . . . Dangerous crazy!

"Even after all this time," the man said in a hollow
voice, "I'd think you at least remember what my *name*
is. Don't you, *Jeff?*"

"How do you—"

Jeff's voice cut off with a sharp click in his throat.
He wanted to close his eyes and beg for the darkness
to come crashing down on top of him and sweep him
away, but try as he might, he couldn't pull his terrified
gaze away from his brother's eyes.

"Jeremy," Jeff managed to say, his voice nothing
but a ragged whisper.

"I don't give a shit *who* you are, you fucking *bastard!*"

Katherine's voice cut through Jeff's flood of panic.
He turned to see that she was still kneeling beside
Danny, holding his arms straight out to expose the
thick red welts that lined both of his arms all the way
up to his shoulders. She gently nudged him forward
and raised his shirt to reveal a network of puffy, red
welts that lined his shoulders and back. They looked to
be an inch wide, and Jeff immediately recognized

them. They were exactly like the ones he used to get from Kirby! Some of them had been crushed over with dried blood, that looked brick red in the lantern light. Katherine gingerly touched the wounds, her hands fluttering above them like butterflies.

"How *could* you?" she said, turning to the man with tears gleaming in her eyes. "How the *hell* could you *do* something like this to a boy? . . . To *my* little boy?"

"He needed to be punished," Jeremy said, his voice low and level, sounding absolutely matter-of-fact about it all. "They brought him here and told me he needed to be punished."

"They?" Katherine squealed. "What do you mean, *they?"*

Jeff didn't need to ask; his first thought had been that, like himself, Jeremy heard voices inside his head, but he immediately knew the real answer.

Kirby and Mildred!

They were the ones who had told Jeremy to punish Danny . . . the same way he had been punished.

"You . . . you're a . . . you're a fucking *monster!"* Katherine shrieked.

Holding her hands out like claws, she waved them wildly in front of her as she leaped to her feet. With a low grunt, she charged at the man, but Jeff quickly stepped between them, grabbed her by the arms, and shook her roughly, spinning her around. She looked at Jeff with wild-eyed fury, and for a fleeting instant, he was positive he saw the suspicion in her eyes that he was a part of this—that he had helped this monster bring Danny down here, and now they had *her,* too!

With a low, shuddering moan, Katherine collapsed into his arms and let out such an agonized wail that it sounded like the flesh of her throat was tearing.

"How could you?" she said again, her voice weaker and muffled against Jeff's shoulder as she sobbed and beat her fists uselessly against his shoulders. Jeff could feel her body shaking in his grasp as a tearless cry convulsed her body.

"How in the name of God *could* you?"

"Well, it *did* take some doing, I'll grant you that much," Jeremy said simply, his eyes twinkling like a fire, throwing off sparks.

He still hadn't budged from where he stood. Jeff was eyeing him cautiously, wondering . . . hoping that he would get a chance to strike. Now that his initial burst of fear had subsided, at least a little bit, he realized that Jeremy was no taller than he was, perhaps even an inch or two shorter. But he looked well-muscled, and Jeff didn't want to risk all of their lives by having to wrestle with him. No, if anyone was going to get out of here alive, he was going to need something else—a weapon, just to make sure.

"Well now, big brother," Jeremy said.

Jeff directed Katherine back over toward Danny and watched as his brother took a single, menacing step forward. "What the hell are we gonna do now, huh? You got any idea?"

Jeff sucked in a breath, held it for a moment, then shrugged and said, "Why not just let all three of us leave?"

Jeremy's reply was another loud burst of laughter that was so loud it hurt Jeff's ears.

"No . . . I'm afraid I can't do that, big brother," Jeremy said once this fit of laughter had passed. "I think we may have a bit of catching up to do, for old time's sake and all, but after that—" His eyes darted up at the ceiling for a moment and he winced. " 'Specially if *they* tell me to, I think I'm gonna have to do it."

Do what? Jeff thought but didn't have the strength to say.

As if in reply, Jeremy reached behind his back and pulled out a wicked-looking hunting knife. He held it up in front of his face, twisting it back and forth so the six-inch blade caught and reflected the light from the lantern. The blade seemed to glow white-hot in his hand. Then, with a soft grunt, he swung the knife around quickly a few times so the blade *whisked* in the air before pointing it straight at Jeff's chest.

Still sounding absolutely rational and in complete control, he said, "I'm afraid I'm gonna have to kill all three of you, and just pray to the good Lord that the cops don't find out."

"So, what did *you* do to survive?" Jeremy asked.

With the knife still pointing at his chest, Jeff cringed away from Jeremy and pressed his back hard against the cold stone wall. He closed his eyes for a moment, vividly aware that *this* was the sensation he had been imagining all those times—this was the *real* stone wall of the dark room!

The room where I always thought I was so safe!

He wedged his eyes open and chanced a glance at his wristwatch. By his estimate, they had been down here less than fifteen minutes. It felt more like a couple of hours. Katherine was kneeling beside Danny again, and Jeremy didn't protest when she started to untie him. Once he was free, she gently hugged him, rocking him back and forth, trying to bring him back around. Danny's face actually looked a bit livelier than when they had first entered the room. He forced a smile and whispered something into his mother's ear, but Jeff didn't quite catch what it was.

"What did *I* do?" Jeff said, dragging his voice.

The question had caught him off guard. He shook his head, shrugged, and rubbed his forehead. For a moment, he thought he heard voices, muttering in the darkness; but as soon as he focused his attention on them, they started to fade away. He could feel his pulse throbbing hard in his neck, and far behind his eyes, in the center of his head, a hot pressure was starting to build up. He knew he was going to have a blinding headache soon, but he told himself it didn't matter. It might be only a matter of minutes before he was dead, anyway.

"I just . . . just lived my life," Jeff said after a tension-filled moment. "I . . . I got married. Had a kid, a little girl named Robin." Jeff cast a quick glance over at Katherine, but she seemed not to be paying attention to anything he was saying.

"Why, then I'm an uncle, ain't I?" Jeremy said, sniffing with laughter. "Uncle Jeremy! I like the sound of that!"

Jeff nodded, trying to calculate just how far Jeremy was gone and how dangerous he really was.

"We live out in Denver. Colorado. I teach at the University of Denver . . . history."

"Isn't that nice?" Jeremy said.

His knife hand never wavered an inch to either side. The gleaming tip remained pointed straight at Jeff. Jeff's eyelids fluttered as he tried to imagine the cold, ripping sting of the blade that would end his life.

"But do you mean to tell me," Jeremy continued, "that in *all* this time, you never even *suspected* that I might still be alive?"

"How . . . how could I have known?" Jeff said, painfully aware that his voice sounded thin and reedy. A hot, salty taste flooded his mouth, almost choking him. "The cops and half the town combed the woods and river for weeks after you disappeared. They finally decided that you must be dead, either drowned in the river and washed out to sea, or else lost in the woods. I . . . I—"

A long-repressed memory suddenly resurfaced and hit Jeff with such a solid impact it made his body shake.

"Jesus! I remember . . . we even had a funeral service for you."

"Huh! Really?" Jeremy said. "Tell me, did Kirby and Mildred attend?" His voice rose with a lilting edge of humor in it.

"Yeah, I . . . I think they did," Jeff replied.

In truth, he had no idea if they had or not. He wasn't even sure if he had attended. The only funerals he had clear memories of were much later in his life, those of his parents and his sister.

Jeff looked around at the dingy surroundings and wrinkled his nose involuntarily when he took a shuddering breath.

"But do you mean to tell me that *this* is where you've been living?"

Jeremy nodded, his eyes narrowing slightly.

"And you—" Jeff continued, "I mean—Jesus, didn't you miss your family? At least me and Judy, if not Mom and Dad? I'm your brother, for Christ's sake!"

"I know that, but you'd better watch your mouth, big brother," Jeremy said. He frowned deeply as he shook his head. The expression on his face was an odd mixture of rising fury and deep, ineffable sadness. His knife hand shifted a bit to one side and dropped. Jeff could see Jeremy thinking, trying to reconcile the opposing forces inside him. He flexed his arms and legs, coiling up inside himself. He was thinking now was the time to make a move, but Jeremy seemed to notice immediately, and he raised the knife again.

"After a while, it didn't really matter," Jeremy said in a hollow-sounding voice. A dull, pained look lit his eyes. "They . . . they kept me down here for a long time . . . a *very* long time. And they—" His voice choked off, and he winced as he glanced again at the cellar ceiling. Jeff cringed with his own memories of the torture and torment they had suffered down here. He couldn't imagine a whole lifetime of it. After a moment, Jeremy shook his head and said, "But—hey, I have a place to sleep, and they feed me. After a while, this *was* home. For the longest time, it was the only home I remembered."

Jeff nodded as his own understanding deepened.

"After you disappeared," Jeff said haltingly, "that must have been when Mom and Dad stopped sending us out here to stay—me and Judy, I mean."

He remembered, now, that the visits to his aunt and uncle's house had abruptly ended, obviously following the supposed death of his brother. Try as he might, he couldn't remember anything about how either of his parents had reacted to his younger brother's supposed death. Had they known or ever suspected what Kirby and Mildred had done? Did they blame him for his younger brother's death? Jeff knew that for years after Jeremy's disappearance, he had been haunted by an overwhelming guilt until the pain had become so bad, he had blocked everything out of his mind and created a whole cast of alter personalities to keep the truth hidden from himself. His body began to tremble as he wondered how many other memories might still be buried deep within him . . . and how many of them were going to rise up like reanimated corpses, lurching out of the graveyard.

"You're probably right," Jeremy said, his voice cutting through the rising flood of Jeff's panicked thoughts. "I was Kirby and Mildred's little secret, hidden away down here in the cellar. In the cold and damp. And after a while . . . it didn't matter any more. This was my home. I *belonged* here."

His voice kept sliding up the scale, but then it abruptly cut off. He winced again noticeably before continuing.

"After a while, they *convinced* me that living here was for my own good and that I could never go home again. That I shouldn't! It was for the good of my soul, they said, and I *believed* them. They were going to save my soul. They taught me how to read so I could read the Bible." He nodded toward the opened Bible on the wooden crate beside his bed. "They told me that they had wanted to save you and Judy, too, but that they could only save one soul at a time. I was the lucky one, they said, because they had picked me to raise as their own child and keep me out of the clutches of Satan."

Jeremy was shaking so badly, the knife in his hand was wavering wildly back and forth. Splinters of reflected light stung Jeff's eyes.

"But they made you *live* down here, in the dark!" Jeff said softly, not wanting to frighten Jeremy or push him too hard.

He was tensed, ready to react. He could see that Jeremy was getting really upset, and he knew the danger of stirring up buried memories like this. He had suffered plenty of his own over the years. This could spur his brother to fury just as easily as it could get him to drop his guard.

"If they loved you so much," Jeff went on, "and if they wanted to save your soul, how could they do these things to you? . . . How could they do something like that to *anyone?*"

Again, Jeremy shrugged, and this time he didn't seem to notice when his knife hand dropped down below his waist.

"I . . . I got used to it . . . eventually," he said haltingly. He sounded absolutely defeated. "They . . . they used to make me memorize passages from the Bible, and they'd whip me as I recited them. Kirby used a leather strap. I spent a lot of time down here. A lot of time . . ."

His eyes were glazed over as he stared past Jeff.

"And they never let you out of here?" Jeff asked.

Jeremy shook his head as he suddenly pulled his attention back.

"No. Not at first. Only at night, so I could help with chores around the farm. But after a while, once I was older and honestly had given up on ever going back home again, I used to sneak out of here late at night. Sometimes I . . . I'd go back to the old house. The first time I went back there, I didn't even know where I was going. It had been so long since I had seen the house, it was like . . . like something out of a dream. I used to hide in the woods, out in the backyard and watch the person who lived there, especially at night, when she was up in her bedroom."

"Judy," Jeff whispered.

Jesus Christ! he thought with a violent shiver. *He's the one I saw out there! . . . The person who was lurking out behind the house! He's Judy's "twilight lover" . . . and my "fetch!"*

"I never even realized she was my sister until a little while ago," Jeremy said.

Even before he had finished speaking, Jeff noticed that his brother's eyes were unfocused. He was breathing shallowly and staring far off in the distance at something. A subtle chill skittered up Jeff's back as he wondered if now was the time to go for him. Even if Jeremy fought back, even if he got hurt or killed, it would give Katherine and Danny the opportunity they needed to get away.

But maybe Danny's still too weak to run, Jeff thought. *Maybe his legs aren't strong enough to support him yet. If they don't get out fast enough, Jeremy's going to finish me off and then kill them. That's what he said he would do!*

You gotta go for it! whispered a different voice inside Jeff's head, but Jeff knew he couldn't chance it.

Not yet.

He had to make sure Katherine and Danny were

ready so at least *someone* would get out of here alive.

He could see that Jeremy was starting to lose control of himself as memories of his own past came rushing back at him. If Jeff was going to get him off balance, he knew he was going to have to push him *hard*.

"And then one night," Jeff said, his voice low and even, "just around twilight time, you came to her, didn't you?"

The expression on Jeremy's face suddenly tightened. His mouth stripped back in a pained grimace, and a crazy gleam flared behind his eyes.

"That's what you did, didn't you?" Jeff said. "Even after you *knew* she was your sister, you came into her house, went up to her bedroom, and you . . . you got into bed with her."

"No, I . . . ," Jeremy said, but his voice faded quickly.

Jeff could hear his brother's rapid breathing and see the panic rising like a firestorm in his eyes.

"Oh, yes you did," Jeff said, pressing his advantage. "You *sinned* with her, didn't you, Jeremy? You made love to her . . . to your own *sister!*"

Completely unnerved now, Jeremy let his arms hang loosely at his sides as he stared straight ahead, wide-eyed and slack-jawed. He was shaking his head from side to side and making a low, moaning sound.

"But I . . . but I didn't know," he said in a hollow, shattered whisper. "Not then . . . not until—"

"Oh, but I think you *did* know," Jeff said, cringing at his own guilt about what he and Judy had done when they were young. He took a single step forward, watching to see if Jeremy noticed, but his brother's eyes reflected milky white in the lantern light.

"You *knew* she was your sister. You recognized the house, but you went up to her bedroom anyway, and you lay with her. You had *intercourse* with her! You committed the sin of incest, and now you're living with

the fear that *they'll* find out about it, that they'll punish you for it before you die, and that you'll go to hell
where you'll be punished . . . *forever!"*

Jeremy groaned as his body slumped forward.
Keeping a wary eye on the knife in his brother's hand,
Jeff took another quick step closer to him. The room
was filled with a tense silence that throbbed like a
drumbeat in Jeff's ears.

"I . . . I think they already know," Jeremy finally
said in a shattered, twisted voice. "I think that's why
they brought *him* down here." He flicked his head in
Danny's direction, a sneer curling one side of his
mouth. "They wanted me to punish him the same way
I was punished. It's the *Lord's* will, big brother, not
mine!"

Jeff glanced quickly over at Danny and Katherine
and was glad to see that, while he and Jeremy had been
talking, she had gotten the boy to stand up. He looked
weak and unsteady on his feet, but Jeff was hoping
they'd be ready to run when the moment came.

And it's gonna be soon! Get your ass ready!

"I-I knew they were going to replace me—because
I'd sinned," Jeremy said, his voice rising in an agonized howl before it finally cracked. He licked his lips
furiously and shook his head. "They—they didn't
want me anymore! They didn't *need* me! I was—was
already going to hell . . . because of what I had done.
They had lost me to Satan, so they—they needed a *new*
boy to save! It was *God's* work they were doing!"

Jeremy looked over at Danny and Katherine, who
were standing side by side now, cowering in the far
corner of the room. Katherine had one arm around the
boy's back and was supporting him. The insane gleam
Jeff saw in his brother's eyes got frighteningly bright.

"They were finished with me, don't you see that?"
Jeremy wailed. "They were going to let me die and go
to hell because of . . . because of what I did!"

His voice choked off as tears streamed from his eyes, glistening like quicksilver in the lantern light. His head dropped forward as he covered his face with his hands. Jeff could see that his grip on the knife had loosened. He was prepared to leap at him, but he was unable to move when he saw Jeremy's shoulders heave and heard the long, anguished cry of torment sounding deep within Jeremy's chest.

"Hey, come on. Take it easy," Jeff said softly, feeling a rush of tender feelings for his brother. He took a few more steps forward, but was still tensed and ready for Jeremy's knife hand to lash out at him.

Jeremy gazed up at Jeff. His features were so twisted that he looked like a different person. Once again Jeff was riveted by the terrifying thought that—somehow —one of his alter personalities had taken shape and substance. He watched in mute horror as his brother—a frightening, distorted mirror image of himself—stared straight into his eyes.

"You're not gonna hurt me again, are you, Jeffy?" Jeremy said in a whining voice that sounded much higher than normal, almost like a little boy's. He still had the knife in his hand, but it was forgotten as he pressed the heels of both hands against the sides of his head and shrank back, shielding his eyes.

"Please don't! Not like last time. Please tell me you won't hurt me, Jeffy!" Jeremy wailed. "Even if he—if Uncle Kirby tells you to . . . even if he tries to *make* you, please don't use the strap on me again! *Please!*"

"I promise . . . I won't," Jeff said, his voice shaking, nothing more than a ragged whisper.

Jeff's heart felt like it had stopped cold in his chest. He cringed, waiting to hear the voices start up inside his head again, but the only sound he heard was his own ragged breathing and the raw, gasping sounds as Jeremy cried.

"You . . . you didn't come down here to . . . to hurt

me, to kill me, did you? To kill me for real this time?"

The tormented expression on Jeremy's face tore into Jeff's heart much deeper than the knife could have penetrated. He felt a twinge of guilt for having used as a weapon the same thing he and Judy had done back when they were kids, but he knew it had been necessary to get Jeremy to lower his guard. Now all he had to do was get the knife away from him.

"No," Jeff said mildly. "I didn't come here to hurt you. Honest I didn't."

He was shaking his head from side to side as he took another few steps closer to his brother, all the while keeping a wary eye on the knife in his hand.

Jeremy's eyes suddenly widened; his mouth dropped open as he looked up at the cellar ceiling again as if he had heard something that Jeff hadn't. He cowered, looking like he was trying to fold up inside himself.

"They're gonna be really mad at me, you know," Jeremy said, his voice now low and gruff. "They'll be mad at *all* of us. And they might want you to do it—to kill me for real this time."

Jeff found it almost impossible to speak, but he cleared his throat and said, "No they won't. I-I just want to take the boy and his mother out of here. That's all I want, Jeremy. I didn't come down here to hurt you."

"But *they'll* want to hurt me once they find out he's gone! Or they'll *make* you do it, just like they did before! And they'll hurt you for being here, too," Jeremy said. His voice ended in a rising, keening howl.

"Trust me, Jeremy. We'll be all right," Jeff said. "I just want you to let us leave. It isn't right that you're keeping Danny down here like this."

"Danny? Is that his name? Danny?"

"Yes, and his mother's been very worried about him, just like our mother was worried and upset when you disappeared."

"But he'll start to like it down here. After a while, he'll get used to it, and it'll be home for him, too. Just like it was for me."

Jeff shook his head. "No, Jeremy. It's wrong, and you know it. That's why you're going to give me the knife now and let us all leave. We'll take you somewhere where you can get help."

Jeremy stiffened. Clutching the knife handle, he made a quick move as if he was going to slash out at Jeff. He turned the knife back and forth in his hand, mesmerized by the orange light that reflected off the blade. Jeff took one step back, but then he saw his brother's body relax. His shoulders slouched forward, and he stared blankly down at the floor for what seemed like much too long. The silence pounded like a hammer in his ears. Finally, Jeremy raised his head and held the knife, hilt-first, out to Jeff.

"That's it," Jeff said softly.

"You promise you won't let them hurt me?" Jeremy said, still sounding like a terrified little boy.

"I promise," Jeff said.

It took a great deal of effort not to move too fast, but Jeff didn't want to frighten Jeremy, and he didn't want him to know just how scared he was, but his hand was shaking wildly as he took the knife from his brother and then tossed it off to one side. It hit the stone wall with a loud clang and sent a shower of sparks flying.

"Yeah, that's it," Jeff said. "Nice and easy now."

Jeremy was staring at him. They were close enough for Jeff to see the hot, blue core of the lantern, mirrored in his brother's watery eyes.

There's a fire, deep inside him, and it's burning him up, he thought. Remembering the mental anguish he'd had to suffer throughout his adult life made him feel all the more for what his younger brother must be experiencing. With a long, rasping sob, Jeremy collapsed forward into Jeff's arms. Surprised by the sudden weight, Jeff staggered back as he clasped his arms around his brother's back and gave him a bracing hug as he patted him on the back.

"Take it easy now," he whispered, but he glanced over at Katherine and nodded reassuringly. "No one's gonna hurt you. We're gonna take good care of you from now on."

Just as Jeff was turning back to look at Katherine, an ear-shattering explosion split the air. Katherine screamed, and Jeremy pulled away quickly from Jeff and dropped down onto his knees on the floor, groveling on the floor with his hands covering his ears.

Dazed with terror, and with the blast still ringing like chimes in his ears, Jeff looked all around the room until he saw the dark figure that was looming in the doorway. Behind it was another indistinct shape. As both of the figures moved forward into the light, Jeff saw that it was Kirby with Mildred a few steps behind. Kirby was holding a double-barreled shotgun and aiming it straight at Jeff. A thin thread of blue smoke was coiling up from the end of the barrel. Kirby's lined face was set in a deep, angry scowl.

"I got one shell left, boy," he said. His voice was a dry, gravely growl, but Jeff could barely hear him above the high-pitched sound still ringing in his ears.

"One shot, and I ain't afraid to use it on either one of you if I have to."

Chapter Twenty-nine
Wounds and Death

After the initial rush of panic, Jeff's first clear thought was that he wished he hadn't thrown Jeremy's knife away a moment ago. A cold ache filled his chest as he turned and glanced down at the floor. The knife was barely lying, hilt toward him in the dark corner where it had fallen, a little more than arm's reach away. But he knew if he went for it, the second blast from Kirby's shotgun would end his life. He also knew that, if he died now, Kirby and Jeremy would no doubt kill Katherine and Danny, too, and that would be the end of it for all of them.

He had to think of *something!*

Kirby's mouth was set in a hard, lipless line. His eyes were gleaming wildly as he took a few steps into the room. The whole time, the shotgun was leveled straight at the center of Jeff's chest. Jeremy was still on the dirt floor in front of Jeff. He shifted into a kneeling position and cowered as he watched his uncle advance.

The sound of the shotgun blast was still ringing in Jeff's ears, but it seemed to be fading, only to be replaced by a heavy *whooshing* sound that throbbed like squeezing fingers in Jeff's head and neck.

We're all going to die! wailed a frantic, high-pitched voice which, at first, he thought was Katherine's, but then he realized the voice was echoing inside his own head.

All of us! We'll all be dead soon!

Like a stroke of lightning, sheer, blinding panic coursed through Jeff. He wanted to push aside the thought, deny it, but he honestly couldn't. He was unable to move or speak as he watched Kirby's eyes slide back and forth, trying to take in the situation. As soon as the old man apparently realized that he had everything under control, one corner of his seamed mouth twitched into a thin half-smile. Jeff wasn't sure if it was from humor or self-righteous anger.

Probably both, said a different voice inside Jeff's head. *You remember how much he used to ENJOY hurting you!*

"You don't want to move," Kirby said softly, squinting one eye as if already sighting down the gun barrel as he looked at Jeff. "And you don't even want to *think* about trying anything, 'cause I'll do it, boy. I'll drop you in your tracks without a second thought and send your blackened soul to hell, where it belongs!"

Jeff licked his lips, wanting desperately to reply but unable to think of anything to say.

Turning to Jeremy, Kirby nodded in Danny and Katherine's direction.

"First thing you do, Son, is get that boy tied up again. And while you're at it, tie up his mother, too, so's she won't give us no trouble."

Katherine bristled, her fists clenching as she took a threatening step forward; but after casting a helpless glance over at Jeff, she let her shoulders drop and slammed back against the wall. Jeff could see the tears of frustration and rage that filled her eyes. He wanted to say something about how sorry he was for bringing her down here and getting her involved, but words failed him. Only one thought registered that provided the slimmest ray of hope or consolation.

At least she got to see Danny again. . . . She found out what happened to him!

"Well, are you gonna just sit there on your skinny ass all day, or are you gonna do what you been told?"

Kirby's voice resounded in the small room, filling Jeff with a jolt of the same primal terror he had experienced down here as a boy. Anger and hurt, blind rage and pain exploded inside him, but instead of sparking him to action, they paralyzed him. His arm and leg muscles felt like they were locked up as firmly as if he were bound with iron bands.

Jesus, we'll all be dead soon! the voice hissed again. It was screaming so loud inside his head that it blocked out every other sound.

Still kneeling on the floor, Jeremy looked back and forth between his brother and Kirby. His face was streaked with tears and smudges of dirt, and his expression was one of absolute, utter confusion. His eyes were staring and his lower lip was trembling, but Jeff couldn't tell if it was because he was trying to say something or because he was blubbering in terror. The control Kirby had over him, maintained by fear, was obvious.

"Since *when* have I *ever* had to tell you something twice, boy?" Kirby said, eyeing Jeremy with a deepening scowl.

Jeff stiffened when he saw the shotgun swing a bit to the side and point at Jeremy. He was debating whether he should jump Kirby now or go for the knife; but as if he could read Jeff's mind, Kirby turned and glared at him.

"I said don't even *think* about trying something, boy, and I *meant* it!"

Jeff focused on the old man's gnarled forefinger as it curled around the trigger.

"You . . . you'll never get away with this," Jeff said, frantically trying to sort out the raging confusion that filled his mind. He couldn't ignore the feeling that he was still a terrified ten-year-old, and that this man—this *monster*—was going to tie him over the oil drum and beat him with a leather strap for even daring to speak against him.

Kirby regarded him with a smoldering stare before glancing over his shoulder at his wife, who was standing quietly in the shadowed doorway. Then he laughed, a single, sharp burst that didn't have a trace of humor in it.

"I already *have* gotten away with it, for better 'an twenty years," he said. His shoulders hunched forward as he laughed, but the aim of the gun at Jeff never wavered. " 'N I don't see as there's much of a problem here—nothin' I can't take care of, anyway. Sure, I'm gonna have to kill you and the woman, and I regret that, I honestly do, but the boy is gonna be staying down here with Jeremy, 'n I'll keep him here till he gets used to being here. And he will . . . eventually, by God, he will!"

"Never, you fucking *bastard!*" Danny shouted, his voice high and nearly breaking.

Kirby turned his head slowly, like a cobra getting ready to strike, and looked at him.

"Oh, you will, believe me. But you'd better watch your mouth, young man. 'Cause I don't *have* to let you live, and you know it!"

"The police already know we're out here," Katherine chimed in.

She had one arm protectively around Danny's shoulder, pulling him tightly against her. The expression on her face was one of desperate, helpless horror.

"We told them this morning that we were coming

out here. If we don't show up, this will be the first place they come looking. The state police are still searching for my boy, you know."

Kirby snorted with laughter and wiped a trace of snot away from his upper lip.

"They've already been out here, ma'am, askin' all sorts of questions and lookin' around. But they'll never find you. Least not while I'm alive."

"But I told my friend, Eddie Dearborn," Jeff said. "He's going to meet us out here if we're not back before noon. What time is it now? For all I know, he may be upstairs right now."

"*Lying* is a *sin* in the *eyes* of the *Lord,* boy!" Kirby said. His deep, resonating voice made him sound like a television evangelist. "I guess that's something you just never learned, did ya? Neither from me or from the Good Book! But lying certainly isn't the least of your sins, is it, boy?"

Jeff started to reply but fell silent.

"No," Kirby went on, obviously enjoying Jeff's reaction. "It isn't the worst you've done, not by a long shot . . . *Adulterer! Fornicator!*"

Jeff stared at Kirby, wondering frantically if he knew the truth about what he and Katherine had done, or if he was just guessing, trying to throw him off balance.

"You can think what you want," Jeff said, after a tense moment. "But I-I know what you did! I remember it all! Anything I might have done is nothing—*nothing* compared to what *you* did! Kidnapping . . . and child abuse, and . . . and trying to *kill* someone!"

Kirby was silent, smiling grimly as he listened to Jeff, but then he snickered and shook his head.

"Anything you know ain't gonna do you a damned bit of good—not when you're dead and rotting in hell. Will it? *Will it?*"

His face went suddenly livid, and his eyes glowed

with righteous indignation. With a quick snap of his head, he turned back to Jeremy and shouted, "I'll tell you just once more, Son, and if you don't do what you've been told, I'm gonna have to punish you. You wouldn't want *that,* now, would you?"

Jeremy started mumbling senselessly under his breath and was vigorously shaking his head as he slowly stood up. He moved stiffly, but instead of moving toward Katherine and Danny, he took a step toward Kirby, all the while wringing his hands in front of himself as he stared at his uncle.

"I . . . It isn't . . . I can't . . . this . . . this isn't *right!*" he said in a high, whining voice that almost broke on every syllable. Jeff thought he sounded like the frightened six-year-old he had been the last time he had seen him, and he felt an almost overwhelming surge of pity for his brother.

"What's *right?*" Kirby growled, his eyebrows lowering like storm clouds. "What's *right* is doing what you've been told to do by your *elders!* The commandment is: 'Honor thy father and mother that thy days may be long in the land which the Lord thy God—"

"But *you're* not my father!" Jeremy shouted, waving his arms as he pointed his forefinger at Kirby and shook it wildly. "And *she's* not my mother!"

Jeremy glanced over his shoulder at Jeff as fresh tears started from his eyes; then he turned back to Kirby.

"You took me away from them . . . *stole* me from my mother and father . . . from my family, and you're trying to do the same thing with *this* boy." He hooked his thumb over his shoulder to indicate Danny. "But that . . . it's not right! You can't do that!"

"It's not *my* will. It's the *Lord's* will!" Kirby bellowed as he swung the shotgun around and aimed it straight at Jeremy's head. Jeff knew he had to do something—soon—but his body was still locked with fear. Several voices inside his head were screaming.

"You . . . you're not thinking of replacing me, are you?" Jeremy said in a wildly trembling voice. His face was deathly white beneath the tearstained grime. When he took a halting step forward, Kirby raised the shotgun and pressed it into the crook of his shoulder. His finger on the trigger twitched.

"I tried to save your soul, Son," Kirby said, sounding almost forlorn as he drew a steady bead on Jeremy. "I honestly did, but I know the truth about you. You, too, are a *liar!* And a *fornicator!* You've allowed yourself to indulge in carnal pleasures!"

Kirby's shoulders slumped forward, and Jeff thought he actually saw tears fill the old man's eyes.

"We've tried," Kirby said in a halting voice, "but we failed with you. But with *this* boy, we can try again. His soul isn't as stained and rotten as yours is! We might be able to save him!"

Jeremy remained perfectly motionless for several seconds, staring at Kirby as though unable to believe or accept what he had just heard. Utter silence filled the room, making the rapid, muffled pulse in Jeff's ears sound like heavy drumbeats.

"You don't want me anymore, is that it? You don't need me?"

Before Kirby could respond, a sudden, ear-piercing scream filled the room. With his hands propelled in front of him like claws, Jeremy launched himself at Kirby. Within two steps, and before the old man could react, he hit him hard and low, like a tackling football player. The impact knocked Kirby clean off his feet and carried him backwards. As he fell, twisting to one side, the shotgun went off with a deafening blast. Jeff turned and ducked protectively as Katherine—at least he thought it was Katherine—screeched shrilly.

Jeff had no idea if he had been hit or not as he

crouched and watched as both men landed hard on the dirt floor. Jeremy was on top of Kirby, and he easily overpowered the old man. Screaming wildly, like a man possessed, he squatted on top of Kirby's chest and started raining down blows onto the old man's face.

For a terrifying, frozen moment, Jeff could do nothing but watch them fight, but then he became aware of another movement in the darkened doorway. He looked up just as Mildred lurched forward into the light. She moaned softly as her hands clutched at her chest and in a slow, graceful spin, she collapsed to the floor, landing on her back. Beneath her hands, he could see a ragged hole in the front of her dress and the dark, widening stain that was slowly seeping through the cloth. Even through his shock, Jeff knew that it was blood. At close range, the shotgun blast had made a fist-sized hole in her chest, just below the left shoulder.

"Jesus! She's hurt!" Jeff shouted as he jumped past the struggling men and went to his fallen aunt.

Mildred was lying on her back and looking up at the ceiling, her eyes glazed and distant. She tried to speak but coughed instead. Her throat rattled with a thick, watery gurgle, and a spray of foamy blood gushed from her mouth and nose as her lips moved soundlessly. She focused on Jeff for a moment, and then her eyes widened and went dim. Her body shivered once, violently, and with a deep, shuddering groan, she went lifeless.

The sounds of Kirby and Jeremy, still scuffling on the dirt floor, were like a distant memory as Jeff stood there, staring down at his dead aunt. Contrary to everything he knew and had experienced, he couldn't help but feel a pang of sorrow for her. After only a few seconds—but they were seconds that felt like dragging

minutes or hours—Jeff shook himself and looked over
at the men.

They were still fighting, but it wasn't much of a
contest. Jeremy had his uncle's shoulders pinned to the
dirt floor with his knees and was moving with a rigid,
clockwork motion as he alternately punched Kirby in
the face.

Left. Right. Left. Right.

Each punch made a loud *whack* sound. Jeremy
grunted fiercely as every punch landed, snapping
Kirby's head sharply from side to side. Thick ribbons
of blood, showing bright red in the direct glare of the
lantern, were streaming from Kirby's mouth and nose,
smearing and staining Jeremy's clenched fists.

"Stop it!" Jeff shouted, so loud his voice cracked.
"Jesus Christ! You're killing him!"

Realizing there was nothing he could do for Mildred, he darted over behind Jeremy, grabbed him by
both shoulders, and tried to pull him off. Over
Jeremy's shoulder, he could see that Kirby wasn't of-
fering any resistance. His features were slack, and his
eyes were puffy and looked as death-glazed as Mildred's. He was already either unconscious . . . or dead.

Turning to Katherine and Danny, who were still
cowering in the corner of the room by the mattress,
watching all of this, Jeff shouted, "Go on! Get out of
here! Go upstairs and call the police!"

For a moment or two, Katherine didn't move. She
looked like she wanted to help but had no idea what
to do. Then she snapped to and, grabbing Danny by
the hand, yanked him forward so fast he almost lost
his balance. Side by side, they started for the doorway,
hesitating only a moment to look down at Mildred's
corpse. Then Katherine and her son disappeared
through the doorway, their footsteps echoing in the
narrow corridor.

"Hurry!" Jeff called after her. His voice echoed in

the small room and for a frozen instant sounded like several voices. "Call for the ambulance, too! I think she's dead, but she—she might not be."

Jeremy's arms and legs were flailing wildly as Jeff struggled to pull him off Kirby. His brother was much stronger than Jeff would have expected, and he was charged with adrenaline and rage. They struggled silently, each trying to get the better of the other, but Jeff had the advantage of being behind Jeremy. With some effort, he got his brother into a full nelson and managed to pull him away from Kirby's motionless body. Jeremy was still kicking and screaming as Jeff dragged him over to his mattress and pushed him face-first onto it.

"Calm down! For Christ's sake, you practically killed him!" Jeff shouted as he crouched and threatened Jeremy with his clenched fists.

Jeremy's face was a mask of anger and torment as he glared at his brother. Flecks of foam and snot speckled his face. His bloodshot eyes were bulging from his head, and his whole body was trembling like someone having an epileptic seizure.

They remained frozen like this for several tense seconds, but once Jeff saw the fight go out of his brother, he looked back at Kirby. The old man was flat on his back and groaning as he rolled his head from side to side. Blood from his nose and mouth smeared his face and shirtfront. His eyes were closed up behind puffy, purplish swellings.

Good . . . at least he's still alive.

Suddenly Jeremy uttered a low moan that quickly rose into a high, warbling scream. Boosting himself up off the mattress, he tried to dodge around Jeff so he could get back at Kirby again, but Jeff caught him with both arms and, hugging him tightly, flopped back onto the mattress with him. They clutched each other, squeezing hard as if they were wrestling. After a moment or two, Jeff felt his brother's body go slack in his arms. After that, the raw sounds of crying filled the small room.

"There, there," Jeff whispered, not even sure that Jeremy could hear him above the agonized sounds he was making. He patted his brother firmly on the back, but all the while he kept an eye on Kirby's prostrate form. Jeremy dissolved into tears as he pressed his face hard against his brother's shoulder and started rocking back and forth like a child, needing to be comforted. All the misery and fear of a lifetime came out in one long, agonized wail that sounded like it was never going to end.

Just as he always did whenever he was in the dark room, Jeff lost all track of the time. He closed his eyes and held onto his brother, willing what little strength and love he had to fill him.

It could have been minutes or hours later when the police arrived. With guns drawn and flashlights shining, two policemen burst into the room where they found Jeff and Jeremy sitting on the bare mattress, both of them crying as they embraced each other and rocked back and forth.

"Well, for starters," Eddie Dearborn said, "there's kidnapping, conspiracy to kidnapping, possibly murder, and attempted murder. Any one of those is probably going to be enough to put him away for the rest of his natural life."

Jeff nodded. "That's probably the best news I've had in a couple of weeks," he said, although he wasn't really sure he felt that way.

He squinted in the bright afternoon sunshine as he looked at his friend. They were standing on the front steps of Kirby and Mildred's house, looking out at the small, weed-choked front yard. Parked in the driveway, as close to the house as they could get, were two state police cruisers with their emergency lights flashing, one town cruiser, an ambulance, and the medical examiner's car. The autumn air had a sharp chill to it, but Jeff repressed the shiver he felt inside as he said, "How about my brother? What's gonna happen to him?"

Simultaneously, both men looked over to one of the two state police cruisers and at the dark silhouette that was sitting motionlessly in the backseat behind the metal protective screen. Jeff's eyes began to sting with gathering tears.

"That's not up to me to decide," Eddie said as he craned his head to one side and scratched the back of his neck. "You know, if it was, I probably wouldn't even press charges. I mean, from all indications here, your brother was an innocent victim, doing whatever your uncle told him to do."

"And *that's* the ironic thing, you know?" Jeff said, forcing a smile as he shook his head and looked back at his friend. "All these years, Kirby and Mildred had him out here, and we all thought he was dead. And they did what they did, so they said, because they wanted to save him, save his soul." Jeff sniffed with laughter. "And in the end what they really did was end up creating a monster. God! Just think of all the time . . . the lifetime that was . . . wasted."

Eddie was silent, but after a moment he cleared his throat and said, "But you know, even if the state doesn't press charges against your brother, he's probably going to have to be put away in a mental institution."

"Yeah, I know," Jeff said, nodding.

"That probably would be the best thing for him right now, anyway," Eddie said.

"Who's to judge, huh?"

A clang of metal from the side of the house drew

their attention, and both men turned to watch as a sheet-covered form strapped to a stretcher was wheeled out into the sunlight. A dark, flower-shaped splotch of red had soaked through the white sheet. Obviously not in any hurry, the medical team wheeled the stretcher down the walkway to the waiting ambulance and slid it into the opened back door. Following a few paces behind it were two state policemen escorting Kirby, whose hands were handcuffed behind his back. The old man's face was a mess of prune-colored bruises and bleeding lacerations. He paused and almost collapsed when the ambulance door slammed shut. One of the policemen grabbed him by the arm to support him.

After the ambulance started up and drove away, Kirby turned and locked eyes with Jeff, staring at him with obvious hatred. Jeff resisted the impulse to turn away as he waited for his uncle to break the eye contact, but he never did as the state troopers led him down to their waiting cruiser, opened the door for him, and guided him into the backseat. Just before the door closed, Jeff saw that his uncle said something, but they were too far away for him to hear what it was.

The door swung shut, and Jeff watched silently as one of the policemen got into the car, started it up, and drove away. A plume of yellow dust swirled in the cruiser's wake as it drove down the driveway and disappeared behind the screen of trees.

"Overall, though, I think things turned out for the best," Eddie said. "Don't you?"

Realizing that he hadn't taken a deep enough breath in quite a while, Jeff inhaled slowly.

"Yeah . . . at least everyone else is okay."

Katherine and Danny had left more than half an hour ago for the hospital. Although Danny was terribly frightened by what he had just been through, his injuries weren't serious. Jeff felt confident that, with time and maybe some therapy, he would be just fine. Now that Mildred was dead, and Kirby and Jeremy were being hauled off to jail, this had ended about as well as he could have expected. Placing one hand on Eddie's shoulder, he gave him a bracing squeeze.

"I guess so, Eddie," he said. "I just want to thank you for—"

"Think nothing of it," Eddie said. "I was just doing my job." He scratched his brow as he shook his head. "I just wish I had . . . Shit! I dunno. I mean, maybe none of this would have even happened if I had followed through—you know, on some of the things you were trying to tell me."

"You did the best you could," Jeff said. "At least it's all over now."

Jeff looked up as the other state policeman who had led Kirby out to the cruiser walked over toward him. The policeman's face was set with a firm, all-business expression.

"We'll need you to come down and make a complete statement, Mr. Wagner," the state policeman said. "But whether or not you choose to press charges, the state will. We'd appreciate your cooperation."

Jeff nodded. "Do I have to go right now?"

The officer shook his head, the flesh of his neck looked squeezed inside his uniform collar. "Later today or even this evening would be fine."

He turned to go, but Jeff stopped him.

"Excuse me, Officer."

The policeman turned back to him with one eyebrow raised.

"Yes?"

"Before he left, my uncle said something. Did you happen to hear what it was?"

The officer's eyes narrowed a moment; then he nodded and said, "Yes, sir, I did."

"What was it?"

Again, the officer's eyes narrowed as he regarded Jeff steadily.

"Are you sure you want to know, sir?"

Jeff didn't even consider for a moment before he nodded. The state policeman cleared his throat and said, "Your uncle said his one prayer is that you'll rot in hell for what you've done to him."

"What *I*—"

"That's what he said."

A cold, clutching sensation took hold of Jeff when a faint voice started whispering inside his head. He took a shallow breath and forced himself to smile as he said out loud what he had just thought.

"I—I hope he does, too."

"Yes, sir," the state policeman replied, and then he turned and walked away.

Chapter Thirty

Endings

"Would you like to come in for a minute?"

It was late, almost eleven o'clock. Katherine was standing in the lighted doorway of her house, leaning against the doorjamb and looking utterly worn-out. There were dark circles under her eyes and a sad, downward drooping to her mouth even when she tried to smile.

Jeff didn't move from where he was standing on the front steps. His hands were folded in front of him, and he kept squeezing them nervously. Faint moonlight silvered the lawn behind him. The evening was cold and almost unnaturally silent. In the distance, a dog barked, and the sound echoed hollowly. Jeff shivered as he cast a worried glance over his shoulder, more than half-expecting to see the shadows under the trees seething with activity. He imagined faces and dead smiles and cold, staring eyes. Looking back quickly at Katherine, he smiled and shook his head.

"Uh—no . . . no thanks. I just stopped by to let you know that I'm leaving first thing in the morning."

"You are?" she replied, half statement, half question.

"Yeah."

Jeff wanted to look away but couldn't.

"You know," Katherine said after a moment, "I've been calling you for two days straight." She sounded too tired to be accusatory. "I left messages every time. Why didn't you return my calls?"

Jeff shrugged.

"I've had a lot of things to take care of. The house is pretty much empty and ready to be sold now, but I've been busy—you know, talking to my brother's lawyer about what . . . what's going to happen to him."

"How's he doing . . . and your uncle?"

Jeff shrugged again as cold tension twisted in his stomach.

"They're facing a lot of shit. I think it's gonna be a real nightmare, for both of them. I could just about give a shit about what happens to Kirby. That son of a bitch more than deserves whatever he gets, but with Jeremy—"

His voice stopped sharply. Batting his eyes to fight back the gathering tears, he looked up at the night sky and shook his head.

"It's really sad, I know," Katherine said. She reached out and gently laid one hand on Jeff's shoulder. He looked at her, trying to deny the strong attraction he still felt for her, even after all these years and everything they had been through recently.

"How about you?" he said, his voice catching and threatening to break. "You're doing okay, aren't you?"

Katherine nodded and smiled. "Sure. A lot of friends have stopped by to help, just to talk and keep me company. I think what makes it hardest is I've been bombarded by newspeople with requests for interviews for TV and the newspapers."

"Yeah. I've been pestered a little, too. My wife even heard about the story on the news out in Denver."

He paused and took a deep breath.

"So how's Danny doing?"

Katherine cast a furtive glance over her shoulder. The warm glow inside the house filled Jeff with an aching loneliness. He was painfully aware of the dark night, closing in around him. Even though he had talked to Sally and Robin several times over the last two days, the reality of the warmth and security of his own family seemed so far away it might just as well not be real.

"Oh, he's fine. They kept him in the hospital over-night for observation, but he's been home since yester-day morning. He's sleeping right now."

Jeff nodded. Katherine's facial expression seemed to contradict what she said, but he didn't say anything about it.

"Tell him I said 'hi,' okay?"

"Are you sure you don't want to come in?"

You know you do! whispered a voice inside his head. *And you want to do MORE than go in . . . you want to stay the night, don't you? Admit it, at least to yourself!*

"I . . . I really can't," Jeff said.

Even to his own ears, he didn't sound very convinc-ing.

"The flight's pretty early, and I'm really anxious to get back home and . . . see my family."

"I understand," Katherine said a trace wistfully.

As she said that, she moved close to him and laced her arms around him. Before he could stop her or himself, they embraced and were kissing—long, warm, and passionately. The tip of Katherine's tongue darted between his lips, teasing him. He felt himself becoming aroused and shifted his hips away from her so she wouldn't feel it, too. Their embrace lasted a long time. Jeff lost all sense of who he was and where he was, but a corner of his mind told him that, if she were to take him by the hand and lead him upstairs to her bedroom, he would follow without a word.

When they finally broke off their kiss and they separated, Jeff felt like a part of himself was being ripped away from him. He gazed into Katherine's eyes and thought he could see reflected there the hopes and dreams and promises of a life they would never have.

Maybe you could have, once upon a time . . . but not any more!

The cold, lonely ache inside him got worse, but he knew he was going to have to leave.

"That's just my way of saying thank you," Katherine said. Her voice was husky with emotion. "For everything you did to help."

She was still standing so close to him he could smell the subtle scent of her perfume as she gazed into his eyes the way she used to back—a lifetime ago—when they had been sweethearts.

"Thank *you*," Jeff said, knowing even then how stupid he sounded.

"You're going to be all right, aren't you?" she asked. He could see the dark worry in her eyes.

Biting his lower lip, Jeff nodded.

"Of course I am," he said. "I know it isn't really over for me. I'm not sure it ever will be. We'll just have to wait and see what happens to Jeremy, but no matter what it is, I'll have to work out on my own what I think and feel about it."

"I . . . I wish there was some way I could help," Katherine said.

Tears filled her eyes and glistened as they ran down her face. Jeff felt a warm flood in his own eyes, and his throat constricted when he tried to speak.

"Believe me," he said, his voice little more than a strangled rasp. "You have helped, more than you'll ever know."

They stood there a while longer, silently staring into each other's eyes. Then Jeff cleared his throat and, wiping his face on his jacket sleeve, he said, "Well, I guess I'd better be going."

He leaned forward and gave her another quick kiss on the cheek, then turned and started down the steps.

"You'll stay in touch, won't you?" Katherine called out after him.

Jeff turned and looked back at her. Framed in the doorway with the soft lemon glow of light behind her, she looked more like an angel than a real person.

"Absolutely," he said. "And I'll come by to see you if . . . no, *when* I come back. I don't know when the first court date is yet, but I have to—I *want* to do everything I can to help and support Jeremy."

Katherine nodded. "And what about Kirby?" she said.

Her voice seemed to echo in the night. Jeff opened his mouth to say something, but words failed him, and he ended up simply shaking his head.

"I have no idea."

"You know," Katherine said, "my minister was by, and he gave me a book to read about how to deal with sadness and anger. There was one line in particular that made me think about you. It said that the resolution of anger is either vengeance or forgiveness. I've been . . ." Her voice caught and almost broke, but she forced herself to continue. "I've been trying real hard to find it in myself to forgive your uncle for all the horrible things he did especially to Danny, but to you and your brother and sister, too. I hope you can find some way to forgive him."

Jeff stood there, the cold night surrounding him like a blanket. He continued to stare up at her silhouette in the backlit doorway until his vision began to blur. A confusion of thoughts and voices filled his head, but

through it all, he carefully picked out what he wanted
to say.

"Yeah," he said, forcing himself to smile. "I think I
might be able to . . . eventually."

He leaned his head back and, looking up at the
star-filled sky, took a deep breath of the brisk night
air.

"I might be able to forgive . . . but I *sure* as hell am
never going to *forget!*"

YOU'D BETTER SLEEP WITH THE LIGHTS TURNED ON!
BONE CHILLING HORROR BY

RUBY JEAN JENSEN

ANNABELLE	(2011-2, $3.95/$4.95)
BABY DOLLY	(3598-5, $4.99/$5.99)
CELIA	(3446-6, $4.50/$5.50)
CHAIN LETTER	(2162-3, $3.95/$4.95)
DEATH STONE	(2785-0, $3.95/$4.95)
HOUSE OF ILLUSIONS	(2324-3, $4.95/$5.95)
LOST AND FOUND	(3040-1, $3.95/$4.95)
MAMA	(2950-0, $3.95/$4.95)
PENDULUM	(2621-8, $3.95/$4.95)
VAMPIRE CHILD	(2867-9, $3.95/$4.95)
VICTORIA	(3235-8, $4.50/$5.50)

Available wherever paperbacks are sold, or order direct from the Publisher. Send cover price plus 50¢ per copy for mailing and handling to Penguin USA, P.O. Box 999, c/o Dept. 17109, Bergenfield, NJ 07621.Residents of New York and Tennessee must include sales tax. DO NOT SEND CASH.